THE
BRADFORD
STORY

AMELIA ELIZABETH WALDEN

THE
BRADFORD
STORY

APPLETON-CENTURY-CROFTS, INC.

New York

THE
BRADFORD
STORY

Chapter 1

It was going to be a big party. Not especially big in terms of the number of guests, but because of the amount of preparation Nina Galloway had put into it.

Nina's parties were always big. She adored fussing, and while she would much rather have been putting the effort into a party for Mark's and her friends, she could do no less than her best for the Bradfords. After all, it was only once in five years that she entertained her own family formally, *en masse* at the Bradford Thanksgiving party.

It was not yet Thanksgiving. Everyone else in the town of Bradford celebrated Thanksgiving on the last Thursday in November. The Bradfords, however, with the rugged individualism of the family after which the town had been named, held their party a week, to the day, before Thanksgiving was celebrated. This in itself was not so remarkable as the fact that you could get Nina's family together socially. She had always felt that the annual party was a stupendous achievement, a unique concession to that school of thought which claims that blood is thicker than water, no matter how thin the blood flows.

Nina walked over to her dining table. She glanced over it with the thoroughness of the meticulous hostess. It was a beautiful thing to behold with its heirloom damask cloth, the Bradford solid silver with crested pattern, custom-made by a friend of her late father's and presented to each Bradford as a wedding gift. The glassware was from Sweden and the bone china from England, a brilliant wreath of turquoise and yellow flowers on pure white, and it gave her a special satisfaction whenever she looked at it to know that this pattern was imported only once a year by a New York firm and that no one else she knew had it.

Nina did not think of herself as a snob. There was no connection in her thinking between snobbery and enjoying beautiful things which no one else could afford. This was her prerogative by heritage. She had been born to it and had become as used to it as to the air she breathed, and it had nothing to do with social distinctions or snobbery. You took life as you found it and she had found it full of beauty, color, and charm. Life was a gracious thing, shot through sometimes with pain and sorrow—Mark and she had lost one of their children, their only son, a few months after he was born—but on the whole, life had been extraordinarily good to her. She could see no reason for quarreling with it because it had not been equally good to everyone else.

There would be seven guests at Nina's table tonight, all of them Bradfords or their spouses, but among them, there would be three who would predominate. Nina selected three red roses from the crystal bowl on the buffet and, together with a stiff white place card, set one down before the setting of each of the three guests who most compelled her attention.

First there was Spencer who, rightly or not, Nina knew to be the recognized head of the family. Nina felt her lips pucker and the corners of her mouth turn involuntarily down as they might if she had bitten into a sour apple. Sometimes it bothered her that she had so little taste for her own brother. This, in spite of the fact that they had never openly quarreled about anything. Despite the even more salient fact that Spencer appeared to possess all the Christian virtues.

It was apparent to Nina, as it must be to anyone of discernment, that Spencer was a Yankee through and through. She envisioned him now in her mind's eye, lean to the point of tautness, immaculate in dress with clothes that would not dare to show a wrinkle; a face that had in the youth Nina so well remembered been handsome, even sensitive, but that had been molded and set, then hardened into the firm, Gothic lines of middle years.

There was no joy in Spencer and for this Nina disliked him most. She had fallen in love with her husband, Mark Galloway, partly because of his great zest for life. She liked jovial people about her, people who could laugh heartily, people who were not stingy with their smiles. Spencer's heaviness oppressed her. Nor was this all.

She knew that Spencer was not well liked among the men at Bradford Tool. This troubled her. Her father had not been the strong man old Jared Bradford, Nina's grandfather, had been, but he had been popular with his workers. Nina knew that the men considered Spencer snobbish and unsympathetic.

It's his way with people, she thought, as she straightened the rose before Spencer's place in the center of one side of the long table. It's that moody, sharp way he has. On the surface he's smooth enough, but underneath you feel the barbed edge. Ready to cut and bruise. He doesn't try it on me. He doesn't dare.

Her head shot up at the thought.

I'm a Bradford too. It takes a Bradford to handle one!

She smiled at the thought as she placed the second rose with its place card in front of her sister Evelyn's plate.

She knew how to handle Evelyn too, although it required different methods from those used on Spencer. After all, Evelyn was her sister, and she was closer than Spencer in years

3

and interests to Nina even if she was not closer in nature. Unlike Spencer, Evelyn did not look at all like a Yankee. She favored their mother, with the same tendency to plumpness which their mother had ignored but which Evelyn viciously fought by semistarvation. Evelyn was dark, with heavy hair, fiery eyes, and a cleft in her chin.

As children, Nina and Evelyn used to lean on their elbows before a table that held the gilt frames containing the pictures of their mother and their Aunt Nina.

"I'm like Mother," Evelyn used to say in a voice that was even then deep-toned and calculating. "You're like your namesake, Nina. See, you have Aunt Nina's blond curly hair." Evelyn would touch Nina's hair, saying, "It's so fine it falls away when I touch it. Your eyes are like hers too, and wideset." Then she would laugh provocatively. "Always looking as if you expected something wonderful and fine to happen to you wherever you turned." Then Evelyn would draw her fingers across Nina's cheek. "You've got too much jaw for a girl. Girls ought to look soft and appealing, even if they aren't. You look too strong, as if you were built to take it."

Then, back at the picture again, Evelyn would comment, "But our mouths are the same." Evelyn traced her fingers along the curve of Aunt Nina's mouth. "My mouth isn't like Mother's at all, I've got the Bradford mouth."

The Bradford mouth. It was Evelyn who had first called attention to it, who had pointed it out in portrait after portrait of the old Bradfords, and who had coined the phrase. The Bradford mouth.

Its sensuousness always came as a surprise, even to Nina, when she looked into the faces of her ancestors, when she found herself studying Spencer or Evelyn or any of the others. That mouth seemed generally not to belong to the faces it graced. Spencer, with all his hardness, had it. Her other brother

4

Bob had it, and Evelyn and Nina and Nina's younger daughter, Jill.

It was the feature that identified a Bradford, even as their bodies were identified by tall, straight lines, an enviable slenderness that persisted no matter how heartily they ate, a back so straight that it seemed to be made for horseback riding and sitting erect on ladder-back chairs.

Victoria has the Bradford mouth too. And Nina set the third rose down at the head of the table. Even in his own house, Nina's husband must concede this place to Victoria Bradford. It was not just because of her great age—Nina could only guess that Victoria hovered somewhere between seventy and seventy-five years, for Victoria would never tell on herself. It was not even because Victoria was the last of the old Bradfords left, the daughter of old Jared who had established Bradford Tool and given the town its name.

It was because of Victoria herself that Mark willingly yielded to her his place at the head of his own table. Mark had always admitted to Nina that her Aunt Victoria was the one person he knew who completely dominated a scene the moment she entered it.

"So we might as well put her where she belongs," Nina said softly, setting down the card.

Of all the people who would be at the dinner party tonight, Nina was sure that her husband and Victoria Bradford understood each other best. They were strangely and, to Nina, inexplicably alike. By all the rules, this should not be so. Nina saw Victoria for what she was, the proud descendant of a family of power and wealth, reared in culture and refinement, always taken care of. Nina also saw Mark for what he had been. He had been born into poverty, in one of the tenements erected by the earlier Bradfords to accommodate the cheap labor that had flowed into the town. But he had been blessed with two other heritages besides poverty: a brilliant mind and the kind of individuality that forces its way to the top.

His brilliance had won him a scholarship to M.I.T. and then had assured him first rank in his class. It had obtained for him the fateful position in Bradford Tool that had thrust him upon Nina's notice and led to her falling in love with him.

In love with him she surely was, even to this day, seventeen years after their marriage. She fondly chose a rose from the bowl on the buffet, the largest and reddest of them all, and set it down next to Victoria, at the place that would be occupied by her husband.

This is my husband, she thought, forming the words with tenderness, and remembering how proud she had been when she first uttered them. The moment she had set eyes on Mark, she had known he was the man for her.

She could even now hear the words ringing in her mind. "That man will be my husband. Someday I'll marry him."

All her important decisions in life were made like that, quick, direct, almost masculine in their sureness. She had never once regretted marrying Mark. The very idea seemed so preposterous as to bring a smile to her lips now.

People had prophesied that she would regret. They had warned and advised, and she had listened to everyone and then done as she wished. It was not just because Mark was so big and physically attractive that she had been drawn to him. It was not even because of his brilliance. Deep within herself she had felt he was more a man than her brothers or Evelyn's husband, more a man for the job to be done at Bradford Tool where he had become vice president and general manager. Yet these were not her reasons for marrying him. She would no more have thought of marrying Mark because he would fit into the Bradford need, the Bradford scheme of things, than she would have thought of not marrying him because he had been born in a tenement on River Street.

6

She wanted him for himself, for what he was. She knew what Mark Galloway was, a straightforward, lovable man, somewhat too impetuous, with a plain manner of speaking and a way of drawing a person to him and holding that person in a bond of affection. She had been drawn and she had been held. He was so much a man, she had never even desired another.

It was easy enough to like Mark Galloway, she thought. Almost everyone does. Even Spencer, fussy and hard as he is, has no complaints. Not serious ones anyway.

In his picky way, Spencer sometimes dropped minor criticisms to Nina, hoping she would pass them on to Mark. But they seldom amounted to anything.

Spencer did not particularly care for the democratic way Mark had with the men. He would hint to Nina that it was not necessary for Mark to roam through the plant so much, to learn the first name of almost every man working for the Bradfords. It was hardly important for him to know whose son was co-captain of the high-school football squad and whose wife was expecting a baby. Spencer reiterated to Nina almost every time he saw her that there was no special profit in Mark's interest in the lives, hobbies, and gripes of the men at the plant.

Nina was convinced, however, that except for these minor complaints, Spencer enjoyed working with Mark. She realized, of course, that Spencer did not wholeheartedly like her husband, but then, Spencer had never in his life wholeheartedly liked anyone, even his wife Christie or their children. His was the psychology of restraint and caution. "All human beings have faults," he was fond of saying. "We mustn't expect too much of each other." Consequently, not expecting much, he did not get much in return. His wife had a quiet contempt for him, going on her social whirl of life and meeting him only when she had to. His daughter Marilyn had run away and married a ne'er-do-well when she was eighteen. His son, having been asked to leave five reputable colleges in the East, gained a subsequent reputation for excellence in three activities: horse-back riding, ski jumping, and breaking speed laws.

But for all his distrust of the human race, Nina felt that Spencer enjoyed, in spite of himself, a fundamental faith in Mark. He had admitted as much to Nina. It is true that she had to force the admission from him, but he did concede that Mark had been a healthy shot in the arm for Bradford Tool.

"Mark is the best general manager the plant has ever had," Nina was fond of flinging into her brother's teeth.

Spencer's grave face would not flex a muscle as he nodded in acquiescence. "The relationship has been mutually beneficial," he would answer. "Mark is industrious. He's a worker, not a playboy."

Nina would discern that the curl of Spencer's lip and the scornful emphasis on "not a playboy" was intended for Evelyn's husband, Thornton Watrous, who was head of public relations, with an innocuous "Vice President" lettered on his office door. Nina was amused at Spencer's contempt for Thornton. She knew it was because Thornton got too much fun out of everything, including his job. He was not serious enough. He did not work for the sake of working. Work, as Spencer had been happy to tell Nina upon many occasions, was the cardinal virtue of life. You couldn't be anyone unless you worked hard, worked every minute, worked with a zeal that amounted almost to fanaticism. Work was Spencer's god.

"Yes, Mark's a worker," Spencer would say. "I admire him for that."

It was because of Spencer's admitted admiration for Mark's ability that Nina felt a tiny cloud of worry about the party tonight. Had her older brother been openly antagonistic to her husband, she would have brushed off her recent conversation with Spencer as carping criticism, nothing more. This man Steve Emrich, this engineer at the plant who was so clever that Mark set him up on a pedestal even above himself, calling him

8

a "genius" as an inventor. This Steve Emrich might be going to cause Nina some trouble.

Nina glanced once again over her table and quickly set down the other place cards but she was not thinking of her party now. She was thinking about Steve Emrich.

The other day when she had dropped in at the plant to bring Mark some papers he had forgotten, Spencer had called her into his office to talk about Steve. Oh, it had not been done that bluntly. There had been family talk and plant talk and discussion of policy but eventually Steve's name had popped up, with a rather startling suddenness that warned Nina this was the real reason for the chat.

This afternoon Nina boiled down the conversation in retrospect and it could be summed up neatly. Beware of Steve Emrich. He's dynamite for Mark. He wants Mark to get him the job of chief engineer. But beyond that, he wants Mark to help him climb, climb, climb in the firm. He has aspirations to do what Mark has done, to be accepted as part of Bradford Tool. Mark did it, why shouldn't Steve Emrich?

Because he's not married to a Bradford, that's why! The words were Nina's, not Spencer's. She knew a thing or two. She had chosen her man, Mark Galloway, on her own. That was true enough. But that did not mean she was breaking entirely with Bradford tradition. She was a Bradford, first, last and always. She knew what it meant to be a Bradford. She, like the other members of her family, held a unique position in this town. They had a responsibility. Their brains and acuteness and common sense and money had built up the business that was the backbone of the town. They owed something to the town. They had to keep their tradition as a family—the Bradford tradition—intact.

To marry into the Bradford family and virtually become a Bradford as Mark had done was one thing. To push your way up as Spencer indicated that Steve Emrich was trying to do was another.

She had to go easy with this. It was tricky stuff, a touchy matter with Mark. She had to be careful how she handled him and what she said. The last thing she wanted was trouble in her own home, trouble with the man she loved.

It was not a simple matter at best and it was further complicated by the fact that Mark had that dream of his tucked at the back of his thoughts, the dream that kept cropping up every so often.

"It would be swell to have my own business," he'd say sometimes half-humorously to tease her, but sometimes with a wistfulness that frightened her more than she dared to admit even to herself. "It's a dream every man has," he would elaborate upon his favorite theme. "His own name over his own door."

Steve Emrich was all tangled up in this dream of Mark's, because Steve had the dream too. She had thought of talking to Mark about Steve but her wisdom told her to let the subject alone.

Let it alone! her thoughts hammered away at her as she walked toward the living room. You're on thin ice. *Let it alone!*

She did, by main force. She pushed it out of her consciousness and concentrated on the job before her.

I must think about the party, she said to herself. It's enough of an ordeal.

With a determined effort, she put out the worry about Steve and concentrated on her home, checking everything to be sure it was perfect. Her house was especially beautiful on this late autumn afternoon. With the family Thanksgiving party in mind and with both their daughters away at school for the first time, Nina had had the Galloway house done over this fall. It had been a nightmare for a month, with Mark and Nina living down in a suite at the Harrington Inn while the decorating was being done, but as she stood here, looking around at it, she knew it had been worth the inconvenience.

Actually this had been old Jared's house. Nina herself had chosen it from the half-dozen fine houses owned by her father, as Mark's and her wedding present.

Mark was proud of her choice because he shared her devotion to the old gentleman whose portrait hung in the place of honor over their mantel.

"He was the best of the Bradfords," Nina was fond of saying. "I try to be like him but I don't always succeed. Because I'm only a woman," she would finish.

And Mark was fond of gathering her to him and saying, "You're the best of the Bradfords as far as I'm concerned, and believe me I'm glad you're a woman. *All* woman." And he would smile down at her.

She looked now from Jared on the mantel to the sweeping view she had from the doorway of his house, *her* house, the house in which she and Mark had loved and suffered together.

Yellow and blue were her colors, for she had from the Bradfords the blond hair and blue eyes of the family, and she had decorated her living room this time as a foil for herself. When her children had been younger this particular luxury had not been feasible for she was not one of those mothers who believe in keeping children cooped up in a nursery. She had let them have the run of the house. But now the house was hers and Mark's, and she had exploited this new-found freedom, this togetherness again, to the hilt.

So all the downstairs walls, with the exception of Mark's study, were varying shades of yellow, from palest cream to deep gold. She had combined wallpaper with the solid effect of painted walls, tossing aside for once her conservative taste, and choosing lively patterns in distinctive colonial designs. The floor-length draperies were topaz and there were muted tones of gold and rose in the Kermanshah rug. Blue had been used in the upholstery on the chairs and there were accents of rose in the figurines, the priceless bric-a-brac of other eras, the quaint Victorian footstools. All her furniture was very old, with the mellowness of cherished antiques, but these Hepplewhite and Sheraton and Chippendale pieces were not merely collector's items, accumulated with the feverish desire to possess something of the past that attacks so many newly arrived American families. These chairs and tables and chests, the spinet piano, even the primitive paintings on the wall had belonged to her always. And before they had been hers, they had belonged to other Bradfords. They had the pleasantly old look of long use and long possession and long memories.

She amused herself sometimes wondering how much they would have been able to tell, if they could have talked.

What scenes of love and hate, what whispered conversations, what brawling arguments, what high joy and numbing grief had they witnessed? She asked herself this question, standing among them, loving them because they were hers and because they had belonged to her ancestors before her.

"Mrs. Galloway. Excuse me, please." Nina turned to face Effie, the regular maid who lived-in with the Galloways. Today she was bolstered by two other servants hired for the occasion, a young girl to help with the kitchen chores and an experienced maid, Mildred, who was called in when any of the important families in Bradford gave a party.

"What is it, Effie?"

"The ice-cream molds are some pumpkins and some Pilgrim hats and not all Pilgrim hats like you asked for. I sure hope we have enough turkey but seems like the birds get smaller every year and you know the way Mr. Bob and Miss Victoria eat. Excuse me, I meant to say they both take third helpings. And if I'd picked out the sweet potatoes myself, I'd have picked them bigger, but the cranberry's just right, and so's the pie, and the watermelon rind couldn't be better. When do you want me to serve the *hors d'oeuvre?*" Effie pronounced it exactly the way it looked, making it sound like "horse doovree," and she rattled off what she had to say, reading most of it from scratchy notes on bits of brown wrapping paper. She prided herself on running the Galloway kitchen as efficiently as the Bradfords ran their tool company.

"Mr. Galloway just called," she said, reading from the last bit of paper. "He said not to interrupt you if you were busy, but if you weren't too busy, would you put out what he ought to wear tonight. He said you'd know best, and that he'd be late." Effie spoke the last sentence with an editorial fillip to her voice that said more plainly than words could have done, "You'd think that tonight of all nights that man would quit work on time and get home early for a change. The way he works himself to a frazzle for Bradford Tool!"

Nina smiled, careful not to let Effie see her, turning toward the mantel and old Jared's picture.

"I'm not too busy," she said. "You and Mildred and the girl" —she never could remember the girl's name—"have been wonderful."

"Just the same you ought to take a rest, Miss Nina." Effie had been inherited from Nina's mother and she still called Nina by her girlhood title, even as she called Bob and Spencer and Evelyn, "Mr. Bob" and "Mr. Spencer" and "Miss Evelyn," but she referred to Mark, the head of this household, as Mr. Galloway always, with the same primness and propriety she had used when she had addressed Nina's father as "Mr. Bradford."

"I'll rest awhile, before I dress," Nina said. "Don't worry about me. Or anything else, Effie. The party's going to be fine. You've done a good job."

Nina expected Effie to withdraw, for surely it was these last words of praise for which she had been waiting. Ordinarily they would have been enough to send Effie clicking back to the kitchen in a state of self-gratifying human goodness. Not so today.

She stood there, seeming undecided what to do.

Nina helped her out. "Is there something more?" she asked.

"Well, yes. One little thing." Effie shook her head with sudden determination. "I had a mind not to mention it this afternoon. It being such a big day for you and all. And I think I just won't talk about it, with your leave, Miss Nina. I'll save it for tomorrow."

"Tell me now, Effie. If it's important, I want to know now." Effie's mouth was a grim line.

"It's about Miss Ginger."

"Ginger?" Effie nodded, her mouth thin and unrelenting. "Oh, no! Effie, she hasn't called up again!"

"Yes, Miss Nina, she has." Effie's tongue was loosed. "And I just told her. I took it upon myself. 'Your mother has a big party for tonight and she's busy and she's worried enough and she has a million things on her mind. Now you behave yourself like the good girl you can be when you want to and let your mother alone. You go back to your classes or gym or wherever you should be and behave yourself.' I just told her."

Nina tapped the edge of the nearest table with her fingers. This was the last straw. All afternoon she had been fighting off the strain of the party and now it settled down on her. She felt suddenly very tired. Ginger like no one else could get her down.

"It's a shame," Effie was saying. "The way she keeps nagging you, Miss Nina, to take her out of that school."

"Did she talk about it today?"

"Not much. She was all set to but I didn't give her the chance. I told her what for, I did, bothering you at a time like this. And always the same thing. I wanna come home. I wanna come home. You'd think she was the baby instead of Miss Jill. I just up and told her so."

Nina's fingers tapped restlessly on the table. The whole thing was completely distasteful to her. Not so much that Ginger had called today. The calls were so frequent and persistent that she was building up a personal immunity to them. She did not like Effie to be drawn into these family matters. It did not look well. Effie was a trusted and reliable servant but if this business with Ginger kept on, it would hurt the Bradford family throughout the town, and at the plant. Worse even than that was a nagging worry that Mark was completely on Ginger's side in this campaign to have her taken out of private school and let her attend the local public high school.

Effie misinterpreted her quietness. "Did I say the wrong thing, Miss Nina? I didn't mean to butt in but I wanted to help."

"No, no. That's perfectly all right. You did the right thing. Ginger should have known better than to call this afternoon."

Effie's face relaxed.

"Can I do anything more, Miss Nina? Get you a cup of tea or hot soup? You haven't eaten enough today."

"No. No, thank you. I'm fine." She forced a smile. "That's all for now, Effie."

Effie left. Nina walked over to the portrait of Jared. She stood looking up at it. It was hung fairly low so she could easily look into Jared's eyes. They were her eyes, her Aunt Nina's eyes too, the Bradford eyes, wide-set and blue, and Jared's had a twinkle in them. She loved this portrait of him. It had been her selection from several he had sat for during his lifetime.

This was the real Jared. Proud, firm, unyielding in the right, uncompromising with those who disagreed with him, not giving an inch when he felt he had a point. But kindly and warm and human withal. There was a sparkle of fun in the eyes and around the corner of the mouth, the sensuous Bradford mouth which he carried so proudly and held so firmly in place.

Old Jared. The man with a vision. A vision and a dream like

15

Mark's dream. A business of his own. A town to give his name to.

Steve Emrich and Ginger. Nina sighed. How small these problems would have seemed to a man like Jared Bradford.

Take life in its stride, he had been fond of booming, even with the rasping voice of his later years. Nina remembered the line, flung out like a challenge to his grandchildren. "There's nothing human that's big enough to worry about!"

She remembered it tonight. Tonight was indeed a good time to remember it. She needed all the strength she had, and she herself knew that this was considerable, to face the crowd of Bradfords who would pour through her doors tonight for the traditional Bradford Thanksgiving party.

Chapter 2

MARK GALLOWAY LOVED THE FACTORY IN THE LATE AFTERNOON like this, when most of the men had gone and only the hangers-on, the men who were kept overtime for a special job, or the draftsmen with blueprints that had to be put into the mail before eight o'clock, or men like Steve Emrich were staying on in the research laboratory for sheer love of their jobs.

On the catwalk that separated the executive offices from the plant, he paused and listened. Back of him one of the secretaries, kept past her quitting hour, slammed back the carriage of her typewriter in complaint. Before him rose and fell the groaning of a machine as the workmen tried to find out what was wrong with it, testing, tinkering, trying again to get it moving with rhythmic ease. There was pounding, some intermittent hammering, the reverberation of voices calling back and forth across the long room between the groans of the machine. Mark knew what was wrong with the machine, and it gave him an indescribable satisfaction to anticipate the pleasure ahead of him, of going down there into the plant and pulling off his coat and rolling up his sleeves and pitching in.

With his arms halfway out of his coat sleeves, he paused, remembering. This was the night of the Bradford party. Only once during the day had he thought about it and that was when

Spencer, leaving early, had looked in on him and said, "Be seeing you later, Mark." The party had rushed into his mind then, and he had called home to say he wouldn't be as early as he had promised, and would Nina please put out his clothes, but he had forgotten about it again.

Now it loomed before him, an inevitability that couldn't be put off any longer. It descended upon him with an imminence that pushed out everything else, including the anticipated pleasure of a half hour's work on the defective machine. The best he could do now was call to the men and tell them what he thought was wrong.

As he passed the research laboratory, the door was open and he caught sight of Steve Emrich bent over a drafting board. He paused a moment, torn between his curiosity over how Steve's new invention was coming along and the pressure of the Bradford party. Bradford Tool had always specialized in one product: lathes. It had been a good, steady, rising business from the days when the first Bradford, old Jared, had opened up his shop to make the hand-controlled lathe that had given the family its fame and fortune. A lot had happened since then. The old shop that had been little more than a big, oak-beamed shed, had become a sprawling brick structure that spread itself like a noisy giant along the Pontatuck River.

The old hand-controlled lathe was now merely a relic in an exhibition case in the main lobby of the plant. *One of the first Bradford lathes, manufactured and sold on this site by Jared Bradford*, read the typewritten card beside the glass case.

Mark smiled whenever he looked at the exhibition. It was so laconically Yankee. It told the whole story in its concise, smug little way, and it was so typically Bradford.

The lathes that bulwarked and buttressed the family fortune today were a far cry from that primitive hand tool. They were heavy precision lathes, called in the trade "turret" lathes, and they had automatic controls. They were in demand by every big industry in the country. Aircraft, automobiles, tractors and farm implements, electrical motors. Name anything important that came to your mind. They needed Bradford turret lathes.

And Bradford Tool needed men like Steve Emrich, Mark thought as he watched the small, slight figure bent over the board. They were the brains and the lifeblood of the business. They were more than that. They were its very soul.

Back in the good old days, the ingenuity of Jared Bradford and his few trusted foremen had been enough. It was not enough any more. That was one of the things that had changed. The ingenuity of a whole family of Bradfords wasn't enough.

And there's precious little Bradford ingenuity left, Mark thought ruefully. Both Spencer, nominal head of the firm, and Bob Bradford, director of sales, graduated from engineering colleges, but this had been a token gesture at best. They had both hastily supplemented their engineering education with a stiff course in business administration to which they took like ducks to water. The engineering background was desirable. It was good to have a theoretical knowledge and an adequate vocabulary to meet the functional problems of their factory. But what they were both most concerned with was the double-entry bookkeeping. They were money-makers, both of them, hardheaded, shrewd businessmen who knew what they were doing every minute of the day and made everything pay to good advantage.

They had no special love for the factory. Not the way Mark loved it. Mark loved it the way old Jared Bradford had loved it, with a compelling passion second only to his love for his wife. For this reason he had sometimes almost come to look upon the factory as "his" plant. It was in his blood and under his skin and he could not imagine what life would have been without it.

It was true that tucked away in the back of his mind was a dream of owning his own business. But aside from an occasional bull session with Steve Emrich, when they talked about that dream, Mark had accepted old Jared's vision for Bradford Tool as his own. Nina teased him about it, saying that she did not enjoy playing second fiddle to her own grandfather's factory. Actually Mark knew she was pleased.

Spencer and Bob on the other hand could only be persuaded to go into the factory upon the most important occasions or the most urgent need. They were not like Mark, who was always finding an excuse to jump out of his office chair and run across the catwalk. They would not, for instance, have been able to tell, just by listening, what was wrong with the lathe the men were testing tonight.

For that very reason they needed men like Steve Emrich. Steve had risen, much as Mark himself, up through the testing department, into draftsmanship and design and thence to the research laboratory. There he had proven his worth within the last three years by developing a unique type of cam action to operate the feed mechanism in Bradford lathes more automatically and yet produce work to close tolerances. This had been only one of his inventions, including several devices for use with the new carbide-type cutting tools. He was as smart as Mark, a whole lot more inventive, but he stayed where he was, doing an honest job, earning a little extra on royalties in accordance with the strict policy of the Bradford Company that all inventions developed on Bradford time be absorbed into the company with reasonable royalty payments to the inventor.

Mark had a great fondness for Steve Emrich. They spoke the same language. They would rather tinker over some improvement in a turret lathe than eat. During the eight years that Steve had been here, a firm friendship had sprung up between them. Steve and Mark often worked late together and then knocked off for a snack at a corner diner where they could continue their shop talk. Sometimes, if it was summer and the weather was good, Mark and Steve would park near a sand lot and watch the kids play a Little League game. Mark had taken Steve out in his sloop three or four times to Cockinoe Island where they had had a swim and eaten some lunch put up by Effie. Twice he invited Steve to Ivy League football games. He had even suggested to Nina that she ask the Emrichs in for an evening, but Nina had always pleaded previous engagements, or absorption with little Jill.

It wasn't that Nina was a snob, Mark assured himself. It was just that she didn't like to entertain people unless she had a great deal in common with them. Why, she didn't even care much about giving this dinner party for her own family.

Mark had big things in his mind for Steve Emrich. All these years as he quietly watched his friend whose inventive ability amounted to genius, he had bided his time. And now he thought that perhaps the time had come. With the chief engineer's place empty due to the recent death of a cousin of the Bradfords, Steve was the logical man to fill that place. Steve knew more about the mechanics of Bradford lathes than the Bradfords did themselves.

"Hi!" he called to Steve. "How's it going?"

Surprised, Steve swung around. "Not bad. Come on in and I'll show you what I'm doing."

"Can't. Got to rush home to a party. Can it wait until to-morrow?"

"Sure."

"Let's make it for lunch. Take a half hour extra and we'll run over to the Roadside. Bring along your drawings."

"Swell," Steve said. "How're the kids? Or isn't that a fair question when you're in a hurry?"

Mark laughed. "Jill's pretty well adjusted now at school. Wrote a five-page letter to tell us about a new horse."

"She'll be winning prizes for horseback riding one of these days. Just like Mrs. Galloway."

"I guess so." Mark was frowning. He wasn't thinking about his youngest daughter, Jill. He was thinking about Ginger.

Tall, rebellious Ginger, the only redhead in a family of blondes and brunettes. Nina swore there must have been a redhead somewhere in Mark's family. "She certainly doesn't get those gold-flecked eyes and tawny skin and carrot top from mine!" Nina would say when Ginger wasn't around.

"How's the other girl?" Steve asked.

"Oh, fine, fine." Mark answered, preoccupied. "Well, see you tomorrow for lunch. Good night, Steve."

He went down the stairs toward the testing room, slowly now because he wanted his thoughts to run out before he reached the room where the men were still working.

Ginger was a problem. She had always been different from Jill who was a quiet, well-behaved child, falling into the pattern her mother chose for her, docile almost to a fault. Ginger was fifteen. Born during the war while Mark was overseas, she was as turbulent as the era into which she had been born. Her personality was like her hair, flamboyant, compelling attention. As a small child, she had resisted Nina, stubbornly holding out for her own way when she felt she was right. She had a positive talent for rubbing her mother the wrong way, bringing in mongrel dogs and stray kittens and dirty-faced little girls and boys whom she magnanimously called "my friends."

"Mother, I want you to meet my new friend," Ginger's resonant voice would call from the doorway, and Nina would turn to face a mangy mutt, half cocker, part collie, part almost anything, or a grubby urchin with a fist full of Effie's chocolate cookies and Ginger's new sweater on his back.

Yet, on the whole, they had managed nicely as a family and even enjoyed Ginger's personality differences. Until recently, that is. You might say until two months ago when Ginger was sent to Nina's old school up in Massachusetts in preparation for her entrance to Vassar. Until this year, Nina had kept Ginger at home, thinking she would be good company for the younger Jill, and enrolling her in a country day school. Aside from the

fact that Ginger spurned horseback riding and preferred softball to field hockey, there had been no open rebellions. Ginger
had learned to ride, albeit protestingly, and she had played field
hockey.

But now there was open rebellion, as open as Ginger could
stage with all these miles between her mother and herself, and
with only the telephone and the mail service to abet her.

Yet the letters and the telephone calls came. They came with
a regularity and a persistence that was beginning to be harrowing even to Mark who understood Ginger better than Nina did.

More and more, with every letter and call that came, it was
being brought home to him that Ginger was not going to be
tractable. She wanted to come home. It was her theme song,
her leitmotif. She wanted, with shocking clarity, to go to public
school. She had fortified herself with excellent reasons. All the
interesting people she knew went to public school. Her friends
went there, girls she had met the past summer at Claire Elliott's
dramatic school.

That had been the big mistake, Nina assured Mark every
time they discussed Ginger. It had been wrong to let her enroll
at Claire Elliott's school. It didn't matter, Nina said, that Claire
knew her theater inside and out and that she had done a lot to
give her students poise and self-assurance and some grand fun.
What mattered was that Ginger had caught the bug. It happened to other people. If anyone was crazy about acting to begin with, if you gave them the least encouragement, they went
overboard. It got in the blood. All their lives they went around
joining theater groups and wanting to act. No wonder this re-
belliousness. Ginger wanted to come back and go to public
school where Claire Elliott was teaching this year. She wanted
to join a dramatic club and be with the people she liked. She
hated horseback riding and field hockey. She was fed up to the
neck with both of them. She didn't want to be a lady. She

wanted to go to public school and eventually she wanted to be an actress. Or so she thought now.

It was appalling. It was appalling even to Mark who viewed the whole situation with more perspective and humor and composure than Nina. Ginger was so much his kid that he was crazy about her. She looked like him with her large frame, not tall the way the Bradfords were tall, with a ramrod straightness, but like a big overgrown Great Dane puppy, a little clumsy. She had Mark's features, if not his coloring, the same heavy brows meeting in a slight scowl of concentration rather than ill-humor, the same strong nose and long, firm mouth, the same prominent cheekbones. She walked like him, all determination and purpose, always hurrying to go somewhere, a bit stooped over because she was so tall. She was an ungainly girl now but she would grow into a handsome woman like his mother. She would be striking enough to make a good actress, but he did not want her to go on the stage any more than Nina did.

This child of his, so like himself, so violent in her affections and hatreds, so generous and so stubborn, frightened him a little. She frightened him because he knew himself, and he knew that no one had ever turned him aside in anything that he had proposed to do. Now here was Ginger, his own flesh and blood, standing up to her mother and to him, begging, pleading, threatening, anything to get her own way, determined to have it at any cost. He saw the humorous side of it, but as he and Nina were being dragged into argumentative discussions about what to do with Ginger, he also saw the serious side of it, and he found himself fervently wishing that she would quiet down and behave herself. He was inclined to indulge Ginger. Nina accused him of it. Maybe she's right, he thought as he went down the steps to the factory. And I'd better watch my step. Because I don't want to quarrel with Nina over Ginger unless I have to.

"Hello, Mr. Galloway." It was one of the men in the testing

department waving to him as he threw open the door upon the momentarily quiet room. The men had stopped testing the machine and were examining it again.

"Hi," he called over to them. "Sorry I can't join the party, but I think I know what's wrong."

"What, Mr. Galloway?" The men came toward him and he met them in a huddle near the doorway.

"Try changing the gears. Get a new set from stock. The ones on that lathe apparently weren't made to specification. You've got to have zero backlash in the teeth, or you won't get running smoothness." The men were already hurrying back to the testing machine. "Better try a lighter oil in the gear box, too," he said. "That might help."

"Thanks," the men called over their shoulders. "Thanks a lot, Mr. Galloway."

He turned and went out of the testing room and hurried toward the parking lot where his car stood in the spot under the shed reserved for it. As he turned on his dashboard lights, he noticed that the clock indicated it was eight minutes past six.

He whistled and said to the darkness around him, "Brother, I'm going to catch it. And this time I deserve it."

He smiled at the thought of Nina pretending to scold him because he was so late. She wouldn't mean it. Not really. After seventeen years of marriage, they were still desperately in love with each other. He knew it wasn't according to Hoyle, not the way people held marriage so lightly nowadays. You were supposed to get sick of each other. You were supposed to get so fed up and so jaded that you fell in love with someone else, anyone but your wife.

It hadn't happened to him. He was sure it would never happen. There had been quarrels and disagreements and days of pouting and sullenness but those had been few and far between. The vast majority of their days together had been wonderful.

Quietly, only to himself, he admitted that he had two loves

in his life. It was the price he paid for being a man and especially for being Mark Galloway. He loved his work. He loved it with a devotion that could be called passion. He would have been miserably unhappy if anything ever happened to wrench his work away from him. But he loved Nina too. He loved her because she was beautiful and alluring and chic and the epitome of good taste in everything she did. But even above this he loved her because of all they had suffered and overcome together, the tense separation while he was overseas, the bitter loss of their only son, the hundred and one little things that go to make up the adjustment of two personalities called marriage. He loved her especially because she was, in every sense of the word, his wife.

Chapter 3

MARK FOUND HIS WIFE STRETCHED OUT ON THE ROSE DAMASK chaise longue in her dressing room, her lovely, slender body wrapped in a turquoise robe and her yellow hair spread fanlike as a frame for her delicate face. He sat down on the edge of the couch and bent over and kissed her, long and hard.

"This is worth coming home for," he said.

She laughed, pleased. "You're late." He sighed in answer, waiting for the scolding. "I'm not going to scold tonight. We've both got a big enough evening ahead as it is." This time they laughed together, sharing their feelings about the party.

"It's only once in five years," Mark said. "Maybe by the time our turn shows up again, there won't be any party."

"What a lovely thought, darling. Do you expect all the Bradfords to die off?" She slanted her eyes, teasing him.

"Of course not. I meant we might be moved to Alaska or somewhere."

"Hypocrite," she said. "You'd disintegrate if you were moved five miles from the Bradford Tool Company. You love the place more than any Bradford."

Mark grunted his acquiescence, getting up and ripping off his tie and coat. He invariably did this when they were going out or entertaining for the evening, starting to get undressed in

27

Nina's dressing room and scattering his things in a trail to his own sitting room beyond the bedroom which they shared. It was a compliment to Nina's wifely wisdom that she had spurned the custom of so many female relatives and friends who had set up separate sleeping quarters for themselves and their husbands.

Shortly after his return from the war, as they had gone the round of homes, visiting relatives and friends, Mark had expressed himself plainly on this matter of separate bedrooms.

"Look, Nina," he had said, "this thing frightens me. These people don't sleep together. It's a kind of disease." Nina had chuckled softly. "I'm not being funny. I'm being dead serious. If you ever spring this separate room stuff on me, Nina—" He had interrupted his threat, not knowing exactly what he wanted to say, not even knowing exactly what he felt. It was a primitive instinct which rebelled against a husband and wife not sleeping together, but he could not put it into words. Nina had saved him the trouble by putting her arms around him and calling him darling and kissing him and saying she understood exactly what he meant and she felt the same way.

So they had always shared this huge bedroom on the second floor of the beautiful old house that had once belonged to Jared Bradford. At one end was Mark's sitting room, different from his downstairs study where he sometimes held business interviews, seeing people whom he could not conveniently work into his schedule at the plant. The study was orderly and tidy and fitted into their home. The upstairs sitting room was an answer to Mark's wail for a place which he could call his own.

"I need one place in this spotless house where I can be sloppy. I'm not a tidy person. I've got to have someplace where I can stretch my full height and throw things around."

So the sitting room was this place for him, with its simple furnishings, mostly dark leather, a drafting board in one corner under a blazing arc of light, a glassed-in cupboard to hold his collection of curious antique inventions which he doted upon gathering at auctions and fairs. Then in the bedroom you passed again to the world of Nina Bradford Galloway, all elegance and order with its old canopied four-poster, its long bed-chest at the foot of the bed, the pair of saffron-colored wing chairs and the two lowboys and massive highboy, the mauve-colored gauzelike curtains and the flowered chintz overdrapes in tones of deep saffron and Wedgwood blue and the hooked rugs, so old that the colors had faded into a pleasant softness.

Actually, Mark enjoyed most of all Nina's own dressing room, a long room at the other end of the bedroom with a French dressing table and chairs, and the damask chaise longue, white rugs on the floors, and on the walls eighteenth-century French prints of dandies and ladies in their laces and satins. He liked it because it was feminine. Being all man, his instinct went out to the warmth of this delicate white-and-pink thing that was Nina's dressing room, and that was, in its way, the epitome of Nina herself. It was fragile and delicate like Nina. It was refined and dainty. It reminded him of a woman and for that reason he loved to come home and stand here in this room and rip off his tie and coat and bend down and kiss Nina again, three times, four times, until his mouth ached from the hardness and eagerness of his kissing.

"I've got to get dressed," she said, stretching lazily. "Everyone will arrive promptly at seven thirty. This dreadful family affliction of punctuality. For once, just once, I wish I could be deliberately late for something. But I never will because I wouldn't enjoy it."

Mark lingered, pretending to be so tired he had to stretch out on the couch for a few moments, but actually he stayed because he enjoyed watching Nina dress. His eyelids were only half closed as she threw off her negligee and tossed it beside the things she had placed on one of the chairs and which she would wear to the party.

Whenever she tossed off her robe like that, his mind, even

seventeen years later, raced back to their wedding night. Nina, in her long-lined strapless satin brassiere, white and shining above the lace-trimmed white petticoat, was his bride again. She was as slender as she had been then, and her figure, after three childbearings, was still as good. For all her slenderness, she was full-breasted and below her long, tiny waist, her hips rounded out with feminine provocativeness.

All woman, Mark always thought when he watched her toss off her robe. And what a woman!

"Mark," she said. He closed his eyes as she turned toward him and murmured a faint "Mmm?" pretending to doze.

"You're not a bit asleep," she said. "So don't make believe. I want to talk to you about Ginger." He didn't answer. "I had both a letter and a telephone call today." His eyes were shut tight, but he knew that Nina, who missed nothing, would be watching the twitching of his jawline and know he was much too tense even to be resting. "Effie took the call but I read the letter myself. She says that if we don't let her come home, she'll do something desperate. She doesn't say what. Just threatens. She keeps repeating how much she hates the school." Nina was silent a moment and he listened to the rustle of her gown as she slipped it over her head.

Her voice came to him again. "Darling, I'm frightened about our oldest daughter. Why isn't she like Jill?"

Mark rebelled at the question, even as his daughter was rebelling at Nina's school. It was an idiotic question, but he would not let Nina suspect he thought so. Nina was a smart woman; she ought to understand that no one could be exactly like anyone else. She might, with as much sense, ask why Jill wasn't like Ginger. He didn't uphold Ginger in this particular shenanigan of hers, this open rebellion against her mother and him—for Nina's sake he had stood staunchly by her in her choice of a school for Ginger and her insistence that Ginger stay there—but Nina had no right to question Ginger's individuality. Ginger might be wrong, but the kid had a right to be wrong in her own way. And when the time came—the right time—he would make Nina see it.

"Mark, are you taking Ginger's side in this?"

The question bolted him right out of his pretense at dozing. He opened his eyes wide and faced the loveliest woman in the world. Nina was fully dressed now, in something so beautiful that it took a man's breath away. As usual, he missed the details in the blurring effect of his wife's startling loveliness. He just knew that her dress was something airy and palest blue, and he saw her hair like a halo of gold above the blue dress and the whiteness of her throat and shoulders.

He jumped up and took her in his arms. "Did I ever tell you how much I love you?"

Her laugh, tinkling and charming when she was pleased, eased the moment for both of them and turned the talk away from the ticklish subject of Ginger. She drew gently back. "Darling, go dress this minute. As it is, I'll have to meet the family alone. Or is that the way you planned it?" He looked at her eyes, almond-shaped as they always were when she teased him.

"You don't have a very high opinion of your husband."

This time it was she who kissed him, taking his face in her hands and pulling him toward her.

"I adore my husband and I have the highest opinion a woman could possibly have of him. Now, does that satisfy you?"

"Enormously," he said, winking at her and making his hurried, half-clumsy way from her dressing room. At the door, he turned, "Don't worry about that redheaded brat of ours," he said. "I'll find some way to bring you both to terms."

In the bedroom, alone, Mark went about his dressing in a far more leisurely manner than the occasion demanded, enjoying this interim of solitude before he went down to face the Bradfords. For a few moments, as he came out of the shower, wrapped in a huge terry-cloth towel, he stood there and drank in the atmosphere of his home. It was a good place to be. It was an especially good place to be when you had come out of one of the cramped little houses, those drab boxes chopped up into three- and four-room apartments down on River Street.

At the factory, he seldom had time to think so self-consciously of what he had been, and of what he was now and of how far he had come. Tonight, perhaps because of the very nature of the occasion, an awareness of these facts pressed against him.

He was Mark Galloway, husband of Nina Bradford, and he owned half of this house and everything in it. He was one of the vice presidents and the general manager at Bradford Tool. He knew that many people—all the people who mattered really —said that he was the most vital wheel in the firm because of his key position between the men and the management.

He was secure. For the last ten years or so, he had felt that growing awareness of security that was the most important thing in life. Make no mistake about it, brother, he told himself when he talked it over with himself, security is what counts. A wife like Nina, a job you are crazy about, a home like this, a couple of kids. Sure, he would rather have had one or both of them be boys. What red-blooded man doesn't want at least one son, but that was a minor tragedy when you took in the whole full span of a life. He had so much to be thankful for that for a moment he wanted to get down on his knees and thank God. He wasn't ashamed of this thought. He was on speaking terms with God. Sometimes he asked for things like guidance and wisdom. He had a rough, clumsy way of praying that he had picked up on mine-infested battlefields. He had prayed hard and long when Nina had her children—their children—and he had prayed when his son was sick and he had prayed when Nina was ill for so long after their son had died. He knew how to

32

talk with God and he did that tonight, not hurriedly, because he knew you could never hurry God about anything. But slowly and quietly as he went about his dressing and breathed in the love and comfort all around him, he thanked God for it.

Then, suddenly, as he was putting his studs into his dress shirt, he paused. This room was so perfect in every way, with its rare antiques, its simple elegance. Downstairs he could hear the sounds in the kitchen, muted and shushed by the watchful Effie, but perceptible none the less. And even Effie could not keep the house from being permeated tonight with the mouth-watering smells of turkey and chestnut dressing and warm pie. There was Nina's laugh, a thing he loved to hear because it was so free from constraint and fear, as she talked to the first of the Bradfords to arrive. All this was well-being. All this was good. Yet by some strange perverseness his mind would go back to-night to the boxlike house on River Street with all the walls painted a sickening shade of bright green, dirty and pock-marked by generations of pictures hung by various occupants, and the old black kitchen stove, and the broken furniture with the shabby upholstery. This had been home. This was what he had come from and he had hated it. When he was a boy, he used to tell himself that he would fight his way out of it. He would break noses and arms and legs and heads if necessary to climb up out of that squalor and poverty.

He had done it so much more easily than that.

He had done it by using his intelligence and his ability. He had also fallen in love with Nina Bradford. His marriage to Nina had saved him time, valuable time, in reaching his goal. But he would have reached it anyway. He had never doubted that. He would have got out of that house on River Street. Squalor and poverty could never have held him captive. Man had a better birthright than that. This he felt deep inside him and all his life had been proof of what he believed must be inevitably true about all men.

33

He was thoughtful now because he remembered something Jason Evans had preached in his sermon last Sunday. Jason was his minister and his friend. Except for Steve Emrich, Mark looked upon Jason as his best friend. Steve and Jason. They were as far apart in interests and temperament as two men could be, but Mark had put his hand upon both of them, in much the same manner as Ginger would put her hand upon people she liked and say, This is my friend.

The first Sunday Nina had taken Mark to her church and he had looked into the face of Jason Evans as the latter stood greeting his parishioners on the way out, Mark had said to himself, This man I like. He'll be my friend. He's a good man.

Mark had been a religious man but never a churchgoer until Nina had persuaded him that he must become one. Then Jason had finished the job Nina had begun, calling on them, asking Mark to stop by and see him, going out in his sloop with him, cementing their friendship with long talks about everything under the sun and a few things above it.

But more than anything it was Jason's sermons that drew Mark to church Sunday after Sunday. Jason had the athletic mind of a man of letters. His sermons were literary gems, but in addition to this, he could preach them, which was something else again. Mark remembered whole passages of Jason's sermons. They came back to him throughout the week in odd moments, even as one quotation came back to him now. It was from Psalms.

"He brought me up also out of an horrible pit, out of the miry clay, and set my feet upon a rock, and established my goings."

"He did," Mark said aloud to his reflection in the mirror, as he deftly tied his black tie. "That's exactly what's happened to me."

He used two brushes to flatten his wavy hair, and grimaced as it bounced up again. In fifteen minutes, it would look as if he had run his hands through it in a frenzy. He strapped on his wrist watch and walked down to meet the Bradfords.

Going downstairs, he could make out voices and thin, nervous laughter. Then there they all were, as Mark stepped to the wide door of the room, not seeing him as they stood absorbed in their conversations. He had that fleeting moment to appraise them and it amused him to do just that.

His eyes went involuntarily to three corners as three of the Bradfords formed a magnetic triangle in the Galloway living room.

Victoria was the apex of the triangle. She drew and held Mark's eyes first. Straight and standing, she gave out, for all her years, an aura of timelessness. Her hair was snow-white but her face did not have the shriveled look of ancient parchment one finds so often in the elderly. There was natural color in her cheeks, her eyes were still the candid blue of Nina's eyes, and her mouth had retained much of its sensuous fullness.

Her gown was extremely chic, of a muted apricot color, and she wore it with an air, as a Parisian gown should be worn.

Watching her in animated conversation with Spencer's wife, Christie, Mark could not help remembering all the things he had heard about her. Victoria's past read like a sentimental novel of the era into which she had been born. She had once been the most talked-about woman in Bradford, but the touch of scandal had never drawn its ugly shadow across her path.

Mark reviewed the gossip. Although Victoria had never married, there had been four or five love affairs, one with an actor, one with an artist, and one, so rumor had it, with a duke.

Now that would have been something to see, Mark thought. The valiantly American Victoria and a foreign duke!

Victoria herself had been a painter of sorts and she had published some poetry. Mark had read the six volumes of verse and it wasn't at all bad stuff. The paintings were something else again. Monstrous impressionistic canvases that Mark loathed and could not understand. Yet her house and her studio were full of this weird stuff and you had to admire it if you cared to remain Victoria's friend, something which Mark very much wished to do. Except for Nina, Victoria was to Mark the best Bradford left.

His ears, rather than his eyes, pulled Mark's attention to the second point of the triangle. Evelyn Watrous, buttressed by her husband on one side and Bob Bradford on the other, was holding court. Her laugh, a peculiarly provocative laugh that turned most men's heads but sent shivers through Mark, pierced the room.

He disliked Evelyn. It was an unreasonable, and, so far as Mark knew, a completely groundless dislike, and yet he could not help it. This dislike bothered him on two counts; first because Evelyn was Nina's only sister and he felt he should feel at least a certain cordiality toward her. Secondly, there were so few people he disliked that when he found himself rubbed the wrong way by a personality, it bothered him.

He was not sure just what it was about Evelyn. He never had been able to put his finger on the trouble and he was no more successful than ever as he watched her tonight, laughing, talking gaily, keeping the fawning Thornton Watrous in tow much the way a great queen might keep a courtier in attendance. It did not become a husband and wife to act like this in public. Mark resented seeing it in his own house, not only because Evelyn's subtle and elusive character went against the grain with him, but also because she antagonized him in behalf of all the males in the world. She was an insult to his sex. She dominated and browbeat, not openly, but in that sensuous, insinuating way of hers, and he hated her for it. A man should be a man. He should be in control. He should be his own man and not his wife's man. Therefore, if Mark distrusted Evelyn, he held her husband, Thornton Watrous, in contempt.

They're quite a pair! he thought, quelling his emotions as best he could. Thank goodness Nina doesn't feel she has to be too intimate with her sister. We'd be in for some real trouble if she did.

He heard a short, nervous cough and turned to the third point of the invisible triangle he had drawn in his mind.

Spencer Bradford. Mark smiled inwardly. Most people were not amused by Spencer. They were either frightened or infuriated. Mark had belonged to the latter group long ago, very long ago. That was before he had learned what a really small man Spencer was.

If Victoria represented the best of the Bradford tradition and Evelyn formed the inscrutable middle element, Spencer revealed the worst of the Bradford strain.

There must have been Bradfords like him before, Mark thought. Maybe the first one that stepped off the boat in Guilford in 1639 was like him, maybe not. This may have been a later breed that cropped up somewhere in the relentless march down through the centuries, but here he is in all his pettiness and narrowness, hammering away at Nina and Bob's wife, Alice, about heaven only knows what. Money, business, work. Those were the only things Spencer could talk about intelligently, with a special emphasis on money.

Money was fine and important and Mark would be the last one to deny the fact, but it didn't come before everything else. Profits in business were not more important than the men who worked for you, their welfare, their happiness.

Spencer had been fighting Mark for years on every important progressive move Mark tried to make at Bradford Tool. They had come to grips over the recreation building project, vacation-with-pay and benefit-insurance program, the more liberal policy for older employees plan, incorporating a workable system for using older men in the factory. Sometimes Mark had won as on the latter count, sometimes he had lost.

All the fights with Spencer had not in the least squelched Mark's zest for the plant. Spencer may have become Mark's gadfly, but he also tested his metal. Mark knew his own worth. He knew that Spencer knew his worth too. Spencer may not have liked him, but he respected him and he knew that Mark was there to stay, as much a Bradford as anyone who had that precious blood flowing in his veins.

Mark sized up the man back of the nervous cough. It was a puny cough, as small in sound as the man was in character. Mark knew the significance of it. Spencer had something on his mind, something important that disturbed him, and Mark was pretty sure they'd hear what it was before the evening was out.

Spencer teetered back on his heels, rocking back and forth as he talked and nodded to Nina. Mark's eyes swept down the tall, slender frame in the dinner jacket, taking in the almost bald head, the pinched nose and chin, the two spots of high color in the cheeks, the watery blue eyes.

People who had known him well said that Spencer had once been a fine-looking, sensitive young man. It was inconceivable. Mark could not believe it, even when they showed him the old photographs. Yet he had to believe it. Even if he could not believe his eyes, he must believe his experience. Mark knew that life could touch you and scar you indelibly. He had been touched and scarred himself. Or was it rather that you touched life and left your own stamp, your own scars upon yourself?

"Mark!" It was Victoria who called his name, spying him first and hurrying over to meet him. She threw her arms around him and kissed him. It was a firm, hard, family kiss. Then she stood back and looked at him. "Here's a man," she said, dramatically, in her deep voice that filled the room. "If I must ever have been loved by any man, I'd have chosen one like this." She winked solemnly at Mark while Spencer coughed and coughed.

She jabbed Mark with her forefinger. "Tell them you still love me, Mark."

"Victoria, you witch," Mark said affably. "I'm crazy about you." Victoria put her arm through his, with a sudden primness that only he and she knew to be the act it was. "You're late," she thundered. "What right have you, a mere upstart and pretender to the throne of Bradford, to arrive at this royal feast ten whole minutes late?"

"I couldn't get my hair to stay down," Mark said, helping himself to an anchovy.

"Now that's the first sensible remark I've heard all evening." Victoria nodded her approval. "This is a very bright young man you've got, Nina. Hang on to him. Don't let him get away from you."

Evelyn laughed much too loudly and Thornton joined her.

"I'm hungry," Victoria said. "Mark, take me in to dinner."

The dinner which was to prove so memorable a one for Mark began as every other Bradford Thanksgiving dinner had. Victoria, at the head of the table, said grace, reading from the family Bible the Hundredth Psalm. Then, while the fruit shrub was being served, there was some trifling self-conscious conversation. Victoria, who might easily have done so, did not try to grasp the conversation and steer it whichever way she liked. She listened. Mark, watching her, had the feeling that she was listening to learn, and perhaps to be amused.

Spencer talked about a possible forthcoming trip to Missouri, Christie complimented Nina on the newly redecorated house, and there was a lengthy discussion about interior decorators. None of it was important but the Bradfords, gathered around the table, found it easy to exchange banalities while they let their thoughts wander to the more important or merely interesting topics in their minds.

Nothing might have happened that evening that had not happened, with variations, at the dozen or so previous Bradford Thanksgiving dinners which Mark had attended. Even the question that set the thunder rumbling across the room and the lightning crackling about all their ears came only as a minor conversational theme of no real importance.

It was Victoria who asked it.

She asked it with a casual twist of her wrist as she indicated to Effie that she would have her second helping of turkey.

"Who's going to take poor Sheldon's place at the plant?"

Sheldon was the cousin whose recent death had left the chief engineer post vacant. There was no sympathy in Victoria's voice, even though she used the word "poor" in describing Sheldon. He had been a weakling, a little mouse of a man, and although he did know something about engineering, his picayune traits had caused him to be thoroughly disliked by both relatives and strangers.

"Have you anyone in mind, Spencer?"

Spencer coughed. He was a nervous man at best and he had the nervous man's dislike of blunt questions, except when he was asking them himself.

"Nothing's settled, Victoria," he said, rather brusquely. "These things take time. Poor Sheldon's death was sudden."

Victoria sighed and Mark would have sworn there was a twinkle in her eye. "Poor Sheldon," she repeated. "He was such a tiresome man. I'm sure he wore himself out with his own company."

Spencer and Bob looked properly shocked. Christie snickered and Thornton Watrous almost rolled off the chair.

Spencer's cough was sharp and personally directed at Victoria, in much the way a schoolteacher will tap her ruler at an insolent student.

"Sheldon was a very fine engineer," he said. "He was a valuable asset to the firm. I'm sure we'll all miss him."

"Such nonsense," Victoria said. "You know very well that Sheldon was only a second-rate engineer and that he held his job only because he was a Bradford. I don't know anything about engineering and very little about the mechanics of the Bradford plant but my intelligence tells me that Sheldon was about as essential down there as a woodchuck in a garden of young vegetables. From what I heard he made trouble and stirred up the men."

The silence around the table was broken only by the tapping and clicking of Victoria's fork and knife as she tackled the succulent turkey.

"Mark," she said, "you know I'm right. You tell them what a dreadful liability poor Sheldon was."

Mark shifted uneasily on his chair. He did not like to be drawn into a family quarrel right here in his own dining room.

Victoria saved him the trouble of answering. "Oh, you don't have to say anything, Mark. I know what you're thinking. You know as well as I do that Sheldon was one of the most disliked men in this town." Victoria grabbed the stem of her water goblet and thrust it forward as if to make a toast.

"To the late lamented poor Sheldon Bradford," she said. "Wherever he may be, I hope he's causing less trouble than he did here."

Bob gasped and Spencer bent double in a paroxysm of coughing. When he was able to talk, he glared at Victoria through watery eyes.

"I think that's going a bit too far, don't you?" he asked in a shocked voice.

"Nonsense." Victoria took the glares of the two men in her stride. They did not ruffle her in the least, these two hardheaded nephews of hers. "People make too much of death, as if that in itself were a virtue and that by being pushed over the line from one phase of existence to another, the poor departed had gathered some kind of immunity from all the evil they've done here. Now take poor Sheldon for instance, he was a mean, petty, backbiting man. There wasn't a man at the plant who had any reason to feel gratitude or love for him. He browbeat inferiors.

He bootlicked superiors. He had a mean soul. Do you think that just by dying he's become some sort of sanctimonious hero? Nonsense!"

Spencer pushed back his chair. "I don't think I want any dessert," he said.

Victoria reached across the table—he was near enough to her so she could touch him—and pushed him back.

"You can't run away from me, Spencer," she said. "I haven't finished with you. You stay and eat your dessert. Nina's cook makes the best pie in the county. And besides, I want you to answer my question. Who's going to take poor Sheldon's place?"

Spencer sat down again, tapping his fingers against the table in irritation. "I told you I didn't know who was going to take his place. It takes time. We've got to look the field over."

"You mean the field of Bradfords?"

Bob came into the fray. "Well, naturally, Victoria, we'll want someone from our own ranks"—he emphasized the word *ranks*—"for an important post like chief engineer."

"I've already looked over the ranks. There isn't an eligible Bradford available," Victoria retorted.

Spencer seized the bait.

"That's a rash statement, Victoria. There are plenty of Bradfords available. Cousin Ollie Muthersbaugh has two boys who were graduated from engineering school seven or eight years ago. They've been cutting their wisdom teeth on some good jobs. I think we ought to have them in and talk to them."

"Cousin Ollie Muthersbaugh!" Victoria sniffed. "Cousin Ollie didn't know enough to come in out of the rain and her husband was a yes-man who married her for her father's money. What kind of sons do you think might come of a union like that? Now if Mark down there had a son and if that son were the right age, I'd say, let's take the boy into the firm. Mark's a man, a big, strapping he-man with guts and strength, and Nina

42

married him because she loved him. That kind of marriage might produce a son that could amount to something."

Mark and Nina exchanged glances and then looked hurriedly away from each other. Victoria, in her onrushing way, had unwittingly touched a sore spot and she seemed to sense this herself because she changed the subject.

"Spencer," she said, "I came here tonight with something on my mind. You won't let me go to board meetings. You find all sorts of ways of keeping me away. So I'm determined to have my say here tonight. I want a man for this job of chief engineer who's not a Bradford."

"That's ridiculous," Spencer snorted. "It's a policy of the firm. You can't change policies."

"Policies aren't law," Victoria thundered. "I'm fed up on this inbreeding. Mark here has proved that the best chance we've got to stay as big and important as we are is to take in new blood. There's not a red-blooded Bradford left. You might as well face it, Spencer, because it's true. This family hasn't specialized in engineering. They've specialized in horseback riding."

It was fortunate that at just that moment, Effie and the young girl who was helping her appeared to clear the table and bring in the desserts. Victoria's final remark had set up an undercurrent of unrest down the length of the table because everyone except Mark felt the barb of it. Nina had been champion amateur horsewoman of the state for many years. Spencer, Bob Bradford, and his wife Alice were members of the Hunt Club. The Watrouses were fond of being photographed in riding clothes for newspapers and magazines and even Christie, who had acquired a nice disdain for everything characteristically Bradford, rode for the social splash it gave her.

Victoria was unabashed. "Now I've hurt everyone's feelings," she said. "Everyone but Mark." She softened a bit. "I'm not trying to hurt feelings," she explained, "but I've got to speak my mind. I think we should pick someone for chief engineer who's qualified because of his training and brains and not because of his family connections."

"I agree with you on that." It was Thornton Watrous. Mark looked at him curiously, wondering what he could be thinking of. He was here tonight solely because of this inbreeding policy of the Bradfords and he held his own job only by virtue of family relationship. Perhaps he was saying this to needle Spencer. Thornton would not readily take a position in the open against Spencer at board meetings, but here, under the protection of Victoria's family prestige, he could antagonize Spencer by taking Victoria's side. Mark guessed that Thornton did not care two hoots whether the new chief engineer was a Bradford or a Smith or a Jones. He just liked to see Spencer writhe.

Then Thornton did a remarkable thing, something which almost jolted Mark right off his chair.

"Victoria," he said, "you've been asking for candidates. I think Mark has a candidate for the vacant job." He turned to Mark. "What about Steve Emrich?" he asked. "You're rooting for Steve, aren't you, Mark?"

Mark felt every eye in the room turn on him. There were Spencer's cold, cynical eyes and Bob's shrewd eyes lost in a mountain of fat and Christie's bold, inquisitive eyes and Victoria's frankly admiring ones and the Watrouses' greedy, restless eyes and Nina's beautiful, appealing ones.

Her look was pleading with him, asking him to stop this monstrous family row. He could do it. He could be a man of great tact and gentle diplomacy when he wanted to. He could, by saying that all this was so much nonsense and he had never thought of Steve Emrich as anything but a man he liked to talk to in the shop, a man who had special know-how in the research laboratory, deftly terminate the discussion.

As host, it was his place to do what he could to stop this squabble, but he knew he would not stop it.

He looked away from the focus of his wife's imploring eyes, down at his plate. This was his moment. He might never have it again. He would have wished to have it in a less dramatic way. He would have chosen to drop quietly into Spencer's office some afternoon and point out Steve's good points and suggest that they consider him for chief engineer.

But he was too much Mark Galloway to overlook the opportunity before him. He had a family hearing. Now, here tonight, in his own home, at his own table, he could win over Victoria and possibly the Watrouses and certainly Christie Bradford who took an opposite stand from her husband in everything. He could place his case before his wife in a way he might not have been able to do at any other time. He felt sure that if Nina really knew Steve Emrich, knew him as he knew him, and understood that Steve would have been a good man in any job, any place, any time, she would want him to get ahead as much as he did.

He looked up, staring into Victoria's eyes and realizing that they were the only genuinely friendly eyes at the table. All the others were filled with fear or selfishness or anxiety. Even Nina's were clouded with concern, worried about what Mark would say next.

He decided to give it to them straight, no holds barred.

"You're right, Thornton," he said, in a voice so loud that it carried the full length of the table and enabled his listeners to hear without straining. "I am rooting for Steve Emrich. One hundred per cent. From where I'm sitting he's the only man for the job."

There was a momentary silence. Then a chair scraped. Spencer got up and Victoria did not detain him this time.

"I refuse to stay and listen to such idiotic talk," he said. "Steve Emrich for chief engineer! That climber! Why, it's preposterous." He was fuming, punctuating his speech with that little, hacking cough of his. "You know he could never fill the job, Mark. He's not man enough." In his anger he leaned across the table and shook a finger at Mark. "You know it as well as I. You're just doing this to oppose me. You've opposed me all along the line on policy. You're an impulsive, headstrong man, full of whims, wanting your own way, wanting to show your admiring little world how strong you are." He wheeled on Nina. "Mark my words, Nina, you'll live to regret the day you married this man and brought him into our family."

Chapter 4

THE DAY AFTER THE THANKSGIVING PARTY HAD AN INAUSPICIOUS beginning for Mark. Nina did not come down for breakfast. This was something that happened so seldom, only when she was seriously ill, that in itself it was a momentous event. It portended for Mark, whose whole life was wrapped up in two things, his job and his wife, a very bad day indeed.

He knew what was troubling Nina. The party last night had not gone well. There had been that frightful squabble between Spencer and Victoria and then, to climax it, had come his own catastrophic remark about Steve Emrich, with Spencer's nasty retaliation. The party had broken up early.

If Nina had let Mark talk it out with her, they might have cleared the atmosphere between them. But no, she would maintain that painful silence, speaking only when he spoke to her and then in hurt little sentences that made him feel boorish and guilty. He had spoiled her party. He had taken sides against Spencer in favor of an ambitious upstart, Steve Emrich. So she had slept away from Mark, on the far side of the bed, with her back turned to him, spending a restless night. He knew because he had not slept a wink himself.

Now this morning in the small dining ell between the formal dining room and the kitchen, that cheerful place which Nina called their "breakfast room," he sat alone, jabbing at his grape-fruit and splintering his toast.

He hated Nina to be angry with him. He wanted her opposite him in one of her colorful housecoats, chatting about the hundred and one unimportant things that married people who are still in love with each other like to talk about. Before he left, he ran upstairs, planning to scoop her up in his arms and kiss her and tell her that he loved her, but when he entered their bedroom and tiptoed across the thick rug, he saw that she had fallen asleep at last, curled up, kittenlike, with her face half hidden under the covers and her blond hair tousled as it never was when she was awake.

He loved to look at her like this, rumpled for a change. She was beautiful even in sleep, and there was a little-girl quality about her expression that reminded him of his daughter Jill. Looking down at her, wanting so much to awaken her with his love, he thought that Jill and she might have passed for sisters at this moment.

Then he turned and tiptoed from the room.

At the plant he met with even more pronounced coldness from the Bradford family. Spencer usually dropped into Mark's office during the morning to leave a list of things he wanted taken up in the factory but this morning he sent his secretary with an interoffice memo. It was a direct snub. Mark understood it for what it was.

Bob, who was usually all over the place, popping his head in and out a half-dozen times during a busy morning, today did not put in an appearance either. He telephoned Mark once, about something that had to be talked over, but he did not mention last evening.

Thornton, on the other hand, went out of his way to look Mark up. He was full of talk about the party. It had been a great shindig, the food wonderful as always, the house had quite overwhelmed Evelyn, who was talking about using the same decorator for their own home. Nina was a charming hostess, Thornton assured Mark. And Victoria was quite a girl, wasn't she? Plenty of spunk for her age. Remarkable woman. He was careful to avoid any mention of Steve Emrich, or Mark's defense of his friend. Thornton was obviously on his best behavior, eager to please Mark, saying only the right things.

But they were not the right things after all, because Thornton's approbation was something Mark felt he could do without. While the aloofness and displeasure of the Bradford brothers had left him feeling nipped with frost, Thornton's overdone affability gave him a sticky feeling, as if he'd like to run home and take a long shower and change his underwear.

Late in the morning Mark jumped up from his desk and ran across the catwalk to the factory. As he shook off the stuffiness of the executive offices, a wave of relief swept over him. The men called good morning to him as he went, more hurriedly than usual, through the various departments. It made him feel good to hear the ringing sound of his name as it echoed through the rooms through which he passed. "Hi, Mr. Galloway!" "Hello, Mr. Galloway, how are you this morning?" or "Hi, there, Mark," from someone with whom he had worked before he married Nina Bradford. He stopped in the testing department to ask the men how they had made out with the defective lathe last night. He looked in on the tool room and then ran down to the stock room and chatted a few minutes with old McGovern, the longest-employed man still with the company, and just about the most outspoken.

McGovern was a great gossip, a regular old woman with his tongue, and it sometimes amused and enlightened Mark to talk with him. Mark often used him when he wanted to get to the bottom of something that was going on in the plant and needed to be straightened out. McGovern knew everything about everyone. His information was startlingly accurate. He culled it from every department as the men came down with their orders for tools and other equipment. Many a time Mark had averted serious friction in the plant by listening to what Mc-Govern had to say.

McGovern had already heard something about the Bradford Thanksgiving party.

"What they trying to do to you, Mr. Galloway, those two up there? Don't let them push you around. You got all the men back of you." McGovern, chewing gum with the stubs of teeth he still owned, stared over his long nose at Mark. He cackled, almost swallowing his gum. "I heard Miss Victoria told them off in high style. By golly, there's a woman for you. Real chip off the old block. Her father's daughter down to the last shoelace. Old Jared Bradford was a regular guy. Too bad some of the men in his family didn't inherit his know-how."

Mark left the stock room wondering how much McGovern had heard and who had told him. Not anyone in the family, certainly. Even Thornton would not be so rash. It had probably crept out through those extra girls Nina had hired to serve dinner last night. The secretaries in the offices had a remarkable intuition for ferreting out what was going on behind the scenes. They were thick as thieves. One of their greatest pastimes was to get together for gossip during coffee break. Mark always said more Bradford business was settled there than at board meetings. Someone had, no doubt, started the rumor about the squabble of last evening and it had been pushed along by the grapevine, inflated and distorted until heaven only knew what it sounded like by now.

Mark shrugged it off. It happened all the time. It wasn't of any real importance in itself. What was important were the repercussions in the executive offices themselves. He didn't like the way Spencer and Bob had conspired to shut him out. It was bad for everyone's morale.

As he headed for the stairs to run back over the catwalk,

Mark heard his name called. Steve Emrich was standing in the doorway of the laboratory, beckoning to him. Mark retraced his steps. Steve had some blueprints in his hands and he shuffled them as he talked.

"Mark, I don't think I can make it for lunch today. I'm sorry, but I got behind on these blueprints. I'll have to grab a sandwich in the cafeteria on the run."

Mark looked at Steve, studying him, but Steve kept his eyes on the blueprints. Mark knew what was going on in Steve's mind. The grapevine story had reached his ears. Steve was a modest man, and a considerate one. He thought big and far. He was worried about Mark, about getting him into trouble with the Bradfords. It wasn't the blueprints that would keep him working this noon.

"Are you sure you can't make it?" Mark asked.

Steve looked up then, their eyes met for a second but Steve glanced away. "Yes. I'm sorry, Mark."

"Forget it. We'll make it next week."

Mark turned and ran up the stairs, taking them two at a time in his anger. He was, by nature, a self-controlled man, seldom given to violent outbursts of rage by way of a safety valve. When you have been brought up in a large family that has managed somehow or other to live together in four small rooms, when you have been disciplined by a tired mother who has had to work hard all her life, and whose children too have learned to work as soon as they were able, you have no time for coddling temperament. The luxury of a fine rage was something he had learned in his youth to do without, along with expensive clothing and rich foods and a beautiful home and plenty of spending money. All the other things, the material wellbeing, he had acquired, but the early training still stayed with him. He had none of the disposition traits of pampered affluence.

But today he was angry. He felt his fury mount, sending his

blood pounding through his veins, flushing his face, clenching his fists. For that moment as he paused on the catwalk to get control of his emotions before going back to his office, he hated the Bradford family and everything it stood for. Toward Nina who had turned her back on him last night and who had not come down to eat with him this morning, he felt an undeniable resentment because she was acting so much like a Bradford. This startled him, it even frightened him, because he knew he loved his wife as much as any man can love any woman.

He did not return to his office. Glancing at his wrist watch, he saw that it was almost noon and he took the turn that led out to the sheds where his car was standing. He did not want to go back and face his stenographers and his secretary and whoever else would be around. It was raw and damp and he ran, hatless and without a topcoat, toward his car. He opened the trunk of the car and pulled out an old army coat and a weather-beaten hat he kept there and, still shaking with anger, pulled them on, yanking the coat into place and tying the belt with a vicious pull. He caught sight of his face in the mirror as he backed out and it was flushed and set under the battered old hat that cocked over his forehead.

He drove at high speed, as high as he dared, through the traffic of town and out into the country. He was acting with deep-seated instincts now, not thinking, not caring. He had only one impulse pushing against him, to get away from the Bradford Tool Company with Spencer and Bob sitting in their high and mighty thrones of offices and the silly smirks of secretaries, and the grapevine of gossip.

Suddenly, somewhere along the road, the anger left him and his vision and his head cleared. The experience of this morning stood forth in his mind, as distinct and separate as the pain a patient feels as he is being put under anesthetic. Everything else fades out, the surroundings, the nurses and doctors, the patient's body; only the pain stands forth. So it was with him today. This place called the Bradford Tool Company to which he was so devoted, which he had loved with an emotion that amounted close to the passion he felt for his wife, stood forth as sharply as pain.

He saw it as a thing apart from himself for the first time in his life. Always before he had been part of it, working there as a young boy during the summers when he was going to college. Then coming into the plant as a beginner and regular work-man. Then there had been that day when Nina at a Christmas party had singled him out, had talked to him with such anima-tion, and had practically asked him for their first date together. At first he had let her take the initiative in their love affair, thinking that it would be wrong for him, a nobody named Mark Galloway, to force himself upon Nina Bradford, but he had fallen in love with her from the start.

She was in nothing so much a Bradford as in her determina-tion to choose the man she wanted to marry. Mark had been that man from the first moment she set eyes on him. It had been a hot love affair, a burning romance, all fire and absorption in each other, the kind of love affair in which neither can get the other off his mind for five consecutive minutes of the day. People thought it wouldn't last. It was such a burning desire with both of them. It had lasted. It had lasted beyond all ex-pectations. Now, last night, Nina had turned away from him in their big bed because he had hurt her brother's feelings. It was preposterous. It was unbelievable. He couldn't believe it. All because of Bradford Tool.

Bradford Tool.

What was Bradford Tool? It was a lot of things, a lot of dif-ferent things to a lot of different people.

It was a living wage to about one third the families in Brad-ford. It was a place where young women fresh out of high school could find a position as file clerk or stenographer or mail girl, easy work to do while they kept their eyes open for a possible husband among the hundreds of young men who poured daily into the factory. It was a place where due to Mark's efforts elderly men might now stay on, men like McGovern in the stock room, long after they would have been turned away from other shops with a less liberal policy toward the aged. It was a testing ground, an apprenticeship for young engineers eager for experience. It was half their lives to men like Steve Emrich and Mark Galloway. It was a ready-made situation for almost anyone related to the Bradfords, and in some cases, like that of Thornton Watrous and a half-dozen other Bradfords scattered throughout the plant, it was a sinecure.

Livelihood, matrimonial clearinghouse, trysting place, stop-gap to marriage, last desperate hope of the elderly, career, or cushy job. Mark stood off and looked at it, not physically because it lay far back of him now, something he had left behind in much the way that an angry man will walk out on a woman whom he loves and with whom he has quarreled. That was the trouble. Bradford Tool wasn't a factory or a business to him. He saw it now. It had always been a personality, even from the beginning, alive and variable and compelling as any human being of great stature. And, like a person, you could love it and hate it, and today he hated it.

It was inevitable that the anger that had risen so suddenly within him should as suddenly subside, and with the passing of emotional turbulence came the quick realization that he was hungry.

He was driving toward one of those settlements that nestle themselves on the outskirts of busy towns in an answer to the housing problem. Greencrest was its name. It had the unreal, picture-postcard look of developments, houses jammed close to each other, all alike in construction and individualized only in the owner's pathetic attempt to give his home a bit of distinction, yellow blinds on this one or a red door here or a pair of old wagon wheels flanking a front stoop or perhaps a coat of bright pink paint. These developments invariably depressed him, hearkening back as they did to his beginning down on River Street. But Greencrest, far from depressing him, brought a swift lifting of spirits. Claire! Claire Elliott. She lived somewhere near here. She had her headquarters for her dramatic work right here in the Greencrest School.

When Claire rushed into his thoughts, she pushed everything else out. Long ago, before he had met Nina and fallen in love with her, he had been in love with Claire. He had put her behind him when they broke up over some foolish quarrel but he had never fogotten her. A year ago she had returned to Bradford from New York to open a summer theater school for teenagers. It had done surprisingly well, and this year she had a position as dramatic supervisor for the public schools, continuing her private dramatic work on the side.

Suddenly he wanted very much to see Claire. The few times he had run into her around town she had been friendly but restrained. There had always been other people around and they had never had a chance to talk. Now his disgust with the Bradfords drove him to want to see someone who had known the old Mark Galloway, known him well. Someone who spoke his language, or used to. He pulled into one of the parking spaces in front of the Colonial Restaurant where he had heard Ginger mention that Claire often lunched.

The restaurant was crowded. There was no hostess, but a waitress, hurrying past him with a tray, nodded toward the back.

"A couple is just leaving," she said. "That table way back."

He started toward it, passing between the row of tables and the booths on one side, his eyes searching for Claire. Then he saw her, alone in one of the booths. He hurried toward it.

"Hello, Claire," he said, stopping beside her.

"What are you doing here?" she asked, smiling up at him.

Her smile had not changed. It had never changed since he had first known her, years ago when he was a senior in high school and she was studying at Teachers' College. It had been the first thing he had noticed about her the night they had met on a blind date. Her smile was as it had been then, a little mocking, if mockery can ever have a warmth and friendliness in it.

"Mind if I sit down?" he asked.

She looked at him, searching his face. He could see that her quick mind was wondering what it was all about, trying to piece together his being here in this place, especially his being alone. She must know that he had been looking for someone and that he had finished his quest when he had found her.

"Sit down," was all she said. "I'm glad you came."

Her poise had been one of the things he had always most admired about Claire Elliott.

"I've just ordered," she said. "What luck for me. I'll have you all to myself during lunch. Tell me what you want and I'll use my influence to get you quick service so we can eat together." She was beckoning to a waitress who knew her, calling her by name.

"Yes, Miss Elliott?"

Claire's smile was turned on him again. "Let's see, your favorite lunch was jumbo beefburger, French fries, and cole slaw. Coffee and apple pie."

Mark nodded, smiling a little himself. "That will be all right," he said to the waitress. He sat back against the leather-cushioned seat, watching Claire. It had been several years since he had taken a really good look at her. Last summer when Ginger was studying dramatics or acting or whatever they called it at Claire's summer theater school, he had seen Claire a few times when he had gone to pick up Ginger or drop her off at a play rehearsal or to attend the two performances in which Ginger had taken part. But that had not been like this. It was interesting how different a woman looked when you sat down opposite her. This past summer Claire had been a vague, shadowy figure flitting about, always busy, calling orders and instructions to stagehands and the young students at her theater.

Today she was Claire Elliott again, and by the simple magic of remembering his favorite menu, and smiling at him, she had carried him back so many years that it set up a positive aching inside him.

It was because she had not changed. It was remarkable. It was startling. Everyone else he had known in those old days had changed. He had changed himself. He was heavier. He felt older. He was more serious. These things he knew about himself because you could not run away from such obvious facts. But Claire was still the same.

Strangely enough, sitting here with her today, she seemed younger than he. There were no lines in her face, a fact which he found himself wondering about because Nina, even beautiful Nina who was certainly a few years younger than Claire, showed fine lines around the eyes and at the corners of her mouth.

Claire had never been beautiful as Nina was beautiful, with a graceful loveliness that almost took your breath away. Yet Claire had that kind of handsomeness that mellows and deepens with experience. Her coloring had always been striking, with that deep chestnut thatch through which, with some coaxing, ran a silver streak, with eyes to match the color of her hair and ivory skin and thick dark brows, arched in perpetual good humor, and only her mouth made up, but that quite madly, with a brilliant shade of lipstick that refused to be overwhelmed by the garish hair and eyes.

"Take a good look," she said, laughing deep in her throat, and her voice was throaty too, just as he remembered. "Then tell me what you've found."

"You look good," he said, slipping into the casual ease that had always characterized their friendship. "You haven't changed."

"Music to these ancient ears," she said. "Thanks."

He looked around him at the crowded room. "You eat in this place often?" He did not want to appear too well informed about her activities.

"Several times a week. You've probably heard that I'm dramatic supervisor for the town this year. An experiment. I float around and help teachers put on assemblies and pageants. The annual school plays. Greencrest is my headquarters." She was searching his face now, trying to find things in it.

"Now are you going to tell me how you happen to have strayed out into this foreign territory for lunch? Or is it a secret?"

"No secret. I lost my temper and instead of blowing my top where it would do some good I jumped in my car and just drove."

It was strange the way he slipped so quickly into the habits of those years so long ago when Claire and he had been close. Then he had told her everything that happened to him, the good and the bad, the comical and the important, the petty and the big. He was starting to do that today, telling her about getting angry when he might just as easily have given her some noncommittal answer that would turn the conversation away from personal matters.

She didn't pump him. It might have been better if she had, because then he would have clammed up. Instead she turned her attention to her food, since the waitress had just served them, and made no comments. She was waiting, as she had always done, for him to go on and he did go on, with alarming candor, telling her everything, about the party last night and the way Spencer and Bob had reacted this morning and the Bradford grapevine and what it was doing to his friendship with Steve Emrich. From time to time he gulped down some of his food and occasionally Claire would move her hand toward the table and nod toward the booth in back of them, indicating that he must keep his voice down. But he managed to get it all out, every bit of it, and it brought him great relief.

Only one thing he kept from her and that was the way Nina had cut him short when he wanted to talk to her last night and the way she had turned her back on him in bed, even when he had wanted to take her in his arms. That was none of Claire's business.

They were eating their dessert when Claire said, "I get letters from Ginger. One every week."

"You do?" His voice was sharp with surprise.

"We're very fond of each other, you know, Ginger and I. We have more than red hair in common." She was smiling at him, and now he felt there was a bit more of mockery than friendliness in that familiar smile. Claire went on.

"I was rebellious like Ginger when I was her age. I wanted to go on the stage. I was not allowed to. I had to settle for teaching. Remember, Mark?" He turned away instead of nodding, although he did remember, very well. "Your daughter and I are a lot alike."

He looked back again. "That's funny, I thought she was more like me than anyone else in the world."

"She is, Mark. You and I are alike, too. That was the trouble. We were too much alike, in the final analysis, to make a go of it." She was mocking again. "Don't tell me you've forgotten." She reached for her check, and he took it away from her. She did not make a point of it. "Because I haven't forgotten, you know. I never will."

He crawled out of the booth, following Claire toward the door. He was disturbed now, but by something besides the upset at the plant this morning. He was disturbed by Claire, by these things she had said to him, by the way she could, with that peculiar charm of hers, catch him up in the net of the past, the way she could bring him to her again as if he were a boy in high school pouring out his heart to a sophisticated girl who had experienced so much more than he. Most of all, he was disturbed because Ginger was writing to Claire. He knew how kids were. They opened up with much greater frankness to strangers, especially if they felt their parents were against them.

He wanted to say something of this to Claire, but where he had been articulate enough about his troubles at the plant, he could not pour out all the confusion and doubt that surrounded Nina's and his relationship with Ginger. It stuck in his throat when he tried to say something about it.

So he stood with Claire at the door of her car, feeling that there was much more to say to her but not knowing exactly what it was that must be said. "I'd like to see you again, Claire," he blurted out. "Just for old times' sake. May I?"

She ignored the remark as she got into her car and he thought she was offended.

"Don't worry too much about Ginger. She's a grand girl. She's too much like you not to make a big go of life," she said. She was looking down at the steering wheel of her car, not smiling. Then quietly she said, "I'm going to the movie in Bradford tonight. The first show."

She started the motor up and backed out, waving to him, smiling again, so that his last picture of her was the one he always carried around in his mind's eyes when anyone said "Claire Elliott," the picture of a handsome face, alive and vital, beckoning him on, slightly mocking him.

Chapter 5

HE DID NOT STAY LATE AT THE PLANT THAT NIGHT. NINA WAS too much on his mind. He had a plan worked out to mend the breach between them. His hope was that he would find her in her dressing room. After he had taken her in his arms and kissed her again and again, he would say, "It's silly for us to quarrel, because we're head over heels in love. Look, let's forget what Effie's cooked for dinner. Let's go over to Brampton, to that little Polish restaurant we used to go to when we were first married. We'll have chicken Polonaise and we'll ask the piano player and the violinist to play all our old favorites. Let's be just a couple of kids who were crazy about each other again. Maybe we'll even go to a movie."

Nina was not waiting for him in her dressing room. When he came into the front hall, prepared to bound up the stairs toward her, she called to him from the living room.

"Mark, I'm in here."

He went in and there she stood, in a yellow wool dress that turned her hair to palest gold. She appeared sweet and smiling, the old Nina, so he kissed her with the special tenderness of a man who has quarreled with the woman he loves and is now ready to forget it. Something in the way she responded surprised him. Her kiss was not wholehearted, as if she were warning him that something was not yet settled between them.

There was a cocktail shaker of fruit juice on the coffee table and a plate of appetizers. The two stemmed champagne glasses looked intimate and friendly and he watched Nina fill them, but her kiss was still upon his lips, that restrained little kiss that had come to him as a slight shock.

She held out a glass and the plate of appetizers and he helped himself.

"To us," he said, holding up his glass, but now he was wary too, watching her and wondering what was going on in her mind.

"To us," she said. "And to our children." She drank slowly, saying nothing, but when she set down her glass again, she spoke. "Families are wonderful things, Mark. Being part of a family is the most important thing in the world."

He did not answer.

"I had a long talk with Evelyn today," she said. Ah, he thought, now we're coming to it.

"Evelyn and I are in perfect agreement about everything. I invited myself to her house for tea. Her maid is out Friday afternoons and I knew we couldn't talk here with Effie puttering about."

Nina went on. "We talked over what happened last night and we're in perfect agreement about everything."

"In perfect agreement about everything?" The repetition of the phrase nettled him. "I'm not sure I understand you, Nina."

"I think you do, Mark. I mean about filling the position of chief engineer at the plant. It's not going to be your friend, Mark. It's to be one of Ollie Bradford's sons."

He had to hand it to Nina, she was giving it to him straight, without flinching.

"So you and Evelyn decided all this this afternoon," he said, sipping his juice and looking at her. "I was under the impression that the bylaws of the Bradford Corporation required that all important positions be filled by the vote of board members. In case you don't recall the fact, I happen to be a member of the board."

"You know very well that's a token gesture. You've been on the board long enough to know these things are talked over in advance. You're not naïve, Mark."

"When you talked this over with Spencer this morning on the telephone, was it he who called you or you who called him?"

"He called me, of course. You know very well I wouldn't—" She bit her lip, angry that he had trapped her into telling him that it was Spencer who had prompted what she must do. He went over and stood near her chair, looking down at her.

"Let me see if I can fit together the pieces of this interesting puzzle. Spencer telephoned you to see what you could do to get me to change my mind about Steve. Then, just possibly, he suggested you might talk the matter over with Evelyn, knowing that of his two sisters, you, being the Bradford, the true Bradford, that is, are the stronger. You might influence Evelyn but Evelyn could never influence you. Thornton Watrous, in turn, is weaker than Evelyn and she dominates him, so you were to win Evelyn over to Spencer's point of view and she in turn will dictate to Thornton how he will vote about the chief engineer's job. A very skillful handling of the matter. Your brother is a clever man."

"All Spencer is thinking about is the interests of the company."

"Correction, Nina. All Spencer is thinking about is the interests of Spencer. He's afraid to get new blood into his company unless he can control it. You see, darling, if Thornton could not be persuaded, with Victoria and your husband sold on Steve Emrich for the job, Spencer might have been overruled. That's one thing that frightens your brother, the day when he will be overruled, when he won't have his own way. Last night he was trying to pin his own worst fault on me. It's Spencer

63

who's got to have his own way. He's got to have his way about everything."

"You're that way, too, Mark. What about this stubborn attitude of yours about Steve Emrich? Aren't you as stubborn as Spencer because Steve Emrich grew up on *your* side of the tracks?"

"I happen to be right about Steve, Nina. That's the joker in the pile. I just happen to be right. Steve is the best man for the job. It's crazy not to give it to him."

"Is one man really so important?" she asked him with honest eyes.

"One man, no, Nina. Not just one. But two, three, a half-dozen men, yes. That's bad for morale. Bradford Tool is studded with men in important positions who are there only because they are related to the Bradford family. Sometimes that doesn't hurt if the men are good. But when are they good? How often are they really good?"

"You mean, how often are they Mark Galloway." Her eyes, watching him, narrowed.

"All right, call it egotism if you want. But it's honest egotism. And honest egotism is better than dishonest stupidity."

"You mean this policy of the firm about key positions."

"I mean Spencer calling you up today and dragging the women of the family in on it. What kind of men does he think you and Evelyn are married to?"

"Thornton is a very grateful man," she said, slowly, measuring his full height with her eyes as she answered. "He knows that if he had not married Evelyn, he would not have been where he is today."

"Say that again, Nina."

"Must I?"

He turned away from her for a moment, letting the full significance of her words sink in. Then, with a deadly quiet in his voice that should have given fair warning, he said, "Nina, I'm not Thornton Watrous. I'm where I am by my honest contribution to the company. I like to think I might have been general manager of some plant, maybe not Bradford Tool, but some equally big company on my own. I like to believe I've got what it takes." He turned on her. "Not that I needed Nina Bradford to get it for me." He saw the quick flush of anger in her cheeks and neck.

"It doesn't happen that way," she flared back. "Do you think our company is the only one that operates this way? All right, call it playing politics. Anything you want, Mark. But whatever the differences in your characters, you're general manager because you married me just the way Thornton is head of public relations because he married Evelyn."

He walked toward her again, and his voice was still ominously quiet. "Nina, do you realize what you're saying? I just can't believe you mean that. I can't believe that all these years you've been thinking that if I hadn't married a Bradford I wouldn't be what I am today."

She got up and faced him. The angry flush of color was drained from her face as she answered.

"Would you, Mark? You talk about honesty. That's your creed. Always the honest answer, always the truth. No punches pulled. Well, I ask you again, Mark, would you?"

He did not answer her question. Instead he walked out into the hall and picked up his hat and coat. It was the same old topcoat and hat that he kept in the car for an emergency. In his haste to come home to Nina tonight, he had forgotten to change back into his good coat. As he picked up his hat, the thought crossed his mind. This is sure my day for running out on things.

"Mark, Mark, what are you doing? Where are you going?" It was Nina calling to him as she crossed the living room. He turned, intending to answer, but he had nothing to say.

I don't know what I'm doing, he thought. I don't know

65

where I'm going. So, without answering her, he went out and let the door close behind him.

It was a different ride from the one he had taken this noon. There was no anger in him now, only a kind of numbness. No feeling at all. He drove through the traffic of the town, down to one of the community parking places, facing the river, and pulled in with his car headed toward the water. Across the water flickered the lights of small factories and warehouses, an apartment house or two, and far down, so that he had to crane his neck to see it, was the black hulk of the Bradford factory sprawling every which way, with one side lighted up where a night shift was working to fill a rush order.

He looked away from it, hunching over the wheel, watching the reflected lights on the black water, feeling a kinship with the loneliness of the river.

It was the first time in seventeen years that he had ever walked out on Nina. This was a fitting climax to a day that had begun badly and grown worse as it progressed. But why did she have to say that dreadful thing to him, letting him know that in her eyes everything he was today had come to him through his marriage to her? He wondered if she could honestly believe such a thing or was she, like him, edgy and quick to anger. The party last night, the Bradford squabble, their disagreement about Steve Emrich, and Ginger. Ginger was there in the picture of tension, this war of nerves between them. Make no mistake about it. Ginger, with her stubborn determination, her threats to leave the school she was in, her anger with them, was a source of the trouble between them.

All right, so they were both jumpy. But Nina could have said something else, anything else, but not that. It was almost the worst thing she could have said to him. Only one thing might have cut him more deeply and that was if she had said she did not love him.

Maybe she doesn't love me as deeply as I believed she did,

he thought. Maybe that's what I've been really kidding myself about. Could she love me all the way and take sides against me in anything so vital as a Bradford squabble? They had been perhaps closer to each other than most married couples. They had lost their only son. Things like that pulled a man and woman together for good. Especially if they were as much in love to begin with as they had been.

Then why this open antagonism about Steve Emrich? It bothered him because he could not understand it. Vaguely, deep in his thought, was the suggestion that in some way Nina's attitude about Steve was tied up with Ginger. It was so ludicrous a thought at first that he hesitated to bring it into the open, but the more he dwelt on it, the more he thought there was something to it. Ginger was his daughter, the way Jill was Nina's. Ginger was acting up. She was being a hellion in her own individualistic way, and Nina sensed that Mark was siding with Ginger.

He could understand why a kid might not like the sort of private school Ginger was enrolled in. He would have hated it himself. It would have seemed like imprisonment to him and he could see why it would seem like that to Ginger. She needed free air. Plenty of space to move about. To sprawl herself around in, be sloppy and independent and noisy and magnanimous and hearty. Like him. Like Mark Galloway in Nina's elegant house on top of Turkey Hill with its antique furniture and its Oriental rugs and everything in its proper place. Something within rebelled against the finical orderliness. There were times when he had wanted to bust out, to take his two big paws and wipe away the priceless bric-a-brac from tables and shelves and bookcases and send the porcelain and the Wedgwood crashing to the floor.

Ginger was the bone of contention. When you got down to rock bottom, it was Ginger rising between them. For a moment he envisioned her standing there between Nina and him

67

and shaking her fist at both of them. Then gradually she faded out, growing smaller and smaller until she was a redheaded toddler of two or three, running into his arms the day he had come back from overseas. He was in his uniform again, holding out his arms to her, and she was laughing and screaming, "Daddy, Daddy!" and running to him. He had been so overwhelmed and excited that all he could do was catch her up in his arms and hug her. It was hours later that he thought to ask Nina, out of the mist of love as he lay next to her, "Say, how did the kid know enough to call me Daddy?" And Nina had laughed and said, "I've been teaching her. From your picture. Every day we rehearsed the scene."

Even then Ginger had been an actress. And a darn good one, too.

In a way, Ginger was all he had left to remind him of River Street. She was like him when he had been fifteen, a crazy, loud, noisy kid having to raise his voice to be heard either out on the street or in their crowded home.

The one who could yell the loudest won the argument, got the attention.

Ginger was flesh of his flesh. He saw his mother again in Ginger's face. His pigtailed and dirty-faced sisters in torn overalls, always begging for something to eat. Ginger was here to remind him and Nina of what he had been. Mark himself had almost lost the stamp of those beginnings. He had the suavity, almost always anyway, of a gentleman. He could move about freely at the Hunt Club when Nina rode there. He fitted into her country-club and Bradford society. His personality and brains made up for any deficiency in his breeding.

"He's such a b-i-g man!" Nina's friends would exclaim on first meeting him. "So strong-looking. Where did you ever find him?"

He got by. He more than got by. Everyone had forgotten River Street. Everyone but Mark Galloway himself.

Everyone perhaps but Mark Galloway and Nina Galloway. She remembered, too. She must remember or she would not so much resent Ginger for being herself. She resented Steve for the same reason. Nina was afraid Ginger and Steve would pull Mark back to what he had been, to his beginnings. That was it! But it was a mighty peculiar reason for hating Steve Emrich. Mark shrugged, watching the lights across the river.

You couldn't figure women out. Even when you were married to them. They were all enigmatic.

Take Claire Elliott for instance.

No, don't take Claire Elliott. Let her alone. Stay away even from the thought of her. This is no time to drag in Claire Elliott, on the night you've walked out on your wife.

Claire sure looked good today. Happy, he guessed was the word for it. Contented and at peace with herself. But then she had always been like that, with a spirited nature that acted like a wellspring of happiness. Always on top of things. Never a gripe on her lips the way so many people had. Always the best construction on everything. It had always made him feel good to be with her.

Now that he thought about the meeting with her today, it occurred to him for the first time that he hadn't found out much about her. She had not talked about herself, except to explain her new job. He began to wonder about her. She wasn't married. Although Claire had been in New York for years the local paper would have announced her marriage. Nina, who read all the papers, would have looked up one evening and said, "Your old girl friend is married. Did you know, Mark?"

Nina always referred to Claire as "his old girl friend." It wasn't any secret. Half the town had known about it then. But that was long before Nina. That was way back on River Street, with the kids screaming, "Hey, Joe, run for first base! You can make it, Joe!" With the cheering and booing of a baseball game going on in the middle of the street and Claire edging her car through the crowd of boys to pick up Mark for a date and the kids yelling at her, "Hi, beautiful. Hi, Red. Give us a lift. Aw, shut up, she's Mark Galloway's girl. Hey, Mark, have you kissed her yet? How many times, huh?"

Laughs and more yells as they drove off through the summer night.

He had been in love with Claire, yet not with the feverish intensity with which he loved Nina later on. He was a man then. He was still a boy when he knew Claire, but she had been fascinating to him, pulling him to her, binding him with a devotion he had never felt for anyone before. Claire was his first love. Tonight, sitting here looking over the river, he smiled a little at the thought of that love affair. So green, so terribly, terribly green, he thought. Claire was tall, taller than Nina, and she had been an ample-bosomed girl who was not afraid of a few extra pounds. Friends, kidding them, would say they were the right size for each other. Big, handsome, vivacious Claire. Full of life, but with a radiant quietness about her, too, that made her a good listener, that made the young and still-growing Mark Galloway pour out his whole soul to her.

"Mark Galloway's girl is a redhead!" The kids on River Street chanted it. He could still hear them chanting it, merciless in their youthful teasing.

Mark Galloway's daughter is a redhead. He said it himself. *She's like me, Mark. I was rebellious, too.*

I thought she was more like me than anyone else in the world.

She is. You and I were always alike. That's why we couldn't make a go of it.

If Ginger had been Claire's and Mark Galloway's daughter, there would be no problem. Ginger was devoted to Claire, as Mark had been. She adored her, idolized her. All they had heard last summer was Claire Elliott this, and Claire Elliott that, until Mark wondered how Nina ever stood it because he had a hard time standing it himself.

"Claire Elliott is just a person," he would say to his redheaded kid. "So I knew her when she was a kid herself. Forget her for five minutes, won't you?"

"But I can't. She's so wonderful. She's just, well, just sort of perfect. She makes you feel so good, just to be with her."

Mark, remembering, would answer Ginger without speaking to her, merely in his mind he would say, I know how it is. I thought she was wonderful once too. I felt good just to be with her.

He shook himself, trying to throw off these thoughts about Claire. It gave him a guilty feeling, as if he were doing something wrong to be thinking about her on the night he and Nina had quarreled.

This is fine, he thought. I'm getting a guilt complex over nothing, over having lunch with an old friend and thinking about her afterward. Next thing I'll be looking up a psychiatrist. Or was it a psychoanalyst you went to for a thing like that? He never could get those two straightened out in his mind.

He pulled out of the parking place. This was stupid. It was bad business sitting around in the dark by yourself and just thinking. He couldn't yet go back home. He didn't know why. He just knew he couldn't. Claire's parting words came to him. *I'm going to the movie in Bradford tonight. The first show.* The car clock said nine and if he hurried, he might just catch her. He turned the corner into the main stem of town and slowed down. As he slowed almost to a stop, he glanced over and there she was again. She had evidently just come out of the movies and she was standing for a moment, buttoning up her collar against the cold and pushing her thick hair back from her face —she never had worn a hat, as far as Mark could remember.

She spied him at the same moment he spied her and came over to the car. She was wearing a pair of large silver hoop earrings and they gleamed in the half-light cast by the movie marquee, bringing out the silver streak in her hair.

71

"Get in," he said. "I'll drive you home."

"You don't have to, really. The taxi stand is just around the corner. They give excellent service."

"So do I," he said. "Get in.

"You'll have to tell me where you live," he said. "I know it's near Greencrest."

"On Easton Road. I bought a little house last summer. Mortgaged to the hilt, but that will disappear in time. It's a place to call my own, anyway."

He turned the car toward Easton Road and they did not talk. He wondered what Claire was thinking. She was sure to be thinking that it was strange that he should have looked her up twice in one day. Or maybe it didn't matter to her. Maybe he was so far removed from her life now, from anything that did matter to her, that she didn't care what he was doing or why he was doing it. Maybe he was just a lift home to her on a cold night.

"You live alone?" he finally asked.

"Yes. I had another teacher with me at first but she was transferred. It doesn't always work out. Having someone with you. It's easy to take someone in. Harder to get rid of them. I guess I've always been sort of a lone wolf."

"You in a hurry?" It was an impulse, a crazy impulse, compounded partly of his pique with Nina, partly his fear of facing her again. And mixed with all that was an interest in Claire. Where this noon he had been filled with his own troubles, tonight he wanted to hear more about her. He wanted to know what she was like now, really like, and he thought she might give him, too, some key to the mystery of handling Ginger. So, spying the same little shopping center where they had had lunch this noon, he pulled up in front of the brightly lighted restaurant.

"How about a sandwich and a hot drink?" he said.

Another woman might have hesitated, but Claire had never

hesitated about anything. She knew her mind without the agonizing wrenchings over a decision that plague so many females.

"I'd love it," she said.

For a moment he paused. He was the one who hesitated. Now
that he had extended the impulsive invitation, he questioned the
wisdom of it. There was nothing wrong with having a snack
at nine thirty in the evening in a brightly lighted restaurant
with an old friend who had been teaching his daughter how to
act. Yet Bradford was in many ways still a very small town
and it had the small town's love of gossip. If someone who
knew either Nina or him should see him with Claire! Claire was
so darned attractive. It would look like only one thing. Especially since Claire, by the magic of attentiveness, gave the
impression that she was involved with anyone she was talking
to. Of all the women he might have chosen for a tête-à-tête in a
restaurant on the night he had quarreled with his wife, Claire
was the most dangerous choice.

Claire, unaware of his thoughts, was out of the car, stamping
her feet against the increasing cold, bundling herself up like a
child, a big child, enthusiastic, running head on to meet life.

He couldn't back out now.

The place was much less crowded than this morning. A noisy
party of teen-agers in one booth, a few lone diners. Claire led
the way toward a booth near the back and slid in opposite him.
She looked even better tonight. Whereas this noon he had not
even noticed what she was wearing, tonight he took in the
moss-green dress with the turtle neckline. This was one of the
colors he remembered her wearing so much, and it had always
impressed him as a worldly color, sophisticated and subtle, a
suitable color for Claire's special kind of good looks.

They ordered hot drinks and sandwiches and, in contrast
with his earlier talkativeness, tonight he was withdrawn and
almost silent. Claire seemed to understand, filling in the conversation with remarks about the movie she had just seen.

73

Then suddenly somewhere in her talk, she switched to Ginger. It was done so adroitly that he hardly noticed when she began. She was talking about Ginger's talent, how well she had done last summer at the theater workshop, how willing she was to work, any time, any hour, nothing was too much, nothing too difficult.

"That's what makes an artist in any field," she said. "That willingness to work hard."

"Isn't Ginger a little young to be put in the artist class?" he asked. He always felt a bit superior to this talk about the theater. He could never be persuaded to take Claire's workshop seriously, although other people in town, important people, said she was doing a good job. Perhaps she sensed something of his attitude because she looked away from him for a moment.

Then, like a slap, her question came at him.

"Mark, why don't you be sensible and let Ginger come back home? She wants so much to go to school here."

To himself he could admit that Ginger might have a reasonable case, but never in the world to Claire, especially since she was challenging his common sense, asking him why he wasn't sensible enough to let Ginger come home. She misunderstood his silence.

"Maybe it's her mother's idea," Claire went on. "Well, no matter whose idea it is, I'm against it. It's a mistake to keep Ginger in that school. She's miserable. It's not just a case of making an adjustment. The child is unhappy. She'll never be happy there. I can tell from her letters."

"Have you written anything to encourage this attitude of hers?"

"Of course not. You know better than to ask that. But I'd like to. I'd like to tell Ginger that once upon a time, a long time ago, I could have talked some sense into her father. He would have listened to me. He used to say I had a way with me." She was laughing, leaning toward him. "Remember, Mark? You

74

used to say, 'Honestly, Claire, I don't know what it is about you. You're not as cute as a lot of other girls, but you sure have a way with you.' "

Her face was thrust toward him, alive and eager, as her face had always been, and he remembered, not only what Claire was asking him to remember, but other things too. How he would take her face in his hands and kiss her when she leaned toward him like this. In a shocking backlash of memory, he remembered what it had felt like to kiss Claire.

All those innumerable kisses of a half-forgotten past rushed back at him in a wave of reidentification, and there was longing in the remembrance of them. Sharp, poignant longing. He remembered everything now.

There was the long ride into the country the first night she had let him drive her car and the long stop in the moonlight at midnight on some forsaken beach. There was the night of his high-school prom when she, just home from a year at college, slipped out into the darkness with him for a stolen kiss between dances. She had worn a white dress that night, a billowy white dress that stood out among the motley group of pastel evening dresses, and he could recall her in it still, the one night when he had thought her truly beautiful. There was the night before he had gone off to college and Claire had been the only person he wanted to be with on his last night home. There was his first Christmas vacation back, when feeling so much older, he tried to lord it over her and she had taunted him with that smile of hers, ridiculing his intellectual pretensions until he was badly hurt by her sharp wit, and then putting her hand to his face and kissing him. There was one New Year's Eve. No, no, he mustn't bring that kiss back.

He tried to tear himself free from her, to look away from her eyes, but he couldn't. Suddenly he felt trapped by his own remembered emotions, the way you will come unexpectedly upon some keepsakes in an attic trunk and feel the quick inrush of an old pleasure, an old pain. Only this was all pleasure, swift and heady, compelling him, pulling him back again. She was so near and yet so far away. He wanted Claire again, wanted her to love and kiss, to feel her in his arms, smiling up at him. It was an emotion so strong and sudden that it swept over him headlong, turning him hot, then, as he resisted it, ice-cold in panic.

He had to get away from her, out of here, away from the past into which she was dragging him on this fateful night.

He was surprised at the calmness of his voice.

"Had enough?" he asked. "Do you want some dessert?"

"No, thanks," she said, lightly, unaware of the storm of emotions she had stirred up in him.

"I think we'd better leave," he said. "I've got to get back."

"All right," she said, again lightly, as if it made no difference.

Back to what, he thought. What am I going back to, to Nina, to the house on Turkey Hill. Back to Mark Galloway as he is today. That was an odd thought. Back to himself as he was today. He should be going forward to today, not back to today. Yet as it seemed now in his mind, with Claire and the past hovering over him, any step away from the Mark Galloway he had been when he had known Claire was a backward one. That made no sense. He had success now. A lot of money. Position. Everything. Then he had had nothing. He had been nothing. Really? the voice within asked him. How interesting. I would have put it the other way round.

All the time his thoughts were tumbling over themselves like this, he was smiling at Claire, picking up the check, paying it, steering her out toward his car, helping her in and driving off toward her little house on Easton Road.

It was an even smaller house than he had expected, just a tiny cottage tucked among some evergreens that grew twice its size, but it looked snug and inviting with the lights Claire had left burning both on the porches and inside. A dog raced to

76

meet them, a miniature collie all affection and joy at Claire's presence, and she picked him up, laughing and ducking from his kisses.

"Hey, there, Galahad. Stop it."

"Galahad." Mark got out and walked toward the porch with her. "You haven't really named him that."

"Why not?" she said. "I haven't found my own Galahad yet."

She turned and looked up at him from where she stooped to rub Galahad's ears. Her look could have held a special significance for him, or it might have been casual humor. "I almost found him once," she said.

"Sometimes the things we've almost found, and lost," he said, "seem better than the things we've got our hands on. What we lose stays a part of our dreams, and what we manage to get—" He stopped, raising his hands in a futile gesture to indicate he could not, or would not finish what he had started to say.

She finished for him. "What we have sometimes becomes a stubborn reality we can't flee from the way we can from dreams."

This was dangerous. This was the way they used to talk to each other. Talk like this, coming so swiftly on the heels of that sweeping nostalgia he had experienced when looking into her face before, was more than dangerous. It was mad.

"Would you like to come in and see my little place?" she said.

"No," he said quickly. "Not tonight. I've got to get back. Some other time perhaps."

Again it did not seem to make any difference to her, one way or the other. She was merely being polite.

It should make a difference to you, he thought. It makes a difference to me. I wouldn't trust myself to go in. I'm not sure just why. I wouldn't kiss you again. Not tonight. I know I wouldn't. But somehow I couldn't bear to stand with you alone

77

in this house of yours. All the dreams might come back. I might not want to go back ever then. The way I feel tonight, I might want to stay.

"Well, good night." She had unlocked her door and Galahad rushed in before her, barking, exploring the place.

"Good night, Claire." It was the first time tonight he had spoken her name, and the sound of it bothered him because it seemed as if it were the first time he had spoken it in years, since the days he had gone around with her.

"Thanks for the lift," she said. "It was nice."

He turned without another word and walked quickly to the car. Her words and her voice followed him. She shouldn't have said that. *It was nice.* She meant more than the lift. She meant seeing him again was nice, the way seeing her again had been nice for him. All the old emotion, the old enthusiasm pulsed through him and he was young again, very young, and not tied to anyone or anything, not Nina or Ginger or Jill or Bradford Tool or the whole family of Bradfords. He was free because Claire would not have anything around her that was not free. He was young and he had been with Claire Elliott and, as his daughter Ginger had told him again and again last summer, you felt good just for having been with her.

The fever was still racing through him as he raced his car back to town. *It was nice.* So all the indifference, the magnificent poise had been just a cover. It did matter to her. She had liked being with him, just for this half hour or so.

What was it she used to say to him, clasping hold of his arm, linking her hand through it as she bent his elbow? "I just love being with you, Mark Galloway." She used to use his full name when she said anything especially nice. "It's a storybook name," she would tell him. "A hero's name. Like Siegfried or Tristan or Lochinvar or Galahad. Be a hero, Mark Galloway. Don't ever settle for anything less. Keep life always sitting in the palm

78

of your hand. Like this." And she would hold out her expressive hands. "Never let life push you around. You're not the type. You were made to be a hero."

It was appalling the way it all came back. A ride out Easton Road, a sandwich in a little place he'd ordinarily never go into, that crazy, appealing little house of hers snuggled among all those trees. A glance, a smile, a pair of silver earrings and a moss-green dress. Her charm. Always, always the charm that was Claire. It had pulled him before. It was pulling him now. It could make him forget for a moment that he had quarreled with Nina.

The thought sobered him, grabbed him by the shoulders and set him on his feet again.

Nina. Now he had to go back to Nina. He slowed up. All thought of Claire gone. *What we have sometimes becomes a stubborn reality we can't flee from.*

He drove around the town, still trying to summon the courage to face Nina. Then, as he drove down Church Lane, he thought of Jason. The lights of the church building were still burning as some stragglers from choir practice lingered. He slowed up as he passed it, intending to pull into the driveway of the rectory and if Jason's light was still on, run in as he sometimes did to see him. Friday night was a good night for barging in on Jason and Mark had often done this when he worked late at the plant. Jason wrote his sermons early in the evening and by ten o'clock he would be relaxed enough to let go, but too wide awake from his intellectual work to want to go to bed.

Suddenly Mark remembered this was Friday night and Jason would welcome a call from his friend.

He looked at the church, its outside lights illuminating the steeple and façade. It was a beautiful building, very old, rich in tradition, one of the finest examples of early architecture in this part of the country. Feature writers were always dropping in to ask Jason for permission to take pictures or write stories about it. Mark knew that secretly his friend lamented the fact that more attention was paid to the historical value of the church than the value of the work he was doing.

Mark turned into the driveway and before he was out of the car, Jason, who had heard the noise, came out to greet him.

"Hello, Mark!" he called, his voice bouncing out before him. "Come on in." There was the resilience of unquenchable good spirits in Jason's voice. It had great range. He could whisper or thunder when he preached a sermon, but the fundamental quality of his voice never changed. Joy was the key word. It was a voice that had been in touch with grief, with despair and frustration and failure, with death itself, and yet you felt that, underlying the voice, there lay an unspeakable sense of joy that nothing in this world could quench.

Jason's hand was on Mark's shoulder as they walked up the side steps that led to his study, set off from the rest of the house, "so the women folks won't get too mad at me," Jason always said with a twinkle in his eye.

Inside the study, a fire burned in the fireplace and chairs were already drawn up to it and there was a table with a pitcher of milk and glasses and bread-and-butter sandwiches, Jason's usual Friday-night "sermon supper," as his wife called it.

The two men sat down and Jason did the talking, about the things uppermost in his mind. He was that kind of man, never secretive or withdrawn, always bubbling with wit and intellectual vitality. There was a spot in his sermon—several typewritten pages were spread over the old walnut desk—which was bothering him and he talked it over with Mark.

Jason's subject was "meekness" and he had chosen the text, from the Twenty-fifth Psalm, "The meek will he guide in judgment: and the meek will he teach his way."

Jason was talking to Mark, informally, about his subject. He didn't see meekness as docility or submission. It was a strong thing, a quality allied as much to power, spiritual power, as to gentleness. True meekness, he thought, was a kind of quietness. That's what "meek" had meant originally, "spiritually quiet," and the more he thought about it, the more he realized that only from this inner quietness could man find his true relationship to God.

It was a phrase Mark had often heard Jason use. *Man's true relationship to God.* He himself did not have time for thinking much about such things. There was always business demanding his thought, or Nina and the girls. Yet his attitude of listening, and especially so tonight, was hardly one of impatience or superiority. Jason had that burning enthusiasm, whatever he talked about, that compelled you to listen, and even to believe. Mark did not always understand the full import of his words, but he was ready to believe them because Jason was speaking them.

He watched his friend now, sitting on the broad arm of one of the club chairs, bending slightly toward him in his earnestness. He was a young man, incredibly young in looks although he must be several years older than Mark. His face was unlined, and his dark-blond hair, straight and thick and bristling, added to the youthful impression made by a fresh, deeply tanned skin in contrast with startling blue eyes and a mouth that smiled easily. Yet it was not boyishness you saw in Jason's face. The wisdom of the ages rested there. This was a kind of perennial quality, the youthfulness of buoyancy that springs up like the returning spring.

Tonight, more than ever before, Mark reached out toward Jason, wishing that he possessed some of his friend's faith. These things of the spirit, this spiritual strength and joy that nothing could crush out of Jason, seemed to come so easily to him. Yet their coming had not been easy really. All of Jason's past was known to Mark. Jason had told about it himself, snatches here, a bit dropped there, until Mark had the whole picture. An unhappy childhood with a neurotic mother who had been deserted by his father. Always on the move. No home life to speak of. Those bleak years when he was shifted from one boys' school to another, not the fine boys' schools either, but dingy affairs, little obscure places in Godforsaken areas that no one ever heard of, no one ever came to. Certainly not his mother. She was glad to be rid of him.

Then, out of the blue, a scholarship to Yale, arranged by a sympathetic teacher who thought he saw possibilities in the young Jason. That had been the turning point. A full life and a good one. Intellectual companionship. The good things of life. Phi Beta Kappa. Then, as he was finishing his last year, the desperate plea for men to drive ambulances in Africa. The war looming ahead. America not yet in it but almost there. Jason signed for the ambulance corps.

"Until then I had one compelling ambition in life, Mark," he had told his friend. "Security. Make enough money for the good things in life. The things I thought were good. Never be in a position again where I could be shifted about the way I had been as a child. Thrust my stake deep into life. Make my claim solid. Money. Security. That was the thing. The *all*. But out there in Africa, something happened. Suddenly money seemed very unimportant. There wasn't any security. Not in the agonizing mass of humanity around me. I saw what security really was. It wasn't human at all. It was to be found in only one place, in the continuity of whatever it is that controls the universe. Intelligence. God. Call it whatever you want. I saw that's where it was."

Hence, the switch in careers, the abrupt decision to give up business administration and study for the ministry. Not a moment's hesitation. Not a pang of regret. It was remarkable. Mark, staring into his friend's animated face, wondered how he could have done it. They had a lot in common, these two men, and Mark saw it perhaps a bit more clearly than Jason, for Mark was always quick to see the mundane similarities.

82

The humble origin, the determination to get free of it, the brilliance and ambition, the way of escape. But the logic of events had taken Mark one way and he had got everything they both had wanted. And Jason had taken the other and given up all of it. Strange that he gave out no sense of loss, no aura of martyrdom.

Never a pang of regret.

"Jason." Mark stopped the flow of words that poured from his friend's thoughts. "Jason, I've quarreled with Nina."

"A serious quarrel?" Jason was married, too, and he knew how inconsequential the disagreements of marriage can often be.

"I walked out on her. The first time in seventeen years."

Jason whistled. "That is serious." Jason managed to look sober without appearing depressed by Mark's news. "Do you want to talk about it?"

"I think I do. I think I'd better." Jason slipped off the arm of the chair and sank into the leather depths. He rested his elbows on the arms, in an attitude of waiting.

"It's too much family," Mark said. "The Bradfords. We had them all to dinner last night." Jason nodded. As rapidly as he could, Mark pictured the party and the conversation for Jason. Then he recounted the events of the day, from breakfast through the early-evening encounter with Nina in their living room on Turkey Hill. He did not mention Claire Elliott. There was no point in involving Claire.

Jason heard him out, with no further comment than "Yes, I understand" or a nod of the head as Mark paused in his recital. Even when he finished, Jason did not comment, seeming to understand that it was neither sympathy nor advice Mark wanted, but just the opportunity to talk things out.

Mark was standing, facing the fire, not looking at his friend. It had cost him something to tell all this to Jason. The clamor of emotion, the mixed anger and bitterness and strife that rose and fell and struggled for precedence in his consciousness, left him exhausted and spent.

"It's not Victoria," he said. "She's a great old gal. Not even so much Bob. He's just a henchman. But Spencer. There's a fine upstanding Christian gentleman who has no idea how the other half of the world lives. He's drawn a circle around himself and everything belonging to him. No one can step beyond the imaginary line. And now he's pulling Nina into his circle with him." Mark faced Jason. "Have you any idea what this does to me? Having my wife yanked away from me by her brother. The nerve of it. Instructing Nina. Manipulating her like that. Telling her to stand up to me and let me have it."

"I have a very good idea what this does to you," was all Jason said. He poured some milk for both of them and offered Mark a glass. Mark shook his head. Jason ate a sandwich and drank his milk.

In the silence between the two men, only the snapping of the logs in the fireplace gave sound to the room.

"Mark." He looked at Jason. "Go back to Nina."

"If you mean go back and reason with her, it's impossible. Have you ever known a woman you could reason with?"

"Yes, quite a few."

"Not Nina. Under the charm and gentleness there beats the Bradford heart. She can be as hard as Spencer." He stopped. His own words bounced against the walls of Jason's study and came back at him, striking against him with the weight and force of living things. This was his wife he was talking about. The wife he found so beautiful and desirable. The woman he loved. He could not say he was sorry because he was not sorry. This had been something in him, rising to a crescendo of feeling and tonight it must burst forth.

"Nevertheless," Jason persisted, "I would go back to Nina."

"What can I say? What shall I do?"

"I can't tell you that. I can only tell you that you'll know. When the moment comes, you'll know."

"You don't know the half of it, Jason. It's not only this Bradford mess, this unholy interference. It's Ginger, too. We can't agree on Ginger. Nina wants to keep her in that school. I've backed her up, but I'm not with her, Jason. I want Ginger to do what she wants to do. We've all got to have the right to push up and out in our own way. We can't map out lives for each other, even the lives of our own kids."

Jason got up and came over to him.

"I don't know what's happening to us," Mark went on. "All of a sudden. Like a tornado rising up without any warning. Look, Nina and I have had a marriage. A real marriage. None of these makeshift affairs. None of these sham marriages held together by a scrap of paper and a whole lot of fear. We've loved each other. All the way."

"I know."

"Then what's happening? *What is happening to us?* Overnight, almost, this thing has happened. No, not overnight, but in a few weeks, a few bitter, crazy weeks. First Ginger and now the Bradfords." He looked into Jason's face. "I keep asking myself. All day I've kept asking myself, what next?"

"Nothing next, Mark. It happens to most marriages. Some get this sort of thing over at the beginning. In the early stages. Scraps and disagreements, the human ego resisting a fusion of two personalities. You and Nina were fortunate. You've had a lot of happy years."

"Were we really so fortunate?" Mark asked. "It would seem almost better to have a series of knockdown fights right off. This way it's bad. When you go along the way we have and now suddenly find yourself disagreeing. You can't believe it. You have to pinch yourself to be sure it's happening."

"It's not really happening."

"I don't follow that kind of double talk, Jason."

"You don't have to. Go back to Nina, Mark. You'll see."

Mark shrugged. He picked up his coat and hat where he had dropped them and stood reluctantly by the door. Jason walked out with him and stood there in the dark, waving as he pulled out of the driveway.

He didn't want to go back. He had no idea what he wanted to do, but anything besides face Nina with all that Bradford coldness about her. But he turned his car toward Turkey Hill. He was fighting Jason's advice, but he knew he had no choice but to follow it.

He did not know what he expected. Darkness throughout the house since it was late now and Nina was not one to read in bed. Good heavens, could she have read anyway on a night like this!

There would be silence in his home, too. The cold indifference of last night. So little to say to each other now, and that little painful and unimportant. Strain. The deadly, agonizing weight of strain.

As he held his car steady on the long climb up Turkey Hill, he was surprised to see his house all lighted up. Something's happened, he thought. Nina's sick, or maybe something worse. But there were no cars in the driveway. Nina's car had been put up for the night and the station wagon, too, and the garage was closed. Then why the blaze of lights?

He jumped out without putting his car in and ran up the steps, pulling out his key. The door was unlocked. He slammed into the hall, looking around him. The living room, upstairs, where was she? He glanced into the brilliantly lighted, empty living room. She was not there. He stalked through the downstairs rooms, his study, the dining room, the breakfast room, even the kitchen. Effie had left a note saying there was a snack for him in the refrigerator and he'd just better eat it. Crumpling the note in his hand, he took the front stairs two at a time.

She was not in their bedroom, not in her dressing room. His

86

concern became panic, but he followed the trail of lights into his den at the other side of the bedroom.

Then he saw her. For a moment he paused, trembling with anxiety yet wanting to burst into laughter with relief at the sight of her. She was asleep. Sitting bolt upright in his chair, she had fallen asleep and her head drooped to one side. Her hands were stuffed with tissues and they lay in tight little wads around her feet. A half-empty box of them stood on the small table beside his chair.

She must have cried herself sick! he thought. Her face was stained with tears where they had run down her cheeks and some of her lipstick had smeared, leaving a red scar near her nose. She was, in her misery, a petulant child and a grieving wife at the same time.

I love her, he thought. Tremendously.

He leaned down and kissed her, wanting to see the look on her face when she saw he was here.

"Mark!" She jumped, as one who has been awakened from so deep a sleep that she does not know what time of day it is, or where she is. He picked her up in his arms and held her close to him, the way he would have done with Jill.

"Dearest," he said.

"I was so lonely." The words came out in little gasps as if she might cry again. "I couldn't stand it. I went through the house and turned on all the lights. But that didn't help. I wanted to call up people we knew. Places you might go, but I didn't want to seem that kind of wife. I thought people might begin to ask questions."

It hurt him to hear her talk this way, more even than their quarrel earlier this evening had hurt him.

"Don't, please," he said close to her ear, kissing her face again and again. "Don't, dearest."

"Why did you do that, Mark? Please don't ever do it again. No matter what you do, don't leave me."

It was a pathetic plea, almost childlike in its simplicity, and it cut him across his ego and his pride more effectively than a lashing might have done.

"Don't, dearest. Don't try to talk."

She was sobbing against his shoulder, her face buried against him.

"Darling, don't," he said. "I love you."

"I love you, too, Mark," she said. "I'd die without you."

Where was the coldness? he thought. This was no Bradford talking to him now. This was no tall, regal lady who had been born into the aristocracy of power and position and wealth. This was his wife and she was all woman.

He gathered her more firmly toward him, and she clung tight, unwilling ever to let go.

Chapter 6

Nina drove up to Briarwood on the day before Thanksgiving to bring Jill home. Another time, under different circumstances, this might have been a pleasant trip. The day was bright and sunny, almost balmy for this time of year, and Jill was a sweet and amiable child.

This afternoon she was agog with the excitement of homecoming, full of emotion when she parted from her friends at Briarwood, saying good-by as if she would be gone for a year instead of a few days, and then rushing headlong into the anticipation of being back in the house on Turkey Hill.

She talked rapidly, in breathless, disjointed sentences, about everything that came into her mind.

"I didn't like to leave Darling Boy." He was her horse at Briarwood. "Most of all I didn't like to leave him. Alone without me, Mother, all that time. I cried this morning when I said good-by to him. And I think he wanted to cry too, if he could have. Why can't horses cry, Mother? It helps. I felt better this morning after I cried over Darling Boy."

She exclaimed over everything of interest along the road. The fruit stands with their piles of pumpkins, baskets of apples and jugs of cider fascinated her.

"Let's buy Daddy a pumpkin, Mother," she exclaimed. "I'm sure he'd like one. A big one. The biggest we can find."

So Nina pulled into one of the outdoor marts and helped Jill pick out the largest pumpkin on the stand and a basket of apples for Effie, "because," as Jill explained to the lean-faced farmer who served them, "when you buy something for one person in a house, you have to remember everyone else too." She wheeled on Nina. "Couldn't we send something to Ginger? It must be lonesome up there. Why won't they let her come home, Mother?"

Nina in a quiet voice explained that she had already sent Ginger a box for Thanksgiving, with some of Effie's cookies and a layer cake and candy and some new things to wear and lots of love from all of them along with the package. And she explained, too, why Ginger couldn't come home, that it was much too far and the trip would take a whole day coming and another whole day going. Besides, Susan Thompson's School was not like Briarwood. The girls were older and the headmistress preferred them to stay there for Thanksgiving. There would be a traditional hockey game between the upper and the lower classes and a fine dinner with a concert in the evening.

"Plenty of turkey?" Jill asked anxiously.

"Plenty of turkey." Nina smiled in response.

"But it won't be the same as being home," Jill persisted. "Ginger's going to detest it, Mother. She's going to hate every single minute of Thanksgiving Day."

The lean-faced man was taking it all in with a broad smile. Obviously he was enchanted by Jill. He left his stand to carry their things to the trunk of Nina's car and he let Jill supervise him as to where they should go. Then he stood by waving and calling "Happy Thanksgiving" several times as they left.

Driving along, Nina stole side glances at her bubbling younger daughter. Little charmer already, she thought, not blaming the farmer at the roadside stand for being captivated. Jill had the Bradford fairness, pale blond hair, now the color of champagne, later to deepen into pure honey. Her blue eyes seemed overlarge in a face that would have to grow to a size suitable to accommodate them. She had the Bradford mouth, full and sensuously appealing, and nature had given her the deep cleft in her chin that belonged to Nina's mother and her sister Evelyn, and a dimple in her right cheek, too, so that, when she smiled, she had the appearance of an Italian Renaissance angel bent on mischief.

Mischievous she was not, not as children went nowadays, for although she was lively and full of fun, she was a sedate, well-behaved little girl who liked to keep herself clean and her playthings and room orderly. This was, however, a strictly personal taste which she confined to herself since she admired her older sister, sloppy and swashbuckling Ginger who was often grimy from hard play on the softball diamond or sailing her father's sloop or digging in someone else's garden. Her sister's noise and heartiness and untidiness pleased rather than irritated Jill, who eagerly made herself Ginger's shadow whenever she was allowed, as much as to say, "This is what I like so long as I don't have to be it myself."

Today Jill was adorable in a blue woolen suit that was an exact copy of one of Nina's, even down to the tiny white collar at her throat. Her hat was a Scotch plaid perched in saucy arrogance over her bouncing blond curls and she wore tiny gloves and carried a boxlike handbag.

Completely satisfying, Nina thought, suppressing a sigh and wondering why everyone couldn't be like Jill who had never presented any real problems.

"Mother, you're so quiet," Jill said. "Is something wrong?"

Nina quickly covered for herself. "No, dear. It's just this winding road. I have to watch every curve."

"Does it bother you if I talk?"

"No, dear. You go right ahead."

Jill did. She chatted on about Briarwood and her new friends and Darling Boy and the interesting events at school. Every day was new, with something unexpected to look forward to, Jill explained. Letters from the girls' parents which they shared with each other and presents and boxes of good things to eat which they shared also. Nina listened, pleased that Jill was so well adjusted, that she had so many friends, even among the older girls at the school, and that Jill found life such an altogether good thing.

She's like me when I was her age, Nina thought. So much like me that it takes me back, back so far it hurts to remember. I can't believe it now but I must have looked like Jill, too. Everyone mistakes my own little-girl pictures for Jill. So Nina let her thoughts ramble back to what it had been like to come home from boarding school for a holiday. She could still remember the old Bradford limousine pulling up to the side door of the school where she had waited. Avery, the Bradford chauffeur—her father never drove—had jumped out and run up the walk for her bags and her mother had leaned forward with the back door open, to catch Nina in her arms the moment she reached the car. Sometimes there had been tearful partings with girl friends, for Nina and Jill were alike in that respect too, a little sentimental, unwilling ever to leave the enjoyment of any moment behind them, intense in their desire to cling to the pleasant things of life, then, strangely enough, the next moment racing forward to meet the good things that lay ahead of them.

The holiday at home had been intense and delightful, with skating and toboggan parties if there were ice and snow enough, with family gatherings and days spent among old friends and cherished possessions in her room at home, her dolls and toys and books, for she had always been a voracious reader even as a very young child. Then, when she was a little older, there had been the thrill of dances and parties and flirting with boys. She could, with no effort at all, recall the very dresses she had owned then, a dance frock of orchid satin and another of black velvet, tight around her tiny waist and billowing into a full, gathered skirt, and one quite mad holiday when she had worn a scarlet taffeta dress. It all came back, flooding her consciousness with the joy and happiness of other years, young years that were so precious in their freedom from care.

Here, throw open that door of memory and there is the Christmas she was given her own car, when she was just past sixteen, and her own checking account. She could see the Bradford house again, the big old house that people in Bradford had almost reverently called "the mansion." For all its hugeness, her mother had managed to make it warm and homelike, drawing her family together in the bonds of affection and understanding. Nina could see the Christmas trees, three of them, one in the big drawing room and one in the family sitting room and another in the hall upstairs near the servants' quarters. She could smell the house the way it had smelled through holiday time, a delicious mixture of warm gingerbread and pumpkin pie which refused to be kept in the back part of the house where the two kitchens were humming with activity from dawn until late at night. Her mother's perfume assailed her nostrils even now, poignant and caressing, a perfume imported from France for her, which Nina had never smelled since then. There was always company in the Bradford house, because Spencer and Bob and Evelyn and Nina had dozens of friends and they would at one time or another bring them all home. They were that kind of family. So at holiday time, with each of them returning from a different school or college, and bringing overnight guests with them, Nina might stumble over a strange young man or woman in the halls of her home and inquire laughingly, "Who are you!"

What wonderful days, she thought, as she nodded acquiescence to Jill's almost unheard question. What great roaring days full of the joy of living!

Her thoughts fell at last upon the present, but the thoughts were anxious ones and they found no repose.

93

I have been happy with Mark, she said firmly within herself. I have been ecstatically and beautifully content with him, beyond all complaint, far more so than most women have been with the men they have married.

But you're not content now, the voice within taunted her. Something is marring that happiness and you know it.

It would have been perhaps more pleasant, especially at Thanksgiving time, to minimize the discord and pretend that things were not so bad as they seemed. Nina was too honest for that. Now, riding home with Jill, pretending to be absorbed in her younger daughter's chatter and keeping her eyes intently on the road ahead, she faced for perhaps the twentieth time in the last week this thing that had risen between Mark and her. To call it "a thing" was to give it a far more tangible form than it really had. She did not know actually what the matter was. On the surface it appeared to be several things. It appeared to be their dissension over the policies of Bradford Tool, and their disagreement over Ginger. She knew for sure now that they were on the opposite sides of the fence where Ginger was concerned. At first she had thought Mark was on her side, but her intuition was thrusting home the fact that Mark was wholeheartedly with Ginger in her willful desire to leave Susan Thompson's School.

She asked herself the question, What's the matter with us? Suddenly, after all these years together, years of living in happiness and harmony, something was out of whack.

It couldn't really be Claire Elliott. It was inconceivable that Mark could, after all these years, be drawn back to her. Nina was not naïve. She knew that sometimes even the finest men were tempted, and Claire had been an early love. But she knew too that there was always a reason back of the temptation to wander. The reasons could be innumerable, and in her mind she ran through them. A wife who is too absorbed in other interests, her children or her career. No, she had never been guilty of that even when both Ginger and Jill were home.

Failure any longer to satisfy each other, physically or emotionally. Ridiculous. Mark and she were still in love.

Carelessness on the part of the wife, postmarital slump in appearance or intellectual buoyancy. Out of the question. She was the most chic woman in Bradford and men still turned to look at her when she passed them on the street. Her mind was keener than it ever had been, she kept active in community affairs, and she was still the avid reader she had been as a girl.

Sometimes the trouble was in the man himself, so the marriage counselors said. Frustration of the male ego could cause about as much breakdown in marriage as any other one thing. Mark, frustrated! The idea struck her as ludicrous; Mark with his big booming personality and his success in business and his total success in life itself was the least frustrated person she knew. So she chuckled involuntarily at the humor of it, causing Jill to ask what she was laughing at.

"Nothing, dear. Just something I happened to think about."

"I do that, too," Jill said. "Things are funnier sometimes when you look back on them." And Jill was off again, about her interests and her life, and leaving Nina to her thoughts.

They were not pleasant thoughts, despite the humorous interlude while she tried to contemplate a frustrated Mark Galloway.

She knew that Mark had been seeing Claire Elliott. Bradford was a small town at best, and where malicious gossip was concerned, its inhabitants became one big happy family intent that there should be nothing hidden but that all should be revealed. The very day after Mark had walked out on Nina during their quarrel, Evelyn had telephoned and brought up the subject of Claire Elliott.

Evelyn was adroit. She had not thrown the information at Nina without tact or deftness. She had started the conversation with trifles and then, in the spirit of sisterly helpfulness, had said, "By the way, Nina dear, there's something I think I should tell you because you're bound to hear it from someone else sooner or later. Meg Sheldon called me up this morning and said she wondered if you were away or something because Mark had been seen having lunch with his old girl friend Claire Elliott."

Nina had drawn in her breath and turned her head away from the phone, pressing her lips together so she would not answer Evelyn, but her sister's voice came at her relentlessly, "They were eating together in some impossible restaurant over in Greencrest. Isn't that near where Claire lives, Nina?"

Nina had almost choked on the words but she got them out. "I don't know anything about her, where she lives or anything else."

"But I thought Ginger worked with her last summer in that playhouse of hers."

"Yes, but I saw very little of Claire Elliott myself." Nina's voice had sounded strained and tight even to her own ears.

"Are you angry with me for telling you, Nina?"

"Of course not. I'm sure there's nothing to the story. You know how Meg Sheldon is."

"Of course I do." Evelyn was conciliatory. "She balloons everything. Avid for something to gossip about. She knows everybody's business better than they do themselves." Nina did not like the way Evelyn said it, a note of falseness came through the voice that belied her words. "And even if several people did see Mark with Claire Elliott as Meg swears they did, it could have been a chance meeting, you know. Those things happen all the time."

Nina had come away from the telephone dreadfully upset. It could never have been a chance meeting, not way out in Greencrest. Mark had no business that would ever take him out there. He lunched in the cafeteria at the plant, or in a nearby dog wagon with Steve Emrich or some other crony, or if he had an important business deal that required more privacy than the cafeteria would afford, he took his guests to the hotel. Mark was too much the male of the species not to be a creature of habit. He did not break the habits of years without some emotional compulsion that drove him to it.

The luncheon with Claire Elliott at some impossible little restaurant out in that impossible little development had not been a chance meeting. No one knew that better than Mark Galloway's wife.

She agonized over it, hating Meg Sheldon first for being clever enough to find out and then to relay the gossip to her sister Evelyn, the one person who could directly inform Nina.

She would rather not have known about it, but now that she did know, her mind raced through the events that had led up to that luncheon with Claire. She knew her husband very well. She knew her brothers too and she knew that the morning at the plant must have been a grueling one for Mark. So, angry beyond endurance, he had had to thrash out and do something about his fury. He had chosen to find Claire Elliott.

Nina had stood trembling in the middle of her beautiful living room. Now it was her turn to be angry, angry beyond control. She hated Claire Elliott for being so handy. After all these years of being away from Bradford, she should have stayed away. It was a cruel twist of fate that she had chosen to come back just at the time when Nina and Mark were beginning to quarrel with each other. Even above her hate for Claire, there pounded a fiercer emotion, an inrushing resentment toward Mark that he should have gone to Claire in his anger and his hurt.

The morning of Evelyn's telephone call Nina had stood before the two ivory miniatures of Mark and herself in their antique gold frames, paired together even in the portraits. Nina

97

had stared down at his rugged face, and with a fierceness she had not believed she possessed, she hated him for a moment.

This is the man I have loved, she had thought. This, my husband. Can he be foolish enough to go running off to Claire Elliott?

All the sweetness of their reunion when he had returned the night before to sweep her up in his arms and whisper that he loved her, to whisper it again and again, was dissipated in the realization that was gradually flooding her consciousness.

He had been with Claire Elliott again last night. Evelyn did not have to tell her about that. That was something even Meg Sheldon probably did not know, but Nina knew it. Nothing had been said as to where he had gone when he walked out. In the breathtaking emotion of their reunion, all thoughts of what happened during that ghastly interlude had been forgotten.

But as Nina had stood looking down at Mark's picture, what he had done the night before had become very important indeed, much more important than the fact that he had come back to her with love on his lips.

He had gone from the quarrel with Nina to find Claire Elliott again. He was setting up a new habit, a new pattern of behavior. Run away from unpleasantness, from his duty to her and to the Bradford tradition, to find solace with the past, with the old love. Go back, go back to what was once so pleasing and to what I have lost. No matter what their thoughts, no Bradford would run away from reality, no matter how unpleasant, Nina had told herself. Nor would a Bradford be sentimental about a friend like Steve Emrich—a friend who, Spencer said, was using Mark—a friend who could hurt Bradford Tool.

She was jogged from her remembrance of that morning less than a week ago, by Jill's trilling voice. "Mother, aren't we almost home?"

"Yes, dear, almost. Just another fifteen minutes."

Just another fifteen minutes, Nina thought. We'll be home.

98

Only it isn't home any more. It's a house Mark and I are living in together. Just a house, beautiful beyond words, full of all our cherished possessions, not home any more. Something has arisen between us. I don't know what it is. I can't even talk to him about it. That's why I haven't mentioned Claire Elliott. I don't want to know. I don't want to know where he's been with her or how often he's seen her. It can't really be that he loves her. He still loves me, but I can't forgive him for turning to her when he isn't getting his own way. I'm afraid for him. He trusts people too quickly. Steve, Claire, anybody who can reach him through sympathy, he trusts. Mark, what's happening to us? Why isn't our love for each other enough?

Chapter 7

THANKSGIVING DAY BEGAN IN AN AURA OF PEACE THAT MADE Nina's bitter doubts of the last week seem groundless. They had brunch late, in the sunny breakfast room. The meal was hearty and substantial, because lunch would be omitted today and dinner would be in the late afternoon at the Spinning Wheel, so that Effie could spend the day with her family.

As Nina settled down on her chair, with Mark across from her and Jill between them, she felt such an upsurge of security that she wondered for a moment what all the tormenting fear was about anyway. Nothing is wrong here. We're just the way we've always been. The past week has been some bad dream. No cloud is here this morning to cast the tiniest shadow of doubt across our horizon.

For so it certainly seemed. Effie brought in their food and then rustled away in her starchy skirts and aprons to shed this badge of the servant and don her best clothes, a garish royal-blue dress, one of Nina's discarded hats, a bit of green sequin madness that perched atop Effie's florid face like the stem on a tomato, a brown muskrat coat that had ten years ago been Effie's prize acquisition but today, although she did not realize it, was too tight and too short. With a black leather bag clutched tightly in one fist and black glacé gloves worn white at the knuckles in the other, Effie was ready to "dash."

"I've got to dash now," was her favorite way of announcing that she was going. It gave her a feeling of superiority, of being urgently needed both here and where she was going, as indeed she was, for who would cook the Thanksgiving turkey at her son's, but Effie herself?

So she left them, with the precipitous haste of the efficient who know both their value and their ability, flinging some parting words of caution toward her little brood of Bradfords: "Don't forget I've left some fresh-made coffee with a burner still on for you. Please turn it off. I don't want our electric bill run up."

Nina waited until the door had slammed and Effie's heavy heels were clacking down the driveway toward her son's car. Then she looked at Mark and he looked at her and she could see the laughter rising in his eyes and they both burst out laughing, filling the room with their gaiety and drawing Jill into it with them.

"Mrs. Galloway," Mark said, quieting down at last, "I urge you never to buy another green sequin hat."

"Mr. Galloway, I trust you will attend to the burner in the kitchen. Electricity costs money, sir."

They laughed again, not the roaring laugh that had followed Effie's departure, but a chuckling rumble of quiet appreciation.

This is nice, Nina thought. This is the way it should be. Mark, genial and relaxed, and the pleasantness of our home all around us, and Jill with us to double our own enjoyment.

Nina was busy serving from the steam table. She could not resist glancing at her two loved ones in the mirror over the buffet. Mark was smiling down at Jill and Nina watched him as he reached out and caught Jill's hand and Jill, always warm and responsive, jumped up and threw her arms around him and cried, "Daddy, I love you. I love Mother too. I love you both."

Mark held her close, longer even than he needed to, and Nina, watching the embrace, felt the blood pound through her veins with a freedom she had not known in a whole week. Mark seemed almost reluctant to let his younger daughter go.

In her relief, Nina leaned against the buffet, resting her wrists upon the mahogany top and filling her nostrils with the smells of the food in front of her, the sausages and wheat cakes, the mushroom omelet and buttered toast and the dominating fragrance of fresh coffee. The room was bright with sun, sunshine on everything, the old silver and the bright Limoges porcelain, green against white, and the baby chrysanthemums of the centerpiece. Sun touched Jill's silken hair and turned it almost platinum and it gave red lights to Mark's dark crop, and it lay over everything in a haze of benediction, bright, beautiful benediction of Thanksgiving morning.

At last Mark let Jill go, and Nina brought on fresh plates of sausage and omelet and suddenly the room was alive with more than sunshine, for they had all begun to talk at once, rapidly, about the day and what they would do and how beautiful the weather was and how good the breakfast tasted and how nice it would have been if Ginger could be here with them.

Their talk was buoyant and joyous, tumbling out in eagerness, as if something inside the three of them had to be heard, had to shout to the heavens that they were a family and that they loved each other very much.

They went to church together, making it just in time. Nina drove them over in her car because she always seemed more adept at finding parking spaces than Mark. When they entered the vestibule of the church, Nina was conscious of the fact that every usher turned to look and smile. And again, as they walked down the aisle, on the right side near the tall windows, with light streaming through them, she knew that almost every eye was on them. It was always like this. Nor was this vanity on Nina's part. It was, more likely, Bradford matter-of-factness. From earliest childhood she had been taught to face what was, to say this is the way things are, no more, no less, no different.

So she knew today that they were the most watched family in the congregation and she knew why. It was more than their being Nina Bradford and Mark Galloway. It had perhaps something to do with their being part of the family that had given the town its name, part of the big roaring giant called Bradford Tool. That was some of it, but only the smallest part. People envied and hated you sometimes for things like that, and they might stare in covert curiosity, but they did not openly admire.

Nina knew herself and Mark to be admired. Mark for what he was: big, handsome Mark Galloway, a man among men, hard-working as any man in his factory, brainy, ambitious, clean-cut. And Nina they admired for having had the guts to marry him. They loved her for loving Mark.

Once she had overheard a woman standing in the vestibule of the church say, "They're the handsomest couple in Bradford. They're so right for each other." And when Nina had turned to smile at the woman, she had nodded and smiled back.

Nina paused for a moment at the entrance to the pew, to be sure little Jill was with them. She smiled down at Jill and noticed several other people smiling at her pretty daughter, in her tan cashmere coat and matching beret, a doll of a child, all gold from the tip of her head to the toes of her tan shoes. Nina went in, with Jill close beside her, and then glanced back at Mark and exchanged smiles. Brown was his color and in his brown tweed suit, tan shirt, and brown polka-dot tie, he unwittingly blended with golden Jill and made a foil for Nina in her mink stole and yellow suit and hat.

The Thanksgiving service had, from the time she had been a small child, seemed an emotional one to Nina. Today, in her awakened frame of mind, she considered this emotion and what lay back of it.

People were back in Bradford who came home perhaps only once a year, this day. The conscious effort to feel grateful showed itself in faces that might not be touched by a thankful sentiment for another year. Emotions were very near the surface and easily aroused, and a general feeling of good will and happiness, however transient, permeated the congregation. It was as electric as magnetism and Nina, who preferred that her feelings should have the qualities of depth and permanency, recoiled from it.

But it was, on the whole, pleasant to be here, with Jill close by, and Mark just beyond. It was pleasant to feel the sun pouring in through the tall windows, and to listen to the choir, and Jason's sermon this morning was one of the most eloquent she had listened to.

There was contentment, too, in being caught up in the crowd after the service was over and in listening to the greetings and watching the handclasps. All this was something solid and enduring. It was a rock among the quicksands of changing human patterns of experience and behavior. This service and this church and these people, however transient their fervency, reminded you that there was something to turn to when you most needed it. Nina never failed to feel uplifted when she came out of church, and this morning, as they shook Jason's hand and reminded him that he was always welcome at their home, and then later as she and Mark and Jill clasped arms and walked slowly toward the car, Nina felt good. The gladness she had experienced when she had glanced into the mirror over the buffet this morning and seen Mark and Jill clasped in each other's arms was deepened and strengthened.

As she was driving them home—Mark and she never drove each other's cars—she mentioned that she would like to take Jill out to the Hunt Club for a short ride this afternoon. Several gentle new horses had been brought in, safe enough for Jill, and they could be out and back within an hour and a half, with plenty of time to make the Spinning Wheel for a four o'clock dinner.

Mark surprised her by saying he'd like to come along. It was so unusual that she almost let go of the wheel of the car, but she did not show her surprise to Mark, merely saying, "Why, we'd love it, wouldn't we, Jill?"

And Jill, of course, would. It was a gay afternoon. Nina and Jill rode thoroughbreds, a gelding named Dark Phantom for Nina and a mare named Golden Girl for Jill. Mark said he would like to settle for something foolproof like a cow pony and Jill seemed to find this an immense joke, giggling over it all the time they selected a chestnut gelding for Mark and even while their horses were being tacked up and they walked them down the bridle path toward the country roads.

Mark was not such a poor rider as he let on. Nina kept pace with him, watching the way he handled his horse. For a big man whose chief quality was not gentleness, he did surprisingly well. He rode the way he ran the Bradford factory, by having a distinct understanding with the horse from the beginning. It amused Nina a little, and pleased her, that Mark's masculine decisiveness should be in evidence even on the bridle path.

"Don't bother about me," he kept telling them. "I'm just along for the ride. You girls go ahead and enjoy yourselves." But they stayed with him. Nina would not, for anything in the world, have spoiled this moment by breaking into a canter and leaving Mark behind. It was a beautiful afternoon, with thin gold filtering through the trees, with the warm spell of the last few days still holding on like an additional blessing on this day of blessedness.

Jill, in her trim riding habit and velvet hunt cap, rode just ahead of them. They were walking their horses through a wooded area near the club. At one point as their horses' flanks almost touched, Mark reached over and caught Nina's hand.

"Take off your hat," he said. "I want to kiss you."

She snatched off the soft-brimmed fedora and clutched it tightly in front of her as Mark leaned over and kissed her. This was his way, to want to kiss her in a spontaneous impulse of delight, and she was glad to have him do it today, on this woodsy path, because it showed that Mark had not changed the fundamental patterns of his feeling for her. They sat there a moment, looking at each other, Mark's eyes full of approval.

Nina was the first to snap out of their absorption. "Where's Jill?" she asked. She listened for hoofbeats and made them out faintly, in the distance. "She's galloping!" she exclaimed. "She's galloping toward the ridge!" Nina pressed her knees against Dark Phantom and raced through the woods. She heard Mark exclaim, "Hey, where are you going! Nina, wait for me."

She did not wait, and there was no time to call back an answer to him. Jill was somewhere ahead, lost in the labyrinth of bridle paths, urging Golden Girl on. With a sharp intuition of imminent danger, Nina knew that Jill was headed for the ridge. It had never occurred to her to mention the danger to Jill. It had never occurred to her that Jill, the docile and obedient, would take it into her head to ride off by herself.

Nina picked out the quickest path to the ridge. Fortunately she knew every tiniest landmark of this place. She talked to herself inwardly as she raced on. There's no real danger if she stays clear of the fences. Surely she'll know enough not to take them. Jill's no fool. She's a good little horsewoman. She knows enough to let the fences alone. I'm sure she does. Then her thoughts became a prayer, a pleading urgency, Please God make her know enough to *stay clear of the fences!*

Nina came out into the cleared high ground of the ridge. The place was deserted. Only the strident scolding of a pair of jays mocked her from the top of a nearby tree. Otherwise, only silence and emptiness. Her heart pounded with a terror that would not be silenced as she collected Dark Phantom and turned the horse toward the fences, planning to ride the full length of them, dreading that she might see Jill and Golden Girl lying somewhere beyond.

Then suddenly she heard the sound. She swung around and

faced them, Jill and the horse, cantering nonchalantly through the screen of trees and out upon the ridge.

"Jill!" Nina screamed the word. "Baby!" She trotted over, jumped off her horse and snatched a bewildered Jill from the saddle, hugging and kissing her. "Oh, darling, it's my fault. I should have told you. I'd never have forgiven myself. I'm a stupid, stupid mother."

Jill was articulate as always. "What's the matter, Mother? What happened? Did something happen to Daddy? Where is he?"

"Here I am." It was Mark, standing beside them. Nina, in her relief to have Jill safely in her arms, burst into sobs at the sight of Mark.

Mark looked at the two thoroughbreds and then at his wife and daughter. His face was so frankly puzzled as he took in the scene that Nina's sobbing became gasps of laughter and for a moment she was hysterical, laughing and crying at once.

"Would it be asking too much if I wanted to know what this is all about?" Mark said, putting his arm around her.

"The drop beyond the ridge," Nina stammered. "The ground's gone soft over there. See the warnings posted all along the way." She pointed toward the DANGER signs. "I was afraid Jill might try to jump the fences. People used to do it all the time. Last summer the Sunderland girl. . . ." She let her voice trail off, reluctant to go into the details of the accident in front of Jill. The Sunderland girl, a brilliant young rider, had been with some companions and they had dared her to go over. The treacherous ground had given way and the accident had been all but fatal.

"You know, darling," Nina said to Mark, "the Sunderland girl."

"Yes," he answered, remembering the story, "I know." It had seemed a remote story to him at the time, something he hardly paid any attention to, the story of a daredevil young woman, bragging of her horsemanship, her friends calling her bluff, a nasty fall, severe injuries. Now, in a flash, it was brought so close to home that he winced.

He could understand Nina's panic when she had heard Jill's horse galloping through the woods towards this ridge. Suppose Nina had not headed Jill off. Suppose Jill, who loved to jump her horse as much as Ginger loved to act or play softball, suppose Jill had gone over. He could vividly reconstruct what had happened here the day the Sunderland girl had gone over, and what might have happened here today, and he pulled Nina to him in an understanding embrace.

Jill was the only one in the party who kept her head.

"Why, Mother," she said. "And Daddy, too. You don't think I would have jumped those fences, do you!"

Mark and Nina looked at her.

"That would be silly," she said. "It says DANGER plain as anything. And besides, I would have known, even without the signs. I heard about Mary Sunderland. She was a silly girl. Even if she didn't care what happened to her, she should have cared about her horse."

Mark looked at his younger daughter. She seemed incredibly tall for her eight years this afternoon. She was growing fast, she'd be a tall, ramrod-straight woman, like the Bradfords. Like good old Victoria. And this afternoon as she faced them with that look of reproach because they had doubted her common sense, she was dignified like Victoria, and quite formidable for one so young.

Mark glanced from his daughter to Nina. The panic was gone from her face, and the ashen paleness, and she was almost smiling. For the first time, he realized how very upset she had been, and how unlike her it was to go to pieces like this.

"Jill's right," she said, sounding more like herself. "I shouldn't have been so panicky about it. Jill would have known better than to jump."

She got back on Dark Phantom, and Mark went over and picked up her fedora and handed it to her. She smiled again at him as she reached out for it, but her hands, as they closed over his, were cold and trembling.

Chapter 8

IT WAS DURING DINNER THAT THEY MISSED GINGER MOST. THIS was their first Thanksgiving dinner without her. The hostess at the Spinning Wheel brought her absence forcibly home to them when she greeted them in the reception room with its soft pine furniture and crackling fire.

"Just three today, Mrs. Galloway? I thought your other daughter would be home for Thanksgiving."

They had their usual table, the corner one by the picture windows that looked down upon heather-toned valleys. It was pleasant to be in this attractive room with the flicker of lighted candles glowing more brightly in the quick-gathering dusk of late autumn.

Then, as they sat down and Mark helped Jill and Nina out of their coats, and as Nina pulled off her long gloves and folded them carefully on top of the clutch bag in her lap, she glanced up quickly at the empty chair across from her. It brought a swift sudden pain of longing for Ginger. After all, Ginger was her first-born, the child she had carried while Mark was overseas, the child who had been the strong fiber of Mark within her during those months of separation. Ginger was the one who had from the beginning been enough like Mark to bring the presence of him closer just by looking into the open face with its irregular features and its intense intelligence.

They had grown apart these last months, but they had for many, many years been close together, and Nina missed Ginger today as only a mother can miss the one absent member of her family on Thanksgiving Day.

"I miss Ginger." It was Jill, her eyes on the empty chair.

"We all miss her, dear," Nina answered.

"Ginger is fun," Jill said. "If she was here, we'd be laughing so hard everyone in the dining room would be looking at us. Ginger has more jokes than anyone I ever met." It was the tribute of a younger sister to an older, more sophisticated one, but it was well earned. Ginger was fun and she did make people laugh and it was too bad she was not with them.

"I'm going to call Ginger up later on," Nina said, thinking to divert the conversation from her absence. "We'll all talk to her."

"When we get back?" Jill asked. "Right away?"

Nina spoke her answer to Mark's eyes. "I thought we'd call her tonight. After the concert at her school is over. That's the loneliest time for the girls. The excitement will be over and she'll be missing us most then."

So they ordered their dinner, the traditional feast of the day, fruit cocktail and consommé and turkey with all the fixings, boiled onions and turnips and candied yams and whole cranberry sauce with sherbet. There was pumpkin pie for Nina and mince with hard sauce for Mark and a small portion of each for Jill, who wanted to taste everything. They ate and they talked and it was comfortable and cozy in the firelighted and candle-lighted room, snug against the deep gold and purple lights of the autumn sky.

They were a family, and yet they were not a family, for Ginger who was the liveliest of them all, the one the waitresses always made the biggest fuss over, was not here.

They stopped at Victoria's on the way back from the Spinning Wheel. She was giving a tea in her studio, and the place was crawling with all kinds of people, artists and writers from Westport, some show people, a well-known photographer. The studio was bedlamish, with a poet reading some of his own stuff in one corner and a pianist playing Bach on the spinet, and innumerable conversation groups huddled together on love seats and oval-backed chairs, self-absorbed, unaware that anything but their own bombast was filling the room.

Nina drew back from the flamboyance, but Mark was at ease as they circled the room, greeting an old friend or a chance acquaintance on their way to Victoria.

Victoria stood near the refectory-like tea table where some dark young woman, not a day over twenty-five and very beautiful in an Oriental way with black, slanting eyes, was pouring for the guests. Victoria was immersed in a conversation with a small bearded man, and Nina, catching phrases of their talk, knew they were discussing the French painters. Her aunt did not at first catch sight of Mark and Nina—they had left Jill at a young friend's home on the way—and Nina was glad to have this moment to steady herself amidst the confusion. Victoria, quite alone, had always been a strong enough dose for Nina to take, but today, surrounded by her motley group of spectacular friends, she seemed to Nina a bit shocking.

Not that it was an unprecedented shock. Victoria had specialized, throughout a long and turbulent life, in shocking people, but Nina had thought that as she reached the venerable age of an almost completed life story, she would mellow, and grow perhaps less tumultuous. By now it was apparent even to the hopeful Nina that Victoria had no intention of ever settling down. If she lived to be a hundred, she would still be the *enfant terrible* of the Bradford family, in search of new vistas, pulling life toward her in a gargantuan embrace, surrounding herself with jaunty and magnificent people, and with an air of high adventure.

This was Victoria. This was Victoria as she stood here today, somewhere in her seventies, looking more like fifty-five, with her straight and slender figure wrapped in a sheath of mink-colored taffeta, with the Bradford emeralds at her throat and hanging in dazzling pendants from her ears, with her crown of white hair rising precipitously above flushed cheeks and dancing eyes and the Bradford mouth.

She turned and saw them. It was significant that she noticed Mark first.

"Mark, darling. How good of you to come. I've been waiting for you. And Nina, you too. Dear, dear Nina, the only one of my nieces and nephews who comes here any more."

She had them both in her arms at one time and she was introducing them to anyone, everyone in sight. Mark, first. Always Mark's name first, with a glowing pride in her eyes and a triumphant ring in her voice. "This is Mark Galloway, my nephew. Isn't he wonderful? I adore him. It's the one regret of my life that we were born so many years apart." Embarrassed, self-conscious laughter from everyone but Victoria, who turned to Nina and said, "This is Nina, his wife. Isn't she lovely? She's the beauty of the family."

Then, as they got their cups of tea and bread-and-butter sandwiches, Victoria whispered, "Mark, follow me. Let's get away from this madhouse long enough for me to talk to you. Come along, Nina. You, too."

She led them, with remarkable grace and agility, to a little room at the side and after she had turned on a pair of huge Italian table lamps, she closed the door behind them.

"I've got to sit down," she said. "My feet are killing me. You stand or sit as you please." She dropped easily into a straight-backed chair and kicked off her pumps. Smiling up at them, she said, "You can fool everything and everyone but your own feet. They know how old you are."

Nina sat on the arm of a club chair but Mark remained standing, confronting Victoria with a quizzical smile.

"Come on, you witch," he said, "let's have it. What's on your mind?"

She loved him to talk to her like that, with the easy familiarity of a contemporary. It was one of the ways he had charmed her from the beginning.

"Steve Emrich is on my mind," she said, with admirable directness. "I want him to have the job that's open. How can we see that he gets it?"

Mark looked straight ahead of him, not at Victoria who was leaning toward him with compelling urgency, not at Nina who was silently pleading with him not to open this discussion on Thanksgiving Day.

Not today, Mark, please, she was thinking. It's been an almost perfect day, the first peaceful one we've had together in some weeks, so don't spoil it, please.

Victoria, glancing toward Nina, felt the pressure of her thoughts. Her voice was almost apologetic as she went on.

"I don't like to talk business here, on a day like this, but when else can I get to you, Mark? Every telephone at the plant is monitored, whether you know it or not. Leave it to Spencer to see to that."

Mark's answer was an imperturbable smile.

"And as for my going to the plant, you know very well Spencer wouldn't let me get beyond the front door. It sounds ludicrous, but it's true. I wasn't exaggerating the other day when I said he'd kept me from board meetings. By gentle persuasion, my dears, not by force." She mimicked Spencer's soft-spoken voice. " 'Victoria, it's a waste of your time. You aren't needed there, you know. Your proxy is all we need. What's the use of boring yourself unnecessarily? You know what a restless temperament you have, and how you despise the details of big business.'

"It's true," she finished, lapsing into her own resonant huskiness. "I am restless and I get frightfully impatient with Spencer and that pudgy-faced brother of his and simpering Thornton Watrous. I loathe business meetings. Always have."

She reached out with one toe for her slipper and pulled it toward her. "Mark, what can we do about Steve Emrich?"

Nina grew uneasy at Victoria's insistence. She knew her aunt well enough to know that she would not drop the subject until she had got some satisfaction out of Mark.

Nina's eyes were on her husband. He was staring down at the floor where the heel of Victoria's slipper was tapping as she held her foot half in and half out of it.

"Thornton Watrous has backed out," he said. "You knew that, didn't you?" Victoria nodded. "So there are only two of us, Victoria, you and me. Since the sanction of a majority of the board would be necessary to put Steve in, I don't see that we can do anything."

"That doesn't sound like you, Mark."

He glanced down sharply into her face.

"You've never been a defeatist. Never."

"It's not defeatism," Mark said. "It's plain facts. If we wanted to work Steve in, we might have done it with more adroitness. Mind you, I say *might* have, if we'd gone about it differently. My big mistake was rising to Thornton's bait at the dinner party. That brought it out in the open too abruptly. Spencer and Bob were shocked into taking sides against anything so novel. Then they bullied Thornton into taking their side. It's open warfare now, Victoria. A divided camp. The time for quiet policy changing has slipped away from us."

Victoria straightened, her back stiff against the chair. "Open warfare, is it?" she said, her mouth drawn suddenly into a tight line. "Then even if I'm on the side that's outnumbered, I'm going to fight."

"How?" Mark asked.

"I'm a woman," she said. "I have ways and means that are beyond the comprehension of mere males." She smiled wryly, her mouth still a thin line. "If I can't have my own way, I can make myself nasty and unpleasant and mean. I can be a nuisance."

"What are you planning in that female brain of yours, witch?" Mark asked her.

"I'm going to the next board meeting. When is it? A week from Thursday? I'll be there, Mark, with bells on."

Nina watched Victoria. There was a devilish light in her eyes and her mouth was not thin-lined any more, it was the full sensuous mouth of the Bradford family. She seemed girlish, in the half-light of the lamps, young beyond her years, younger in spirit even than Nina, for she had that youthful quality of enthusiasm, the will to strike back at life and fight it to the finish. Then Nina looked at her husband. In the glow of the light, his face seemed shining-glad, and she knew that he admired Victoria beyond anything that could be put into words.

These two are mates, Nina thought. A matched pair like those two table lamps. Victoria is right. If she had been born forty years later, they might have had a love affair that would have rocked their little world. They think alike, they feel alike, they are alike. My own husband is a stranger to me when I see him looking at Victoria like that. Her strength beckons to his. They face life in the same way, flinging a mocking challenge at it, but are they willing always to take the responsibility after they have hurled that challenge? A Bradford had to take the responsibility.

Mark did not speak. He knelt down on the floor and reached for Victoria's slippers and, one at a time, he placed them on her feet.

"How sweet of you, Mark darling," Victoria said, touching him lightly on the shoulder. "To think that at my age I should still have been able to find a prince charming."

She got up. "Will you stick by me?" she asked. "Whatever I say or do on Thursday night?"

116

Mark hesitated. The question was all it implied, an invitation to take a stand against Spencer, to continue the open warfare already begun. It was a crucial question, a vitally important one. Dropped here, in the informal atmosphere of Victoria's studio anteroom with its bizarre furnishings from all over the world, it seemed out of place, and utterly deceptive. A person might underestimate the importance of both the question and the answer. But Nina, watching Mark, knew that he was aware of the power behind Victoria's question and the significance of his answer, whatever it would be.

He hesitated so long that it seemed his answer might not be the one Victoria was waiting for. Nina realized what was holding him back. It was Nina herself. Her presence here and, even more than that, the strength and power of their relationship. More than the fate of Bradford Tool hung upon the answer that Mark would give.

"You've just called me your prince charming," he answered. "Could I have any choice but to stick by you?"

Chapter 9

THE TELEPHONE WAS RINGING AS NINA AND JILL CAME INTO the house. Mark had gone to put the car in the garage after letting them out at the front entrance.

Nina listened to the insistent ringing with no desire to answer it. She had not the faintest notion who it might be at this time on Thanksgiving Day. A glance at her watch told her it was not Ginger. The girls at Susan Thompson's School were just finishing dinner before going to the concert. Business calls for Mark might come through in the evening, but hardly on Thanksgiving Day.

A commotion at the back of the upper hall surprised her and then she heard Effie, stumbling along muttering to herself as she hurried to answer the upstairs phone.

Nina, taking off her hat and coat in the hallway, listened to Effie's grunts and monosyllables, but made nothing of them. At last Effie's head appeared over the banister.

"Is that you, Miss Nina?"

"Yes, Effie, what is it?"

"I thought it was you because I saw Mr. Galloway's car from the back window and then the lights go on in the garage. I got back early from my son's house because the weather looked bad and the radio said snow later on."

Nina smiled to herself as she combed Jill's hair and retied the ribbon that held the pale curls in place. Effie was not to be hurried by a telephone call. Whoever it was must wait until Effie had told the things she considered most important. However, Effie's next sentence jolted Nina from her complacency.

"It's that woman, Miss Nina. She's been calling every ten minutes for the last hour since I got back. She wants to talk to Mr. Galloway."

"What woman, Effie?"

"That Claire something-or-other."

"Claire Elliott?"

"Yes, Miss Nina, that's who it is."

Nina steeled herself against the shock of the words. She must not betray what she felt, not by the tiniest gesture, not by any change of inflection. She stood there in the hall, pulling Jill toward her, straightening the collar of her dress and smoothing her hair, because Jill was something solid and secure in the midst of her own churning emotions.

What does Claire Elliott want? she thought. Calling here on Thanksgiving night. The nerve. The cheek of it. But I can't show how I feel. I must be careful what I say, especially with Effie waiting for me to say something, and with Jill looking into my face with a question in her eyes. I must get Jill out of here. If there's going to be a scene between Mark and me, Jill must be spared the pain of hearing it.

"Do you want to take the call, Miss Nina?" Effie's voice was almost truculent. "Someone better talk to that woman or she'll keep calling all night."

"No, Mr. Galloway will be right in. He'll take it." Nina put her hands on Jill's shoulders and bent down and kissed her. "Dearest, I want you to go upstairs. Be a darling and get into some pajamas and let Effie give you some hot milk. I'll be up later on to say good night."

Jill understood. It was marvelous the way she caught on and

yielded to Nina's pleading, for pleading it was, no mistake about it.

Jill had almost reached the top of the long stairway when the front door opened and Mark, on a gust of November air raw with the promise of snow, walked in. Nina turned and faced him. She was glad to be a Bradford now, glad to have inherited from her ancestors the outward calm that gave away nothing she felt. Back of her poise, deep inside her, were the thundering hooves of memory, the remembrance of her early jealousy over Claire Elliott and what she had meant to Mark, the revolting telephone conversation with Evelyn the other day, and then the crippling realization that had come to her when she knew that Mark had turned to Claire the night he had walked out on her.

These thoughts were there, but they were pushed well below the surface and she could smile at him as she listened carefully to Jill's footsteps retreating in the upper hall along with Effie's. There, Effie had opened the door of Jill's room and taken her inside and closed the door behind them.

"Mark, Claire Elliott is on the telephone. She wants to talk with you. Effie says she's been calling all evening."

Mark flushed, and Nina was grateful for that flush of color because it told her that whatever he felt, whatever he had been doing at Claire's house, he was not hardened to it. Without a word, he started toward the telephone nook at the back of the hall.

"Not there," Nina said. "Upstairs. Effie answered it up there."

Mark hesitated, as if he were reluctant to answer a telephone upstairs while Nina stood close to another phone downstairs. Then, wheeling around, he took the stairs two at a time.

He did not try to lower his voice, letting it boom through the house, but Nina went into the living room, turning up more lights, straightening books that did not need to be straightened and blowing imaginary dust from Dresden china figures.

The conversation was not a long one. She heard the cessation of sound in the upper hall as Mark stopped talking and then the thud of his steps on the stairway. She did not turn as he entered the room, but let him call her name.

"Nina!"

Then, slowly, with not a single trace of the emotions that were beating against her, she pivoted around.

"It's Ginger. She's left the school. Run away. She came down by bus and train somehow. This afternoon she turned up at Claire's."

Nina reached out and put her hand on the back of a chair. "Tell me again, Mark. More slowly, please. I don't quite understand."

"Ginger's run away from Susan Thompson's School. Just walked out early this morning. She had enough money to get back to Bradford and she took a taxi to Claire's house this afternoon."

"Did she come here first?"

"No, I don't think so. No, I'm sure she didn't. Claire said she came straight to her house."

"Why? Why did she do that? Why didn't she come home?"

"I don't know why she did it," Mark answered slowly.

They looked at each other and Nina realized that for the first time in many years she and Mark were feeling self-consciousness in each other's presence. Not since the early years of their marriage when their two individualities were fusing, had she and Mark felt any moments of real discomfort together. Yet tonight, in the face of this startling news, they were embarrassed to be here together. Each would rather have learned this appalling news of Ginger's running away from school alone, away from the other.

Nina, with a woman's quick perception, knew why. It was

because Ginger, by going to Claire Elliott, rather than coming home to them, had said, as plainly as anyone could tell them, that they had failed as a team in this one important thing. Ginger was telling them that they did not understand her, and that she did not understand them, and, what was more, that she was not sure she loved them or that they loved her.

Mark's words, the last that had been spoken, still echoed in the room. *I don't know why she did it*. Yes, you do know, Nina's thoughts screamed back at him. You do know why. You know much more than you're letting on, much more than you're telling me. You and Claire Elliott. You both know things I'm shut out from. You're shutting me out, Mark, out of your life and, eventually, your love, perhaps. Who knows how all this will end? Which of us now, facing each other in the impact of this dreadful moment, which of us can say?

She turned the conversation from what was most in her thoughts.

"What about the school? They should have called us the moment Ginger's absence was noticed."

"Maybe they did. We've been away all day. When would they be likely to notice that Ginger was gone?"

Nina concentrated on the routine of boarding-school life, grateful to have something so far removed from the reality of this moment to think about.

"Not right away. Not on a holiday. Everything is more or less confused on a holiday. Breakfast is straggling. Then during the excitement of hockey games, Ginger would never have been missed, especially since she didn't make any of the teams. At dinner, perhaps, they would first have noticed that she was missing."

The piercing sound of the telephone bell interrupted Nina's reconstruction of the day at Susan Thompson's School.

"That would be the school now," she said, matter-of-factly. Mark started toward the hall, but she held out her hand.

"Better let me answer it. I'll know what to say."

"Let me listen in upstairs," Mark said. "You may need me, Nina."

I'll know what to say. Her own words reverberated in her consciousness as she walked toward the booth in the hall. Effie's steps in the upper hall reached her ears and she called up, "I'll take it this time, Effie." She listened to Mark running up to the other telephone.

I'll know what to say. I always know what to say, she thought. Always the right word, always the correct answer. The thing to do. Always the right thing for the right occasion. This is my training, my whole education for life. No, more than that, it's my heritage. To do and say the right things. Sometime I would like to do and say the wrong thing, the shocking, appalling thing. Like Victoria who has dedicated her life to being different. Like Mark who refuses to be subjugated by anything or anyone. Like Ginger who has brought this unpleasantness upon us tonight. For once, for just one frightening, terrible moment, I would like to reach out my arms and sweep my world away from me in an ugly gesture of rebellion. I would like to turn everything upside down. I would like to throw back my head and scream.

She walked quietly into the telephone nook and in a steady voice spoke into the transmitter.

"This is the Galloway residence."

"Mrs. Galloway?" The voice at the other end was crisp and positive.

"Yes."

"This is Marcia Cromwell, headmistress at Susan Thompson's."

"Oh, yes. You're calling about my daughter. She's home. Back here in Bradford. We know about her leaving the school today and we're dreadfully embarrassed about it." This was the way to do it, take the blame, express sincere but not gushing apologies. "We're having a long talk with Ginger tonight. You must give us a little time, Miss Cromwell, to straighten things out. I'll telephone you in the morning. Will that be quite satisfactory with you?"

She could feel the wind being taken out of Miss Cromwell's sails, feel her responding mentally to the common sense and the unperturbed poise that Nina was showing. If there was any nervousness, it was not on Nina's end of the wire.

"I didn't know you knew, Mrs. Galloway. We were almost frantic to find out Ginger was gone. You can imagine." Miss Cromwell's positiveness had been replaced by a stammering relief.

"I can well imagine," Nina answered, "but there's nothing to be alarmed about, really. My daughter has taken longer than usual to make her adjustments at your school. No one is sorrier this happened than we are, my husband and I. We're most disturbed that you should have been subjected to this, Miss Cromwell, but please trust us to work it out. We will, you know." Her voice was confident, full of hope and promise.

"Good night, Miss Cromwell."

Nina put down the phone. Her hand was moist and shaking and tiny beads of perspiration dotted her forehead. She patted her face with the back of her hand. It could have been worse, she thought. Much worse. Suppose, not having reached us, they had called the police. Suppose Claire Elliott had not telephoned us first. That would have been a nasty situation. There would have been so much more to explain. This was comparatively easy. Now the next step was to get Ginger home, give her a talking to such as she had never had, and then take her back to Susan Thompson's. Not tomorrow. Give her a few days here, but perhaps Sunday, or Monday. Nina had no doubt of her ability to handle Ginger. Ginger was rebellious and wayward, but she respected Nina, more even than she respected Mark. Being tempestuous herself, Ginger feared the determined poise of people like her mother. She resented it perhaps, but she respected it. If Nina laid down the law to Ginger, she would go back to Susan Thompson's and she would stay there. Nina was convinced she could settle this older daughter of hers once and for all.

She went back to the living room and Mark joined her.

"That was the way to take care of it," he said. "I would have said too much. Might have even told her what Ginger actually thought of their school."

Nina looked at him. "Get your coat, Mark," she said, "and bring mine too. We'll go out the back way."

He did not move. "Don't you think it would be better if I went for Ginger myself?" he asked.

"No," she answered, "I want to go too."

Chapter 10

Mark and Nina did not talk on the way out to Claire Elliott's. Mark drove and Nina kept her glance turned away, watching the landmarks of the town whizz by in shadowy hulks. The Bradford Library, the Bradford Elementary School, the Bradford Junior High School, the Bradford Railroad Station, the thickly settled houses near the center of town, then the more sparsely settled sections, then finally the development called Greencrest.

Nina watched this with interest, facing the row of stores as they drew near the shopping center and identifying the Colonial Restaurant where Evelyn had said Mark had lunched with Claire. On Thanksgiving night, it was closed and it appeared desolate and empty, an unreal figment of a dream world, as remote from Nina as Claire Elliott herself.

Mark was more upset than Nina was. She could tell from the way he drove, varying his speed, rushing forward in hurried spurts and then slowing up for no reason at all. Whenever they stopped for an occasional red light, he pressed the accelerator in a preoccupied manner. He could be upset about several things—Ginger, the way she had run away from school and shown up at Claire's house, or even at Nina's uncompromising insistence that she come along tonight.

Each of these in itself was enough to disturb any man, but Nina guessed it was none of them really. It was because he was going to see Claire Elliott again.

As they drew near their destination nothing escaped Nina. She noted that Claire's house was not part of the development, but that they had left Greencrest behind and struck out along a side road, a country road bordered by small woods. Some houses lay along the road, but they were far apart so that they and their occupants would never interfere with one another. A person could be quite alone out here. There would be no neighbors to know what was going on.

At last they turned off the road and Nina saw that they had pulled into a driveway, but not a clearly defined one like the long sweep of paved road that led up to the Galloway house on Turkey Hill. This was an unfinished dirt driveway, all but overrun by evergreen shrubs, and it looked neglected, with piles of leaves lying where the wind had blown them. Neither Mark nor Nina commented on how readily he had found the house. Mark was not equal to the deception of pretending that he had never been here before, and Nina, if she had needed any proof as to where he had gone that stormy night last week, now had it.

He helped her from the car and she walked behind him, shuffling through the dry leaves, pulling her coat close around her, partly because of the biting air, partly because of the task that lay before her.

The house seemed so small from the outside that Nina, who had aways lived in large places, and all of whose friends lived in big sprawling houses, wondered how anyone could be comfortable here. The porch light was on, and so were the lights over both entrances. The summer furniture was still on the porch, with shabby-looking canvases thrown over what appeared to be a couch and several chairs. Leaves had filtered in through holes in the screen and lay over everything. The whole scene was so depressing to Nina that she felt, for one moment, like turning back. Yet she knew she must not do this, she must not leave Mark alone tonight with Ginger and Claire Elliott.

So she went in. A surprise awaited her the moment she stepped over the threshold, where the atmosphere of neglect and disorder was dispelled. Within the house, she saw spotless order. Claire greeted them in a tiny space that was, Nina supposed, a hallway, and then led them into the living room. Nina looked at once for Ginger, but she was not there. Claire must have noticed the searching expression on Nina's face for she explained.

"She's upstairs washing her face. There have been quite a few tears." Claire was smiling and Nina could not bear to face the dazzling quality of that smile. It overwhelmed her. She saw the whole woman in that smile, the tremendous personal magnetism, the drawing power that had pulled on both her husband and her daughter, and she saw its touch of mockery.

This is a woman, she thought, who is afraid of nothing. A woman so big that the vicissitudes of life pound against her in vain. She is not like me, all calm outside and churning within. You cannot simply get to the heart of her. She will not be shaken. I'm terrified of her. She's too strong.

"We heard your car pull in," Claire went on. "So I suggested Ginger fix herself up a little."

So you could have Mark alone for a few minutes, Nina thought. I doubt that you expected to see me too.

Yet, if this was so, Claire did not betray it. She was cordiality itself.

"I met you so briefly last summer," she said to Nina. "I feel this is really our first meeting. But Ginger talked a lot about you, and so have many other people in Bradford. Only nice things," she said, "of course. So I feel I've known you a long time." Then, with that flash of disconcerting directness that Nina was to learn was Claire's most potent weapon, she added,

"I can see now how you stole Mark right from under my nose when we were all very young. Now that I've met you, I don't blame him."

Nina felt nervous. If this was the way Claire Elliott was, determined to say anything that came into her head, she was going to be more than Nina had bargained for. Nina could cope with catty females. She had learned the art during her first year at boarding school and grown increasingly skillful since then. This was something else again. This downrightness was almost masculine in quality and it flustered Nina, making her wonder what Claire would say next.

Claire was evidently finished with Nina because she turned next to Mark. Her voice lowered and softened.

"Be easy on Ginger, Mark, won't you?" she said. "The kid has been through a lot. You remember what it was like to be young and to suffer."

Mark nodded. Nina resented the remark. She resented hearing Ginger referred to as "the kid" and she especially resented having Claire tell her husband how to deal with their child. More even than this, she resented the way Mark responded, nodding his acquiescence, as if he were used to following advice from Claire. It was painful to her now to realize that a special relationship always had and still existed between Mark and Claire, and that it was a relationship which left her an outsider.

She looked around her with awakened interest. Until this moment, it had been merely a place she had been forced into for a few unpleasant minutes, a room she would not ever need to come into again, which she might quickly and mercifully forget. Now she thought of it as a house which, except for the turn of events that had brought her into Mark's life, might have been his home.

Now she exposed her sensibilities to it. She was surprised to see that it had, in its limited way, great charm. A bit too cluttered perhaps, but charming. The furniture was good. The two wing chairs by the fireplace were not antiques but they were excellent reproductions and the workmanship was honest. There were several Victorian pieces, some chairs and a pedestal table and a massive walnut desk, too large for the room, a veritable museum piece. Claire must have a fondness for old ironstone and milk glass because the two Dutch cupboards were full of it. An extravagant amount of lamplight and bright chintz curtains with red predominating in the pattern gave the room an undeniable cheerfulness.

It's a room like Claire herself, Nina thought, alive and beckoning.

She heard footsteps on the stairs and turned toward the doorway. Claire and Mark, hearing them too, also turned. The three of them stood waiting. There was a pause, a soundless moment when the footsteps stopped and hesitated. The three who were waiting reached out in their own ways toward the shadowy figure in the hall. Mark took an aggressive step toward the door as if he would go to get his willful daughter. Claire, for once, had turned off the dazzling brilliance of her smile. Nina's nails clenched tight against her palms, dug deep into the flesh.

Why doesn't she come in! she thought. What's keeping her?

Then, at last, Ginger came in. She walked slowly, her head thrust high and forward with a show of arrogance, but her manner was not so confident, and she stopped short inside the door, facing them bravely enough but not going to meet them.

Neither Mark nor Nina moved toward her, but Mark did speak.

"Hello, Ginger," he said. "What have you done to your mother and me?"

It was the wrong thing to say. Nina knew it instantly, but Mark in his clumsy, well-meaning way did not know that he was touching a match to tinder.

Ginger found her voice. It was a strident voice, full of anger and fear and frustration, of antagonism that lashed out at them.

"I haven't done anything to anyone," she said. "What is everyone doing to me would be a better question to ask. Why doesn't everyone let me alone? I want to be let alone." Tears came, and great racking sobs, because Ginger could not stem the tide of her emotion. It was too full, too ready to burst forth and sweep before it whatever lay in its path.

"Let me alone," she sobbed repeatedly. "Just let me alone."

Claire did not move or speak. Nina had to hand it to her, she knew enough not to interfere at this moment. Nina pushed Mark aside and went over to Ginger. She did not touch her, not at first, but her voice was like a caress as she talked to this first-born child of hers.

"Ginger, dear, no one wants to hurt you. Your father and I want to help you." Ginger looked up at her. Her large-boned face was swollen from crying and her thick red hair hung over her forehead, getting into her eyes, becoming damp from her tears and curling crazily the way Mark's hair did.

"I mean it," Nina said in a steady, reasonable tone. "We want to help you if you'll let us, dear."

"Then take me out of that school," she bellowed. "I won't go back even if you won't take me out. I'll never go back."

Mark took another step toward them, but Nina put up her hand, holding him off.

"Ginger." Nina waited until Ginger looked her in the eyes. "Your father and I didn't come here tonight to make a deal with you. We came to take you home with us."

"Do I have to go back to that place?"

"We'll talk it over."

"There's nothing to talk over. I won't go back. I'll kill myself first." Nina drew back from the vehemence of the words. "I mean it, Mother. I'll kill myself if you send me back there."

Nina did not answer at once. She stood there watching this strange child of hers, so foreign to her own nature.

"Do you realize what you're asking of us, Ginger?" she said. "You're trying to make a bargain with us. Your life against our promise not to send you back to Susan Thompson's." Ginger's head shot forward in surprise. You could see her turning Nina's words over. "If we said yes to that, if we agreed to accept your life in return for not sending you back to Susan Thompson's, we'd be doing you a serious wrong. Every time you met something that baffled or frustrated you, you'd want to bargain your life against it." Nina pushed Ginger gently down into one of the wing chairs and she herself sat down on one of the high hassocks in front of the chair, facing Ginger. She took Ginger's restless hands in hers.

"My dearest Ginger, don't you see we can't do that? We can't set up a pattern for you that will cast a shadow over your whole future. You're not a child any more, Ginger. You can't stand before life and kick at it the way you kicked at the nursery door in anger a few years ago. Life doesn't respond to kicks and threats. It responds to strength and courage."

Ginger had quieted, with some of the belligerence washed out of her, and she was listening to Nina, absorbing every word she said.

"Now this is what I think we should do. You listen and see if you don't agree with me. I think we should all go home and have something to eat together and go to bed and get some rest. Tomorrow we'll talk this all over. Sanely, without threats and without bargaining with each other. Perhaps it is best for you to return to Susan Thompson's, perhaps not. I'll make you a promise. I'll promise you that whatever I think is best for you, the very best thing in the world for you, I'll do. Because I want only what's right for you, Ginger. You may not believe it, but your happiness is very precious to me."

Nina stopped. It was all she had to say. Her daughter, looking straight ahead of her, was mulling over the promise, and Nina could see her brighten.

"All right," she said, "if you really mean what you say, and I think you do, Mother, I'm willing to talk this over. Because I know when you hear my story, you'll know that I belong here. I belong here with people like myself, my own kind, with people like Miss Elliott and all my friends. I can't be like you, Mother, any more than you can be like me. If you want me to be happy, you've got to let me be myself."

Ginger stood up, ready to go. She faced Claire Elliott and it was Claire, not Mark or Nina, to whom she gave her nod of confidence, her smile of friendship.

Nina sat on the hassock, letting her eyes wander about this cheerful room that so much bespoke the character of its owner. She knew that after all was said and done, she was licked. There was no use in kidding herself. She might as well face the truth. Ginger would not go back to Susan Thompson's.

I've had quite a day, she thought. Quite a day for any mother. Within a span of eight hours I've come perilously close to losing both my children. At least I learned what it would be like to lose them. First Jill racing toward the ridge and the dangerous fences and now Ginger facing up to me like this and winning.

Ginger was getting into her coat and hat. The coat was already inches short at the hem and sleeves, and it looked much too snug across the back. Ginger was almost a woman, a dynamic woman who would insist upon carving her own niche in the world and filling it in her own way.

If you want me to be happy, you've got to let me be myself.

What's happening to my world? Nina thought. All this shattering self-assertion. All this self-will flung out on every side. Doesn't anyone want to belong to anyone any more? Doesn't anyone want to be part of a family or a group and work together and give up this self-determination, this willfulness that seems to threaten us and everything the family has stood for? Or perhaps it's me, perhaps the fault is really mine. Maybe my world is passing me by. I still want to belong. I want to belong to Mark and Ginger and Jill. To my family and my brothers and my friends. I don't want to be cast out into loneliness, into the insecurity of fending for myself.

But perhaps that's old-fashioned now. Perhaps I would have done better if I had been a Victoria or a Claire Elliott. Self-sufficient. Strong. A lone wolf. That way you don't get hurt.

Chapter 11

GINGER DID NOT RETURN TO SUSAN THOMPSON'S, JUST AS NINA had intuitively felt that night out at Claire Elliott's house. She stayed home, enrolling at the public high school. Ginger's independence baffled and irritated Nina. She would not even let Nina drive her to school, but insisted on racing down Turkey Hill to join a crowd of friends a quarter mile away where they stood and waited for a school bus to pick them up.

"I want to feel as if I'm really one of them, Mother," she said. "I like those trips back and forth on the bus."

From the first day Ginger attended the high school, Nina had to admit to herself that her older daughter seemed more relaxed and happy. She came home full of talk about her classes and teachers. She talked about the excitement of being in such large classes and the fun of a coeducational school. Two boys had already asked her for dates and she had invited a crowd over after the dramatic club rehearsal on Friday night. She had made Dramatic Club without any difficulty. Miss Elliott's recommendation had acted like magic on Miss Ayres who was in charge of the club.

Nina winced at the mention of Claire Elliott's name, but she concealed her feelings. The last thing she would want was to have Ginger suspect that there was trouble between her father and mother and that Claire Elliott was involved.

Nina was relieved to see Ginger caught up in the activities of the school. She was glad to see her make new friends. They were not exactly the friends Nina would have chosen for her, but they were a well-mannered group of young people, and it was gratifying to see that Ginger was quieting down, losing some of the emotional turmoil that had kept them all disturbed these past months. Here at least was one problem that was not so pressing and harrowing as it had been.

Unfortunately, there were other problems that did not yield so readily. There was Mark himself. That was a problem to keep a woman lying awake night after night, staring up at the ceiling! What was the matter with this husband of hers? He seemed jumpy, irritable beyond all reason, ready to fly off the handle at the slightest remark that did not sit well with him.

As she turned her thought upon him, Nina suspected that the trouble lay within Mark himself, and for that very reason she was helpless to correct it. She could only wait upon the logic of events.

She was worried too about developments at Bradford Tool, and in a wider sense how the policies of the firm might affect the Bradford family, and the whole town. She did not exactly admire her brother Spencer—they were far too different in their tastes and temperament to permit mutual admiration—but she did respect his judgment. She felt his business sense to be sound. He was a money-maker, hard and shrewd, but he was honest in business and his acumen was sharp.

It was the infiltration of a new policy through her head-strong husband that she was most worried about.

Mark was a brilliant engineer and a good businessman, so far as it went. But he had the creative engineer's foibles. He could be visionary. He could be dogged in his devotion to his own ideas, stubborn to a fault. Moreover, he could be misled through personal sympathy. This sentimental strain was something he had brought up from River Street, Nina felt, and she

136

believed from what Spencer said that he was sentimentalizing Steve Emrich and that Steve was taking advantage of Mark. Steve was good enough at his job in the lab at Bradford Tool. Nina never questioned that. What she did question was the overblown concept her husband had of Steve's abilities, his "genius" as Mark was so glibly wont to put it.

Nina did not know Steve very well, but she did know that there was such a thing as opportunism. It was perfectly possible that Steve was using Mark as a step up. Such things were known to have happened.

There was not a doubt in Nina's mind that if Steve were to get the job of chief engineer, a dangerous policy would be established, a policy hazardous not only to the Bradford family but in the long run to the town of Bradford.

What made Nina feel so distressed was the fact that she could not talk to Mark about it. In this one thing they were miles apart. Here was the point of separation, here was the line at which Mark went one way and she another.

He was a better man, a stronger man, and a finer man than her brothers or any Bradford living. Of this Nina was sure. But his great fault lay in his expansive, generous vision.

It was his own vision, it was not the certain, the consciously limited vision in which Mark had been reared. This was the way she talked to herself about Mark and about herself and about her marriage, and she firmly believed every bit of it to be true.

She saw Mark as handicapped by his beginnings in this one thing only: that he did not see his responsibility as part of the Bradford family, the Bradford tradition. He wasn't a poor man any more. He was wealthy and he had, by accepting that wealth, accepted with it some responsibilities. He owed it to the Bradfords to carry along their policy.

It was because she was so vitally concerned with Mark's

place in the family and the Bradford plant that she fretted over what he would do in regard to Steve Emrich.

It was for this reason too that, on the night of the critical meeting of the Board of Directors, she waited anxiously for Mark's return. She sat in her dressing room, unable to read, not even wanting to turn on the television or radio. She had kept the evening open so she might be here waiting for Mark when he returned.

It was her privilege to attend the meeting if she wished, yet such a move was unthinkable to Nina. The Bradford women had always permitted their men to conduct the business affairs of the firm. Her unprecedented presence at this meeting would only have complicated matters. She would have been drawn into the battle between Spencer and Mark and that was the last thing she wanted.

It was Spencer's side she was on. Because it seemed to her this was the Bradford side. Within herself she had no other logical choice. Yet she would not take a stand in public against her husband.

When Mark's car swung into the driveway, Nina jumped up, restlessly pacing the dressing room, waiting for him. This uneasiness was new to her, and it bothered her. She did not like to lose her poise even when she was alone.

Mark came into the house and she was conscious of every move he made, of his stop at the refrigerator for the snack Effie had left, of his brief pause in his downstairs office to gather up what mail lay on his desk, of his quick step on the stairs. She heard him open Ginger's door, heard their voices, their laughs so much alike, then he was coming toward her dressing room.

The moment she saw him, she knew that the meeting had not gone his way. She went quickly to his side. "Tell me about it," she said.

"I'd rather not talk about it tonight, Nina. I'm tired. It can wait till morning."

"I can't wait until morning," she said pointedly. "I want to hear everything tonight, Mark."

He shrugged and his gesture was that of a fatigued man. She saw the deep hurt in his eyes and at the corners of his mouth. For that single moment her heart went out to him and she felt completely his wife. Then the anguish rose within her and she was half Nina Bradford, half Nina Galloway. She crushed the sympathy out of her in one fell swoop, knowing that in the long run, it would be foolish to yield to sentiment at a time like this. Too much was at stake.

Mark slumped down on the chair opposite her chaise longue but she remained standing.

"The meeting convened at seven thirty. The general business was dispatched quickly because of the important nature of the meeting." His voice had a twist of irony in it. He recited the events in reportorial fashion, as if he had washed his hands clean of what had happened.

"We got quickly to the vital question of the hour," he said. "Would Steve Emrich or a Bradford be chosen to fill the post of chief engineer."

"Was Victoria there?"

"She was there."

"And she made a carefully thought-out speech, I suppose."

"Am I to tell this in my own way, Nina, or do you want to take over?"

She drew back from the gruffness, then realized how tired he must be. "Go ahead," she said, "I'm listening."

"Victoria isn't a speechmaker," he said, defending her. "She's a very warm human being, and what she said made sense. She pointed out what some of us have felt all along, that unless this policy of inbreeding is changed, Bradford Tool will become an inept organization, pushed to the wall by the competition

139

that's growing up around us. We need new blood, Victoria said, vital blood with the highest engineering competence and fresh ideas and the guts to carry these ideas out. In today's market—and she is so right about this, Nina—she said you've got to have the best to offer or you drop by the wayside."

"For one who's kept herself in almost complete ignorance of factory methods, Victoria appears to have acquired a rather sudden and overwhelming intelligence. She's never attended an important meeting before."

"If she's been kept in ignorance, it's not her fault. It's Spencer's. He's done everything to keep her out of things."

"Who wrote Victoria's speech for her?" Nina asked.

"If you're insinuating I did, you're mistaken. Victoria is capable of doing her own thinking. For my money, she's the most capable member of the family. She just happens to be a woman and not qualified to run the firm. It's a pity for Bradford Tool that she wasn't born a male."

"I concede she was very eloquent, Mark. Did she persuade the Board to give Steve Emrich the job?"

There was a long pause.

"You know the answer to that, Nina." Mark's voice had a deadly quietness to it. "One of Ollie Muthersbaugh's sons got the job. Frank, the younger one. Spencer favored him because he's married. The older one isn't."

"Surely Victoria didn't accept defeat so easily," Nina answered. "Not if I know Victoria."

"You're right. Victoria didn't accept defeat. Why should she? She holds forty per cent of Bradford Tool stock."

"She said on Thanksgiving Day that she had something up her sleeve. What was it?"

"She's demanding a meeting of stockholders. With forty per cent of the holdings, she's entitled legally to do that."

"But what for? What can she possibly gain since she's already been outvoted by the Board of Directors? Spencer and

Bob and Thornton will stick together. A meeting of stockholders won't change a thing."

"The bylaws of Bradford Tool provide that any amendment can be proposed by a stockholder at a special meeting of stockholders called for that purpose. If passed by the majority of stock-holding interests, the amendment becomes effective."

"I don't follow you, Mark."

Mark spoke slowly, breaking it down for her. "Victoria is demanding a meeting of stockholders to act upon an amendment that would give the general manager rather than the Board of Directors the right to appoint executives who work under him."

"That means you would appoint such men as chief engineer."

"Right."

"They'll never pass it, Mark. It won't go through."

"It could."

"How? I don't see how it possibly could."

"Mind you, Nina, it's the majority of stock, not the majority of stockholders that turns the trick. Victoria was left forty per cent of Bradford Tool stock by your grandfather. Right?"

"Yes."

"And your father was left sixty per cent which he divided evenly among his children. Fifteen per cent to each of you, Spencer, Bob, Evelyn, and you."

"That's right."

"You and Evelyn in turn have given your husbands five per cent of your holdings so Thornton and I could become members of the board."

"I still don't see. . . ." Her voice trailed off as she thought it over. "Wait a minute. I think I do see. Victoria's forty per cent and my ten per cent and your five per cent, Mark, would make fifty-five per cent of the stock. So Victoria is planning to have us vote with her to amend the bylaws and give you power to hire Steve Emrich."

"You're oversimplifying it, Nina. What she's doing is giving Bradford Tool a chance to survive."

"I'd never do it, Mark. I'd never vote with Victoria against Spencer."

"What you really mean is that you'd never vote with your husband against Spencer."

"I didn't say that."

"You don't have to say it." Another pause. "It's what you really mean. You don't trust me, Nina. You just don't have enough faith in my judgment. You have more faith in your brother than in your husband."

"Now you're the one who's oversimplifying. It's not so easy to analyze as that, Mark. This is more than just you and me. This is a family that's involved, and more than that, it's a way of life. A philosophy, and almost a creed. It's what my forebears believed in, what they fought to establish. I can't be a party to throwing it over, certainly not without adequate reasons. This town was built by them. Bradford Tool was built by them. They ran it a certain way. That way has become a tradition and neither you nor I have the right to smash it."

"Not even for a principle?"

"I don't see where principle has anything at all to do with it."

"I was afraid you'd say that, Nina. I held my breath, almost praying you wouldn't say it because principle has everything to do with it. Nobody has a right to establish a dynasty, to build a town and give a family's name to it, to set up a tradition that becomes a creed. I don't believe for a moment old Jared Bradford intended that. I think selfishness and entrenchment and vested interests and greed have fostered those notions. Well, those notions are against principle, against everything I believe, and I don't think I want to live with anyone who subscribes to them."

"What do you mean, Mark?"

"Just that. I'm not your husband any more, Nina. You're not my wife. The way I see it, marriage is a union of hearts and minds and principles. We're losing it, Nina. It's slipping away."

"Are you trying to tell me you don't want to live here any more?"

"Do you really think I should live here?"

"Mark, you can't be serious. You can't mean you want to move out."

"I don't want to, but what choice have I got? What respect will anyone have for me, in the plant or out of it, in your precious family or out of it, when it gets around this town that you wouldn't stand by me, that you cast your vote against me?"

"So to punish me you plan to let it get around that you walked out on me."

"I plan no such thing. I don't want any fuss or talk any more than you do. I'll manage to take a trip, go away for a while, Europe, California, anywhere. You can make plans for our legal separation while I'm gone."

"Oh, Mark, do you think that would fool anyone? Don't you know this town? Don't you know the way things get around? The night after you walked out on me and drove over to that woman's place, someone called me up and told me that you'd had lunch with her that very day." She waited for him to answer. When he didn't, she rushed on. "I think perhaps when we come right down to it, she's the one who's really to blame for this, Mark. She's too convenient. She has too much of a hold on you. You can't seem to tear yourself loose from her. You never really have. You blame me for being bound by family tradition, what about the way you are bound to her?"

"Leave her out of this, Nina. It's no use, it won't do you any good to try to blame your own failure on another woman."

"So I've failed."

"We both have. We might as well face it."

Mark moved toward the door that led to the big bedroom.

"Mark, you can't walk out. You can't do it. We've both got more to think about than ourselves. What about Ginger? You brought her back here."

"I brought her back! She brought herself back."

"No, not really. It's because she's like you, your very own child, stubborn, self-willed. That was half of it. The other half was that you never really backed me up in my struggle to keep her at Susan Thompson's. You wanted her home. Yes, you did. You know you did. Well, now she's here. She's high-strung and impressionable and unsettled. If you leave us now, it will be harder on Ginger than it will on me."

"I believe that, Nina. I believe what you say. You're a Bradford. My going wouldn't shake you to your roots the way it would common stock like Ginger and me. I'm glad to hear you admit it. That's an admission I needed to convince me I don't belong here. But since you use Ginger to make me stay, I'll wait. For Ginger's sake I'll wait and see where I belong."

Chapter 12

So Mark stayed in the house on Turkey Hill. He remained voluntarily and it was for the same reason that Nina wanted him to stay: because he wished, if it were at all possible, to save their marriage. Not, as he had said in anger, because of Ginger.

In the white heat of their argument over the Steve Emrich affair, it had seemed inevitable that he do something drastic and positive. But as he thought it over, and especially as he talked it over with Jason, he changed his mind. You could not build a marriage in a day or two, Jason told him, and neither could you break it off abruptly.

"Stick with it, Mark," Jason persuaded him. "Ride out the storm. Perhaps you and Nina have been through the worst of this business by now."

Mark hoped Jason was right.

In the final analysis, there were more things to bind Mark to Nina than to wrench him away. There were years of closeness, of passionate devotion, and with the Christmas season just at hand, these old associations were touched by the nostalgia of tradition. So, for the time at least, they forgot their differences and joined in the spirit of the season. Nina appeared so grateful that he was letting bygones be bygones that Mark felt a twinge of guilt when he thought how perilously close he had come to shattering her happiness.

Because she did, during the days that followed the bitter argument between them, give the impression of happiness.

How deep it went, Mark was never sure. All he knew was that her smile was quick again, her laugh ready to fill their house with its sound, and that her activity was endless.

The quarrel they had had, full of recriminations and sharp words, seemed to have the same effect as a violent thunderstorm on a humid summer day. The air was clear again. They had both spoken their minds. It had been sheer relief to thrash out at each other and get some of the unbearable tension out of their systems.

Nothing had really changed, and it was the awareness of this that troubled Mark most, for he knew that you could not heal unless you probed to the bottom of the disease and routed out the troublesome cause. Victoria did not demand her meeting of stockholders, holding off at Mark's advice.

He went to see her the very evening he had his decisive talk with Jason, driving out to Victoria's house with Jason's gentle arguments for love and reconciliation ringing in his ears. Mark found Victoria in her studio, clad in a smock, a turban wrapped around her hair, paint brushes in both hands. She talked with him as she dabbed at a canvas that looked to Mark like the meaningless splashes a child might make if you gave him some paper and water colors.

"You don't like it, darling," she said. "I know. But that's because you don't understand it."

"I like your poetry," Mark retaliated. "I understand that."

"My poetry comes from my soul, so it has crystal clarity," Victoria answered. "This comes from my clamoring subconscious, my inner passions and desires and fears and hopes. No one quite understands those, I suppose. Not even I. The human mind is always dark and obscure, even to itself."

146

Then, "You didn't come to philosophize, Mark. You came to talk business. Your face has the grim determination of a man who intends to state his case."

"Victoria, you have a genius for reading people."

"Oh, no, darling. It's just one of the compensations for having lived a very long time. Go ahead, tell me."

So he told her, breaking it down as simply as he could because Victoria had a certain impatience with business details. He had not been able to persuade Nina. He told Victoria something of the quarrel, although he left out much of the bitterness and his threat to leave the house. He did not want to force Nina to side with Victoria and him against her will, he explained. Everyone was entitled to freedom of choice. If Nina preferred to cast her vote on Spencer's side, even though he could not agree with her position, he felt he must let her alone. Perhaps if he and Victoria waited for a more opportune time. . . .

Victoria was outspoken. "That's the argument of a time-server, Mark. It doesn't become you. Neither does this role of appeaser. I have always admired you most for your masculinity, your aggressive, and perhaps at times overbearing, masculinity. I cannot visualize you making concessions to your wife and then excusing her for having won the victory over you. I expected you to support me, Prince Charming."

"It's that I want to do the right thing, Victoria. For everyone. And I'm not sure just what that is yet. The right way isn't always the simple, easy way."

She dropped her brushes and searched his face, his eyes, his mouth, penetrating to his very soul, with that uninhibited stare of the painter and the poet. He knew that she was seeing things he had not told her, perhaps even some things he was not aware of himself.

"You haven't told me the whole story, Mark. I think things are not going well with you and Nina."

"It isn't so bad now. We've patched it up. I don't beat her up any more and she doesn't throw things at me." He smiled, pointing up his somewhat heavy-handed humor.

"If you want to treat it lightly, it's all right with me, Mark," Victoria said. "But if, on the other hand, you ever want to talk about it, I'm here to listen. I'll try not to be too hard on Nina but you must know I'm all on your side."

"That's bad," he said. "There are always two sides, and a viewpoint that takes in only one of them can do a lot of mischief." He was thinking of Jason's fair and just view of his problem, for Jason was almost judgelike in his attitude, refusing to take sides, insisting that Nina's viewpoint be considered as well as Mark's.

"I can see you don't want my sympathy."

"I want your friendship, Victoria. I need it more than I ever have. You're good for me. It's not easy for anyone who has married into the Bradford family to salvage his own ego."

"I know," she said. "I know exactly what you mean. Well, I am your friend. I'm fonder of you than of any of my relatives. I like you better than almost anyone I've ever known. That's why I don't like to see you crawling away into a corner like this, licked. It's not you, Mark Galloway. You were meant for big things, bold big acts."

When she used his full name and told him that he was made for big, bold acts, she reminded him of Claire Elliott. These two, Victoria and Claire, had seen him through glasses of their own coloring, in a way that no one else in life had looked upon him.

Victoria walked out upon the stone terrace of her studio, a bizarre figure in her Parisian smock and Oriental turban, a mink coat thrown over her shoulders.

"I'm not licked, Victoria," Mark said. "Not yet."

"It's going to snow," she said, ignoring him. "In nothing am I so Yankee as in my ability to forecast weather." She smiled at him, her strong teeth gleaming in the terrace lights.

148

"So Steve Emrich will not be our new chief engineer, Mark."
Mark shook his head. "What will you do? This pipsqueak of a
Bradford they're determined to hire—what's his name, Frank
Bradford Muthersbaugh—how are you going to manage with
him, Mark?"

"I don't know," he said. "Steve Emrich was the right man for
the job, the only man. But I can't judge Frank Muthersbaugh
until I try him out."

"What a name." Victoria shuddered. "Only Cousin Ollie
could have found a man with a name like Muthersbaugh."

"The name isn't so important," Mark said, smiling. "It's the
performance that counts."

"The performance will be even worse," she said. "Nothing
that came out of Cousin Ollie could ever be worth its salt."

Victoria was, in this case, a prophet and Mark had occasion
to recall her words many times in the weeks that followed.

One gray December morning, with the first fine flakes of
what promised to be a small blizzard slanting against the windows of his office, Mark looked up to face Frank Muthersbaugh. Spencer himself had not deigned to bring him into
Mark's office for the introduction, but had delegated the task
to Thornton, who dispatched it as if neither the man nor the
position he would fill was important enough to take too much
of his time.

Mark was one of those people who lean strongly on first im-
pressions, so, as he rose from his chair and held out his hand to
Frank Muthersbaugh, his mind, more quickly than his body,
leaped forward to meet this personality head on.

The man before him was of medium height, rather slender
in body but with a fleshy face that held no resemblance what-
soever to any of the Bradfords. Mark knew he was thirty-three
but he appeared older with already thinning hair and the
hunted expression of a rabbitlike mentality. Mark did not like
him. Meeting Mark, his boss, he seemed ingratiating and eager

149

to please, but there was a cruel quality in the lines around his mouth that troubled Mark. Frank Muthersbaugh did not have the look of a man who would get along with other men.

Ordinarily, meeting another engineer like this for the first time, a man almost his own age, Mark would have found many common interests to talk about, their schools, their chief fields of study, the societies to which they belonged. It was fortunate that Frank's vital statistics had been sent in to him yesterday because he had thus been forewarned that they had nothing in common. Muthersbaugh belonged to no engineering societies. His training for his present job had been an almost fantastic departure from the normal. His mother, essentially a Bradford, had been torn between her desire to keep her sons close to the family tradition of being horseback-riding gentlemen and money-makers first and engineers second, and her even more intense desire to have at least one of her offspring absorbed into the executive staff of Bradford Tool.

So Frank had gone to Choate where he learned whatever the curriculum required, and, flung in like a bonus, how to play an excellent game of bridge. He had long ago forgotten most of the skills taught by the curriculum but his skill in bridge had increased to a phenomenal degree so that back where he hailed from, he was known as the champion player.

After Choate, he had spent four years at Bryce Engineering Institute before the army claimed him. Mark, as he read over the interoffice memo apprising him of Frank Muthersbaugh's qualifications, had almost jumped out of his seat when he read the statistics pertaining to Bryce Institute. The school was a standing joke among the engineers at Bradford Tool. It was supposed that the Institute had, in its long career, produced a few noteworthy members of the profession, but on the whole, those who were graduated from it did not rise to any prominence as engineers. They might become good salesmen or personnel directors or publicity men, but their knowledge of engineering was fuzzy. Bryce was a school with easy entrance requirements and Mark suspected that Frank Muthersbaugh, who would apparently prefer to play bridge than do anything else, had enrolled there on that account.

The army had accepted him into their engineering corps and this was unfortunate. For it was here that Frank, as a young officer, had developed the cruel lines around his mouth and had learned that those who were under you had to obey you. It was here too that he had acquired a certain foppish dandiness in his appearance, an excessive attention to the fit of his clothes, the shine on his shoes, the belling out of a necktie.

Mark, forcing himself to relax in the presence of his unpromising new chief engineer, observed this nattiness with an inner twinge of distaste. He liked a man to look like a man, neat and presentable but without such sartorial perfection.

"I'll take you through the factory to meet some of our men," were his first words to Frank Muthersbaugh.

The other looked slightly surprised, and Mark could well understand, for he had purposely neglected to say how glad he was to welcome the newcomer, or how pleasant he hoped it would be here for him.

It won't be, Mark thought. The men aren't going to like him any more than I do.

Mark led the way from the executive offices across the catwalk and into the plant. Arthur Wimbley, the plant superintendent, was the first on Mark's list, and he found the former Englishman in his shirt sleeves poring over some final blueprints just up from the drafting room. He looked up as Mark and Frank entered, his florid face unsmiling and his mind still intent upon the drawings in front of him.

"Good morning, Mark," he said in clipped British accents. "I'm busy." He returned immediately to his absorption in the drawings. Mark smiled to himself. Arthur had been born near London. He had Cockney independence, shrewdness, inso-

151

lence, but he was a first-rate engineer and Mark liked him. The men who worked for him loved him. He had the brawn that men admire in other men. He knew how to be a boss without crushing the spirit, and he had the fire and guts that inspire respect. He was the one man in Bradford Tool who was not afraid of the Bradford family and he spoke his mind whenever he was permitted to, with no concern for hurt feelings and no fear about losing his job.

Mark turned, still smiling, to Frank Muthersbaugh, but there was no return of his smile. Frank was looking around Wimbley's office in evident distaste. It was a messy affair, with books lying in heaps on chairs and desk and floor, drawings scattered about on every conceivable object. Two trays, bearing dirty dishes on which the food had caked, looked uninvitingly up at them. A pot of coffee was boiling away on an electric burner.

Frank, in his nervousness, pulled out a silver cigarette case, offered Mark a cigarette, which he refused, and lighted up himself.

Wimbley came instantly to attention. "Put that thing out," he said. "No one smokes in here."

The abruptness of the rebuff amused Mark, but it did not amuse Frank Muthersbaugh, who scowled darkly as he stamped out his cigarette.

"This is Frank Muthersbaugh," Mark said. "Our new chief engineer."

"Muthersbaugh? I thought it was to be another Bradford."

"On his mother's side," Mark explained.

"Oh." Art Wimbley took stock of the unpromising figure before him. Then his eyes lighted up. "New chief engineer," he muttered. "Good, you're just in time. Take a look at the tolerances on these drawings. Do they look right to you?" He shoved the drawings under Frank's nose, and turned his back to pour them each a cup of coffee in some not overclean pottery mugs. Mark and Wimbley drank theirs but Frank Muthersbaugh did not touch his. His eyes were glued to the drawings in embarrassment. It was clear to everyone in the room that he had no knowledge of tolerances or how to figure them. Mark stepped into the breach for him.

"Art, we've got a lot of territory to cover. I'm showing Frank around the plant. Can't this wait until he's had more time to get acquainted?"

"Cheerio!" Art answered with a devilish wink to Mark that, fortunately, Frank Muthersbaugh did not see.

Frank fared a little better in the chief inspector's office because Pat Clarke was a genial Irishman who liked to keep things even where top management was concerned. Frank and Pat seemed to take to each other, but Mark knew that Pat was smart enough to take an accurate measure of the new chief engineer. He was merely being more politic.

They went on through the plant, meeting Sherman Parker, head of accounting, and another Bradford on his mother's side. Sherman and Frank were noncommittal about each other.

When Greek meets Greek, Mark thought to himself as he piloted Frank out to meet the foremen. The factory was at its busiest in midmorning, and these men, absorbed in their jobs, with the task of meeting production schedules on time so that no money would be lost for the Bradford family through dissatisfied customers, had little time for ceremoniously greeting the new chief engineer.

They reacted in their individual ways; Tom Winters, head of the forging department, choosing this, as he did every opportunity, to complain about being shorthanded, and Mike Conn, foreman of the casting division, booming at the top of his voice that everything was fine, everything was in the pink, no problems, no worries, they'd meet the production schedule on the nose; and Sam Sutherland, head of the general machine shop, a somber little man of few words but enormous knowhow, standing there and nodding at them without saying a word, a little frightening in his glum taciturnity which was misunderstood by those who did not know him.

In the assembly department, however, they were eagerly pounced upon by Bill Seifert, who wanted to show them everything. Bill was always grateful to have an audience. It required all Mark's skill to break away in the middle of Bill's lecture on how a precision lathe was put together, with a promise to bring Frank back to hear the rest of the story.

In the final testing department, Allan Beers was buried among the machines and merely waved at them. There was so much noise that Mark shrugged, giving up any attempt to make an introduction.

"You can meet him some other time," Mark said as they closed the doors behind them. "We'll just look in on the research lab and then take you over to your own department, Designing and Drafting."

Steve Emrich was alone in the research lab, his two co-workers having gone out together for a coffee break. Mark was eager to make the introduction and get on out of the lab. It seemed almost like rubbing it in to bring Frank here to meet Steve. But Steve took it in his stride. If he felt any emotional reaction to the meeting, he did not show it. He was friendly, and for the first time that morning, someone sincerely tried to make Frank at home. Steve talked with him about his army experiences. They had served in the same corps although at opposite sides of the globe, and Steve compared notes with Frank.

"He's a nice fellow," Frank said as they left the lab.

"One of the world's finest," Mark answered, not without a rush of emotion. Then, because he could not control his feelings, he added, "He was a candidate for the chief engineer job."

Frank was interested. "Is that so? I thought the Bradfords rarely took men from the plant. . . ." He broke off, letting the sentence trail amid the distant noises from the factory.

"They don't," Mark said. "That's why he didn't get the job."

They were heading toward the elevator, on their way up to the top floor where the cafeteria was. Frank paused as they passed the simple exhibit in the foyer, the early lathe that had brought Jared Bradford fame and fortune.

Frank, in silence, looked down at it, reading the inscription on the card.

Then, in a quiet voice, he surprised Mark by saying, "You didn't want me to have this job, did you?"

Mark was standing next to him, staring down at the exhibit which he had passed so many hundreds of times. There wasn't any use in beating around the bush. Frank Muthersbaugh would find out sooner or later.

"Steve Emrich is not only a personal friend of mine," he said. "He's an engineer of the highest rank with a designing skill that amounts to genius."

"And you don't think I'm very capable."

"How can I answer that?" Mark asked. "I've never met you before this morning."

"You think I'm unqualified and a little stupid." He suddenly faced Mark and the flabby face was twisted in a vicious grin.

"You'll find out you're wrong," he said. "I may not be as qualified as your friend in the research lab, but I'm not stupid. Not even a little bit stupid. You'll find out."

Mark looked at him a moment, feeling the antagonism behind the words.

So this is going to be even harder than I expected, Mark thought. I've not only got incompetence to deal with, I've got malice.

"Come on, Frank," he said evenly. "This is a waste of time. Let's both go up and get a cup of coffee."

Chapter 13

MARK LIKED THE HOUSE ON TURKEY HILL DURING THE CHRIST-mas season. He had always liked Christmas, even when, as a boy, there was precious little to celebrate the holiday with. Now, as he came into the house in the early evening, the very spirit of the season seemed to reach out to embrace him.

The place was full of good smells. Effie baked endlessly, from morning to night, making elaborate cookies and candies when she was not baking pies and cakes and preparing meals. The sweet, spicy smell of Christmas lay over everything, mingling with the pine of the Christmas tree and the branches tied over the mantel and spreading out in vases and baskets.

And there was such joy in the air. Nina, in self-protection, had given Ginger a playroom in the basement where she might entertain her school friends, but they did not stay there, and Mark found himself stumbling in the kitchen and the halls over gangling boys and giggling girls, and he rather liked this. He could even stand the wail of saxophones and the beat of drums and the oom-chucking of the piano.

Jill came home early in the week. Then she filled the house with her friends, and of course you could no more confine them to the nursery upstairs than you could Ginger's to the basement playroom.

So they were all over the place, eating endlessly, singing, playing the piano, watching television, leaving toys and books and band instruments and miscellaneous articles of clothing behind them and never, never returning to claim anything they had lost.

Mark himself established a "lost and found" department in his downstairs office, and he collected, among other things, four single earrings which had separated from their mates, a rhinestone bracelet, a pack of chewing gum, two dolls, a whistle, a cowboy hat, a neckerchief, one red mitten, one navy-blue mitten, one Kelly-green mitten, a black half mask, two geometry books, a history book, and two copies of *Hamlet*, dog-eared, their bindings torn loose and their pages scrawled with notes on the Bard's more cryptic passages interspersed with such observations as: *What is this thing called love? Ask R. M. and S. W.*

Mark found himself coming home earlier nights, reluctant to miss that exciting moment when Nina gave the signal that the house should be cleared of guests preparatory to the evening meal.

Mark soon discovered that Nina must give three signals, the first at least three quarters of an hour before she expected the slightest response. Nobody took her first announcement seriously. About a half hour later, she would give a firmer warning and there would be some show on the part of Ginger's guests that they intended to leave. Then in fifteen minutes, Mark, if he were there, was called upon to take a hand in the business.

His voice was always heeded, but there were numerous delays, even so. Saxy had lost the mouthpiece to one of his saxophones and Sally had mislaid one of her shoes while she had danced in her stocking feet, or Stretch couldn't find his music sheets and he needed them for the band he was playing with that night.

The kids liked Mark. They treated Nina with the respect due the matron of the Bradford home, but it was Mark they crowded around, urging him to "have a coke" with them or tell about his war experiences. When it was discovered that he could play the piano, with a special flare for jazz in the classic manner, his stock zoomed to the sky and after that they never let him alone. The minute he walked into the house, they seemed to sense it and Saxy or Sally or a tiny brunette named Midge or a willowy blonde named Eileen would fly up the stairs and drag him down to the playroom.

"Play 'St. Louis Blues,' " they would scream at him. "Play it hot, the way you did last night."

It was Mark whom they thanked as they trailed out of the house, in twos and threes, calling back, "Thanks a lot, Mr. Galloway. See you tomorrow, Ginger. Gee, Mr. Galloway, wish I could play jazz like that."

Whether Nina did more than tolerate the shenanigans, Mark never found out. Tolerate it she did, and with style and good humor, for it was she who saw that the playroom was kept well stocked with soda and Effie's cookies, and she never failed to ask the crowd to come back soon. Ginger's friends were neither criticized nor was their natural enthusiasm curbed. They were always made to feel welcome. Mark thought he knew why.

The house had the feeling of a happy, if somewhat noisy, family these days. Mark was at ease in it and Nina was unwilling to do anything that would change that pattern.

So Mark settled down to being a family man once again. It was almost like the old days, when they had had both the girls home. It was like the days when Nina and he had been intensely in love with each other, long before the Bradford feud had cast its shadow over their happiness.

As Christmas drew nearer, the activity intensified. Ginger posted a program of events on the bulletin board in the playroom and Mark, calling it to Nina's attention, commented that it looked like the schedule for a businessmen's convention.

Among other things, Ginger would participate in three informal dances, one formal dance, a coke party, a church party, two afternoons of skiing, two afternoons of play rehearsals, two afternoons of ice skating.

"When is she going to sleep and eat?" Mark asked Nina.

"When you're that age, you eat all the time, mostly on the run, and you think that sleep is a troublesome chore inflicted upon those past twenty-five."

"Past twenty-five being elderly," Mark said, smiling.

"Past twenty-five being ancient," Nina corrected.

They were down in the playroom, looking the place over to consider possibilities for enlarging and improving it. Mark thought red leather booths would be nice.

"This is the sort of place I would have given my right arm for when I was a kid," he said. "You know, I like all this, Nina. A home needs this sort of thing. I think it wasn't such a bad idea having Ginger come back."

Nina didn't answer. She held out swatches of linoleum and asked him to tell her which he thought would go with red leather cushioned booths.

Mark did his Christmas shopping for the family, alone, on Christmas Eve. It was a custom he had established during those first busy years after the war and he had kept it up because he enjoyed it. The plant closed at noon and he drove over to Brampton where the stores were larger and more numerous. He liked being caught up in the crowd of last-minute shoppers. Because he did this so seldom, the Christmas carols seemed new and fresh to his ears. They reminded him of the years when he was a boy. He remembered singing "First Noel" and "Silent Night" and "Hark, the Herald Angels Sing!" in school. So his mind went back over the years, to that last assembly before Christmas vacation. He remembered himself, restless and eager, sitting on the edge of his seat and waiting for the assembly to be over because then his class would have ice cream and cake and soda and a grab bag.

Those were the days. Those were the golden days.

It was almost like that this year, with Ginger home. Ginger got a big bang out of everything. She was dynamite around the house, but she was life and originality too. He was glad she was home.

He walked through Redfern's, the store he had chosen as his base of operations, checking off his list as he bought the presents he had settled upon in advance. As usual, he found that he had to adjust his requirements to meet the depleted stock. The negligee for Nina which was to have been peacock blue became powder blue in actuality, and Jill's riding jacket which he had thought must be bright red was instead bright green and Ginger's new skis which were to be handmade Norwegian ones had to be special-ordered and he was given a beautiful gold-embossed gift card to present to Ginger on Christmas Day. This seemed not quite right, since he had something concrete for Nina and Jill, so he bought Ginger some new ski poles and a pair of sun goggles and some wax and had these done up in an impressive gift box to make things look better.

He was very careful at each counter where he purchased to have it understood that the merchandise could be returned if it didn't suit. The salesgirls were helpful. They smiled at him, if a bit wanly, and he found himself waiting for their final words, "Merry Christmas to you, sir," and he shouted it back at them, in his hearty manner, "The same to you," and walked off, his arms becoming increasingly full, but very pleased with his world and himself.

As he walked through the stores, people smiled at him, sometimes total strangers nodded and called out, "Merry Christmas," and this pleased him because it gave him the opportunity to send the wish back to them. At the sandwich bar where he settled down for a tardy lunch of beefburger and coffee and apple pie, the waitress was solicitous and asked if he wanted his pie with cheese or à la mode. Here again, the other patrons of the snack bar looked over at him with smiles on their faces.

He was not a self-conscious man, and it would have surprised him to know what most of those who were drawn to him saw in this big man, handsome in an off-beat fashion, with unruly hair and a beaming expression that seemed to include everyone. Most of the onlookers thought they saw a well-settled man, content within himself.

"There's a guy with no problems," one middle-aged man muttered to his wife as they passed him by. "Look at him. Well-dressed, plenty of dough, happy as a lark. You don't see too many of them around nowadays."

Mark, of course, did not overhear the remark, but if he had, it would have startled him. No problems, he would have thought. Me! I'm the original problem guy. Look, I've got this new chief engineer at my plant, I can only guess how bad a time this Frank Muthersbaugh is really going to give me. He's been there less than two weeks and every man in his department hates his guts. A perfectionist, that's what I'm stuck with this time. A puny little guy that knows how to do one thing well, make beautiful drawings with nice closed arrows and neat printing. A perfectionist who doesn't know much more about engineering than the waitress over there who's pouring my second cup of coffee.

And when you want to hear about problems, now just consider what's going on between Nina and me. Sure, it looks patched up temporarily, but that's just what it is, a patch-up job. I'm scared even to think about it because I know that all the old trouble is still simmering beneath the surface and it can break out any minute again.

Then there's the Ginger issue. Nina feels someone cheated her on that one. She feels I ganged up with Ginger against her and perhaps she even blames Claire Elliott a little.

And as for Claire Elliott.

I don't even dare think about her.

This is something I can't understand. Yes, that's right, I don't even understand myself, how I feel about her. It's a strange thing, for years I never thought about her, never cared if I ever saw her again. Now she's back and ever since that crazy night I drove out to her place, I can't seem to forget her. It's because she's so solid. That's what it is. Look at the decent way she handled everything that night Ginger ran away from Susan Thompson's School. A very cool head, Claire Elliott. Plenty of moral courage. Not even afraid to have Nina come out and get Ginger. Someone else would have sent Ginger home in a taxi, or made me promise to come alone, or treated Nina differently once she got there. Not Claire. She just seems to understand. She seems to understand everyone and everything. Never afraid. Or if she is she doesn't show it. You've got to admire her.

Mark finished his pie, thinking about Claire. He had not seen her since the night Ginger returned. He had kept himself away from the little house because he was afraid of his feelings for Claire. He was too upset in his marriage relationship to tempt himself right now with Claire Elliott. He was smart enough to know a danger flag when he saw one.

He had called her up once, just to thank her for being so decent about Ginger—he knew Nina would never do that— and he had thought about sending her a box of roses, but then he had abandoned that idea as impractical. If he did that, he might be feeding the gossip that had already been passed around. Even if he didn't have himself and his marriage to think about, he owed it to Claire to go easy. She would be the last person in the world he would want to hurt.

Mark picked up his check and, gathering together his pile of boxes, made his way through the crowd toward the cashier's cage. He pulled a bill from his pants' pocket and slapped it down, then jammed his uncounted change into the pocket of his overcoat along with his driving gloves and cashmere scarf.

He wrestled his way past Gift Wrappings and All-Occasion Cards, past Fine Leather and Costume Jewelry. The parking place in which he had left his car was just beyond the side door that led into Fairmont Street and he pushed in that general direction. Then, as he headed for the revolving door, he was stopped by the sweet fragrance of jasmine and roses. He turned, wondering where it came from, and spotted one of those revolving fountains of cologne, used for display and promotional purposes. A spray of fragrance shot into the air, falling gracefully down on a pond of artificial roses and jasmine flowers.

A salesgirl caught his eye and said, "Doesn't that smell good?"

Caught, he came back to the perfume counter with its monuments of packages, some black and gold, some brilliant turquoise or fuchsia, some chaste white.

"What is it?" he asked.

"Parisian Nights." The girl hopefully held out a large decanter filled with amber liquid.

"I was thinking of something for my wife," he said. "Christmas doesn't seem like Christmas without perfume."

"That's so true," the girl agreed.

"But Parisian Nights." He smiled, shaking his head. "She'd think anything with a name like that was, well, vulgar, I guess." Then, he added quickly, "She's terribly chic but the conservative type."

"I know." The girl nodded. "I think I know what she'd like. Something like Intermezzo."

Mark shook his head again. "That sounds even worse." Then, "Maybe I'd better pick one for its smell instead of its name."

The girl was most co-operative. She sprayed the air with several fragrances, calling off their names. She pulled out crystal bottles and took out their stoppers and waved them through the air under Mark's nose. He became more confused at each whiff.

"This," he commented to the girl, "is harder than trying to decide how to invest a hundred thousand dollars." The girl laughed, obviously delighted with her democratic male customer.

"If you knew the kind of perfume she likes," she said experimentally. "I mean, does she like heavy perfumes or florals or spicy scents or orientals."

"Wait a minute," Mark answered. "I've got it. She uses something called White Orchid. I've seen it on her dressing table." He sawed the air in what he considered an approximate description of the bottle. "It's an unusual-shaped bottle. Like a pyramid."

"I know," the girl said. "It's a French perfume. We get only a few bottles a year, but I think we may have one left. I'll see."

She called some mysterious person from the next counter who used the telephone to contact an equally mysterious person "upstairs" and after some conversation, Mark was told that if he could wait ten minutes or so, a bottle was available and would be sent down.

"Perhaps you have some other shopping to do," the girl said as a helpful suggestion.

"No," Mark told her. "This is the last stop for me. If you don't mind, I'll just park here and wait." The girl didn't mind and she took some of his packages and put them behind the counter so they wouldn't "get stepped on."

"I don't suppose there was anything else you wanted here," she said. "Some perfume for another member of your family."

Mark said no, his daughters were too young for that sort of thing. Then, suddenly, the idea struck him. There was Claire. He hadn't sent her that box of roses for being so nice about Ginger, but this was Christmas and it was the time of year you

164

said "thank you" to lots of people you couldn't thank in any concrete way at other times.

He wondered if he should get her something. No, perhaps that would be laying it on too thick. She might consider it bad taste. She might even resent it, perfume from a married man. Well, there wasn't anything so wrong with that. He gave his secretaries and stenographers gifts at Christmas and this year Nina, who always selected the presents, had picked out compacts and perfume.

Don't kid yourself, he argued back. Nina isn't going to know a thing about this. This is a horse of an entirely different color.

He wheeled around toward the salesgirl, who was putting back the row of testers she had brought out for Mark's benefit.

"That stuff in the black bottle," he said, "I liked that. Could I smell it again?" The girl waved the black stopper under his nose.

"Isn't it lovely?" she said. "It's French, too."

"I like it, but if it's got one of those fantastic names like Night of Love, nothing doing."

"No, this one is called Touché. It's a fencing term, I believe," the girl added helpfully. "And we do have a bottle of it here."

"Touché." Mark smiled to himself, turning away from the salesgirl. That wasn't too bad. It had humor, and Claire would appreciate it. The very name of the perfume might give his gift a lightness, pointing up that it was not to be taken too seriously.

"I'll take it," Mark said. Then, as an afterthought, "You think it would be suitable for, well, for an attractive woman in her thirties? A dynamic sort of person?"

"Oh, quite," the girl said. "Very suitable, sir. Touché is a provocative perfume."

He flushed. It seemed too intimate to be talking like this about Claire with a girl he had never seen before.

"I'd like to have the bottle of Touché sent out to someone. I suppose it won't get there until after Christmas." He was all business now, trying rather belatedly to establish a formal relationship with the salesgirl.

"Unless you want to pay for a special delivery messenger," the girl said. "The store has that service if the gift isn't going too far."

"To Bradford," he told her.

"We could arrange that," she said. "Do you want to enclose a card?" She reached behind the counter for a white card and a pen.

Panic seized Mark. No, he couldn't do this. It was out of the question that he should send a gift by special messenger to Claire, especially since he would have to enclose a card. That was one he had overlooked, and he couldn't send an anonymous bottle of very expensive French perfume. Claire would be out of her mind trying to figure out who had done such a thing.

He couldn't send this gift to Claire at all. All sorts of imaginative fears crept into his thinking. Someone would be sure to find out, trace the business to him, relay it to Nina. A number of people in Bradford worked in these Brampton stores. Men in his plant had wives and daughters who came over every day to work as saleswomen. Maybe this girl who was waiting on him was one of them. Maybe she had even recognized him. He was known to a lot of people whom he couldn't call by name. He was general manager of Bradford Tool. He was one of the Bradfords, or so people thought of him, even though he was related only by marriage.

He stared into the girl's face, searching for some sign of recognition, some family resemblance to one of his men. His eyes must have held the confusion and uncertainty he felt because the girl, who misunderstood it, said, "Take your time, sir. There's no hurry about the card. You can give it to me when the White Orchid comes down and we'll gift wrap both packages at once."

He shoved the card and pen toward her, moistening his lips.

"I'm not going to send this one," he said. "I've changed my mind. I'll take them both with me."

The girl seemed unaware of the inner turmoil Mark was experiencing. "Fine," she said. "Anything you say."

He watched her wrap the packages and was very solicitous that she keep them separate and marked in some way so he would not mix them up.

"Only don't write anything on them," he added hastily. "Put different bows on them and tell me which is which and I'll remember."

He listened when she placed one in his left hand and the other in his right. "This," she said, pointing to the one with the scarlet bow, "is Touché. The other with the white bow is White Orchid."

He slipped the one with the scarlet bow into the left pocket of his overcoat. It bumped against him as he buttoned his coat. Then he gathered up his bundles and placed Nina's perfume on top of the pile, holding them in front of him and turning at last toward the revolving doors.

"Merry Christmas," he called back to the salesgirl. "Thanks for all the help."

"It was a pleasure." She smiled after him. "Merry Christmas, sir. I think she'll like the Touché. It's a very alluring perfume."

He hurried toward the door, feeling a warm flush steal up from his neck again, glad to be away from the counter and the salesgirl. *Provocative. A very alluring perfume.* He wondered if the girl was making fun of him, if she was laughing inwardly all the time and would perhaps share the story about him later with some of her friends.

"He was such a big man and so sort of helpless. You just felt you had to take care of him. And he was so afraid of the names of perfumes. He wanted something conservative. For his wife. And then he bought Touché for his girl friend. Of course it was his girl friend, silly. He said she was attractive and the dynamic type. And first he wanted to send it and then I suppose he thought he'd better not take the chance so he took it with him. I put a red bow on it. A bright scarlet bow. And as he was leaving I called Merry Christmas to him and said I knew she'd like Touché because it was an alluring perfume. *Touché!* Get it? *Touché!* Oh well, he was a nice sort of guy, he looked rich, the loaded-with-dough type. His clothes, the way he wore them, the way he flipped a hundred-dollar bill from his pocket when I said the perfume came to seventy-three, seventy-five including tax, the way he didn't even count his change. Yeah, he was really a nice guy. I wonder who the lucky girl is. Not his wife, silly. His girl friend."

Chapter 14

CLAIRE'S HOUSE, SNUGGLED AMIDST ITS CLUSTER OF TOWERING evergreens, looked this afternoon as inviting as Claire herself. Because of its tininess, and the piles of snow still banked about it, and the oversize spray of greens she had hung against the front door, it looked very much like a cottage on a Christmas postcard.

Mark had almost made up his mind to drop the package in her rural delivery mailbox, with his card, and then beat it for home, but when he saw Claire's house, he changed his mind. It would not hurt to go to the door and hand her the package.

Her car stood in the driveway. As he pulled in beside it, he wondered what he would say if there was someone with her. It wasn't likely. Claire had made it pretty plain to him that her work was so strenuous this year, getting into the swing of her supervisor's job and making plans for the enlargement of her summer workshop, that she was grateful to have this place in the country to sneak away to. It was her sanctuary, the very seclusion she most needed. Funny thing about people, he thought, those who were surrounded by people were always looking for solitude and those who were forced to lead lonely lives craved companionship. No one was ever satisfied.

He looked for a doorbell and there wasn't any. Then he discovered the knocker was hidden beneath the spray of greens, so he wrapped on the door with his knuckles and listened to the sound reverberate through the house.

Claire opened the door for him. Her face, when she saw who it was, lighted with welcome.

"Mark," she said. "How wonderful! You've come to say Merry Christmas." She took him by the hand and pulled him inside and took his hat and held out her hands for his overcoat. It was that easy. No rough spots. Here he had been wondering whether he should even see her and now he felt that it was the most natural thing in the world to be inside her house.

She hung his coat in the small hall closet and started to lead the way to the living room.

"Wait a minute," he said. "I forgot something." So he fished in his pocket and found the package with the scarlet bow before he followed her into the room.

The awkwardness he felt standing with the package in his hands made him want to get rid of it. "Claire." He paused to find the words he had been forming in his thoughts, something about "this is for being understanding when Ginger came home," but as he looked into her face and saw the expectancy there, he could not put his gift on the basis of paying off an indebtedness.

"Claire," he repeated. "Just Merry Christmas from me to you."

"Oh, Mark, this is nice. What a grand surprise! Can I open it now? You won't mind? I'm such a child about opening packages. I can't wait a minute to see what's inside."

"Sure, go ahead. But blame the salesgirl if it's not what you like."

"Of course I'll like it." She was tearing off the scarlet bow and flinging it into one of the wing chairs. The gold and white striped paper was tossed aside too, into the wood basket, and her eager hands broke the seal on the box and found still another box inside, black leather with the crest of the perfumer tooled in gold on the lid. Instantly she recognized what it was, without even lifting the lid.

"Touché!" she exclaimed. "Touché. A whole ounce of it." Then her eyes grew merry with humor and she sank laughing into the wing chair, pulling the scarlet bow from under her and clasping it in her hands with the perfume.

"I get it," she said. "*Touché!* You would, Mark." Then her mood changed and she held out the perfume in a gesture of unbelief. "I've never had an ounce of Touché in my whole life. It's a fabulous extravagance. No one has the right to spoil me like this." She jumped up and came over to him. "You're a darling to do it, though," and she reached up and kissed him quickly, but full on the mouth and her mouth was as he had remembered it, soft and warm.

"Come on," she said. "Let's have a fire in the fireplace. It's Christmas Eve and what's a house without a fire on Christmas Eve!" She made him help her build the fire, saying that it was so good to have him drop in like this, talking with animation all the time she handed him the kindling and the paper and told him which logs to use first. Then she insisted that they have tea and he said he guessed he might like that since it was cold driving around and his lunch had been a sketchy one at the snack bar of Redfern's in Brampton. She took him into her small kitchen while she made the tea and some sandwiches and got out a chocolate cake from a tin box.

"Not homemade," she said. "I'm no better cook than I ever was."

"You have other talents," he said, entering into the mood. In fact, it was impossible not to share Claire's effervescence. It was so contagious.

Claire had him pull the wing chairs close to the fire and place one of those little Victorian muffin stands between them to hold the sandwiches and cake. "These were invented by someone who believed people should sit close together," she said. "They're just small enough for a cozy tête-à-tête and at tea-time, when people feel intimate. Don't you agree, Mark?"

Mark agreed and Claire went on. "The Victorians were incurable romantics," she said, "despite their reputation for austerity. They gave us the love seat, too, and hassocks. Now what could be more sentimental than to sit on one of those"—she pointed with the toe of her high-heeled slipper to the large footstool—"and look up into your loved one's eyes?" She was laughing, with her eyes and the corners of her mouth, turning that not unfriendly mockery of hers upon the Victorians.

"You see how I surround myself with pieces from the Victorian era. I like them. You wouldn't believe it of me, I'm sure. No one would, but I too am an incurable romantic."

He said he was sure he would never have believed it and her husky laugh answered him, still mocking. There was an immanence to Claire's mockery that seemed to confine it within herself. No matter upon whom or what she turned it, it seemed so subjective that you did not take umbrage. You felt the mockery did not ever really leave her, that she was, in the final analysis, imprisoning her friendly ridicule within her own consciousness.

They talked a lot at first, because there seemed to be so much to say. It was the first time since she had been back that Claire opened up about herself, and he listened with interest, feeling relaxed, sitting before her fire with a majolica cup in his hands, drinking more tea and eating more sandwiches and cake than he wanted to.

"I feel I've found myself here at last, Mark," she said. "That must sound strange to you because I came from here and I was so crazy to get away from Bradford. But now I've come back here to find myself. It sounds unbelievable but it's true."

She leaned forward and poked the fire thoughtfully as she went on.

"When I was quite young, I used to think that my greatest talent was for acting." She turned to him. "You know that. I was so much like Ginger in my intense desire to go on the stage."

"I remember." How could I forget? he thought. The way I used to sweat it out while you played those romantic parts with other boys.

"But I've found I have a greater talent than acting." She laughed. "I have the gift of not kidding myself. It is a gift, Mark." She was serious now. "Never to kid myself about anything, no matter how big or how small. It's the self-deception that gets you down in life. More even than the disappointments and the frustrations. I found out a long time ago that I could never be a great actress, not even a really good one. But I do know something about the stage and I have a great love for it. So if I can expose a few talented youngsters to the enthusiasm I feel, I'll have my reason for being. Everyone needs a reason for being."

Mark said he agreed with her and although he didn't know much about her workshop, he was sure it was going to do a lot of good.

"Teaching, when you have the kind of floating job I have now, isn't too bad either. It has variety and change of pace. I like young people. It keeps you young if you go about it the right way and don't get bogged down in being a stern disciplinarian." She smiled at him, turning the full force of her personality upon him.

It was so blinding that he felt he ought to withdraw in self-protection from so much brightness. It could get under a man's skin, this happiness of Claire's.

He watched her and thought, You're right, Claire. It does keep you young.

For he saw again that youthful quality he had noticed the day he had lunched with her in the Greencrest restaurant. Other

173

people who were his contemporaries grew older, visibly older, all the time. But not Claire. Jason was like that too. These people with an inner something were the ones who stayed on top of things. Even the relentlessness of time could not seem to touch them.

Jason's inner something was his strong religious convictions, his spirituality, Mark supposed you would have to call it. It was not at all the same thing with Claire. This was more human, a spirit of I-don't-kid-me as Claire herself had just admitted, a total absence of self-pity over the compromise she had had to make with life, an honesty and directness you seldom found in a woman.

As she went on talking about her plans for her theater he could not take his eyes off her. She was the same girl he had fallen in love with years ago. Nothing was changed. The spirit was there, the vitality and great surging force of energy. Again he saw how much her physical characteristics had remained the same. Her figure in a Christmas-green dress, a soft clinging wool, was better if anything. The waist was still small, the hips and bosom pleasantly full. Her face still held his rapt attention as it always had, not so much because of beauty as through the vitality back of it. She wore Christmas earrings, tiny clusters of bells that tinkled as she moved her head and they were silver, as her jewelry always was, to bring out the bright silver streak through her dark red hair.

I would like to get right up out of this chair and kiss her, Mark thought, feeling guilty that he was so attracted to Claire.

You can't stifle those things, he thought. It won't do any good to feel guilty. I loved this woman once. I know what it was like to hold her in my arms and feel her mouth pressed against mine and I can't forget it. I doubt if I will ever forget it.

Then, because the question pushed itself to the front of his mind, he had to ask it.

"Claire, why haven't you ever married?"

Another woman might resent such a question, but Claire did not. She sat poking the fire, chuckling softly to herself as if she were alone.

"It would flatter you, Mark, if I said it was because of you. Because of us and the way we once loved each other. But that wouldn't be honest. The simple fact is that no one has ever asked me."

"That's incredible!" Mark exclaimed. "An attractive woman like you. A handsome woman and a brilliant one. You're making fun of me for asking the question."

She threw down the poker, and faced him. "No, it's the truth. No one has ever asked me. You see, I'm too self-sufficient. Men fall in love with me, but they marry someone else. You thought we broke off because of a lover's quarrel. We didn't. We broke off because you thought I didn't need you enough. But you're not the only man who has been in love with me. Right now, as we're talking about this, there's a man somewhere who thinks he's in love with me."

To his surprise, Mark felt a twinge of jealousy. He had fallen out of love with Claire long ago and he had loved and married Nina, but it had never occurred to him that Claire would ever belong to anyone else. It was egregious selfishness on his part, but he could not help it.

Claire intended to spare him nothing. "Maybe you'd like to hear about it," she said, pouring some more tea. She was careful not to look at Mark as she went on. "I lead so public a life in Bradford, what with my teaching and my theater workshop, that no one thinks much about my private life. But I do have one, you know. He's a man I met last summer while I was taking my two weeks' rest between the close of the summer play-house and the opening of school. In New Hampshire. I met him there. A farm boy." She glanced at Mark, smiled and looked away again. "Not the kind you're thinking of. This farmer owns a very modern farm with all the fixings. It's more like a big business, if you know what I mean."

"How old is he?" Mark resented the man, and if he could be proven too old or too young, he felt that might be a good point.

"About our age. No more, no less. He's a widower. His wife died in childbirth three years ago." Mark grunted. "He reminds me a lot of you, Mark. He's big and his hair is crazy like yours, only blond, and he has an off-beat sort of face, too. But he's not as serious as you. His face is full of humor, dry Yankee humor. I think you'd like him."

I'm sure I wouldn't, Mark thought.

"We had a lot of fun together this summer," Claire said. "He likes the things I do. We went swimming, took long hikes, some fishing and boating. He's well-read and a thinker. He talks when I feel like talking and is quiet when I feel like being quiet."

"If you're so perfectly mated," and there was testiness in Mark's voice, "why don't you marry him?"

"I told you. He hasn't asked me."

"Must be pretty hard to carry on such a long-distance romance."

"We write to each other every week," Claire explained. "We've met twice this past month at Great Barrington for a week end of skiing. He's the kind of man you can feel close to, even when you've only known him for a short time."

Now what kind of man is that, Mark wanted to say with a touch of sarcasm, but instead he said, "I suppose he's quite a skier. Coming from ski country, as he does."

"Yes, he is," Claire said matter-of-factly. "He's tops. Everything he does, he does well. I told you he's like you, Mark."

"Are you sure you're not head over heels in love with him?"

"How can we be sure—any of us—of anything in life? We can't be sure of a whole day as it lies before us. Of even the next few hours. But head over heels in love? No, I guess not. Not yet, anyway."

Mark pulled himself up from the chair, forcing lightness. "All those years ago," he said, "I would have raised rim about this. I never liked competition." Claire didn't answer. "Are you going to Great Barrington for some more skiing during the holidays?" he asked.

"No," she said, getting up and standing beside him, "I'm leaving tonight to drive up to New Hampshire."

"I see," Mark replied, "so it really is serious. Christmas on the farm, plenty of snow, good skiing up there, long nights in front of an open fire. Maybe even a moonlight sleigh ride. Watch out, Claire, that's potent stuff."

She laughed and he joined her, making light of it. It was not the way he felt about it. Now that he and Nina were so edgy about each other, he resented having Claire involved with anyone else. He knew he had no right to feel as he did. He had no hold over Claire. She was as free as the air, yet he had never let go of her. Nina had once accused Claire of never letting him, Mark, go. Now this afternoon as he thought about this man whose name Claire had not even mentioned, he realized that it was he who had never let Claire go. That was it. In a compact little dungeon of his mind, he had kept her imprisoned for future reference. He had always felt that when he wanted and needed her, she would be there waiting for him.

"What's his name, Claire?"

"David Wakefield."

"It's a strong name. You're very fond of him, aren't you?" Claire shrugged and he could see she would not discuss her David any further. He held out his hand and she took it, more the way lovers will clasp hands than in the firm grip of a handshake. "Merry Christmas, Claire. No need to wish you one, I can see you're going to have it."

"You, too, Mark," she said. "I want you to have a happy

177

Christmas this year. You deserve it." She shouldn't have said that. It implied too much. It implied that she sensed more than she was willing to admit of what he had been going through this year. It implied that she felt for him and that she understood. Mark could not stand unmoved before Claire's sympathy. His first impulse was to turn away, but she would not let him. She clung to his hand, unwilling to let him go. So, with no alternative, he faced her, looking into her radiant face and feeling incomplete, desolate of happiness himself. The kind of success he had found in life became an empty achievement, based on other people's wealth, at the whim of their directions. Nothing seemed to belong to him any more. To him, Mark Galloway. And he felt restless for what he did not have.

So he did the only thing he could have done. He pulled her toward him and wrapped his arms about her, not in the embrace of old friends, but in the warm embrace of lovers.

Claire pulled back as his lips sought hers. She fought him off but he held her. For a moment there was a tenseness between them as she pushed her hands against his shoulders, unwilling to be kissed.

"No, you mustn't kiss me like that," she was saying.

"Yes," he said. "I've got to, Claire. All afternoon I've been wanting to."

She held him off a moment longer, looking up into his face. "What's the matter with you and Nina, Mark?" she asked.

"Kiss me first," he answered. "And I'll tell you."

She capitulated then, letting him wrap her close in his arms. When he let her go, she broke away from him and walked across the room, standing before the window through which the last pale rays of winter sun sent their light. She was visibly moved. He had never seen her so upset by anything.

"That was wrong, Mark. You shouldn't have done it."

He came up behind her, standing there, looking at her heavy hair, falling in waves to her shoulders.

"I'm not sorry. I couldn't help it. I had to do it."

"We never have to do anything that isn't right. It isn't right for us to kiss each other like that. It's dangerous. Only you and I know how dangerous it is." She wheeled on him. "Tell me what's really wrong with you and Nina. It's not Ginger. It's not the Bradford Company disagreement. What is it, Mark? What would make you kiss me like that after all these years? What's wrong, Mark?"

He sank down on one of the chairs near the window. He was quiet, with his hands clasped before him.

"I don't know," he said. "Unless Nina and I are falling out of love."

Chapter 15

LIKE A COMMANDING GENERAL WAITING FOR THE STRATEGIC MO-
ment to attack, Frank Muthersbaugh chose the week after New
Year's Day to lay down the law to the draftsmen and designers
at Bradford Tool. Like a general, too, he went about it with a
ruthless disregard for everything except the ends he wished to
attain.

When Frank laid off two sixty-year-old men whom he considered too old, he did not consider the psychological effect of
his act upon the men, their families, the other men who worked
at Bradford Tool, and the town itself.

"They were dead wood," he said to Mark, who, in one of
his rare rages, stormed into Frank's office. "Dead wood saps the
life of any industry." Frank was full of aphoristic gems.

"They're men who gave thirty years of their lives to Bradford Tool," Mark reminded him.

Frank shrugged and started to walk away but Mark grabbed
him and held him fast. "Where do you think men of that age are
going to pick up jobs? When you're sixty, specialized jobs
don't grow on trees."

Frank took hold of Mark's detaining hand, and, with a gesture of distaste, removed it.

"Look, we're running a business here, not a court of human
relationships. Go tell it to the judge."

Mark was furious. That evening he went down to their homes and saw both the men. It wasn't so bad at Timmy Baxter's house. His wife was one of those women who meet the trials of life head on and she had a job of her own, selling over in Brampton.

But at Webb Merrick's house, he ran into something else. Webb's wife was a frail woman with a hacking cough and there was an invalid daughter, a girl of twenty who sat in a wheel chair. Webb was brave about the blow and his very courage set up in Mark a tremor of discomfort.

"No one will hire Webb now that your company laid him off," Mrs. Merrick said. "They'll say he's too old."

"Try not to worry, Mrs. Merrick," Mark told her. "Look, if Webb doesn't get a job, I'll find some place for him at the factory. In another department."

Mark left the Merrick house but he could not get what he had seen and heard out of his system. He felt ashamed, not only for Frank Muthersbaugh but for the whole tribe of Bradfords. He knew it wouldn't do any good to talk to Spencer or Bob. They'd back up their blood relatives every time.

The firing of Baxter and Merrick was only the beginning of Frank Muthersbaugh's campaign. In the weeks that followed, Mark often thought that Baxter and Merrick had got the best of the deal. Those who stayed on in the drafting and designing department of Bradford Tool were hastily introduced to the new chief engineer's special brand of hazing.

To understand this hazing, and the mentality that lay back of it, it was necessary to know something of Frank Muthersbaugh's background. Mark, fascinated and horrified by what was going on in the designing room of the plant, became half detective, half psychologist, in his attempt to probe the warped personality of his cousin by marriage.

Frank had been born, to begin with, into a completely loveless home. His mother, a large ugly woman with none of the

Bradford refinement but much of the Bradford strength, had found herself in her late thirties a hopeless spinster. With no special talents except for horsemanship, with no beauty and less charm, she knew at least her worth. She had money. With her inherited hardheadedness, she had no compunctions about letting Joseph Muthersbaugh marry her for her money. She would get in return a man, and a man was what she wanted.

When two sons were born to the union, Ollie Bradford Muthersbaugh interpreted the munificence of nature as a symbol of the rightness of what she had done. Now she had not only one man to dominate, but three of them.

Dominate them she did, with the extraordinary flair with which women dominate the men in their lives who are weak enough to submit to it.

It was plain to even the most thick-skinned observer that her husband and her sons were led about by their noses.

She faked illness. She became a great hulking malingerer when necessary, setting up a hospital room on the main floor of the house, in the family sitting room, where she lay back upon her pyramid of pillows and wheezed and groaned and watched her victims from half-closed eyes. There, in the center of family traffic, with a cry of agony upon her lips, she brought her boys to terms.

It was a monumental job and Ollie enjoyed every minute of it.

Frank Muthersbaugh grew to young manhood in this atmosphere of tension. He became at home a docile child devoted to his mother, with perfect family manners. Abroad, he became a bully, adept in the art of both physical and mental cruelty. As a boy, his victims were animals, girls and boys smaller than himself. As an army officer, his victims were the men under his command. As chief engineer of Bradford Tool, his victims became the men in the designing room.

Mark Galloway's investigations into the past of Frank

Muthersbaugh caused him to unearth Frank's scholastic record while at Bryce, and there he found something of the utmost interest. Frank had graduated fifty-seventh in a class of one hundred and sixty-nine. In everything except mechanical drawing, he had received a grade of C, but in that subject he had managed to get an A throughout his entire college career.

This explained many things. It indicated, for instance, why Frank was so unprepared for his job as chief engineer. He had an extremely limited knowledge of machine tools and their adaptability to the manufacture of parts for which they were designed. He had no practical knowledge of machine shop operation and, as Art Wimbley had uncovered during their first meeting, Frank had a very shaky understanding of dimensional tolerances.

There was one thing, though, in which he excelled. He could make beautiful-looking drawings and he was a stickler for the appearance of anything that came out of the drafting room.

Sometimes the best draftsmen and designers whose work, in every practical aspect, was irreproachable might slip into a relaxed attitude toward the appearance of their drawings. This did not affect the workability of their blueprints and ofttimes it speeded production.

Frank Muthersbaugh would tolerate none of this casualness. He continued to insist that all arrows be closed, whereas the men of long experience who worked under him did not bother themselves with this minute detail. Frank was fussy about printing. Although he could not himself have made a working drawing for use in the Bradford factory, he did know how to print beautifully. It was an unfortunate fact, and one that set the cruel lines around his mouth working overtime, that some of his best men were slipshod printers.

Perhaps the greatest bone of contention between Frank and his men was the matter of final tracings. Frank insisted that hereafter, so long as he was chief engineer of the plant, all final tracings be done in ink. There was something to be said for his stand because in many factories this rule obtained and was enforced. However, at Bradford Tool there had been much leniency permitted the designers and draftsmen on this point. There was such a rule, hidden in the archives of the executive offices, but for fifty years, or as long as the rule had existed, no one had even tried to enforce it.

The reason for such laxity was a practical one: for ordinary factory work where changes were frequently made, pencil drawings were more satisfactory. They were easier to handle if changes and corrections were numerous and this saved time. Ink tracings were in use only for what were called "frozen" designs, those designs which remained static over a period of time. In a progressive plant like Bradford Tool, there were not many of these.

When, one fine morning early in January, Frank Muthersbaugh showed up in his department with the dictum that hereafter he would put his official stamp of approval only on final tracings done in ink, the men howled in protest.

From their standpoint, they were justified. Some of them had never heard of the rule which Frank quoted. Those who did know of its existence had long ago forgotten about it. The important thing was that their work, already made onerous by Muthersbaugh's picayune faultfinding and meticulous attention to unimportant detail, would now become irksome beyond endurance. Even aside from the extra burden which this unnecessary fussiness would impose upon them, there was a problem of morale to be considered. The men felt hunted and oppressed. Although they knew nothing of Muthersbaugh's background, they did know enough about human nature to know they were dealing with no ordinary chief engineer. They discussed Muthersbaugh behind his back. They discussed him frequently and exhaustively, and the consensus of these discussions held during coffee breaks and lunch hours and in cars coming to and from work was that Muthersbaugh was slightly off his trolley.

Nothing dangerous, you understand, but just a little cracked.

They decided, with the healthy tolerance of the normal for the abnormal, to humor him. They decided also on a course of action among themselves. They agreed to bide their time. A long-range strategy was best. It involved no risks to themselves, and they were sure it would work.

Frank was baffled by the treatment he got from his staff. He was, as he had assured Mark on his first day here, not even a little bit stupid. He sensed that he was being treated by his men as if he were not quite right in the head.

This made him bear down harder. He was more exacting than ever, and cruel in his enforcement of the rules he arbitrarily laid down. Frank Muthersbaugh became, in fact, as the days wore on through bleak January, a man possessed.

Mark was aware of what was going on in the designing room. What he did not gather from his own observations, he culled from old McGovern in the stock room.

He visited the stock room often these days. Eleven o'clock in the morning or three thirty in the afternoon were the best times for garnering information, for those were the hours when McGovern was comparatively free. The old man took his breaks at his own time, and since he was a tea addict, he brewed his own strong beverage in a chipped green pot he had brought from home twenty-five years ago.

Mark would join him over a cup of this strong stuff, often bringing down with him a bag of Effie's doughnuts of which McGovern was fond, and McGovern would spit out his gum, pour the black tea from the green pot, shovel three heaping teaspoons of sugar into his cup, and then settle back with Mark for a talk.

He had one absorbing topic of conversation these days. Frank Muthersbaugh.

"The things I hear I wouldn't believe," he said, "if I didn't know the sources to be strictly reliable. Almost fifty years I've been here, Mr. Galloway, and I've seen all kinds come and go. I've seen love affairs begin, and marriages almost break up, and babies born and men that were young grow old and some of them die. I'll never forget the night Herb Cox came in here to say good night to me just before he left. 'Mac,' he says, 'I'll see you tomorrow morning and we'll talk about baseball.' Only I didn't see him the next morning because he never came back. He was dead. And there I had all the baseball scores waiting to discuss with him."

McGovern drank his cup of tea and poured another before he went on. "Like I say, I've seen all kinds of things happen in this place. But to tell you the truth, Mr. Galloway, I never seen nothing like this Frank Muthersbaugh." Mark nodded.

"You heard about the drawing lesson, didn't you?" Mc-Govern asked. "Or maybe you didn't."

Mark acknowledged he had not heard about that one. So McGovern helped himself to another doughnut and settled back to tell him.

"It happened just last Monday. The men in the designing room came in like any other Monday. A little tired from the week end. You know how it is. Too much celebrating. Parties and families and such stuff. Well, what do they see when they get there but a row of chairs all lined up like a Sunday-school class and one of them portable blackboards at the front of the room. Then Muthersbaugh comes in, very businesslike, the way he is." McGovern paused to give an imitation of Frank rubbing his hands together and leering around.

Then, in a fairly good imitation of Frank's steel-edged voice, McGovern continued, " 'Men,' he says, 'this morning we are all going to learn how to print.' Print! Ain't that a laugh. Print!" McGovern paused to laugh derisively. "He's going to teach those hardened old guys under him, men who forgot long ago what he ain't ever going to learn, he's going to teach them to *print!* Another cup of tea, Mr. Galloway?"

Mark shoved his cup over and watched McGovern pour the dark brew into it. After McGovern had poured a third cup for himself and flavored it to taste with sugar and, this time, evaporated milk, he tasted it from the spoon several times, smacked his lips and continued his story.

"Well, it must have been quite a lark, the way I heard it, Mr. Galloway. That Muthersbaugh, he drew letters on the board. The alphabet from A to Z, and he made the men, one at a time, come up and do the same thing. When they didn't do it right, he made them erase it and do it again, and all the time, he stands there with that look on his face, grinning like His Satanic Majesty himself, having the laugh on them. The whole morning they wrote the alphabet on the blackboard while Art Wimbley is screaming bloody murder for blueprints and the machine shop is yapping at his heels and the whole factory is standing still waiting for the designers and the draftsmen to finish having their lesson."

McGovern stopped, letting his head drop forward over his chest, in an attitude of philosophic thoughtfulness. Mark did not violate his meditation. Finally the old man grinned up at him.

"You think this guy is a little off, maybe?"

Mark smiled, but did not answer.

"That's what they're saying around the shop, they're saying he's touched. They got a big word for it, but it means the same thing. Jim Tilly was in here from the tool crib a short time ago. You know, Jim is big Tom Tilly's boy. Jim's a fine smart lad, filling in here for a year or so to make enough money to get a Master's degree in Engineering. He's had a lot of schooling, Jim Tilly has. Well, he told me a name for what this Muthersbaugh is doing. He says its psychotic cruelty. Says something is all

187

twisted up inside of Muthersbaugh and he takes it out on the men who work under him."

"Well, Mac," Mark said, glancing at the clock on the wall. "I've got to shove along now. Thanks for the tea and the chit-chat."

"You ain't offended at what I just said?" McGovern looked up at him from under gray bushy brows anxiously.

"You know better than to ask that."

McGovern flashed his almost toothless smile. "That's what I thought," he said. "You being a personal friend of Steve Emrich who got gypped out of the job. But I just wanted to make sure, Mr. Galloway. See you again."

McGovern did see Mark again. He saw him many times in the days that followed because McGovern was his chief source of information. You might say, his only source. The men might gossip among themselves, but Mark, being an executive, was shut out from their confidences. They might hate Muthers-baugh's guts, they might deride and ridicule him behind his back and pull him to pieces among themselves, but they would never go over his head.

Chapter 16

As the days marched on toward midwinter, Mark was filled with a strange, unprecedented restlessness.

Nothing seemed to satisfy any more.

The gaiety that had prevailed in the house on Turkey Hill during the holidays had lapsed into an unbearable quietness. Jill was back at Briarwood. Ginger was immersed in two engrossing occupations: preparation for midyear examinations at high school and rehearsals for the play in which she was to take part. Most of her afternoons and some of her evenings were spent at rehearsals. Whatever time was left had to be given to her studies.

Once in a while she would take time off to go to a basketball game and then she might stop by in the basement playroom with a handful of cronies. But it was not like before. Mark missed the excitement.

Ginger was moody these days. He supposed that part of this was due to adolescence. She seemed to have things on her mind which she did not share with Nina and him. Mark had thought that once they had her home, she might be caught up in the family life and lose some of her perverseness. It was clear now that merely being home was not enough for Ginger. Mark sensed that a surging force of growing pains, of confusion and questioning, was imprisoned within this elder daughter of his. She was a strange girl. Completely self-absorbed, she made no confidences to them.

In other ways she was as normal as the day is long. She was gregarious, fun-loving and made a host of friends. She liked to be well thought of by her contemporaries. Mark sometimes thought she tried a bit too hard in that direction. Yet where Nina and he were concerned, she seemed almost indifferent. When she had first come back from Susan Thompson's he found her the same girl he had so much enjoyed on sailing trips and picnics last summer. She was full of humor and high spirits. Gradually that had changed and now she was a taciturn, even shy girl, half child, half woman, seldom volunteering any information, given to fits of sensitivity when the slightest remark might offend her, often going off by herself for long walks on Saturdays and Sundays when none of her friends came by to pick her up.

She baffled Mark. It seemed almost as if she disliked him and Nina, the way she shunned their company.

Once or twice he had tried to draw her to him again, taking her up on Rolling Giant for an afternoon of skiing. On the slopes, she was for a short time herself. She did as well in skiing as she did in most sports, for she was a natural athlete. They made a few downhill runs together and Mark encouraged Ginger to teach him the new turns she had picked up. Afterward they drove over to a place of Ginger's choosing, a restaurant which bore the name *Joe's Kitchen* on its sign, but to which Ginger affectionately referred as "Sloppy Joe's." Here they crawled into one of a dozen booths occupied by young people whom Ginger greeted by such names as Dodo, Buff, Saltines, Shark, Boots, Axle, Chips, La-La, and Can-Can.

At five thirty the place cleared and Mark and Ginger were left alone with the few adults who had come in for their evening meal.

It was after the noise had subsided and the crowd had gone that Mark almost reached through to the old Ginger. Over their hamburgers and milk, she began to talk to him, and he was a little shocked at the depth of her conversation. She was reading a lot these days. All kinds of things. She liked her English teacher and the way she taught. She didn't hand out a book list and say, Look here, you've got to read so many books and these are the titles. She encouraged you to find out what your own taste was.

Ginger's taste ran to plays, quite naturally, and she had read all of Shaw and most of Ibsen and Strindberg and Saroyan and now she was reading Eugene O'Neill. She liked a few of the novelists, too. George Eliot, strangely enough since most of her classmates thought this writer "corny," but Ginger liked her. She had discovered some volumes by Katherine Brush tucked into a corner of the school library, and F. Scott Fitzgerald. The latter she did not understand, she frankly admitted. As she did not understand Thomas Wolfe or William Faulkner.

She switched easily from her talk about books to talk about life itself. She had decided never to get married. Mark, who was just biting into his second jumbo beefburger, stopped and looked over at her.

"I'm not sure I heard that," he said.

"I'm never going to get married, Dad. Oh, I may fall in love a few times. That would be fun, but marriage is a big job. I'm not sure I want to take the trouble."

Mark stared in silence, almost frozen by her words. Maybe she was just sounding off. When you were fifteen, you felt you had your life in the palm of your hand and you could choose to do whatever you wanted to. Inevitability, the logic of events, fate, the great pounding universe that pulled you into its cycle, these were forces that could not touch you when you were fifteen. You knew it all. There was nothing anyone could tell you that you weren't sure you knew already. You read the way

Ginger was reading, with an avid desire to gobble down the experiences you had not lived, yet you felt sure you were master of all you surveyed. This was the malady that made Ginger talk like this.

Then, when he thought he had her all figured out, she surprised him by saying, "Marriages don't work out always, do they, Dad?"

He looked away as he answered. "Not always."

She nodded. "I've talked it over with some of the girls. You'd be surprised at how many of them think their mothers and fathers aren't happy together." Mark did not answer. He felt uncomfortable, sitting here under the frank stare of his daughter.

She went on. "What makes people fall out of love, Dad?"

He wondered how much she knew about Nina and him. She knew something, that was a cinch. He had suspected all along that she was absorbing some of the tension that filled the house on Turkey Hill. He had wondered if that was the reason for her silences, her moods, her long, lonely walks. You couldn't hide that sort of thing from an intelligent girl Ginger's age. Yet he had no intention of discussing with Ginger the breach between him and Nina.

"People do fall out of love, Dad, don't they?" she repeated. "I wonder why."

"I don't know," he said. Then, "Maybe you'll find the answer in all those books you're reading."

"One answer isn't enough," she said. "There are too many answers. And no right one."

He stared at her again, unable to take his eyes off her. This was no child any more. This girl across from him who looked so much like his mother was a woman. Her words haunted him. *There are too many answers. And no right one.* This was the special kind of wisdom, the intuitive wisdom, that women have. Ginger was growing away from them so fast that even if he reached out now to catch her—mentally and emotionally—he could not do it. She was leaving him fast behind.

So he let her go, not trying any more to draw her back into the web of childhood when she had been a good companion to him, a child who shared his simple pleasures. He let her go on to be the woman she insisted on being.

He let her lose herself in play rehearsals and novels by authors he had never read. He let her go off by herself when she wanted to, to find in the loneliness of the human spirit, the great yearning for something above and beyond its reach. This loneliness he knew, too, for more and more he was becoming a restless, dissatisfied man who had almost nothing in common with the Mark Galloway he had once been.

Sometimes when he came home late he would look in on Ginger as she sat at her desk poring over her books or writing in her diary. She kept a diary, under lock and key, with a conscientiousness that appalled him. Because he wondered what she could be writing about. Puppy love affairs perhaps with boys like Saxy Aiken. Episodes that happened at school. When you were fifteen you could dramatize the most trivial occurrence.

Once he had, with a note of jocoseness, referred to it. "Are you writing the Bradford memoirs, Ginger?" he asked. "And will we all be immortalized?"

"Maybe," she said, with a cryptic smile. "And maybe I'm only trying to find out what happiness really is."

There it was, another of those remarks that swept her away from him. *Maybe I'm only trying to find out what happiness is.*

When you find it, he wanted to answer, let me know. I'd like to know myself. But he didn't answer. With an air of finality, he closed the door on her, saying good night, carrying away a picture of her in a cerise robe that clashed with her red hair, and that hair flying about her face in snarled waves like his own.

Let her go, he said to himself. This is one of the things you can't hold on to any more.

It was not the only one.

He tried to bring Nina back again, the Nina he had loved so passionately all these years. In a way, he felt that Nina too was trying to bring back some part of him that she had lost.

This searching for something lost was a mutual thing between them. Sometimes he thought it was the one thing, the only thing, they now wholeheartedly shared.

In the way of a male, Mark tried to revive the old courting times. He tried to think of things he might do for her, some gifts he might bring her, and was startled to find out that everything had already been done for her, long before he had stood, a strapping, eager, but poor boy, upon the threshold of her love. There was nothing he could buy for her, nothing important, that she did not already possess. Her taste was exquisite and impeccable and he was afraid that whatever he might choose might be not quite right. Nina would never let him know, but he had always suspected that even his Christmas and birthday gifts were worn only as token gestures to the fondness she felt for him. The gifts, no matter what they had been, had always missed their mark.

He suggested they take a trip together, go south for a few weeks.

"Aren't you needed badly at the plant just now?" Nina asked. "With a new chief engineer."

"Maybe the vacation would do us all good. You. Me. The plant."

Nina thought it over. "Ginger can't be left alone, Mark. Who could we trust her with? She's still going through a period of adjustment. With those moods and everything."

All right, Mark thought, so you don't want to go on a trip with me. I guess I can take a hint.

He let her try, in her woman's way, to bring them together again and he co-operated with whatever attempts she made. When she decided that it had been a mistake to let their social life lapse and that what they needed was to renew all their old friendships in town, he let her drag him along with her. He obligingly left the plant early to attend teas which spoiled his dinner. He went to dinner parties where he ate too much. He played bridge—a game he loathed—with people who disgusted him because they seemed to have no other interest in life. He went to Hunt Club parties, Country Club parties, the little informal *soirées* of Bradford society where overstimulated women tried to flirt with him and stuffy men talked him to sleep.

Once, long, long ago, this had seemed novel and even interesting. That was when he had still been on the way up, when he had been young Mark Galloway, the poor boy who had married Nina Bradford and who was learning to take his place in her strange new world. Then he had needed these social contacts and these people. He had been still untried, unproven. He had to show Nina that he warranted her love, that he could belong to her world.

He no longer needed to prove that point.

So he went along to please Nina, but he withdrew himself. He became aloof, even while he was smiling and chatting and dancing and listening. He became a bit cynical, too, feeling for the first time in his life an intense dislike for a group of human beings. He hated these people of Nina's world. They were bores and stuffed shirts. They were shallow and insincere. They were phonies. Nothing back of them. Nothing to hold them upright on their two feet but the money and the social position and the cars and homes they possessed. Gutted-out, he thought to himself. A bunch of gutted-out nonentities. I can't stand this hobnobbing much longer. It's getting me down. One of these days something is going to happen. I'm going to lose control and forget to smile and say what I think or maybe even take a punch at one of these stuffed shirts when he says something I don't like.

So he told Nina before it was too late. Perhaps this was not the thing to do, but he could not help doing it. He talked it over with Nina one morning at breakfast after Ginger had left for school. He should have led into it with greater tact but he was tired and fed up, with this dreadful restlessness within him.

"Nina." She glanced up with a question in her eyes. Then, when she had looked for a long moment into his face, she laid aside the menu she was working on for Effie.

"Nina." He tried to put some tenderness into his voice as he repeated her name. "It won't work."

"What won't work, Mark?"

"This program you've mapped out for us. This constant activity. I've got to have some rest. I've got to have some time to be by myself and think."

"Why don't you take that trip you talked about, Mark? Without me. Go off by yourself. You'd have time to think then, and you need a vacation."

He jumped up, pushing back his chair and almost upsetting it. "I don't want to go away alone," he said. "I won't go away alone. If you won't come with me, I'll stay."

"If I did go with you, Mark, would it really help? When we came back, would anything be changed?"

He glanced out the window, away from Nina, upon the bleak winter scene that stretched below them. From this window, half of Bradford was visible. It lay huddled under the somber sky, reluctant to wake up on this gray day. With buildings, and its rows of houses, huddling together like human beings for warmth, it could have been anybody's town. But it wasn't anybody's town. It was the Bradfords' town. But it was also Mark Galloway's town. It was the town where he had been born a nobody, raised a nobody, and pushed his way up to be a somebody.

Back of him sat Nina, his wife. Her quiet voice had just given him a momentous answer, the answer perhaps of his lifetime.

She was fed up too. All this restlessness and uncertainty were not his alone. Nina shared them.

It's marriage, Mark thought. It's the vicious, deadly strain of marriage. It's two people trying to live together and fighting to preserve their union and thrashing the waves in desperation so they won't go down for the third time.

Nina would not go away with him, he knew, because when they returned nothing would have changed. It was logic, hard-headed Yankee logic, and it was unanswerable.

Chapter 17

So there was nothing to do but drive out to see Claire. Because of the very strength of the impulse, he did not yield to it at once or without a struggle.

When he had gone to Claire in the fall of the year, he had been motivated partly by curiosity, partly by his anger with Nina. Those, if they were not excusable motivations, were at least transient ones. The visit at Christmas had been spontaneous and uncalculated. Although he had come perilously close to losing his head in the presence of Claire's magnetism, he had known enough to steer clear of the little house out on Easton Road since then.

This time it would be different. His visit would have a new significance. His emotions were no longer transient or spontaneous where Claire was concerned. They were deep-seated. These weeks since Christmas he had been fighting the desire to see her again. All during his feverish attempts to make a permanent place for himself in his own home by cultivating a closer father-daughter relationship with Ginger, by wooing Nina again, by tearing around with her from one nightmare of a party to another, all this time it had been Claire he was fighting off.

Now he knew he would have to go to her. And this time it

would not be as a curious former beau or a momentarily angered husband or a grateful friend. This time he would go to Claire as a man going to a woman.

He chose a Saturday afternoon, and, remembering that there was another man in the picture, he thought it best to telephone ahead that he was coming. Claire took so long to answer his ring that he was about to hang up. Then he heard her voice, breathless as if from hurrying.

"Yes. Hello?" There was a question in her tone.

"It's me. Mark."

"Oh, hello. How are you?"

"Can I come out to see you?"

"Now, Mark? You mean right away?"

"Yes."

"I'm awfully sorry, but I was just leaving to drive over to Brampton for some costumes. They won't hold them after today. They're for a play we're putting on next week."

"Let me drive you over." Claire's response was a long silence. "Wouldn't you like me to do that, Claire?"

"I'd like it all right." She laughed, in appreciation rather than self-consciousness over his directness. "But do you really think you should?"

"If you're afraid someone will see us, don't worry. I'll take the back roads. Brampton's a big city. We'll steer clear of the stores. Don't worry, Claire."

"I'm not worried, Mark. I just don't like sneaking around. If it isn't right for us to be seen, it isn't right for us to go there together."

"I've got to see you, Claire. I've got to."

She hesitated. "Can't it wait until you can come out here?"

"No," he said. "I want to see you today."

"Is it that important really?"

"Yes, it's that important."

"All right, but you'll have to hurry. I'll need more than an hour to go over the costumes and select what I want. And what will you do with yourself while I'm doing that?"

"I won't get in the way. I'll be right over. I'm calling from Greencrest."

"From Greencrest!" There was mild surprise in Claire's voice, then her laugh rolled out to him. "You were sure of yourself, Mark Galloway, weren't you?"

"Not of myself," he said huskily. "But I knew you wouldn't let me down."

It sounded almost adolescent even to his own ears and he was ashamed of his crudeness the moment he hung up. He had no right to talk to Claire like that, to impose on her this way. It wasn't just his own position as manager of Bradford Tool and husband of Nina Galloway that he was jeopardizing. He was asking Claire to risk a lot for the mere privilege of seeing him. Maybe she didn't even want to see him. She might be in love with this New Hampshire character. A farmer! Claire Elliott and a farmer. He tried to work up a nice sense of righteous indignation for Claire's sake as he turned his car toward Easton Road, but he only succeeded in uncovering the fact that he was jealous of the other man. David Wakefield was free and he had the right to love Claire and be loved by her.

Mark Galloway didn't have any rights. With Claire or anyone else. Even in his own home he didn't have any. Nina and Ginger had both shut him out. It wasn't even his home. He owned half of it on paper, but it was Nina's home. It had always been.

Claire was standing in the driveway waiting for him and as he pulled to a stop, his mind and his emotions raced back to River Street, to summer evenings when he would stand out in front of his own house and wait for her to pick him up. Only everything was reversed now. It was he who was picking Claire up. Then he had been an eager kid and she had been a glamorous girl, always seeming older than he. It wasn't summer now, it was winter, with piles of dirty snow banked up and icy roads to watch out for and Claire bundled up in a tweed coat, her red hair tumbling from a parka hood across her shoulders. She wore red boots trimmed in fur and once again he noticed how incredibly young she looked.

Everything has changed but Claire, he thought.

Her greeting was cordial, if a bit restrained, and he sensed that she meant what she had said over the telephone. This sort of thing was not to her liking.

She waited until they were clear of Bradford and driving along the parkway toward Brampton. Then she asked him, "What's wrong, Mark?" From her tone she might almost have asked him, "What's wrong *now*, Mark?" More trouble, her voice implied, always some trouble in that house on Turkey Hill. Can't you keep peace there?

"Let's talk about it later," he said. "I've got to watch the road. There are still a few icy spots."

She did not urge him to talk, settling back into silence. Mark did not try to talk either. He supposed he should feel sorry about this, about having forced himself upon her. He supposed he should feel guilty. He did not feel guilty. He felt rather happy, even with an untalkative Claire beside him, even with the calculated risk he was taking by driving her to Brampton. His dominant emotion was one of well-being. For the first time in weeks he felt like himself again, like the old Mark Galloway who knew where he was going and what he wanted and was sure he would get it.

Claire got out at a little costumer's on a Brampton side street and Mark told her he would leave the car in the parking lot at the end of the street.

"I'll meet you there in about an hour and a half," she said. "Unless you run away."

"Try and lose me," he said.

There was a barber shop nearby and he walked in, remembering that he had been trying to find time for a haircut for the last three days. It was a busy place and he had to wait his turn, but he did this good-naturedly, enjoying the gregarious sensation of the experience. It was a pleasant change from his normal routine. For the last ten years he had been the most privileged patron of Mike's Barber Shop one block away from the main entrance of Bradford Tool. He had not waited for his turn in a barber shop in ten years. Mike saw to that. Even when Mark would protest he could wait, the other customer would shake his head. No one in town minded deferring to Mark Galloway. He was a good guy. He was a busy guy. He was the busiest guy in town. He kept the factory running that fed half or more of Bradford, didn't he?

Today Mark sat down, picking up a newspaper and glancing over the headlines. He let it drop from his hands as his ears picked up a conversation between a stocky barber at the end and the tall young man whose hair was being given a crew cut. They were apparently old friends and the barber was drawing the boy out, asking him about school. The boy played basketball. He was captain of the freshman team. He liked school. He guessed he would be an engineer. When the barber asked him what kind, he said he didn't know for sure, maybe electronics. He just liked to tinker with things, always had a knack with mechanics. Mark became fascinated by the conversation. The boy sounded intelligent. He was clean-cut and lively.

Mark found himself wondering who the boy was, what sort of home he came from. He couldn't even learn his first name. The barber called him "Stretch."

"Stretch, you still got that newspaper route?" The barber pronounced it "rowt."

"Yeah, I got three of them now. I work one myself and I got two boys to work the others for me. I bought out a couple of my friends who got tired of it."

"A bloated plutocrat, huh!" the barber kidded him. "So now you're a boss."

The boy took the kidding in his stride. "Yeah, I guess you'd call it that."

The barber nodded his head philosophically. "You keep on being a boss. That's the only thing to be. That's the only **way** to make any real dough. You can't do anything without dough."

"Yeah," the boy said, "maybe you're right. But other things are important too."

Mark watched the boy get out of the chair and listened to the barber chatter on as he brushed him off. The boy was as straight and tall as a hickory sapling. His hair was blond and his eyes big and candid above his strong nose and broad grin. It was a face you couldn't help liking and it set up an aching in Mark, an aching he had not felt for many years.

Thirteen years old, maybe, Mark thought to himself. Maybe fourteen. Not much older than our boy would have been. He would have been tall like this one. The kids might have called him "Stretch." He might even have looked a little like this. I bet he would have played a terrific game of basketball.

Maybe you're right. But other things are important too.

How do they learn so much so early these days? Mark asked himself. Ginger talks like that. What's in the air nowadays to make these kids so wise?

"All right, Stretch," the barber was saying. "See you next month sometime." Then, as he gave the boy a pat on the arm, "Take it easy, Boss." The barber laughed at his own humor and the boy, easygoing and appreciative, grinned back.

"So long," he said. "Take it easy yourself."

Mark was next. He sat down in the chair and replied in non-committal monosyllables to the barber's attempt to make small talk. He was staring at his own face in the mirror, a dark, scowling face above the white smock and towel. He was not even hearing the barber's remarks. He was thinking of the son he had once had and lost. If that son had lived, he might have given Mark the one thing he needed to hold on to, in this turbulent time through which he and Nina were going. If that son had lived, he might never have needed Claire Elliott.

He was sitting in his car waiting for Claire when she entered the parking space. He honked and leaned out, waving, and she returned his wave and hurried toward him. As he watched her hastening to meet him, the same resurgence of attraction welled up in him. Her walk, even in those ridiculous red boots, was supple and lovely.

All the emptiness and loneliness of these past weeks rose up in Mark and he cried out within, This is my first love. I should never have given her up and I want her again.

There was some argument between them about dinner. Mark wanted to take Claire to a little restaurant in Brampton, but she refused. He coaxed but she was adamant.

"There's nothing wrong in our having dinner together," he said.

"I've got to get back home," she answered.

He turned the car toward the parkway and then changed his mind, choosing instead the long shore road. Claire was silent until he said, "Are you mad at me?"

"No," she replied, "I'm waiting for you to tell me what you wanted to talk about."

"All at once it doesn't seem so important," he said. "I wanted to take you to dinner and talk to you then."

Claire didn't answer.

The dusk came early, and then the swift nightfall, and he was riding on and on along the darkened shore line with Claire so close to him, and yet so far away in that somber silence in which she chose to envelop herself. Yet he felt no unfriendliness in her presence, only restraint and caution.

They rode on through the night, passing the beach colonies

whose houses were boarded against winter, driving fast through the amusement park called Fisherman's Rock. It was an eerie thing to behold, with its row of boarded façades through the midway, its towering roller coaster and stretches of forsaken beach. Then suddenly they were back to civilization where a cluster of year-round residents had settled along the shore. Tonight it comforted Mark to see the lights in houses and the row of stores. He reduced his speed for an occasional pedestrian.

Then the Miramar was ahead of them. Mark swerved sharply and pulled into the parking space in front of the brightly lighted inn. Claire made no comment. He twisted around in the seat and looked at her.

"You know this is plain nonsense," he said. "There's no logical reason on earth why we can't have dinner here. You're hungry and so am I. The food is tops. We're not likely to run into any snooping Bradfordites. How about it, Claire?"

She sat there, taking off her mittens and slapping the leather palms against each other in preoccupation.

At last she looked up at him. "I'm remembering last Christmas Eve," she said slowly, "and a certain breath-taking kiss."

"I know," he said. "I know what you mean. But I won't kiss you again unless you say I can. That's a promise."

She smiled at him for the first time that afternoon, smiled in the old way, with the touch of mockery which implied she was never quite revealing all of what she was thinking.

"Let's go," she said. "I could do with a cup of coffee."

The Miramar was a charming place run by a family called Bertini. The specialties of the house were Italian dishes like lasagna and chicken cacciatore and veal scallopine. But there were good steaks and chops too. The place had an old-world atmosphere with red-checked tablecloths and majolica pottery displayed in shadow boxes hung on the walls. A piano on a level with the dining tables stood off in one corner and here one of the Bertinis played nightly during the dinner hour while another Bertini brought in his accordion or violin, as the mood pleased him.

Mark had known and loved this place for a long time. Oddly enough, he had never brought Nina here. Italian food held no appeal for her, so the Miramar had grown into a quiet hideaway where Mark could come when the pressures of business drove him almost beyond endurance. Steve Emrich had come up here with him once or twice, and one night he had brought Jason here, but most of the time he came alone.

A Bertini met Mark and Claire at the door and took their coats, chatting about the clearness of the evening and the cold, not forgetting to mention how glad he was to see "Mr. Mark" again.

They were all glad to see "Mr. Mark." Like a procession, several Bertinis escorted Mark and Claire to a favorite booth at the side.

"The second booth next to the end one. There. That's Mr. Mark's place. Here, light the candle, Giuseppe. Here, Lisa, take away this cloth. Bring a fresh one for Mr. Mark. And bring some flowers from the center table. The yellow roses. Quickly, Catherine, the bread sticks and plenty of butter. Mr. Mark likes lots of butter. Right?"

"Right."

They were properly appreciative of Claire, eyeing her from dark eyes filled with friendly curiosity, but in their sophisticated Latin way, refraining from the presumption of calling her "Signora" until they were sure. All through the ritual of ordering their meal, Mark felt pairs of penetrating eyes turned upon Claire, felt the questions back of those eyes and saw the lively faces around him decide that the handsome woman with Mr. Mark was not his wife.

In the spirit of the evening, Mark went along with Claire on whatever she ordered. She did not feel like having Italian food.

She wanted a steak, very rare, and vegetables but no potatoes, a tossed green salad, anchovies to begin with, no soup but later she would have some cannoli. She loved Italian pastry.

When they were eating, Claire looked over at Mark and said, "Aren't you going to tell me what you wanted to talk to me about?"

"No," he said. "Not now."

"This isn't fair," she said. "You lured me away because you said you had to see me about something important. All afternoon you've been stalling."

"Let me stall awhile longer, Claire," he said. "This is too much fun. I don't want to spoil it."

It was fun, more fun than he'd had in a long time. The Bertinis outdid themselves with the food and the music. They played all the happy Italian melodies in their repertory, and then they sent over to Mr. Mark's table to ask what else he would like them to play. Mark insisted that Claire do the choosing.

"You really want me to?" she said, with a warning in her eyes.

"But of course. Why not?"

So she pulled the ear of the messenger close to her lips and whispered while the young Bertini smiled and nodded, then returned to the pianist with Claire's requests.

They played Claire's songs while Mark and she were having dessert, and Claire watched him over her cup of espresso coffee, letting her eyes laugh into his.

At first he did not recognize the tunes. He knew only that they were doing strange things to his mind and emotions, carrying him back to some place he could not remember. For a moment, he was like a drowning man, reaching out and up for something solid to grab hold of. Because he was no longer here in the Miramar with Claire. He did not know where he was. He knew only that the songs had pushed him out into space, knocked all his safe little props from under him and yet they had not set him down anywhere familiar.

Then suddenly he knew. Suddenly he was there again, back at Sandy Point in the dance pavilion on a summer evening with Claire. He was wearing a white linen suit and he was worried about his hair which would not stay down. Claire was in billowing yellow-green, a frothy dress with yards of skirt and no shoulder straps and her beautiful throat and neck made lovelier by a silver medallion hung on a green velvet ribbon. He saw her as she was then, as plainly as if this young Claire were sitting across from him now. The same flamboyant hair, the same mouth, the same smile. Only this younger Claire seemed closer to him than the woman across from him. She was farther away in years but closer in memory. That Claire he could have taken in his arms and loved and kissed. He could have rested his face in her thick, wiry hair. He could have smelled her perfume, feeling it linger long after she had left him. He knew the softness and the warmth of her.

This Claire across from him was near in space and time, but she was far away in actuality. He could not touch her. He had promised never to kiss her again unless she gave her permission. And then even, he could not let his love flow out to her because he had no right to.

It would have been possible to touch her hand by just reaching out to it, yet even this he could not do. Claire would withdraw it. He watched her hand, resting lightly upon the red-checked cloth. It was startlingly white and as smooth as a child's. She wore one ring with a large topaz that flickered in the candlelight.

An aimless line from some long-forgotten poem reached out and touched his mind, even as the music was touching his feelings.

She walks in beauty.

Claire was that line of poetry. She was beauty in motion. Her laugh, her gestures, her walk, the tilt of her head, the laughter in her eyes, the curl of her lips. She was the antithesis of his wife because Nina represented static beauty, perfection in everything, but that perfection still and passive, the beauty that waits for all things to come to it. Claire went out to meet life, running, falling over herself in her eagerness, and that was the beauty of the woman. He wanted to gather her in his arms, to clutch that eagerness to him, to catch and imprison it forever, but he could not. He could only sit here and watch her.

"Do you remember the songs?" she asked him.

"I remember them."

"Sandy Point," she murmured. "Your last year of high school. And all the next summer too. I had a yellow-green dress."

"I remember," he said.

"You were still learning to dance and you were awkward."

"I know."

"I was the only one who believed in Mark Galloway then," she said. "I knew then the sort of man you would be one day. I used to tell you."

"I remember that too," he said. He paused, then went on. "For a while I was the man you said I'd be. The man who could hold life in the palm of his hand. Oddly enough, it was during those years that I lost you. Now I'm not so sure about myself, about anything, but now I've found you again."

"Have you? Have you really?"

"I hope I have."

She glanced away and then back to his face. "Would you go back to those years again, Mark, the years we loved each other, if you could have them?"

He waited, knowing that whatever he answered, it would set the pace for whatever was to follow between them. Claire was asking him to let her know what was in his mind about them.

"No," he answered slowly, "I would not go back there even if I could, but if you would let me, I would go forward, reaching out for you as you are now."

She did not reply, but her hand moved along the table, closer to his, and the topaz stone in the ring was like a beacon light drawing him on. He closed his hand over hers. Her lashes flickered nervously as she looked into his face, but the hesitation lasted only a moment. Then her fingers curled up and grasped his hand, pressing it in response.

It was on the way home that Mark finally talked to Claire about Nina. Driving through the night, with only the flash from occasional headlights passing them, he spoke to her about what was on his mind. In the fall he had been reluctant to draw Claire into his family squabbles but so much had happened since then. Ginger had, by running to Claire in her panicky departure from Susan Thompson's, already drawn Claire into their disagreement.

This time he did not spare himself the pain of revealing what was happening to his love for Nina and Nina's regard for him.

For the most part, Claire listened without comment, but occasionally she asked a question to clarify something in her mind, and once, as he was telling her about the scene in Nina's dressing room, following the fateful meeting of the Board of Directors that ruled out Steve Emrich, Claire made a soft murmur of protest and said, almost to herself, "How dreadful that must have been for both of you."

She did not take sides against Nina. She did not openly declare her allegiance to Mark. All the catty things another woman might have said under the circumstances she left eloquently unsaid. Here was a woman who had loved and lost a man to another woman and now, facing the opportunity to even that score, she chose silence rather than the articulateness of anger or scorn, or even revenge.

Mark, who had once loved Claire for reasons too numerous to recount, now found another reason for loving her. She could be generous in victory.

He left her, shortly before midnight, in her living room. After his lengthy confession to her, he felt gutted out, tired beyond even the normal fatigue of a busy day, but Claire was still fresh and radiant.

As he got ready to leave her, he said, "Will you forgive me for burdening you like this with my troubles?"

"Nothing to forgive. That's what old friends are for."

But he felt the need to explain. "I've got no one else to talk to. No one but Jason and he's so busy straightening out the whole town's troubles, I don't like to bother him."

She nodded. "Besides," Mark went on, "there's a special comfort in spilling your troubles to someone who once loved you."

"I did love you once, Mark. Very much."

"And now you love someone else." She didn't answer. "Very much?" he asked.

"That's not a fair question," she countered.

"You're right. You should put me in my place," he said. "Don't let me get away with things like that."

"I won't," she said, smiling. She held out her hand to him and he took it. "I've loved tonight, Mark. Even if we shouldn't have done it, I'm glad we did. And I think it helped you."

"It did," he said. "You have no idea how much."

He held her hand, searching her face, and she, with a sudden gesture, moved toward him. He did not make any move to take her in his arms, remembering his promise, but she moved closer. She reached out and put her hand on his shoulder and her eyes told him before she said the words what she wanted him to do.

"Kiss me good night, Mark," she said. "And make my evening complete."

With one arm encircling her, he pressed his free hand against her cheek and drew her face gently toward his. Her lips were soft against his, and yielding.

She doesn't love this other man, he thought. She still loves me. What he said was, "Claire, I need you. I need you more than I did when we were kids together. Don't shut me out of your life."

Chapter 18

THE IMMEDIATE EFFECT OF MARK'S RENEWED FRIENDSHIP WITH Claire was one of freshness and renascence. The night at the Miramar gave him a new lease on life, on his work, on himself. It was faith in himself, in the old Mark Galloway, he needed, and for the time being at least, he found the self he would like to be reflected in Claire's eyes.

He telephoned her every day. He would drive some distance from the center of town to find a booth in a side-street restaurant or corner drugstore and wait, with all the eagerness of a boy calling his first girl, to hear her voice again.

It was a lilting voice, full of vitality, and he loved it. He loved her laugh too. In a world made dreary by home problems and factory problems, Claire was a star to pin his hopes to. He needed her buoyancy and cheerfulness. He needed her contagious happiness.

There were times when he called her from Greencrest in the evening when he had been working late at the plant, and then, with some coaxing, he would get her to invite him over for a little while. They would sit in her living room, in front of a blazing fire, with a cup of tea and some muffins or cake or a sandwich, and they would talk.

Or rather, Mark would talk, and Claire would listen, asking

an appropriate question or two, nodding her head or murmuring sympathetically from time to time. Claire was no yeswoman, but Mark did feel that she understood his problems.

So he brought his troubles to her, and talked them out, and listened to her minimize them or bring him to the threshold of a solution with a resiliency that refused to accept defeat. All the people in Mark's life, like hulking shadows of a dream, came and went in Claire's little house. Nina, Ginger, Victoria, Spencer, Bob Bradford, Steve.

Frank Muthersbaugh was the one most present in their conversations. The effect of his presence at Bradford Tool was proving disastrous. Since his advent, everything in the plant was slowing up. His preoccupation with details, the details of drawing and draftsmanship, kept him in the drafting room. He seldom got into the plant to see what was going on there. Art Wimbley was always running into trouble but instead of going to Frank, he went to Steve Emrich.

At the weekly plant meetings of foremen and executives, Frank's ignorance of his job showed up most sadly. This was the place for the discussion of problems concerned with the machining of parts, and Frank proved irrefutably that he knew nothing about machine shop practice. He didn't even know when a drawing specified the proper manufacturing tolerances and operations.

The result of this ignorance, if not checked in time, showed up in the assembly department. Even though the component parts of a precision lathe might pass inspection because they had been made according to the drawings, when they reached the assembly process they might not go together properly. Fortunately, there had been no vast damage as yet, since Frank's mistakes had been discovered early enough to correct them. Steve Emrich had saved the day time after time and Art Wimbley's insistence on going to Steve instead of Frank for final check-ups had avoided enormous waste, but the situation was a treacherous one. They were all treading on thin ice. The day might come when some small event, some minor happening, might result in a catastrophe costing Bradford Tool thousands of dollars. No one knew the pitfalls of production better than Mark. No one knew where the blame would fall better than he.

"When that day comes," he said to Claire one evening, "I'll be the fall guy. The top guy is always to blame. Some one of these days I'm going to be sitting down on a junk pile of scrapped parts, in an inferno of top management fury, because of Frank Muthersbaugh's ignorance."

"But can't you stave it off somehow?" Claire asked him. "Can't you stop him now?"

"How?" he asked. "How could I do anything short of firing him? And how can I fire him when he's a Bradford? Spencer and Bob selected him themselves."

Claire talked occasionally about her own work. She enjoyed her dramatic work in Bradford and she liked working with young people. Her real dream, however, was to have a professional theater of her own one of these days. She knew she could direct well enough for summer stock since she had tried it. However, the problems surrounding such a project were numerous. To start with, you needed considerable capital. You needed the right spot. Bradford was not such a place. It was too close to New York. She always had her eye out for some spot farther out, a country barn that could easily be converted. That was her vision for the future.

She seldom talked about David Wakefield, and then only casually. He was renovating his stables and barns in preparation for the spring and summer seasons, so he had to stay there and supervise the work. Claire heard from him often. He telephoned and he wrote and he sent her gifts. Some of these she showed to Mark, a pair of brass candlesticks with carved dragons for their bases, a crystal wedding bowl, a set of Staffordshire teacups.

"He knows my fondness for such things," she said, but she never elaborated upon her feelings toward David. For this Mark was grateful. He did not want to discuss David Wakefield. He did not want to acknowledge his existence. He was jealous of the man because Claire, by the raising of her little finger, might have married him. It was a selfish attitude on Mark's part and he knew it, but he could not help it. He wanted Claire for himself, or not being able to have her, he did not want anyone else to have her either.

Claire would not go out with Mark around Bradford again, but twice when she was going to New York for costumes and make-up for her plays, he managed to have business there too. He met her late in the day at a small hotel and they had dinner together. Claire chose the place, a little Hungarian restaurant named the Chardas up in the Seventies, "because I like gypsy music," she said.

They sat on seats along the wall, close to each other, and he insisted that Claire order for both of them. She did this gracefully, familiar as she was with the Hungarian menu, ordering chopped chicken livers, and a thick soup, then chicken paprikash with nockerel, red cabbage salad, and apple strudel for dessert.

They ate in a leisurely way and tonight Mark did not talk about business. They sat holding hands—above the table where anyone might see since there was no fear of running into anyone who knew them here. They listened to the gypsy orchestra with its violin and cello and cimbaloms. There were two singers, a man and woman, not very young but with plenty of fire still in their voices, who sang continental songs in Hungarian and German.

Mark was entranced with the place. He liked its quietness and charm and he was happy to be here with Claire.

"This is the sort of thing I've been wanting to do for a long time," he told her, "without knowing I wanted it."

"It grows on you, doesn't it?" she said, nodding toward the musicians. "That music pulls you on and on. It's sad and happy all at once."

Mark closed his hand more tightly over hers. "You grow on me, too," he said. "I don't think I can ever give you up again."

"You can't give up what you've never had," she answered him.

He drew back, a little shocked, because what she said was so true. "Suppose I told you that I'm falling head over heels again for you, Claire. Suppose I told you that there are times when I think I'll have to do something about having you."

She did not look at him as she answered. She was studying the goblet in front of her. "I wouldn't say that, if I were you, Mark. I wouldn't even think it."

"Why not?"

"Because it wouldn't work out," she said. "It would never work out. You can't build anything right and constructive between two people on the ashes of something they've destroyed."

He was tempted to argue with her, to tell her that you couldn't destroy something that had destroyed itself and that if she meant his love for Nina, Nina had set the match to the tinder that had reduced it to ashes, but he did not argue. He did not even answer. He was caught up in the spell of the moment, content to sit here next to Claire, to listen to the bittersweet music, to press her hand within his own.

So near and yet so far, he thought. I have her close to me and yet I can't have her.

It became a theme for him for that evening on the long ride home in his car, on the lingering kiss when he held her close for just that brief moment or two.

So near and yet so far.

Chapter 19

MARK DID NOT SEE CLAIRE FOR SEVERAL DAYS AFTER DINNER AT the Chardas. He was urgently needed at the plant, working all day and into the evening on a rush order from Merriman Pump Company.

Merriman was an old customer of Bradford Tool, having done business with them for some thirty-odd years. They manufactured marine pumps and at present their firm was undergoing an expansion program. They needed fifty lathes for their new extension and they needed them in a hurry.

Bob, who made the commitment for Bradford Tool, did so reluctantly. He did not like rush orders, even from old customers, even when he was sure his factory could fill them on time. They were ticklish business and they could be a prolific source of ill will if you did not come across on schedule. However, the purchasing agent of Merriman was a good friend of Bob's and he felt obliged to do what he could.

So, on a bitter cold morning in late February, Bob consulted with his production and engineering departments about the proposed order for fifty Merriman lathes. Merriman wanted them within thirty days. Under normal circumstances, this would have been an impossibility, but Bob found out that the type of lathe used by Merriman was already in production.

Except for minor variations such as a special spindle, this lathe was standard production for Bradford Tool. The fifty lathes could be got ready in thirty days. It would be a tight schedule and some workers might have to put in overtime, but it could be done with maybe two or three days to spare.

Mark stayed close to the plant because he did not dare leave it. He was well aware of the mental atmosphere in the factory —it was like working on high-tension wires in an ice storm. The sparks were flying out in every direction. Rush orders created nervous irritation and short tempers even when everything was running smoothly in a plant. Things were not running smoothly at Bradford Tool.

The tempest over Frank Muthersbaugh was reaching a climax, goaded on by Frank himself. Lately he had discovered that Art Wimbley was taking the drawings from the drafting room to Steve Emrich for a final check-up and it infuriated him. He had threatened Wimbley about it, offering to go over his head, if need be to Spencer Bradford himself. Wimbley had brushed aside Frank's objections with about as much concern as he would brush a fly off his arm.

"My job is to produce good lathes," he boomed back at Frank. "No one cares how I do it so long as I do it." And Frank, strangely enough, cowered before the tight-lipped Wimbley. He never went over his head, not even to Mark, although Mark heard about the squabbles between them from his old crony McGovern, in the stock room.

"That man is afraid of Art Wimbley," McGovern would cackle. "Just plain scared of him. Wimbley's a big man and powerful and not one to be afraid to strike a blow if anyone provoked him enough. He's got Muthersbaugh bamboozled."

Bamboozled or not, it was not a healthy atmosphere for production, and that production accelerated by the Merriman order to the breaking point.

For three days Mark practically lived at the plant, having

all his meals there and even throwing himself down on a couch in his office, exhausted, to sleep for a few hours in the evening before the night shift came on. He did not even see Nina and Ginger in the morning because he had his breakfast early and left for the plant before they came down. For three days he could not get far enough away to telephone Claire, although during that time it was brought forcibly home to him that it was Claire more than anyone whom he missed. He promised himself that as soon as the rush was over he would buy a big box of flowers and run out to her place, and maybe even coax her to find some business in New York so that they could have dinner again at the Chardas.

On Thursday night, sheer exhaustion forced him to knock off at eight o'clock. He went through the plant for a last check-up before leaving, then grabbed his coat and hat and ran out to his car. He had one thought in mind, to have a shower, a big bowl of crackers and hot milk, and fall into bed.

As he crossed the parking lot toward the shed under which his car stood, he heard someone call, "Mark! Mark! Is that you?"

He wheeled, unable to see anyone in the dark, but instantly recognizing Claire's voice. Then he saw her, standing in the shadows near the shed. He recognized the outlines of her tweed coat and saw her red boots with the fur tops.

"Claire," he said, hurrying over to her, "what are you doing here?"

"I'm sorry to bother you," she said. "I've been waiting in my car two hours. I've got to talk to you, Mark. It's very important." He took her arm and felt her shivering under the heavy tweed. Her teeth were chattering.

"Hey, you can't do this to yourself," he said. "This is no good. Come on, we'll get some hot food into you."

"No," she said. "There isn't time. We mustn't be seen together."

"What's the matter?" he asked. "What happened?"

"That's what I came here for," she replied. "To tell you all about it."

He walked to her car where she had left it near the entrance to the parking lot and they both got in.

"I don't dare drive you out to my house," she said. "I think it's being watched."

"Watched!" He twisted around in surprise. "Say, what is this?"

"Where can we go?" she asked. "I'm freezing and it's too cold to sit here, but where can we go?"

"Drive along the river," he said tersely. His mind was racing ahead, figuring out what he thought might have happened—Claire afraid to take him out to her place, waiting here for him for two hours in the cold—"There's a little restaurant down there by the water. Run by a Polish family. Strictly for people we don't know. The food isn't bad."

"Are you sure no one we know will see us?" she asked.

"Not unless you know someone who speaks Polish."

"But what about men who work in the plant? Won't there be some of them there?"

"Not this time on a Thursday night. Friday night, yes, it could happen. They're all home with their families and television."

She drove as he directed, but he could see the tenseness in her movements. She was following his directions with her body but her mind was on whatever she had to tell him.

The restaurant he was taking her to was called Turn-of-the-River, and it was tucked away on a wharf that jutted out into the Pontatuck River.

"You were right about not seeing anyone here," she said as they walked into the plainly decorated place with dingy booths, finding one for themselves at the back. "There's not only no one we know. There's no one at all."

For a moment, her sense of humor returned and she smiled. When a tired-looking woman in a soiled apron came for their order, Claire said she wanted just coffee, but Mark felt hungry and wanted bacon and eggs.

"Better bring the coffeepot along," he said to the woman. "We're going to want a lot of it."

As he looked at Claire, her face twisted into a fixed smile, he could not help thinking how different tonight was from their dinner parties at the Miramar and the Chardas. This place, with its ghastly décor, jarred Mark's already raveled nerves. The food was well cooked and the kitchen clean, but he had never lost his distaste for ugliness learned during the bleak years of his boyhood.

Claire waited until she had drunk half her coffee before she began talking. She glanced toward the kitchen to be sure the door was closed and the waitress nowhere in sight.

"I don't know where to begin," she said to Mark. She paused, drawing one of her hands across her forehead in a gesture of confusion.

"It's been a nightmare of a day, Mark," she said. Then, "I thought twice about coming to you tonight, knowing how busy you are, but I felt this was something you should know. For your protection as well as mine."

"If it's something that's hurt you, I want to know about it."

He had never seen her so upset. The surface poise was still there and she appeared almost the same Claire as always, so that a stranger might not have known about the inner struggle. Mark knew about it. He had known this woman a long time, from girlhood, and he had long ago learned to read the nuances of her emotions even as she had done with him. Something had happened today to touch a wellspring deep within her. She had been hurt—badly hurt.

"Tell me the whole thing, Claire," he said. "What touches you, touches me."

"I was called to the superintendent of school's office early this morning." As she talked she gathered some crumbs that had dropped from his plate of toast and rolled them together in a mound in front of her. "There's nothing unusual about that. I have to report to him every couple of weeks anyway. I thought perhaps he wanted to change the schedule of plays for the schools. So I wasn't prepared for what followed."

"What did follow?" Mark asked.

She managed a feeble smile. "The moment I entered Mr. Cameron's office, I knew something was wrong. I knew intuitively, if you know what I mean."

"I know."

"He acted ill at ease, and while he's usually very smooth, today he was testy and abrupt. He asked me to sit down, but he didn't talk to me at first, just kept straightening the things on his desk. Finally he said something about liking the way I'd taken hold of a new job quickly, that I'd got good results with the young people. Then he switched to what was really on his mind. Some talk had been getting around about my relations with one of the men in the community. A married man. Of course he didn't believe a word of it, but he thought he ought to, well, not exactly warn me, that was too strong a word, but he ought to let me know about the rumors. They were getting stronger. In fact, yesterday someone had come to his office to speak to him about me, about me and this married man."

"Did he mention any names?" Mark asked. "Because if he did that's defamation of character."

"No," she said. "No names. He didn't even make any accusations. It was all put to me on the basis of rumor. Mr. Cameron said he didn't believe a word of it himself and that his natural inclination would have been to ignore the whole thing, but on having given it his serious consideration—that's the way he put it, Mark, *on having given it his serious consideration—*

he thought he ought to talk to me about it. 'Forewarned is fore-armed' was his final remark."

She smiled ruefully. "You know Mr. Cameron?"

"Not very well. I've met him at a few public affairs. He made no special impression."

"That's just it. He's a colorless little man, thin and pinched-looking with a smooth tongue and no backbone. A clever politician, I suspect, playing both ends against the middle. I also suspect he believes every word of what he heard and has given free rein to his imagination. Of course everything he said was supposed to be in the friendliest manner. You know, I-am-your-best-friend-and-feel-I-must-tell-you. Actually, he was warning me, Mark. He was telling me in the plainest language he could use that I'd better watch my step if I don't want to be asked to resign."

"He told you someone came to him yesterday and talked to him about you and me."

"About me and some man. No names, Mark."

Mark let his fork clatter against his plate. "If I thought Nina would do such a thing to you—"

"It wasn't your wife, Mark."

"Did he tell you who it was?"

"Certainly not. But Nina wouldn't do it. Believe me, I know. She's too proud. She would never do a thing like that because of what it would do to her."

"You're right," he said. Then suddenly he knew who had done it. "Evelyn!" he exclaimed. "Evelyn Watrous. Nina's sister."

"Would she do a thing like that without first consulting Nina?"

"You bet she would."

"But her own sister."

"Her own sister!" Mark laughed. "Evelyn has always been jealous of Nina. Nina is more beautiful and she's stronger.

Evelyn's afraid of her, and when you're afraid of someone, you don't love them."

"What a dreadful family," Claire said.

Mark laughed grimly. "You don't know the half of it."

He turned back to his food, but now he did not eat it with the hunger he had felt when he came in here. He drank his coffee slowly, sipping it, and staring across the room at the garish wallpaper, not even conscious of its ugliness.

"What are we going to do?" Claire asked. He had to ask her to repeat the question. "What are we going to do, Mark?" she asked again.

"I don't know," he said. "I honestly don't know."

"I know what I'm going to do. I mean right now, in the immediate future."

"What?"

"Next week, we have our vacation break—we have the eight-weeks system here, every eight weeks we get a week off. I'm going away, Mark, where I can think things through."

"Where are you going?" he asked.

"Don't you think it would be better for both of us if you didn't know?"

"I don't think so at all. Where are you going?" The thought of losing Claire even for a week or ten days was more difficult to bear than the news she had told him about the danger to both their reputations.

"I've decided not to tell you, Mark. Please don't coax because it won't do any good."

"Tell me one thing," he said. "Are you going up there to him? To New Hampshire?"

She smiled again, with the same mocking curl at the corner of her mouth.

"You're jealous," she said.

"Yes, I'm jealous. Are you going to him?"

"No," she said, "I'm not."

The tension eased for him. "But you won't tell me where."

"Why should I?" she said. "You've got to stay away from me. Promise me you will."

"I can't promise that," he said. "I'll promise to try, but I can't promise I will. That's a big order and I'm not sure I can fill it." She turned away from him and he knew what she was thinking. "All right, I'm being selfish. I'm not thinking of what this is doing to you."

"I didn't say that, Mark."

"No, but I'm saying it. Well, you're wrong. I'm thinking about you more than you realize, Claire. But not to keep you here in this tight little hole of a town where you'll rot away. I'm beginning to think Bradford isn't big enough for us, Claire. Too many things have happened here. Too many things I don't like and won't stand for any more."

Chapter 20

CLAIRE WAS EVEN BETTER THAN HER WORD. SHE HAD GIVEN Mark to understand that she would leave early Monday morning. On Saturday, he stayed close to his job until late afternoon, knocked off around six o'clock and drove out to Greencrest with the intention of calling Claire.

He knew he had promised to try to stay away from her, but he felt there was no harm in telephoning to find out how she was. If she hinted, however slightly, that it would be comforting to talk with him, he'd use that as an excuse for running over to her house.

She did not answer the phone when he called and, curious, he drove out Easton Road to find out what was going on. Her house was dark. When he knocked, there was no barking response from her dog. She had gone. The very air of desertion about the place told him that. She had left before he could persuade her to tell him where she was going.

The prospect of spending an entire Saturday night in the house on Turkey Hill with a silent, brooding Nina did not appeal to him. Nina had made it plain to him in many ways that she was self-sufficient. Now that their earlier attempts to mend the break between them had failed, they had fallen into the habit of going their own ways. They ate together when Mark was home. They still shared the big double bedroom on the second floor, but it was a token gesture, maintained by two people who had seen the sparks die out between them. Nina had withdrawn her love from him somewhere along the line; the exact day, the exact night when she had ceased to reach out for him was lost in the dramatic and unhappy chain of events that had taken place since the memorable Bradford Thanksgiving party.

They were husband and wife in name only and sometimes he wondered which of them was more hurt and frightened by this fact, Nina or himself.

So, with the intolerable prospect of a dull evening, full of silent tension, he turned his back on Bradford and drove along the shore, purposely taking the route he and Claire had gone over on that evening at the Miramar.

He was going back there again to find the presence of Claire. She would not be there, but the memory of her smile and her voice and her laughter would be there, and these he wanted tonight more than he had ever wanted anything in his life.

The Bertinis were delighted to see him again and they ushered him to his favorite booth, the one he had shared with Claire. He ordered Italian food tonight, antipasto, veal parmegiano, salad, and coffee. The Bertinis were solicitous while he ate his dinner and listened to the Italian songs played by the two Bertinis on the piano and accordion, but it was not the same as that other evening.

The impulse to come here, hoping that he might find the shadow of Claire lurking somewhere in this place, had been a foolish one. She was not here. No tiniest vestige of her was here. She was too alive, too much in motion to leave the ghost of her anywhere. He, of all people, should have known that.

When the pianist, thinking to do something pleasant for their favored guest, began to play the songs Claire had asked for that other time, Mark could not stand it. To have the memory of those golden days with her forced upon him like this, and not to have Claire herself, was more than he could bear. As soon as he could, and as tactfully, he asked for his bill and left the Bertinis and the Miramar behind him.

He rode along the shore in agitated depression. Suddenly nothing was right with his world. These weeks of uncertainty and restlessness were crystallized in his mind at last. He felt unhappy and unwanted, with a tremendous sense of not belonging, of having failed. This was not like him, he told himself. All his life he had been reaching up to become the Mark Galloway he now was. All his life he had wanted and worked for the position, the prestige, the wealth, the importance, the power he now theoretically had. Yet he felt no sense of its belonging to him or of his belonging to it. It left him with a tastelessness he had once experienced after a severe cold, when nothing, not even the most delectable food, tasted like anything in his mouth.

Tantalus has nothing on me, he thought. Everything in sight and nothing within reach. Me, I've got everything in the palm of my hand and I still haven't got it.

Maybe something's happening to me, maybe my nerves are shot, what with the accelerated program at the plant and all this family stuff and Nina withdrawing from me and my being responsible for Claire's trouble with the school superintendent and then having her run away from me.

He recalled a period during the war when after the strain of days of unrelieved flying, he had almost gone to pieces. He remembered what that had been like, extreme irritability at first, then fits of blazing temper, then sudden rushes of heat throughout his body so that he seemed to be on fire, then a cold sweat. He became obsessed with trifles. A slight word passed by someone was cause for indignant offense. His mind was never free, but held in bondage to anxiety in one form or another.

The very thought of that agonizing period set up a reaction

in him now. He had closed his mind to it, shut it out, never went back over it, because at the time he had believed he was coming close to a crack-up.

Tonight the remembrance of that time was so strong that it forced out everything else, Nina, Claire, the upsets at Bradford Tool, the insecurity and failure he felt even at the peak of his success.

He was suddenly full of fear. It was a nameless fear, an un-identifiable one. He could not put his finger on any one thing, and say, Here, this is what I am afraid of. He knew only that he was terrified of something nameless and unseen, of life itself perhaps, of its uncertainty and meaninglessness. He felt the wheel swerve beneath his hands and he pulled off the road into a wide shoulder, slamming on the brakes.

He hunched over the wheel, limp, first feeling a rush of heat, then of cold pass over him. He shivered, pulling up the collar of his coat, in a futile effort to keep warm.

How long he sat there shivering in the grip of this nameless fear, he did not know. It could not have been more than a few moments, but it seemed much longer. A few cars flashed by, lighting up the road, but for the most part, he sat paralyzed in the darkness surrounding him.

The emotion was gone as it had come, with startling sudden-ness. He felt drowsy, but he shook himself and, pulling out a handkerchief, wiped the cold sweat from his face. He had to get out of here, to get off this road and back to something familiar. He had a great urgent longing to find something familiar to cling to, something familiar to see and touch. He wanted to talk to someone and Jason would be the only one he could seek out. He broke all speed laws in his pell-mell race back to Bradford because in the face of these inner complexi-ties, man-made laws seemed to lose their validity.

He felt for that dreadful three-quarters of an hour that it took him to get back to something as familiar as his home town like a man alone in the world, beyond the reach of human touch, of human sympathy, or human laws. Only his own ego stood forth, naked and distressed, reaching for something outside itself, for exactly what he had no true concept, but for something that would shelter him from that devastating emotion of fear that had swept over him.

He found the street on which Jason lived, Church Lane, and turned down it, slowing his speed at last. Jason's study was dark, but as Mark went up the walk, he could see through the bay window on which the shades were only partly drawn. Jason was in the living room reading a book and his wife, Charlotte, was doing some kind of handwork, knitting or crocheting. He could see her look up and smile at Jason and say something and saw Jason put his finger in his book to answer and smile back.

Mark hesitated. He had no notion of disturbing Jason's tranquil domesticity and yet his own need was so imperative that he could not turn back. For a moment, with his hand on the bell, he paused. Then he pressed the button and listened to the chimes echo through the house.

Jason came quickly. He opened the door and pulled Mark into the lighted hallway. Then as he grasped the meaning of the expression on Mark's face, he said, "We'll go to my study."

"I don't want to interrupt," Mark began. "I don't want to bother anyone."

"You never have bothered anyone," Jason said. The words themselves were so kindly and the tone in which they were spoken so gentle that Mark drew back from them.

Jason led the way, lighting up his study. The brightness was a welcoming gesture.

"Sit down, Mark," he said, dropping into his own favorite chair.

Mark slumped down across from him but not for long. He jumped up and paced restlessly, stopping at the library table to finger the books.

"I can't sit still," he said in apology. "I don't know why, but I just can't."

"Had supper?" Jason asked.

"Yes. Hours ago. I'm not hungry." It wasn't hours ago, but it seemed so.

"I thought maybe with Nina away, you weren't eating."

Mark stopped, wheeling on him. "Nina away?"

Jason looked disturbed. "Didn't you know?" Mark shook his head. "I'm sorry," Jason went on. "Charlotte had to call her up for a donation for the fair and your maid, what's her name, Effie, said Nina had taken Ginger away for the week's holiday." Jason was looking into the fireplace. "I'm sorry if I've broken some news I shouldn't have. But I thought that was why you came over. Because of loneliness."

Mark walked over and looked into the black emptiness of the fireplace. One evening last fall he had stood here and looked into a blazing fire. He had come that night to talk about Nina and him. It was he who had run away from Nina that night, walking out on her during a quarrel. Now tonight Jason had just told him something he should have found out in some other way, that Nina had taken Ginger away.

This plan must have been in Nina's head for a long time. Yet she had never breathed a word to Mark. She had not even called him up at the plant to say good-by. Maybe she had just left word with Effie, the way she left instructions about what meat to order for the day's meals, what vegetables and salad greens and groceries and flowers. Perhaps she had left a note, one of Nina's terse Yankee notes that said nothing. He had never had a real love letter from her, not even during the years when they were madly in love and he was overseas and she was back here bearing his first child for him. Her letters had been bleak little affairs, but he had cherished them because they were all he had of her and because he had felt their coldness belied her warmth. He knew that she was not readily demonstrative, that she would not reveal her complete feelings in a letter any more than she would show her affection in a public place. Formerly he had found this reticence appealing because he knew she could be warmly responsive. He forgave her her inarticulateness, sometimes even teasing her for being thrifty, in true Yankee fashion, even with her words.

So, even at best, all that awaited him in the darkened house on Turkey Hill were a few sentences from Nina, brief, untelling sentences, written in an admirable hand, tall and bold and individualistic, a beautiful hand for so cold a message.

"She should have told me," he said. "But she wanted to hurt me and she chose this way to do it."

"What's wrong with you and Nina, Mark?" Jason asked.

It was the same question that Claire had asked on Christmas Eve when he had kissed her.

What's wrong with you and Nina, Mark?

And he gave Jason the same answer.

"I don't know for sure, unless it's that we're falling out of love."

He tried to talk to Jason. He had come here for that one purpose, and yet when he tried to put his thoughts into words, the words would not come. The shock of Nina's running off like that without a word, without so much as a good-by, coming as it did on the heels of his recent upheaval, left him numb and speechless.

"I can't talk about it, Jason," he said. "I came here tonight to talk to you, and now I can't open up. Let me come back again some other time."

Jason did not urge him to find words when no words would come, but he walked out with him to the car. Throwing a topcoat over his shoulders, he sat a few moments in the car with Mark before he drove off.

Mark drove into the night, not seeing the things around him. Back there on the shore road, he had felt a compulsion to drive back to something familiar. Now that he was here, there was only that numbing sense of loneliness.

Almost without thinking, he turned his car toward the far end of town where he had lived as a boy. Down River Street, between the rows of plain little tenements, he made his way. There were a few changes. The houses were older and even more impoverished-looking than they had seemed to him as a boy. Time and the evolution of human thought had brought about changes that only added to the general ugliness. There was a machine shop on the ground floor of one of the buildings, an automobile repair shop in another, a few stores, a pizzeria, a newspaper shop.

It was a long street that wound its way in sinuous reluctance toward the river, ending abruptly in an abandoned wharf and some mud flats.

Mark pulled in near the wharf and shut off the engine.

This is what I came from, he thought. From this. Then, as he sat there in the dark, his mind, still disturbed from the events of the evening, did a treacherous thing to him. It went back to River Street as he had known it years ago and it carried Mark along, pushing him, protesting, into what he had known and what he had been.

The street was no longer drab and colorless. It was alive with activity. Kids everywhere, sprawling over doorsteps and on sagging porches, spilling out into the road. Young men and old men, young women and old women. Babies crying. The self-conscious laughter of young lovers. It was not winter, but summer. Somehow or other, his memory always reconstructed his boyhood in summertime, perhaps because summer had been more fun, or perhaps because summer had brought Claire to him.

There was, strangely enough, no poverty in this scene from memory. There was plenty besides the sounds of the street. Smells by the carload. Heat, the humid, oppressive heat that rolled in from the river, and the aromas of a hundred different dinners cooking on stoves in hot kitchens—poor people had not learned the luxury of cool meals on hot days and everyone believed that "a hot meal is good for you, no matter how warm the weather gets."

The Italians cooked their spaghetti sauces and lasagna, and the Germans, their sauerbraten and sauerkraut, and the Hungarians, their stuffed cabbage, and those who were just Americans cooked what they wished. The smell of sweat mingled with the smell of food, and then there was the smell of babies, and of cheap perfume on the girls who were waiting for their boy friends, and the ever-present smell of fish and garlic. And, of course, there was the smell of the river and the mud flats. Some of this was distasteful or offensive to the young Mark, but he never thought of rebelling outwardly. He had always known he would come out of it. He had always felt it was a temporary stopping place for him on a journey up.

That had been the wonderful thing about River Street, there was no place to go but UP. You looked forward, you planned, you reached out, you knew the time would eventually come. And it had come, with lightning rapidity. It had come through his job at the Bradford plant.

No, if he were going to be honest, it had come through Nina. Nina Bradford. Nina herself knew it. She had told him this in that first angry quarrel last autumn. All those early years of their marriage stretched back of him now in a haze of self-delusion. Nina was right. He knew that now. It had been a bitter pill to swallow, but he had managed to get it down at last. He was where he was and what he was because Nina had pointed her finger at him, put her Bradford mark upon him, lifted him up. Up out of River Street that wound its serpentine way down to the mud flats.

Up, up, up, until he was the Mark Galloway Nina wanted

him to be, the Mark Galloway he had thought he wanted to be, himself.

Nina had declared that it was she who had built him up.

Nina was now bent on tearing him down. For what purpose he could not tell except that presumably she no longer loved him. He felt it. The thought was as dark as the blackness around him tonight on River Street. The murkiness of the river flats, the gripping cold, the acrid smells of the neighborhood oppressed him. He felt the tentacles of River Street reaching out for him.

Then his depression was replaced by sudden anger. Nina had no right to despise him. True, his marriage to her had been a short cut to success. But he had never viewed it in that light. He would have got to the top anyway. If not at Bradford Tool, somewhere else. He hadn't had to marry Nina Bradford to reach the top. He had his own potentialities, his own true worth.

Nina was wrong about him. She had always been wrong. She had placed too great a value on the hand she had reached out to him on the way up.

Claire was different. She had him figured out. It was Claire all along who had realized his worth.

I need Claire, he thought. If I can get to her and talk with her, it will help. I can talk to Claire more easily than to Jason. Claire's a woman. She loves me. More than I've ever needed anything, I need to feel that someone loves me.

Right now he wanted something hot to drink to take away this clammy cold that moved in from the river. He started the car and drove over to an all-night restaurant on the street.

Parking close to the curb, he flung himself out of the car and without bothering to lock it hurried in. All at once he felt that nothing he owned was important enough to put under lock and key.

The restaurant, once he was inside, was surprisingly clean

236

and cheerful. Czechs, he thought, glancing at the triangular faces of the two waiters behind the counter. He sat on a stool and hunched over the counter.

"Coffee," he said. "Good and hot. And one of those." He pointed to a plate of pastry.

"Cold out," the man commented as he set Mark's coffee in front of him and slid one of the buns on a plate.

"Yes," Mark said, shoveling the sugar into his cup.

"You new around here?" the man asked in a friendly tone.

Mark looked up at him, stared into the man's face, then let his eyes rove around at the polished coffee urns, the stacks of cups and saucers and plates, the glass cases with doughnuts and cookies, before he answered.

"In a way I am, and in a way I'm not."

It was the man's turn to stare at him, and this he did with penetrating directness.

Mark felt an impulse to shock this friendly stranger. He might never see the man again and it would give him a certain relief from the burden of the moment.

"I was born here," he said, in a chatty tone. "I was raised here, lived here as a kid." He jerked his thumb toward River Street. "Played baseball and marbles and raised general Cain out there. I fell in love here, too, for the first time in my life."

The man was staring harder, in fixed amazement, and Mark, pleased with the effect he was creating, went on.

"But I wanted to get out of here, you understand." He stirred his coffee hard as he spoke. "I wanted to be someone important. So I got out, and I guess you'd say I got my wish about being important too. But I did it the easy way. I didn't realize it at the time but now I do. Never do anything the easy way, brother. It doesn't pay. You find you've got to do it all over again."

He gulped down his coffee, shoved the untouched bun away from him, and slapped down fifty cents on the counter.

"Keep the change," he said to the waiter. He got up and started for the door, then turned upon the astonished man.

"Am I new around here?" He threw back his head and laughed. "Listen, once upon a time, I could walk up and down this street and name every family living in every house, every house full of garlic and stuffed cabbage and babies and sweat and noise. Noise! Brother, you should have heard the noise on a hot summer night!" Mark laughed again, and shook his head. "Am I new around here! That's funny. That's a whole lot funnier than you realize." He shook a finger in the man's face. "In fact, you'll never, never know how funny that really is."

Chapter 21

HE WAKED UP SUNDAY MORNING IN AN EMPTY HOUSE WHERE he felt a stranger. From the moment he got up he knew that he was going to find Claire. He was pretty sure she was at Great Barrington. She had given her word that she was not running off to New Hampshire to join David Wakefield. Where else would she go for a winter holiday but the nearest good skiing country?

By the easy expedient of telephoning every ski lodge in the neighborhood, he would have his answer. He had breakfast by himself, in the sun-filled breakfast room, with Effie serving, and in the anticipation of seeing Claire soon, he enjoyed his wheat cakes and bacon.

He packed a few things in an overnight bag and took it out to his car. Then he came back to the kitchen and told Effie not to count on him for meals the rest of the day. He would, he told himself, telephone her from somewhere along the road if he planned not to return that evening.

He was more quickly successful in locating Claire than he had expected he would be. His first call at a corner drugstore revealed the fact that she was staying at the Skyline Lodge.

"Yes, Miss Claire Elliott is registered here. She's on the ski slopes at present, but if you wish we could get a message to her."

"No," he said to the operator almost too quickly. "No message, please. Just cancel the call." At least I know where Claire is now, he thought with relief.

The ride to Great Barrington was a pleasant one. Last night seemed like a dream from which he had awakened to a world in which there was at least some hope. He took his time. The trip to Great Barrington could be made in three hours. He knew something of the habits of skiers and he figured Claire might return to the lodge around one o'clock for lunch.

He thought once, but quite comprehensively, about the consequences of what he was doing. There was no immediate danger to either Claire or himself. Nina was away. She had left of her own free will, and she had left without even discussing her plans with Mark. The note from her which was tucked into the folds of his wallet said, *Dear Mark, Ginger and I both need a change. We're going south for ten days. The address where you can reach me is attached to this note. Effie will see that all is in order for you. Love, Nina.*

Rereading it last night in his study, he had thought, Where is the warm and vibrant girl I married? Where is the devoted woman I picked up in my arms and carried across the threshold of this home of ours?

Bleak and proper—you could not call her note anything else. Oh, very proper. No recriminations, no emotion, not the tiniest spark of fire between the lines. *I am going away. I will be in such-and-such a place. Your house will be in order while I am gone.*

Dear Mark. I'm not your dear any more, he thought. You know that as well as I.

Aside from Nina's absence, there was Effie to think about, but he had already telephoned her, at a dog wagon where he stopped for coffee, and told her that he had suddenly decided to take a long ride, and he might not be home tonight. If it developed that he did not come home for two nights, or three,

Effie might think he'd taken a vacation too. Nina, by going away, had left the door wide open for Mark to do likewise.

He thought about who might see him together with Claire at Great Barrington and decided the chance of their running into anyone they knew was very slim. Claire had told him that she had never met anyone from Bradford or the surrounding towns. Bradford had few ardent skiers. A few families went up to the nearby slopes but their skiing was in a class with playing a game of softball in the corner sand lot. He knew of no one else in Bradford who would, like Claire, travel miles for the pleasure of a long downhill run.

There were no real risks in what he was doing except that which might lie within Claire and himself. That risk was a calculated one.

When he reached the Skyline Lodge, he was surprised to find it so huge and sprawling. He had stayed at a skier's inn once in New Hampshire. It had been a small place, quaint and old-fashioned with two small dining rooms, together no bigger than his living room on Turkey Hill, with no elevator service. He had been obliged to climb to the top floor on a narrow stairway and his room had been charming, with an old-fashioned wood stove to give added warmth during bitter cold weather.

The Skyline was vast and modern, with a St. Moritz air, and a St. Moritz gaiety about it. There was music everywhere he turned, in the lounge, in the outdoor terrace where some hardy skiers were eating their lunch from a buffet set up there. The lobby was decorated in ultramodern fashion, with lounge chairs so big a man might lose himself in their depths and with impressionistic murals done in what were to Mark terrifying shades of coral and chartreuse and olive green. Fresh flowers beckoned from tall vases on every conceivable flat surface in the big room. The cavernous stone fireplace, constructed of massive slabs of rock, was blazing away and a few lazy skiers in checked shirts and slacks lounged in front of it.

Mark did not register at the desk immediately. He knew better than to do that without first finding Claire and seeing how angry she would be with him for coming after her.

She was not in any of the three dining rooms. Someone at the desk suggested Miss Elliott might be on the terrace with the sun-worshipers who were having sandwiches and coffee, but Mark could not find her. She failed to answer the insistent telephone call to her room.

Then another clerk brightly suggested the waxing room. "Skiers go there sometimes after lunch to wax an extra pair of skis for the next day's run."

Mark had never heard of a waxing room, but he soon learned that it was a tomblike stone cave, deep in the basement, where skiers were encouraged to leave their equipment. And it was in these somewhat sinister surroundings that Mark found Claire, her red head bent over a pair of skis. He heard her laugh roll out as she chatted with a fellow skier. He stood there a moment and watched her, knowing that once she saw him, she would react one way or another, and he would perhaps lose her as she was now.

She was free. The strain which he had seen in her face as she had sipped her coffee in the Turn-of-the-River Restaurant was gone. She had thrown off the worry over that nasty interview with Mr. Cameron. She had laughter on her lips and in her eyes and everything about her bespoke that exulting freedom for which he most loved her.

Gallant spirit, he thought. Nothing from the outside will ever succeed in breaking it.

She turned suddenly, as if she felt his thought, and her face told him what he wanted most to know, because there was only joy in it when she saw him. After that quick changes of mood followed: amazement, concern, bewilderment, annoyance. But the joy had come first.

She walked slowly over to him, dropping her skis against the wall as she moved his way.

"This is something you should never have done," were the first words she spoke, low, so low that he could barely hear them. "Let's get out of here, where we can be alone. If there is such a place in this big city of a hotel."

"I haven't had lunch," he said. "What about you?"

"I've eaten, but that's an idea. They'll bring sandwiches and drinks to the club lounge. It's usually deserted in early afternoon."

The club lounge was smaller than the main lounge. Paneled in knotty pine, with small low tables spread about between club chairs, it had the appearance of a large living room. English hunt scenes and scarlet draperies of heavy monk's cloth gave warmth and color to the place.

"This is better than all that elegance." He nodded toward the main lounge.

"I know," she said, "but lots of people like a splash. I prefer this too."

"At least then we're starting in accord," he said, smiling at her as the waiter came to take his order. "I'm not sure of what's to follow."

When the waiter had left, he said, "All right. Let me have the scolding I deserve."

"It's no use to scold any man," she retaliated. "They all do what they want." There was no malice in her voice, only a kind of amused tolerance, and the early annoyance she had shown when she realized what he had done was already gone.

"Aren't you angry?" he said. "If you're not, I'm disappointed."

"Yes, I'm angry. I was at first. But anger is such a devastating emotion to indulge. I'd rather save my energy for the ski slopes."

"Aren't you even going to let me talk about it, to explain why I came here?"

"If you like."

He told her about last night, about finding out that she had gone sooner than she had planned, about his frustrated attempt to recapture her presence at the Miramar, about his learning from Jason that Nina had left without a word to him and then how he had driven back to River Street to find, if he could, that sense of belonging and how he had almost found it.

He did not tell her about the attack that had gripped him on the shore road back from the Miramar, or that he had gone to Jason in terror, fearing a return of the malady that afflicted him during the war. Later on, perhaps he could speak about that. But not now.

"How did you know I was here?" she asked, and he told her about the telephone call.

It was only after Mark had finished eating that anything was said about plans for the afternoon. The subject was approached casually by both of them. This very casualness assured Mark that Claire shared with him his unwillingness to separate now that they were together.

Claire had thought of going out to the slopes again. A new cross-country trail had just been opened to skiers and she wanted to explore the first half of it this afternoon. You skied across open country until you reached the halfway mark, a ski hut called Top Kick, and you stopped there for hot food and kept warm until a bus picked you up late in the afternoon.

"I'm not sure I'm a good enough skier for that sort of thing," he said. "But I'd like to have a try at it."

They rented his equipment in the shop run by the hotel management, skis and poles and a complete outfit from cap to boots. The trousers were a little too small—the man in the store kept turning to Claire and saying, "Your husband is such a *big* man, he's hard to fit." Mark checked his clothes with the man, promising to pick them up before nine o'clock when the shop closed.

As they walked out, Claire turned to Mark. "You look so ridiculous in those rented clothes," she said. "Everything's too small except the boots."

"You forget, my dear, that your husband is a big man."

"That was a bad moment," she said. "I thought I'd laugh in the poor clerk's face."

"How would you like a big man for a husband, Claire?"

"I don't know right now," she said. "Sometime, if I ever find a really big man who's free, I'll let you know."

The ski jaunt across country was exactly what Mark needed. Claire insisted on skiing ahead of him, saying she knew this terrain better than he. He followed close behind her and, for a couple of miles, they were the only ones on the trail.

He could not help thinking as he watched the trim figure in the Kelly-green suit ahead of him, her red hair flying out from under her snug-fitting green cap, that this was Claire's element. She belonged out here with all this space, this expanse of white hills rolling away from them on every side.

He was not the skier Claire was and several times she had to whirl around and wait for him as he extricated himself from a gully.

But he kept going, feeling a primitive delight in the struggle to stay on his feet, to stem-turn from the path of an evergreen, to make a terrain jump over a jutting ledge of snow.

This was the kind of conflict he liked, a struggle with a force of nature, out in the open, where a man could keep his eyes on his opponent. It was these inner struggles, these psychological wrestlings between human beings, between human minds and emotions, that he hated. Those were deep, hidden and treacherous, and a man had all he could do to know the truth about what was going on in his own mind, no less someone else's. His own motives were often so amorphous and poorly defined that he was hard put to it to judge the motives of another person whose inner mind, far below the surface of social amenities, was a mystery to him.

Truth, he thought. That's the big question. What is truth? If a human being could come into life fully equipped with truth, how much easier everything would be. Or would it? Truth was dangerous. It was costly. It was so often unwanted by the world. Maybe it was better not to know what it was. No, he couldn't go along with that kind of thinking. Truth, at any price, was desirable.

Strange, how being out here in this blinding brightness, with trees whizzing by and no other human but Claire in sight, strange how much more clearly a man could think. He wasn't afraid up here. That other man who had been huddled over a wheel in a car on the dark road last night wasn't him. This was his true self, this man who could span the heavens in seven-league boots.

They reached the hut called Top Kick. It stood lonely at the foot of a hill where a country road, recently ploughed clear of snow, ran up to meet it.

When they pushed open the door, there was no one inside.

"Hey, I thought you said there'd be someone here to give us hot food," Mark said to Claire.

"No, I said we could *get* some hot food here. Get it ourselves." She walked over to a row of cupboards. "The management of the hotel keeps this place equipped. What would you like, hot tea, soup, coffee?"

"What about water?" he said.

"We use melted snow for that." She smiled. "A little too rugged for you, Mark?"

"Not for me!"

They built up the fire, embers of which were still glowing

from the party of skiers that had been here before them. They made some soup and tea and found a box of crackers among the supplies. For a half hour they sat around the fire and talked about the things that were closest to both of them. Claire told him about her Christmas visit on David Wakefield's farm.

"There's a simplicity about that way of life, Mark. A simplicity and a kindliness about those people up there. They're strong, not as you and I are strong, with a callous resistance we've built up from fighting our way ahead. Theirs is a more quiet strength that doesn't have to hurt anyone to hold its own."

"Did he ask you to marry him?" She looked away from him. "He did. He did ask you to marry him."

"What if he did, Mark? What concern can it possibly be of yours?"

"Have you accepted him?"

"That's none of your business, Mark."

"It is my business. Everything that concerns you is my business, Claire."

She walked away from him, busying herself with the bindings of her skis where they were propped against the wall.

"You're a funny man," she said. "I should be angry at your arrogance. But I'm not angry. I'm amused." She whirled on him and despite her words her eyes were full of fire. "Years ago you could have had me. Now for some perverse reason you think I still belong to you."

"It's not a perverse reason, Claire. It's a highly logical one. You and I are mates. We belong together."

"That's no way to talk to me."

"How would you have me talk to you then? Like one adolescent to another? In terms of moonlight and roses and romance? You and I are realists. We've always faced everything head on, even little things. When so big a thing as this hits us, what are we going to do about it? Talk in sentimental riddles?"

She came over to him. "Yes, we're realists. Sure, we've always faced things head on, but this isn't realism you're talking to me. There's another word for it. Not a very nice word and I don't want to have to use it." With angry movements she started to clean up the hut before they left. "The bus will be here in another ten minutes," she said. "When we get back to the Skyline, I think you'd better leave right away."

His manner softened, his voice lowered. "Don't make me leave you now, Claire," he said. "I'm sorry if I sounded harsh, but I had to talk that way or I couldn't have said the things that were on my mind. Only in harshness can I convince myself I mean them."

He turned her around. "I'm really sorry. You're right. I should have made up my mind years ago what I could do without and what I couldn't. But you can't hold a mistake against a man all his life. So I made a mistake. Listen, last night out on the shore road, something happened to me. It's a hard thing to describe. I don't suppose I could tell a single other woman about it."

She was changed now too. The resentment and agitation had left her and she seemed full of understanding, as she had always been.

"Mark, what's troubling you?"

As best he could, he told her what had happened last night. "I've had these spells before," he said, "during the war. But then when I came back to Nin—when I came back to Bradford and got busy, they didn't return. I never thought of them." He threw up his hands. "I can't make it out," he said. "They leave me gutted out. I've always thought that if I had a big enough one, I'd crack up under it."

"It's nerves," she said. "And nerves are fear."

"Fear! But what have I got to be afraid of? When you come right down to it, I've got everything I need. I've got all the money I want. More than I can use if I live to be a hundred and eight."

Claire looked at him and then walked away, picking up her ski cap and mittens where she had tossed them on a chair.

"We ought to be getting ready to leave," she said. "The bus is due any minute."

He was close to her. "Let me stay with you, Claire. I need you. You're the only one I've got to talk to."

"You can't stay here with me, Mark."

"Look," he said, "out there this afternoon on the ski trail I was a different man. A new man. No, not a new man. I was myself. The real me. I felt big and generous and immortal." She turned sharply. "Don't laugh at me. I mean it, I felt immortal. The way Jason is always talking. You know how he talks about man in the image and likeness of God. Well, that's the way I felt up there in the hills this afternoon. Let me stay here until I've had a chance to find myself. If you don't want to see much of me, you won't have to."

"You can't stay at Skyline Lodge while I'm there, Mark. It would be madness. For you. For me. It would never work out."

"There must be some other place around here I can stay."

"What about your work? What about the factory?"

The questions slapped at him, stinging him into the realization of what he was planning to do. Claire was right. What about his work and the factory? But the impulse that had made him come here in the beginning made him reckless about his work too. He was fed up on Bradford Tool, on Spencer and Frank Muthersbaugh and the whole tribe of Bradfords.

"I'm fed up," he told her. "I can't stand it another week. I've got to have a vacation. Only a few days. A few days can make a world of difference. I can go back Wednesday."

She turned her back but, as she looked out the window, she said, "The bus is coming," and then, as they went to the door, with their skis over their shoulders, she said, "There's a small place down the road a few miles. It's called the Mountain Inn. Sometimes it takes the overflow from bigger places around here. It's not new, not very attractive, but it would at least be a safe place for you to stay."

Chapter 22

THE PARKING LOT OF BRADFORD TOOL WAS ALMOST EMPTY when Steve Emrich turned his four-year-old Ford into it. He drove past the sheds reserved for the Bradford family and felt a familiar sting of irritation. Those sheds annoyed him. It was a funny quirk in his nature that amused him even while he was experiencing the irritation.

Of all the things he might have been annoyed at in the Bradfords! Their inbreeding policies, their stubbornness and selfishness, their clannish family traits in business although privately they seemed to despise each other, their overpowering wealth and snobbishness. None of these things bothered Steve. They were remote factors that did not touch him. But having to drive past a well-built row of sheds over which each Bradford had his name painted in yellow, this was something to rile a man.

Men in the factory thought he should be incensed because Frank Muthersbaugh had been imported to edge him out of the job of chief engineer. They said the job rightly belonged to Steve. They said it was a shame.

Steve wasn't incensed. He didn't care whether the job rightly belonged to him or not. If it was a shame, so be it. The shame was on the Bradfords' heads, not his. It would have been nice to have the extra money, but it would not have been so very much more than he was getting now. The Bradfords were willing to pay the Bradfords. They paid somewhat more reluctantly when the hand stretched out for the pay check was not fed by arteries of Bradford blood.

What difference did it make in the long run? Maybe the chief engineer job would have been more of a headache than it was worth. He was happy where he was, experimenting in the lab of the shop. He was not a madly ambitious man. He had one ambition in life and that was hardly a mad one. He hoped one day to own his own little machine shop, be his own boss. Anne, his wife, was sure he would. "When you get ready to go into business for yourself, Steve," she said, "I'll stop teaching school and take over the office."

Steve glanced long and hard at the name MR. GALLOWAY in bold yellow letters over Mark's shed.

Mark was a good guy. One of the world's best. It was a shame he had to be mixed up with the Bradfords. But then Mark was ambitious, personally ambitious in a way Steve was not, and maybe he didn't mind the Bradfords so long as he had got where he had. To the top, the very top.

Then again maybe he did mind the Bradfords.

He doesn't seem the same lately, Steve thought. I've noticed a change. Others have noticed it too. He's edgy. Easily upset. Maybe he's finding out the game wasn't worth the candle.

Funny about Mark, the way he had climbed up the ladder. No climbing about it. He just took one long jump and there he was. He was smart, you had to hand it to him. Lucky, too. How many guys that have ever walked through those doors over there could have attracted Nina Bradford? One guy. Mark Galloway. There was only one Mark Galloway.

People said Nina Bradford had been crazy about him, did some of the chasing herself. Steve sat in his car, conjecturing what it would have been like to have a girl with Nina Bradford's looks and money chase after him. The idea didn't excite him. Too beautiful and too much money for comfort. People like that lived in another world, one that wasn't particularly appealing to Steve.

The few times he had met Nina at close range, he hadn't warmed to her, nor she to him for that matter. You felt you had to make the grade with her. People said she had been different in the old days, when she and Mark had been in love with each other.

They weren't in love any more. That was for sure. Whew, what an earful of gossip Anne had brought home from the school she taught in about Mark and Claire Elliott. Steve had told Anne not to blab that kind of stuff around. He remembered with satisfaction his exact words.

"Look, Mark is a friend of mine. He's one swell guy. I don't like that kind of talk anyway. How do you know it's true?"

"Everybody says it is." Anne had flared up in self-defense. "Mark was in love with Claire Elliott long before Nina Bradford set eyes on him. It's just possible he never stopped loving Claire."

"That's the way women talk."

"Maybe women talk that way because it's the way things are."

Steve disliked gossip on general principles. It wasted time. The human equation seldom interested him. He was an engineer. He dealt with facts, with things you could put on paper and then transform into solid material forms. Preoccupation with other people's lives, the fascinating game of poking your finger into something that was none of your business, was sometimes boring, more often disgusting.

So Anne, properly squelched, did not discuss Mark and Claire Elliott again. Others did. The men at the plant had the story too and they were much more graphic in their description of what they thought was going on than Anne had been. Steve wanted to clap his hands over his ears and run every time he heard them tuning up to tell it. Once he had stopped one of the gossipers in the middle of a sentence, changing the subject pointedly.

"Yeah," the man had replied. "Mark Galloway's a friend of yours. I know."

This morning began for Steve in a routine way, much as hundreds of other mornings since he had come here to work. First, he shut off the all-night testing equipment on a new drive unit. He took measurements of wear developing in the moving parts and recorded the results.

Next he picked up inspection reports, looking for flaws and defects in lathes now in production. Sometimes this uncovered useful data for the improvement of new models in his department.

Then he settled down to his baby, a new variable speed drive. This was his kick. He worked with such complete concentration that he lost all sense of time, interrupting himself only when necessary, to give instructions to one of his assistants, Rex Cauldwell. At ten fifteen after repeated reminders Rex got him to quit the job and take his belated coffee break.

He returned at ten thirty and was just about to pick up a socket wrench preparatory to assembling his experimental unit, when the telephone rang. Rex Cauldwell answered it, then turned to Steve and said, "It's for you. Wimbley."

When Steve said "Hello," Art Wimbley's precise accent bellowed. "Steve? That you? Get over here quick. I've got some real trouble to show you." Steve heard the phone slammed down at the other end.

Another morning Steve might have delayed because he was used to getting calls from the superintendent's office. Since Frank Muthersbaugh had taken over as chief engineer, Steve spent much of his time commuting back and forth between the factory and the lab, trying to straighten out the messes Muthersbaugh got into. So Art's S.O.S. was nothing new.

Yet something in his tone as he had said "I've got some real trouble to show you" alerted Steve. This was no ordinary call from Wimbley's office. Something was up.

He traveled the length of the plant, from the lab to Wimbley's office, resisting every temptation to stop for a chat along the way. There were any number of detours he might have taken, especially in the testing department where they were experimenting with a prototype of a new feed mechanism he had been working on. But Art's voice, exasperated in emphasis, pulled him on.

The door of the superintendent's office was almost closed, and as Steve pushed it open, he faced a towering man full of restrained wrath. Steve liked Art Wimbley, for personal as well as business reasons. Art was efficient on the job, and off the job he had a warm human quality that won friends. For a big man, he was gentle; for a gentle man he packed a lot of hidden strength; and for a strong man he was remarkably humble.

Art stood there, staring with ill-concealed disgust at a lathe spindle in his left hand. In his right hand he held a micrometer. Steve glanced from Art to the table before which he stood and recognized the print spread out there. It was a detailed drawing of the spindle.

"This is really something!" Art exclaimed. He pointed to a dimension on the print as he shoved the micrometer toward Steve. "I've got fifty of these parts with both journals made right according to the specifications on the print, all nicely passed by the inspection department, but the print is wrong."

"How did that happen?" Steve asked, already knowing the answer.

"It's that confounded drafting department," Art thundered. "Look. All the prints have nice lines and arrows and the printing is a work of art, but the important part, the dimensions, they don't give a darn about." Art would have brooked no interruption even if Steve had attempted it. Never a patient man, he was almost beside himself with anger and amazement. "Now, what are we going to do about it, that's the question. I'll go up there myself and see the top brass. I'll take my complaint straight across the catwalk this time." His florid face was almost purple and the veins at his temples were swollen with rage. "This ought to fix that jackass Muthersbaugh once and for all with the tribe of Bradfords that put him in."

"They won't blame Muthersbaugh," Steve said quietly. "They'll blame Mark."

Art wheeled around, slapping his forehead with his left hand. "Mark! I forgot about Mark. Where the devil is he anyway?"

"I don't know."

"You've talked with him since Saturday," Art persisted. He pointed toward his desk. "Those factory instructions were dictated by Mark to you over the telephone. You're the only one who's been in touch with him. Where is he?"

"I don't know." The two men looked at each other, their thoughts speaking more forcibly than words. Steve was thinking, I'm telling you the truth, I don't know where he is. I know what you're thinking but it's none of your business. It's none of mine, either. What Mark does is strictly his own affair. If I had a home situation like his, maybe I'd be off somewhere too.

The ringing of the telephone interrupted Steve's thoughts. Art answered with an abrupt "Yes."

"Wimbley speaking, Mr. Bradford," he said. Turning toward Steve, he mouthed the words, "His nibs himself. Spencer." Back at the telephone, he said, "No, I haven't heard from Mr. Galloway. Yes, that's right, I did get some instructions from him. No, I didn't speak with him."

There was a long pause and Art said, "It was Steve Emrich who brought those instructions to me. Yes, he's here with me now. Very well, Mr. Bradford, I'll tell him."

Art hung up and turned with a grimace to Steve. "I had to tell him," he said. "He had us both on the spot. Seems they've been trying to locate Mark since Monday. I got the impression it's a very touchy family matter. Probably hated to admit to us they couldn't find him. I thought it best to tell the truth, Steve. If I tried to cover up that you'd brought in those instructions, they'd have found out some way."

"I take it they want to talk to me," Steve replied.

Art nodded. "Spencer's on his way down now. He said to ask you to wait."

Steve grinned. Strangely enough, he did not feel nervous about the forthcoming encounter with Spencer Bradford. "They must want to know where Mark is pretty badly," he said to Art. "To bring one of the Bradford brothers over the catwalk and into the factory."

Chapter 23

When Spencer crossed the threshold of Art Wimbley's office, Steve looked at him with reasonably objective eyes. Steve was not a man who craved fabulous wealth for himself so he felt no resentment toward this wealthiest member of the Bradford tribe. Steve was not hampered by undue respect for the man, either. He knew him to be an engineer in name only and a phony engineer was worse than no engineer at all.

So he saw Spencer Bradford as he was, an unhappy man well into middle age, with a touch of the arrogance that comes from wealth. Shrewd, brittle, hard, deeply self-contained, not easy to know, with a formidable surface poise. The fundamental insecurity of the man might have escaped a more emotional observer than Steve Emrich, but to Steve it was evidenced in many little things, the downward corners of the mouth, the droop of the eyelids, the too soft-spoken voice, the small cough, the nervous gestures that escaped from Spencer's control only occasionally and were the more significant because of their infrequency.

Spencer did not waste any time. He looked at Steve, but without addressing him by name said, "You've been in touch with Mr. Galloway."

"Not exactly, Mr. Bradford. It would be more correct to say that Mr. Galloway has been in touch with me."

Spencer's eyes flickered at the correction. "But you do know where Mr. Galloway is?"

"No, sir, I do not."

Spencer walked over to Art's desk and thumbed through the pages of notes Mark had dictated to Steve. "These are the notes you made of instructions given you by Mr. Galloway," he said.

"That's correct."

"How did you get them?"

"In a telephone conversation at my home on Sunday night."

"It must have taken some time to give you this information. How long did you talk with Mr. Galloway?"

"Perhaps three-quarters of an hour. Maybe longer."

"Where did he call you from?"

"I have no idea."

"You talked with Mr. Galloway for about an hour and you have no idea where he called from." Spencer's tone was one of ironic incredulity.

"That's right, Mr. Bradford. Mr. Galloway didn't tell me and I figured it was none of my business anyway."

Spencer's eyelids flickered again.

He turned to Art Wimbley. "Would you mind stepping outside?" he asked.

Art hesitated and then went quickly to the door. Spencer moved closer to Steve.

"You can tell me now. Where was Mr. Galloway?"

"I did tell you. I don't know."

"You and Mark have been friends for a long time." There was a question in Spencer's voice, but Steve did not answer. "You've worked closely together. You like each other. You have a lot in common." Spencer paused. "It's natural for you to want to protect him. But this is a serious matter, Steve." Spencer was coming down off his high horse. His tone was cajoling and persuasive, shrewdly so. "I just talked with Mrs. Galloway in Miami. She's taking a plane back tomorrow. She doesn't know

259

where Mark is. You can believe me that she's pretty worried and upset. How would you feel if your wife were in that position?"

"My wife wouldn't be in that position," Steve answered. Again that nervous flicking of Spencer Bradford's eyelids, but his jaw tightened and a hard glint shone in his eyes.

"Did you ever hear of a woman named Claire Elliott?" he asked.

"Yes."

"Has Mark ever mentioned her to you?"

"Never."

"But you do know that he's been seeing her."

"I don't know any such thing. Mr. Galloway and I are business friends. We don't discuss personal matters with each other."

"Come now, you and Mark have gone fishing together. You've gone off for whole days on his boat. He lunches with you more frequently than with any other person. You were his personal candidate for the job of chief engineer of our plant. He's been to your home. Yet you tell me you're just business acquaintances."

"What I'm trying to tell you, Mr. Bradford, is that Mark doesn't discuss his personal life with me. He's that kind of man." Steve measured the man before him, and suddenly he seemed not only unhappy and insecure, but very small. Steve knew the spot he was in, knew what this conversation meant to him personally. It could mean his job. He didn't care. Job or no job, he was going to speak his mind.

"Mr. Bradford, you've asked me repeatedly in the last ten minutes to tell you where Mr. Galloway is. You've implied that I know and that I'm withholding the information from you. I don't know. That's the truth, but even if I did know I wouldn't tell you. I'd figure that if Mark wanted you to know, he would have told you himself."

Spencer eyed him narrowly. Steve had to hand it to him, no matter what emotion was churning inside him, he didn't show it. His voice when he answered was strained and icy.

"Yes," he said. "I rather thought that was the way it was. Now if you'll be good enough to find Mr. Wimbley for me. . . ." He let his frosty voice trail off, but his eyes followed Steve to the door.

Art was only a few steps away from his office, but even if there had been a chance to talk to him, Steve would not have taken it. He did not want Art to know the implications behind the questions Spencer Bradford had just asked him.

Spencer was looking over the prints on Art's table when they entered the office. He did not glance up at once and when he did his face was emotionally ironed out, free of the rancor and spleen that had flared up under Steve's imperviousness.

"While I'm here," he said to Art, "I thought I'd inquire about the Merriman order. The deadline's moving closer and my brother . . . in fact, all of us are concerned."

Art was slow to answer. Steve knew what was troubling him. The ax would fall on Mark's head. Whatever inner tussle Art was having, his answer when he gave it was uncompromising and blunt.

"You're not going to fill that order on time, Mr. Bradford."

"Why not?"

"The reason's in front of you. On those prints." Art walked over to Spencer and put his finger on the drawing of the spindle. He spoke slowly, in the tone of voice you might use to explain the difficulty to a layman. "This is a drive spindle," he said. "It serves to support and drive the part that's being turned in the lathe. The factory has made fifty of these according to specifications from the drafting room. We're stuck with them. They won't assemble."

"What do you mean, they won't assemble? I don't understand," Spencer replied.

261

"The journals on these special spindles don't fit the bearings."

"Is that so serious? Can't it be corrected?"

"Yes, and we have two choices. Either have Purchasing get special bearings made that are smaller. Or else make new spindles ourselves with larger journals." Art's face registered his disgust. "It would be quicker to get new bearings."

"Well, then"—there was a nettled sting in Spencer's voice—"go ahead and do it."

Art was deliberate. "I've already checked the standard ball-bearing catalogues and found none that will do. We could use standard bearings from the lists but we'd have to make up special spacers to fill in on the journals. If we did this we'd have to sell the lathes as 'substandard.' That's not exactly in keeping with Bradford policy."

"Suppose we order the special bearings, what happens then?" Spencer asked.

"If the ball-bearing company works around the clock, we might get them in three weeks."

"Three weeks!"

"That's right, Mr. Bradford."

"But that's impossible. The order has to be shipped from here in ten days."

"Right again, Mr. Bradford," Art replied. "What I'm trying to tell you is that you're not going to ship that order to Merriman. Not in ten days. You'll be lucky if you get it out of here in a month."

"Does Frank Muthersbaugh know about this?"

"Not yet. I just discovered it before you came down."

"Get him." Spencer's voice was barely audible. "Get him in here right away."

Art picked up the telephone and spoke to the operator. Steve stood quietly by, watching the two men in the office. They were a study in opposites: Art, florid and hearty, turning the force of his personality out toward the world. Spencer, pale and lean, turning in upon himself.

"Muthersbaugh?" Art spoke into the phone. "We've got trouble. The spindles won't assemble. Journals won't fit the bearings. Can you come over?" There was a pause and Steve could hear Muthersbaugh answer with what seemed like a protest. Art went on. "I think you'd better make it pretty fast. Spencer Bradford is here, waiting for you."

Art turned from the telephone. "He'll be here," he said.

Frank Muthersbaugh's face, as he stood in the doorway, was drained of color, his ferret eyes almost popping out of his head. They fastened uneasily on Spencer Bradford.

"I got here as fast as I could," he said with obvious truthfulness.

"Frank," Spencer spoke sternly, "what's this all about?" He pointed to the spread of prints. "Wimbley says they've made the parts according to your specifications and now they won't assemble."

"Are you sure?" As Frank asked the question, Steve could see hope fade from his eyes. He knew Wimbley was sure. Frank was no engineer but he understood the human equation well enough.

Art shoved the micrometer toward him and pointed to the print. "See for yourself. We've got to be sure and that's why we're using micrometers instead of regular inspection gauges."

Frank's examination was perfunctory. Steve watched him handle the micrometer clumsily while his mind was working, figuring out how he was going to save his own hide.

Art was unwilling to let him off. "Show him in black and white, Steve," he said. "Put it down on paper for him."

Steve didn't like being mixed up in this business. It was getting hotter by the minute and it struck him as a family affair, a cozy little Bradford party, something they ought to work out among themselves. But under Art's prodding, he started his calculations. It didn't take long. In a few seconds, he proved that even with a minimum diameter bearing and a maximum shaft, there would still be an excessive clearance for proper assembly.

He looked up and, ignoring the two Bradfords, spoke to Art Wimbley. "It would be suicide to use these undersized shafts. Bradford Tool has made its reputation on lathes that stand up. Send out a batch of lathes with sloppy-fitting spindles and you'll never live it down."

"It can be corrected somehow," Frank said.

"Only by rushing through some special bearings," Art retorted. "That's for sure."

Spencer stepped in. "It will take three weeks, maybe longer, Frank. We took this order from Merriman on a guarantee to deliver on time. We didn't figure on anything like this. This sort of thing doesn't happen in Bradford Tool. Do you realize what this will mean to us in terms of money loss and maybe loss of a customer too?"

Frank Muthersbaugh didn't answer. Spencer kept at him. "It's bad enough to lose this order along with a few thousand dollars. These were special-order lathes. We can't sell them to anyone but Merriman."

Frank's eyes pleaded for mercy but Spencer drove home with brutal directness.

"That's not all. That's just the least of our troubles. Merriman is a big account. We do business with them that runs into millions. When we let them down on this order, it's a safe bet we'll lose their future trade. This messy engineering is going to cost us a fortune."

His back to the wall, Frank exploded at last.

"It's not my fault!" he shouted at Spencer. "If you think I'm going to take the blame for this, you're wrong. It's the men who work for me. Go in and look them over. Talk to them. Find out what's going on in your plant. They hate my guts.

They've hated me from the first day I came here. This whole thing was planned long ago. They thought I didn't know what they were up to, but I'm not that dumb. They've been plotting to get me out of here. They hate me because I belong to the stinking tribe of Bradfords."

"Frank!" Spencer tried to stop the tirade but it was no use. "Don't talk here. Let's go to my office." He took Frank's arm but Muthersbaugh yanked himself free. He was wild-eyed, a man possessed.

"Let me alone!" he bellowed. "I'll talk where I want. Let anyone hear who wants to." He pointed to Steve. "The men are for him. They wanted him in the beginning, in my place. That's why they've plotted to get me out. The men in drafting want him. And Mark Galloway wants him. Mark's in on it too. Been mixed up in it from the beginning. He's let the men get away with murder, do anything they wanted just to show me up. He could have stepped in if he wanted to. He could have helped me out, but he hated me too. That's why he ran away this week, just when he was needed here most. That's why he picked this week to run off."

"Frank!" Spencer's voice shot out, cutting through the hysterical tones of the other man. "Stop it."

"Why should I? Everyone else is trying to protect him. Why should I protect him? What has Mark Galloway ever done for me? He's a troublemaker and a climber. A cheap, ambitious climber who married Nina so he could climb over her and get where he wanted to. Now that he's got there, he's throwing her over for another woman. Everyone knows it. The whole plant is whispering about it. Let's bring it out in the open and kick it around for a while."

"Frank!" Spencer started toward him. Muthersbaugh was at the breaking point. Steve had seen men crack up during the war, go temporarily insane. They acted like this. This was it, no mistake about it.

Before Spencer could reach Frank Muthersbaugh, Art Wimbley was there. His arm shot out and he slapped Muthersbaugh across the face repeatedly. Muthersbaugh put up his arms, defending himself like a child from the volley of slaps. He fell back against the wall, whimpering.

"It's not my fault," he yammered. He was a puling child again, defending himself from the attacks of his domineering mother. "I came here in good faith. I've done the best job I could. Why don't you blame it on the man who's responsible? Mark Galloway."

Chapter 24

As NINA STEPPED OUT OF THE PLANE AT BRAMPTON AIRPORT the first thing her eyes lighted on was her sister Evelyn. She was standing at the gate, in a leopard coat, a narrow band of matching fur across her dark hair, her eyes eagerly searching for Nina.

In that moment before Evelyn spied her, Nina recoiled from the encounter that would follow.

I'd almost rather have it be Spencer, she thought. If I've got to come home like this, my head hanging with the shame of what Mark and I are doing to each other, I'd rather face anyone but Evelyn. Spencer would have been glum, but at least he would also have been silent.

Nina's head was anything but bowed as she stepped nimbly across the space that separated the two sisters. Perhaps after all it was better that Evelyn was the one waiting to greet her. Nina would be forced to put a good face on things. Evelyn was the last person Nina would want to show her real feelings to.

She's always been jealous of my marriage to Mark, Nina thought.

It was true. When Evelyn had married Thornton Watrous, the family had considered it a love match. It had never been a love match because neither Evelyn nor Thornton was capable of experiencing real love. They were mates. That much was true. Evelyn had chosen Thornton from quite an array of suitors because Evelyn had been a great belle, more so than Nina. She had been a belle deliberately, with the same calculation she had used in selecting Thornton for her lifelong helpmeet. Magnetism she had possessed in great abundance, the kind of magnetism that turns men's heads and drives them almost out of their minds to possess its owner. She had a flair for style. She had been high-strung, with a compelling vivacity.

It was understandable that she should have chosen Thornton from among all the men who asked her to marry them. He was conventionally handsome, with dark good looks and a mustache that took some of the petulance from his mouth and gave his shallow face a look of distinction. He mixed well. He was considered a bit fast for the Bradfords, but people said at that time that Evelyn Bradford needed someone racy to keep up with her. Because they were so much alike, it appeared to be a love match. But Nina, who herself was capable of deep and overpowering emotion, guessed that it was not. So she was not surprised when Evelyn under the guise of sisterly responsibility tried to stop her marriage to Mark.

Evelyn had fought it to the very day when Mark and Nina had walked to the altar together. On the very morning of her wedding, Nina had been confronted by a sullen Evelyn who implored her to be sure, to be absolutely sure. Mark, she argued, would be out of his depth. Nina and he had nothing in common but this passing infatuation which they called love. Mark was ambitious. He was using Nina to make his way up. The adjustment in marriage was difficult at best, even when two people had everything in common. When they came from opposite poles in the social and economic world, the adjustment was more than painful, it was well-nigh impossible.

Nina had been too young then to understand much about personal frustrations, the bitter rankling of envy and jealousy.

But she had stuck to her decision. She had defied Evelyn, and defied Spencer. She had chosen Mark, chosen him deliberately and with courage and she would not give him up because of anything the Bradfords said. More than anyone she knew at the time young Mark Galloway had possessed the vitality and drive she associated with her grandfather, old Jared. She felt Mark would make the best Bradford of them all.

As the years passed, she had been aware that Evelyn narrowed her eyes when she saw them together and making a go of it. Evelyn clearly hated Mark for being the man he was, and she hated Nina for having had the courage to step outside the close circle the Bradfords approved to marry the man she wanted.

Evelyn was therefore the worst and the best person to be waiting for Nina today. Worst because she would be exultant that Nina and Mark were so near the breaking point, best because Nina would be challenged to fight for the very lifeblood of her marriage in the presence of her only sister.

Evelyn spied Nina and let out a squeal of recognition. "Darling!" she exclaimed, running to meet her. "You poor, poor dear." She clasped Nina about the waist, kissed her with affected tenderness and then led the way, her arm linked through Nina's, toward the luggage desk. Except for an occasional "Oh, my dear, I feel so for you," or "Darling, I can put myself in your place and my heart bleeds," she said little else until they were in her car. Nina refused the offer to stop for a hot drink and Evelyn turned the car toward the parkway.

Every mile they traveled carried Nina nearer the town of Bradford yet she had the strangest feeling of newness and unfamiliarity, as if she were not going home, but setting out on a long journey to some unknown destination.

She did not speak, nor did Evelyn at first. Yet Nina was conscious of furtive glances, oblique and questioning, from her older sister. Evelyn's personality weighed upon Nina, adding to the dreadful burden of the moment. It was an animal personality, basically feline, with the remarkable grace of the cat family, and much of its sensuous beauty. It was fitting that Evelyn chose to wear leopard, although she might have afforded more expensive furs. The spotted pelts suited her. Her features, sharpened rather than mellowed by maturity, reflected the restless mind back of them. Her eyes were too bright, her lips too red, her perfume oppressively heavy. The woman was a worthy successor to the girl she had been, for she could stir up a lusty desire in many of the men she met. She was not a comfortable person to be with, even at best, because her world was so sharply divided into males and females, the former to cajole, flatter and influence, the latter to resent.

Sometimes when Nina looked at her sister dressed for the evening in one of the sinuous sheaths she enjoyed wearing, she recalled a picture from an old Sunday-school Bible they had used as children, and she threw that picture in memory like a stage backdrop behind Evelyn. It was a colored etching of the Garden of Eden, a sprawling and crooked apple tree spread out in all directions, with a serpent coiled about its trunk, and there, in front of it, stood Evelyn with the fatal apple in her hand.

"Darling," Evelyn began, unable to contain herself any longer. "Was the trip a comfortable one? You don't feel too tired?"

"I feel as if I'll never be tired again," Nina replied. The cryptic remark drew another oblique glance from Evelyn.

"I have things to tell you. I wouldn't want to give you the shocking news unless you felt able to stand it."

"Shocking news?"

Evelyn nodded, her eyes fixed on the road, her mouth set smugly at the corners.

"It's a long story, dear. And a hard one to tell. So be patient with me if I do it clumsily."

If it's about Mark, don't tell me, Nina's thoughts screamed. But she said nothing, made no move to protect herself from the impact of what was to follow. It was sure to be more gossip about Mark. Nina did not want gossip at this point. She wanted facts, and she wanted them from Mark himself.

"Mark's been gone for several days. Without a word to Spencer or Bob or anyone. No one knew where he went."

"I know that."

"There was a dreadful scene at the plant yesterday, Nina. This I'm sure you don't know. The Merriman order fell flat on its face. Did you know about the Merriman order?"

"No."

"I'm not sure of the details. Business, especially the engineering business, is difficult to understand. But it seems there was a big order from Merriman Brothers. You know they're one of our biggest customers." Nina nodded. "There was a schedule to make. The lathes had to be delivered at such and such a time. Bob and Spencer committed themselves. It was Mark's job to see that the order was filled. It seems that during his absence the whole thing got messed up. Some of the parts wouldn't assemble because of mistakes in the drafting room. Consequently we can't fill the order on time. We've lost the order and we're sure to lose the Merriman account. All because Mark wasn't there."

"I thought Frank Muthersbaugh was chief engineer." Nina muttered the words. She was numb with grief for her marriage. She didn't care much what happened at Bradford Tool but she did know that Frank, not Mark, was responsible for drafting-room mistakes.

"Yes, but Mark is responsible. That's the way it is in business, my dear. The man at the head takes the blame."

"If that's the way it is, it's wrong. Frank Muthersbaugh should be responsible for his own mistakes."

"Are you defending Mark, dear?" Evelyn's brows arched in surprise and her voice trilled its protest.

"When he deserves defense, yes."

"Then, darling, let me tell you the rest." Evelyn took her right hand from the wheel and patted Nina's gloved hand. Nina withdrew and Evelyn's mouth hardened.

Her voice was not soft with pretended sympathy now. It rasped out at Nina.

"You must understand my motives in this matter, Nina. All of us have interests involved in Bradford Tool. Our financial security as well as your happiness is involved in this sordid business that Mark is being dragged into. You must understand my point of view. Or you won't understand why I took the action I did."

"What action, Evelyn?"

Nina, suddenly roused from numbness, swung around. Her woman's sixth sense shot out toward impending disaster.

Evelyn, bold as she was, hedged. "If Mark is going to act like this, if he's bent on jeopardizing our financial security because the whim seizes him to stay away from the plant at a time when he's most needed, his whereabouts become as much our business as yours, Nina."

"What action did you take, Evelyn?"

Her sister paused, warned by Nina's voice. Then, gulping, she plunged on.

"I had to do it, Nina. It was the only thing to do. Hear me out. Don't interrupt me until I've finished."

"I'm listening."

"I called up Scott Bentley, you know, Thornton's and my lawyer. Scott's very good, conservative but very smart. I wouldn't think of acting without his advice. I told him what I wanted to do and he suggested how to go about it."

"What . . . did . . . you . . . do . . . Evelyn?" Nina dragged the words out, pounding them with a vicious emphasis to compel her sister to come to the point.

"Scott gave me the name of a detective. Not just a common detective. A private one, of course, and a very good one. A man who's discreet and enjoys a fine reputation."

Nina slumped back in the seat. She felt the scenery whizz by the car window, was vaguely conscious of the shapes of trees and bridge abutments and signposts, but everything was blurred. She did not interrupt Evelyn. She could not have found the voice to do so even if she had wanted to.

"It's all right, Nina. It will be kept in the family. There won't be any scandal. This detective we hired—and it was frightfully expensive by the way—got to work yesterday noon." Evelyn gestured with her right hand as she talked, keeping her left hand on the wheel.

"He acted on a lead that Claire Elliott might be involved in Mark's absence from the plant and went over to her house. The schools have a vacation this week and sure enough, he found a cleaning woman there. After a few questions he found out that Claire was up at Great Barrington. He followed her there. She's staying at the Skyline Lodge."

Nina wanted to scream to Evelyn to stop, yet she was hypnotized by the recital, fascinated to learn how it would turn out.

Evelyn was only too willing to oblige.

"He found Mark there too. Not at the same inn, but at a smaller place nearby called Mountain Inn. The detective found out that they'd been spending most of their time together, out on the slopes skiing, eating together, dancing, flirting, having many a comfortable tête-à-tête. Mark went up there Sunday to join her, Nina. He hasn't been home since."

Nina fell back into the corner of the car, too sick to answer. This was something she had intuitively felt was going on yet she had tried with all the strength she could muster not to think

273

about it. She did not want to think about it. She had never wanted to know the truth about Mark and Claire Elliott.

"We can take care of Claire Elliott," Evelyn went on in a matter-of-fact voice.

Nina turned her face away, looking out the window at the blur of evergreens that bordered the parkway. She was not so angry with Mark as she was with Evelyn. She was not even so bitter about Claire. But Evelyn! Evelyn, the pure and untouchable, Evelyn the holier-than-thou who could raise lust in a man just by looking at him, Evelyn ought to have her head cracked for butting in. Nina could have found this out in her own way, at her own time, and from Mark. She should not have found it out from Evelyn.

Evelyn, purposely or not, misinterpreted Nina's silence.

"Don't talk if you find it too great an effort, darling," she said. "I know how wretched you must feel about all this."

Nina said nothing, but continued to watch the trees of the parkway whizz by like relentless sentinels of her doom.

I'm going home, she thought. This is the hardest thing I've had to face in my life. Nothing has ever been as bad as this, not the painful months away from Mark when I knew he was in danger every hour, almost every moment. Not three childbirths, not losing our son. Nothing, nothing has ever been as hard to face as this.

The house on Turkey Hill looked bleak and unfriendly as Evelyn swung the car up the long driveway. Evelyn stopped before the main entrance and jumped out. "I'll go in with you," she said. "Effie's here, but you ought to have some member of the family with you."

Nina was past caring what Evelyn did. Let her come in. It didn't matter. Nothing mattered. Her world had crumbled a few miles back on the parkway as she had listened to Evelyn talk about Mark and Claire Elliott.

Effie opened the door before they had time to knock or ring.

She stood there, her face broken from weeping. As Nina glanced at the deep circles under Effie's eyes, she knew that Effie had heard the story. Effie would understand. Effie would know what to do.

She did it instantly, with a naturalness that brought some slight warmth to Nina. She took Nina in her arms and held her there, rocking her back and forth like a child. She did not speak but she made soft crooning noises of comfort and sympathy and Nina, exhausted and crushed, let herself lean upon Effie's ample bosom.

"I'll get hot tea," Effie said when she released Nina. "You go to your room, Miss Nina, and I'll bring it up there."

"Bring it to the breakfast room. No," Nina changed her order quickly. "The living room. Evelyn's staying."

Effie looked her disapproval as she glanced toward Evelyn but she turned abruptly and marched into the kitchen.

Nina pulled off her coat and hat. She went to the door of the living room. She paused there, fearing to go in. A fire blazed on the hearth. The sudden cheerfulness came as a shock. It belonged to another world, a world which she had left behind. Then suddenly she felt a chafing discomfort, as if something monstrous and obscene were present in the room. She looked about her, feeling the cloying smell of flowers push against her.

The room was full of flowers. Bowls and vases of gardenias and roses and carnations stood everywhere. There were baskets beside the fireplace, filled with more flowers. The smell nauseated her, bringing back a flood of memories, and then she realized what those memories were. She could think only of her son's funeral and the sickening smell of flowers that followed her every step of that awful day.

She wheeled on Evelyn, feeling a fury mounting inside her. "Who did this?" She heard her voice crack on the question. "Who did this terrible thing to me?"

"Who did what, Nina? What terrible thing?" Evelyn came

275

to her side, solicitous, as if she thought Nina were out of her mind with grief.

"Who filled this room with flowers?"

"Why, we all did. I suggested we do it, darling. As a gesture, a token that we love you and intend to support you. I thought you'd find some comfort in coming home to a house filled with flowers."

"You . . . thought . . . I'd . . . find . . . some . . . comfort!" Nina faced her sister, appalled at the cruelty of the woman before her.

"Take them out!" She almost screamed the words. Now at last she had found an outlet for her emotion. "Take them all out!" She shouted the words and as she screamed her order she walked about the room, yanking the flowers from the vases, pulling them out and throwing them in a heap in the middle of the room.

When she had emptied the last vase of its obscene tribute to the marriage that lay dead in her house, Nina faced Evelyn once again.

"Take them out of here," she said. "You brought them here. Now take them away. Make a bonfire of them. Make a funeral pile since that's the way your mind seems to be working, Evelyn. Make a pyre and burn Mark's love for me on it."

She fell back against one of the tables, spent and shaking. The sobs came at last, great convulsive sobs that filled the room and sailed out into the hall and up the stairs, echoing and re-echoing through the house that once had been the home of Mark and Nina Galloway.

Chapter 25

Mark slowed up at the entrance to the parkway, stopped and waited for an opening in the traffic before he eased his way on.

This was the last lap on the way home. The holiday had been somewhat beneficial. Those mornings and afternoons on the ski trail had washed a little of the tension out of him. But in a way, he dreaded going back to take up the job again. The Merriman order would need all his attention for the next four or five days and it was a tough assignment at best. He might have to live at the factory, stay there day and night to see that the job was done right.

The parkway traffic was lighter than usual this morning and it gave him time to think. His thoughts naturally went out toward Nina. With considerable effort, he had been able to keep from thinking about her during the days just past. Now that he was hurrying toward the house on Turkey Hill, no amount of effort could have shut her from his thoughts.

For one strange, beautiful moment, she came to him as he had first known her. He saw her as a young girl again, just out of college. Her eyes were always bright, and her smile sweet and charming. She had been a happy girl.

He let his memory trail her down the years, noting the

changes as they came along. After the war, she had seemed for a time quiet and serious. She was a mother now, and she had been dreadfully worried about Mark's safety. She told him all about that. The quietness had passed off and for a while their life together had been gay. Then they had lost their only son and the quietness in Nina was longer-lasting, deeper. When she brightened, at last, coming out of the long period of grief, she was a woman full-blown. She could be ebullient, but the happiness was fraught with a deep-seated, rather pleasant melancholy. Once she had said to Mark, "I don't think anything from now on will ever hurt me quite so much."

The changes since then had been subtler, harder to put your finger on. She was still as beautiful as she had always been, perhaps more so, since in recent years she had developed a chic which she had spurned as a carefree girl. Yet somewhere along the way, the Bradford overbearance set in. Exactly when Mark had begun to notice it, he could not say. It was a complicated thing to analyze because Nina was certainly not a hard person. She was warm and responsive. She had a sweet disposition. Yet the domination was indisputably there.

He wasn't blaming Nina. No one was perfect. There were things about him, too, that were devilish to endure. It was not anything in Nina or in him. Sometimes he liked to try to put the blame on the institution of marriage itself. It could become a strain, a drawn-out struggle to fuse two personalities in one throughout an entire lifetime. It was harder nowadays to make marriage work. Sure, people did it in the old days. He used to get a kick out of opening up one of the local newspapers and seeing the picture of an elderly couple on the front page with the caption *Celebrate Golden Wedding Anniversary*.

They looked so cute, the two of them, the woman sitting down, sometimes the man sitting next to her, sometimes standing. Cute little old lady with frizzy gray hair, cute little old man with bald head. Great old gal, he used to think to himself. Great old boy. Bet they've had one wonderful time together. Look like they romped through life. Romped through life! Fat chance. Now when he saw a picture like that, he thought something like this: "Whew! What a beating they've both taken. Bet it's been a long haul. Bet they wanted to quit individually and collectively many times. I wonder just how much each one of them has had to sacrifice to make a go of it."

So now he was going home. No, not going home. Going back to Nina's house on Turkey Hill. Only Nina wouldn't be there.

Maybe that was just as well. He would have found it hard to see her at all. He could not live with a woman who had proved she no longer respected him—or cared about his future. Nina wouldn't be back for several days yet, and by then he'd be moved out.

He had decided to leave Nina. To leave for good. Whatever he did about Claire, he was leaving his wife. She didn't need him. He had to get out—he had to think. He wanted to be completely fair to Claire in his plans for the future. But he didn't even know what those plans would be. He had to have some time to himself, a breather even from Claire. After he'd had time to think, he'd go to Claire and straighten things out between them. But he was leaving Nina—Nina and her Bradford tradition.

He didn't know where it was all heading. He honestly didn't know. He was genuinely confused about his feelings for Claire—and hers for him. Were they strong enough for an enduring relationship? If there were some clear-cut signpost, some definite leading to say, Look, this is the way to go, this is the thing to do, he would have got down on his knees and thanked God. Maybe he had the cart before the horse. Maybe if he did get down on his knees and pray about it, even figuratively, he might see more clearly what to do.

He had almost lost his touch with God. Funny, the way life

works, the queer tricks it plays on you. During the war, he had been a religious man, feeling close to God during the worst and most imminent dangers. The safer he got, the more worldly goods and ease he had acquired, the farther away he had got from his religious fervency.

On the ski slopes these last few days he had almost touched the hem of that garment again. He had felt the vastness of the universe. The importance of man. Of all men everywhere. He had felt the touch of deity. He could reach up his arms and almost touch the heavens. Out there a man could find his peace.

His eyes noted the sign *BRADFORD* as he approached his turnoff on the parkway. Then, in a matter of seconds, the exit loomed before him with the sign, *Exit 92, BRADFORD CENTER*. He swerved sharply, taking the curve with too much speed and almost sideswiping the curb. He jammed on the brake at the *STOP* sign, then turned his car toward Turkey Hill.

He would have a quick shower, a change of clothes, maybe a cup of coffee and get over to the factory as fast as he could. Later he'd come back to pack his things and move out.

As he swung up the long hill toward the house, he was surprised to see a column of smoke curling from the chimney. Effie was there, of course, but it was unlikely she would make a fire in the fireplace for herself. Otherwise, there was no sign of activity about the house. No cars stood in the circular driveway at the front or the wide parking space around the garages. He pulled into the parking space and went up the back steps of the house. He poked his head in the kitchen doorway but the room was empty.

He had heard movements in the front of the house, and, changing his plan to go up the back way, he walked along the corridor toward the living room. Effie was there, her back to him, bending over to gather up an armful of flowers from a pile in the middle of the floor. She started toward the fireplace with them.

The strangeness of the scene thrust itself upon him. First the huge pile of flowers, all of them apparently fresh-cut, then Effie's cumbersome movements in her long skirts and apron as she stooped to pick them up, and finally the solemnity of her gait as she crossed to throw them upon the fire.

"Good morning," he called.

She jumped, startled, letting some of the flowers drop as she turned on him.

"Oh, Mr. Galloway, it's you."

"What are you doing, Effie?"

She began sobbing, shaking her head, sniveling like some schoolgirl who was being punished unjustly. As her sobs rose in volume, he could see that she had been crying before. Her face, with its heavy coating of too-light powder and thick rouge, was streaked from tears.

"What's the matter, Effie? What's happened?"

"Don't ask me, Mr. Galloway. It's not for me to tell you."

"Where did those flowers come from?" She shook her head. He walked toward her and she drew away, quickly throwing the armful of flowers into the fire.

"Effie, what's going on here?"

She put her fingers to her lips. Then, glancing around to be sure no one was listening, she lowered her voice to a whisper. "Miss Nina's come back. Alone. She left Miss Ginger with the Lamberts in Florida." She nodded toward the ceiling. "She's up there, not speaking to me, not moving from her chair. Just sitting by the window in her dressing room, looking out, her face set like death itself."

"How did she get back?" Mark asked, his mind racing over possibilities of what might have brought Nina home ahead of time.

"Miss Evelyn. She brought her here from the airport a little while ago."

"The airport! Mrs. Galloway flew back!"

"Yes. There was a dreadful fight between Miss Nina and Miss Evelyn. Over the flowers, as much as I could make it out. Miss Evelyn sent them here early this morning and had me put them in vases and baskets. The whole room was full of them. Like a funeral parlor, Mr. Galloway. I heard Miss Nina tell Miss Evelyn she was trying to make a funeral for your marriage. Or something like that. It was dreadful to hear the two of them, just dreadful. I never heard such a fight in the Bradford family before." Effie stopped sniveling and drew herself up in dignity. "I've worked for the Bradfords a long time, Mr. Galloway. I've heard them fight with each other, but never, never have I heard the likes of this."

"Why did Mrs. Galloway come home?"

Effie began her sobbing again, rolling from side to side, folding her arms across her chest and keening mournfully. "Don't you keep asking me questions, Mr. Mark." In her distress, she broke her own rigid rule and forgot to call him "Mr. Galloway." "Don't you make me tell you things what are none of my business. It's a shame what's going on in this house. It's a bitter, evil shame and I don't want no part in it. I'm fond of you both, I am. You and Miss Nina. I'd give my right arm for either one of you and I don't want no part of this wicked business."

She stopped keening and wiped her eyes. "I've spoke my mind, Mr. Mark," she concluded. "If you want to know anything more, you'll find your wife upstairs." She said the words *your wife* with special emphasis. Then, turning abruptly, she left him standing beside the heap of flowers and walked from the room.

Chapter 26

Nina was sitting as Effie had described her, by the window of her dressing room, on a low slipper chair, facing out upon the town of Bradford. Mark found her there.

At first sight, she reminded him of a small child, bewildered and hurt, and his impulse was to take her in his arms. He stifled that impulse. This was the turning point for both of them, and a show of sentiment, however noble, would only prolong the agony.

He was not afraid to face this moment. In fact, his dominant emotion was one of relief. Whatever she knew about Claire and him, whatever had brought her back on this premature return from Florida, he was willing to hear about. For months now their love had been plunging headlong toward this time of reckoning. This was their one foreseen inevitability. So he faced it, not gladly, for there was no gladness in seeing something die, but stoically, conscious of the easement it would bring.

"Nina." She did not move, did not show by the slightest gesture that she had heard him. "Nina," he said again.

He waited a long time for her to answer. Then she said, "You're back."

"Effie told me you were up here. She said Evelyn brought you from the airport."

Another long silence.

"I know where you were, Mark. Evelyn put a private detective on your trail. I wouldn't have done that myself, but the milk is spilled, so there's no use crying over it."

"I'm sorry you had to find out that way, Nina."

She moved her head, slightly, as if in acquiescence.

"What do you want to do, Nina?" He wanted to help her suddenly, to save her pride. Why not let her think *she* was leaving him.

She thought it over. Then, "I don't want to live with you any more." She got up from the chair and faced him. "This is your house as much as mine," she went on. "You have a right to stay here. Fortunately, it's a big house. That will make things somewhat easier." She spoke in stilted sentences, like an automaton, with no show of emotion, but her lips and hands were trembling, so Mark knew what these words were costing her.

"I'll move my things to the guest suite on the third floor," she went on in her wooden manner. "It's quite comfortable there. There's no use in your moving your things. You've spent a lot of time fixing your den to your liking. With me, it doesn't matter."

"I'm sorry, Nina, but I won't stay in the house. I've decided to leave." He said it slowly.

"What did you say, Mark?" Her tone was frozen and aloof.

"We've lost what we had, Nina. That room doesn't mean anything any more." He nodded toward the big double bedroom.

Her eyes clouded, but he was not sure whether it was with anger or fear.

"Where will you go?" she asked.

"The Harrington Inn. For the time being anyway. When these things happen we have to take temporary measures until we can work out better arrangements."

"When these things happen." She smiled, but it was a smile

full of hurt, and there was no humor in it. "Why do these things have to happen?"

"I don't know," he said. "I honestly don't know."

"Do you want a divorce, Mark?"

"The time hasn't come to talk about that. But I'm leaving you, Nina. I want time to think about what comes next."

"Well, you'd better think. There will be plenty to think about. There will be this house to think about. There will be our money and our securities. Our mutual savings and our mutual investments, and," she said with an ironic emphasis, "our mutual children."

"Not now," he reiterated. "Let's not even talk about it now. I'll get out right away. But I don't want to talk about things like that."

She came quickly to his side. "Are you afraid to face it?"

"I'm not afraid to face anything."

"Yes, you are. You men are cowards when it comes to the showdown. You think big. You even act big, but when it comes to putting all the cards on the table you run away. You don't want to talk about it. You don't want to think. You just want to walk out and leave me here alone." She was shaking and the words tumbled from her with a kind of hysterical insistence.

Mark was angry too. He had promised himself not to lose control. The promise was too big a one for him to keep.

"I'm not a coward, Nina. You know better. I've never done a cowardly thing in my life."

"What do you call the way you've treated me? You could have come to me, told me the truth, told it to me in cold facts. I could have taken it. No, you had to sneak around with her, make sordid little excuses to be with her. You couldn't come to me like a man and tell me the truth. That you've found someone you love more than me."

"What is the truth, Nina? Does any of us know?"

She turned from him so that only her trembling profile was

285

visible. In this moment of anger and recrimination, it was a sad fact that he still found her lovely. The fragile beauty, the delicacy that had charmed him from the first were heightened by the quarrel.

"You were selfish and dishonest, Mark. What's more, you've been a fool."

"Don't say that, Nina."

"You ask me what is truth. This much is truth, Mark. You've thought only of yourself. All you've cared about is your own feelings. Besides that, you've been gulled. Anyone who sympathizes with you can take you in."

He grabbed her by the shoulders and pulled her around. "Don't say that to me."

"You're selfish. Cruelly selfish and dishonest," she insisted. "I could have forgiven you anything else but this." She pulled herself free and walked past him toward the door. He could hear her footsteps running along the hall, running away from him to the end of the corridor, then she was going upstairs. He heard their tap-tap on the floor above him. Then silence.

He stood there watching the doorway through which Nina had fled.

He strode angrily into his bedroom and yanked a big suitcase from one of the closets. With no thought for what he was doing, he began to load it with personal belongings. Undershirts, shorts, pajamas, shirts, socks, handkerchiefs. He swung open another closet and tore a dozen ties from the swivel rack, pulled three pairs of shoes from the shoe caddy.

The suitcase was overflowing and he still had not considered what suits to take. Getting another bag from the closet, he threw it down on the bed and yanked it open. Then, at the closet that contained his collection of suits, he stopped to think for the first time. The row of suits arranged by Nina in systematic order struck him as ludicrous. First there were two dozen business suits, then his dress suits, then his tuxedos, three of them, and his full-dress regalia, then, shoved to the end in garment bags, stood his corded summer suits and lightweight worsteds and seersuckers.

This had never struck him before as absurd but today, in the face of the problem that hung over him, this array of suits seemed ridiculous.

What did I ever want all that junk for? he thought.

He pulled three business suits and a dress suit from their hangers and, as if they were so many rags, hurled them toward the empty suitcase.

That's enough, he thought. I've got all I want.

He went into his den and selected a few items to take with him, some technical books, his journal, some letters, the gold paperweight of a Bradford lathe which the men in the factory had given him on his tenth anniversary with the firm. Impelled by a haste he could not explain, he dumped them in with his clothing. He was in a hurry now. He wanted to get out of here as fast as he could.

He slammed the bags closed and fastened the buckles on the straps. Lifting them from the bed, he heaved them out into the hall.

There. He was finished. He was ready to go.

No, not quite. One last look around. Just to be sure. He must not forget anything he really needed. Any trip back would be more painful than this present moment. He went slowly through the rooms, lingering in his den, looking around at the desk, the table with his experiments and gadgets, the chair in which he had slumped to relax so many times. He did not like leaving it. It was the one place in this house that he would miss.

For a long moment he paused before Nina's picture, an exquisite photograph in a sterling-silver frame. It was in color and her blond beauty smiled up at him, taunting him in this moment of anguish. He put his hand on it as if to take it with him. Then he thrust it from him. It toppled over and he let it lie there.

He strode through the bedroom. The big four-poster in which generations of Bradfords had slept confronted him. He paused to look at it. The heirloom topper of delicate ivory was spread in unwrinkled perfection across the bed. Memory for one terrible moment gripped him in a stranglehold but he cut himself free in much the way a man would fight a raging octopus.

He turned toward the door of Nina's dressing room. The chaise longue and the French dressing table were visible from where he stood. He studied them a moment as if to carry away something of the woman he was leaving behind him. Then he turned from them forever and walked out into the hall.

A suitcase in either hand, he made his way along the corridor, past Ginger's room. No, he would not look inside. Past Jill's room. Past the nursery. No, no more backward glances. On. On and out.

At the top of the stairs, he paused and glanced over to where the staircase ran up to the third floor. Nina was up there. He listened. If he had heard a sob, a single sound of grief, he might have bounded up the stairs even now. He was not a man of steel. He could be touched. He could be reached. He was Mark Galloway who had come up to Turkey Hill from River Street where people felt things deeply and wore their sentiments upon their coat sleeves. But no sound reached him. If she was grieving, it was the voiceless grief of the Bradfords.

He went as quickly as he could down the stairs and out the back way. As he traveled the length of the back hall, the significance of this tiny act impressed itself upon him. When he had first entered it he had come into this house by the front door, but he was leaving by the back door, the one the servants and the tradesmen used. It was a fitting departure for the boy who had made the climb from River Street.

He set his bags down in the foyer and went back to say good-by to Effie.

She was sitting at the table, spreading out a game of solitaire, her jaws clenched, her eyes bloodshot from weeping. When she saw him, she shoved back her chair and got up.

"I'm leaving now, Effie," he said. She looked past him out into the hall at the two bags.

"Oh, Mr. Galloway." The tears started afresh and she came over to him and he took her in his arms and held her there a moment. "Oh, Mr. Galloway," was all she kept saying.

"It's not as bad as all that." He tried to sound cheerful, putting a brightness into his voice he did not feel. "You'll see me again, Effie," he said. Then, forcing a smile, he took hold of her chin and said, "Around town."

This started a fresh outburst of weeping. Gently he took her by the shoulders and held her off.

"It's best this way, Effie," he said. "You'll see. Look," he said, wiping away one of her tears with his finger. "Do me a favor, will you? Take good care of Miss Nina."

"I will," Effie sobbed. "Oh, Mr. Galloway, I will."

He walked out into the foyer and bent over for his bags. They were heavy, heavier than they had seemed as he carried them down the stairs. His whole body seemed clumsy and heavy-laden as he walked down the back steps and turned away from the house on Turkey Hill.

Chapter 27

THE HARRINGTON INN WAS THE ONLY HOTEL IN BRADFORD AND it was very old. It wore its age as some humans do theirs, with dignity and pride and a certain boastfulness.

It sprawled along the main stem of the town, a trifle removed from the heart of the shopping district, a comfortable-looking white frame structure that looked always as if it had just been given a spanking-new coat of paint. At the front, there was no lawn to speak of. The inn hugged and crowded against the sidewalk with the intimacy of early New England buildings. At the rear, there was more spaciousness, with a sweep of fine, aged turf sporting flamboyant painted tables and fringed umbrellas in shocking pink and sharp yellow. That was in summer, of course, but now it was winter, with no tables or umbrellas and only the sere-brown grass rolling down to the river's edge where a lacy border of ice outlined the shore.

The culinary achievements of the inn were widely known. Duncan Hines had put his stamp of approval upon the food. The management was being constantly invited to contribute one of its favorite recipes by editors of cookbooks. The inn's chefs were especially famous for cranberry dishes, their cranberry meringue pie and cranberry spice cake and cranberry velvet and steamed cranberry pudding which made mouths water for miles around.

The Harrington was popular with guests who enjoyed "atmosphere," for it had retained its full New England flavor. The lobby was small, with the original pine floor boards showing at the edge of maroon-colored runners. The Windsor chairs and Governor Winthrop desks and curly-maple tables were genuine antiques. The huge old fireplace had warming ovens at each side and big iron kettles hanging from cranes. There was Waterford glass and Sandwich glass and ruby and amethyst and amber glass on the window shelves where they might catch the light. A Chinese Chippendale sideboard supported gleaming silver candelabra and a Paul Revere silver service. American primitives of gothic-faced colonial men and women and solemn children covered the walls.

This was New England at its finest and oldest and best and there would always be people who would travel miles to bask in its mellowness and charm.

Mark Galloway left his car in the parking lot and entered the Harrington by the side door. His luggage was in the car. He would bring that in tonight after dark. He knew better than to appear in the lobby and reception room of the Harrington with a suitcase in each hand.

One of the women's clubs was having a luncheon and the flutter and cackle of gregarious females assailed him on every side. He had a healthy masculine distaste for high-pitched feminine voices, and he did not like to see a group of women corseted and decked out, hatted and coifed and rouged to the hilt, pursuing the deadly art of female conviviality. Women considered singly were charming, but put them in a group and it brought out the worst in any of them.

He made the best of it, plunging through the milling lobby to the desk where, in a charmed circle of emptiness, he found comparative seclusion. It was a few minutes before anyone noticed him. Then a tall, dark-haired woman with two gray streaks at the forehead, came over.

"Yes?" she said.

"I want a room. Quiet and not too small."

She consulted her board and when she came back with a key in her hand, she held it tightly in her fist as she looked at him. "Mr. Galloway," she said. "I'm sorry I didn't recognize you at first."

He nodded, wincing inside. He did not recognize the woman, but he was not surprised that she knew him. Nina and he had stayed here last fall while the house was being redecorated. They came here sometimes for dinner.

The woman looked at him in curiosity as he registered.

These are the things you've got to face, he thought. This is only the beginning.

"My luggage is in the car," he said. The woman nodded, with that same intensely curious expression.

The room she gave him was not unpleasant. When the bell-boy left him he went to the window and looked out upon the back terrace and the river. This was the quiet side of the inn. Last autumn Nina and he had chosen a suite on this very floor, four or five doors down the hall.

He turned back to the room. It was large, with a double bed, a cherry highboy, a desk, and several comfortable chairs. Everything was spotlessly clean, with the walls papered in a small colonial pattern. The predominant colors in the room were moss rose and a soft green.

This would do. It would do until he had time to think things through and decide what his next step would be. Meanwhile he had to get over to the plant. The quarrel with Nina and his hasty exodus from Turkey Hill had taken up more time than he had figured.

He needed a shower badly and he had better stop to take that because it would improve his disposition. There was no telling how much Spencer knew—plenty, he imagined—and if he was going to be embroiled in another squabble, he'd better be feeling fit enough to take it.

As he was drying himself, he suddenly realized that he was hungry, not just normally hungry, but enormously so. He got into his underwear and glanced at his watch. It was one thirty! He dressed quickly, matted his thick hair with water and, with some difficulty, tamed it with his pocket comb. He felt better. He would feel better yet when he had some food.

Scorning the overflowing dining room of the Harrington, he drove his car over to a diner near the plant. No one from Bradford Tool would be there. The noon hour was well past.

Mark ordered chops, French fries, and a lettuce and tomato salad. He finished off with apple pie and coffee, paid his bill and walked out to his car. It took only a minute to drive over to the parking lot of the plant. He drove under the shed bearing his name, turned off the ignition and slipped the key into his pocket. He got out and started across the lot between the rows of cars belonging to the employees.

The ground was rutted and made for hard walking. There had been a thaw and then a freezing spell, leaving deep ruts. He glanced toward the sky and for the first time noticed the lowering clouds. The damp air penetrated his overcoat and he hunched his shoulders against a raw wind. There would be snow before morning.

He walked into the building and took the elevator to the executive suites. The elevator "boy," Albie Griffin, who had been with Bradford Tool thirty-five years, said, "Good afternoon, Mr. Galloway."

"Hello, Albie," he replied.

"Fixing to snow a bit, I guess," Albie said.

"Sure feels like it."

"You been away, Mr. Galloway?"

"Yes. A few days."

"Missed you. No one else going up there"—he nodded toward

the executive offices—"bids a man the time of day, no one but you. Kinda miss you when you're gone."

"Everyone's busy, Albie," Mark said, smiling. "Too busy for chitchat."

"Busy, my eye," Albie said with the overconfidence of the entrenched. "Too snobby's more like it. They all got a bump on themselves."

It was not the first time Mark had heard Albie talk like this.

"Want me to send you in a cup of coffee, Mr. Galloway?"

"No, thanks, Albie. Some other time. I just had lunch."

"Oh," Albie grunted. "Say the word and I'll git it for you."

Mark got out and walked the few steps to his office. All the executive offices were working behind closed doors, and while this was not unprecedented, it was somewhat unusual. Secretaries had a way of leaving doors open so they could see what was going on. Mark heard the clackety-clack of typewriters, the ring of telephones, but nobody was in sight.

When he opened the door of his own office, the three women inside glanced up and stared at him. Miss Ives, his secretary, was a perennial spinster in her late forties. She had a face that reminded him of a horse, with gentle dark eyes and a bang of frayed black hair that dipped over her forehead. She was soft-spoken, efficient almost to a fault, and her judgment was impeccable. Once someone had bet him five dollars that he couldn't tell a single thing she had worn in the last two weeks. He had taken the bet and lost. After that he had noticed religiously what she wore for one solid week and discovered that it was always a man's shirt, a tweed skirt, and a little ribbon tied into a bow at her collar. The colors varied, but the uniform didn't.

His two stenographers, who answered to the names of Jean and Joan, looked enough alike to pass as sisters although they were not even distantly related. He was always getting them mixed up, not only because of the similarity of their names and looks but because they insisted on dressing almost alike too. If he were a different kind of man, they might have been distracting with their tight skirts and sweaters and high, young bosoms, their artfully lipsticked mouths and crisp good looks.

The men in the plant had a nickname for them and Mark was aware of it. "The Torso Twins." Mark laughed it off. They did satisfactory work and under the eagle eye of Miss Ives there was no nonsense in the office, although Mark knew that most of the eligible young men in the plant cast sheep's eyes at his appealing "twins" in the cafeteria and on spring and summer days when the plant gardens and recreation fields were open.

Miss Ives and Jean and Joan stared at him now as he paused inside his office, his hand still on the knob of the door. Miss Ives' face was disciplined to inscrutability, but the two girls were unabashed in the mixture of curiosity, wonder, and concern which they expressed. Where on earth have you been! their round, slightly opened mouths and wide-open eyes asked as plainly as if they had spoken the words.

Miss Ives recovered first.

"Good afternoon, Mr. Galloway," she said. "It's good to have you back. Was it a pleasant trip?" From someone else the question might have been impertinent and insinuating but not from Miss Ives. Mark had known her a long time. She had heard gossip, no doubt of that, but she had decided that it was none of anyone's business and the best way to handle the whole thing was to pretend that Mark had been away on a business trip of which they had all been previously informed.

Business as usual, was her motto. Act as if everything were normal, everything all right.

"Yes," Mark answered, because what else could he say?

"You had nice weather," she went on, "but now I'm afraid we're in for a storm."

"Yes," Mark said again.

Miss Ives got up from her desk. There, her manner said

quite plainly. That's that. The difficult first moments are over, now let's get down to business. "You'll find letters to be signed, Mr. Galloway. I've got everything in order. The mail and production reports are waiting on your desk. We've done quite well by ourselves, if I do say so. Joan and Jean have been jewels and they've worked hard so everything would be in apple-pie order for you."

Her praise broke the spell for Joan and Jean. They stopped gawking at Mark and, with a simultaneous pat to their hair and smoothing of their sweaters, they returned to work.

"I always say I'm grateful to have two such fine girls working in our office, Mr. Galloway. I don't know what we'll do if they take it into their pretty heads to get married and leave us."

Joan and Jean, almost purring with contentment, were clicking away at their typewriters. Mark smiled inwardly. He was grateful himself, but not for those two sloe-eyed beauties at the typewriters. He was grateful for Ivesy, as he fondly called her, and her inexhaustible ability to handle people and situations.

She followed him into his office and closed the door behind her. Lowering her voice, she came squarely to the point.

"Have you seen anyone yet, Mr. Galloway? I mean here in the plant?"

"No. I came directly up here. Talked only to Albie Griffin."

"Good." She moved closer, speaking even more softly. "Mr. Galloway, we're in an awful mess." She always used "we" when she meant Mark.

"What's the matter, Ivesy? You look as if you had seen a ghost."

"I feel as if I had, Mr. Galloway. Something terrible has happened. It's come to me from three or four sources and most of the stories hang together, including old McGovern's who made a special trip up here yesterday afternoon to see me. McGovern from the stock room, the see-all, know-all."

"Yes, I know. Get on with it, Ivesy."

"Yesterday Art Wimbley discovered that all the spindles on the Merriman order would have to be scrapped. The journals didn't fit and the spindles wouldn't assemble. It would take two or three weeks to make new parts, so that meant the Merriman order wouldn't be filled in time."

"Good heavens!" Mark exclaimed. He came around his desk and stood beside Miss Ives. "That means we lose the order. Maybe the whole account."

Miss Ives nodded. "Yes. Mr. Wimbley showed the trouble to Mr. Emrich and, somehow or other, Mr. Spencer Bradford got in on it. He went down to Art Wimbley's office about something and the whole cat tumbled out of the bag. They got hold of Mr. Muthersbaugh and tried to talk to him about it." Miss Ives paused. She glanced around to be sure the door was closed tightly.

"Mr. Muthersbaugh went to pieces. Excuse me for being so blunt about a relative of yours, Mr. Galloway, but people say Mr. Muthersbaugh is, well, they say he has a sort of nervous condition. If you know what I mean."

"I know," Mark said.

"He went haywire. Right there in Art Wimbley's office. They say Mr. Wimbley had to strike him to make him stop. It must have been awful. They said Mr. Muthersbaugh was stark, raving mad, yelling his head off, saying a whole lot of things he shouldn't have."

"Just what did Mr. Muthersbaugh say, Ivesy?"

She hesitated. "Mind you, Mr. Galloway, we all know it isn't true. Not a word of it."

"What did he say?"

"He said the fault was yours," she stammered out the words, "that if you'd stayed here instead of going off on a trip with . . . on a trip, Mr. Galloway, this wouldn't have happened."

Miss Ives reached in her pocket for a handkerchief and

dabbed at her eyes. "It's not true, not a word of it. We all know it's not true," she said loyally. "I feel awful, Mr. Galloway. I honestly feel awful to be the one to tell you. But I feel it's my duty. If I don't someone else will. That would be harder on you."

He patted her shoulder. She continued to weep, not noisily as Effie had wept this morning, but in muffled little sobs.

This is sure my day for facing weeping females, he thought.

"Look, Ivesy," he said. "It's all right. Don't be upset. I'm glad you told me."

"Are you, Mr. Galloway? Are you, honestly?"

"I am. You're right. If I've got to know it, I'd rather hear it from you first."

She stopped sobbing, patted her cheeks dry and put away her handkerchief. She was in perfect control of herself once again.

"What do you want me to do, Mr. Galloway?"

Mark shuffled the pile of papers nearest him as he made up his mind. Then he said in a voice that was remarkably steady, "Get Spencer Bradford on the phone and ask him if he'll see me right away."

She started toward the telephone and Mark put out a hand to detain her.

"Just a moment. Ivesy, I want to ask you a question, a personal question, and I want a truthful answer."

She flushed. "A personal question, Mr. Galloway?"

"Personal about me, not you."

"Oh, I see."

"Look, Ivesy, I want the answer straight. No bluffing. No soft-pedaling. *I want the truth*."

"I wouldn't lie to you, Mr. Galloway."

"Has the news got around the plant that I've left Mrs. Galloway? That we're separating and I've moved out of the house on Turkey Hill?"

"Oh!" She fell back against the desk, reaching out toward it for support. "It isn't true!" she said instinctively.

"It is true, Ivesy. I'm giving it to you straight from the horse's mouth. I left Mrs. Galloway this morning and moved down to the Harrington. What I want to know is, does anyone here know about it yet?"

"I'm sure they don't. If they did, I'd hear about it. I'd hear right away."

"You're absolutely sure?"

"Absolutely. McGovern would hear it first and he'd tell me. He's on our side, Mr. Galloway. He'd get up here as fast as his legs would carry him. Others would tell me, too." She flushed again. "I have spies. I know it sounds awful, but I've got to have spies, Mr. Galloway. You have no idea the things I've protected you from that way."

"I know the facts of life, Ivesy." He smiled. "So don't worry about any skulduggery you've committed to save my hide." He leaned toward her. "Then you're sure no one knows, not yet anyway."

"Not yet, Mr. Galloway. They'll find out soon enough, but so far I'm sure they haven't."

"Good." He straightened up, relieved. If Spencer didn't know that he had left Nina, he was in a much more advantageous position than he would have been otherwise. "Good," he repeated. "Now call Mr. Spencer Bradford. But keep your voice steady. Just sound as if everything were all right and I didn't know a thing."

She put her hand on the telephone and looked up at him. With a catch in her voice, she said, "Mr. Galloway, I feel like an atom bomb had been dropped into my lap."

He nodded. "I know," he said. "I'm rocking a bit myself. But don't let on. Go ahead, Ivesy. Get the grand panjandrum himself."

Chapter 28

WHEN MARK WALKED INTO SPENCER'S OFFICE, SPENCER GOT up and stood there smiling. "Glad to see you back," he said. The show of friendliness, however insincere, surprised Mark. He made no answer, but waited for Spencer to call the signals.

"Sit down, Mark." Spencer's voice was smooth as silk, his tone affable. "I'm glad you came in to see me. I've got a few things to talk over."

"I figured you had." Mark sat in the chair across from him.

"We had an upset in the factory while you were gone."

"I heard about it. The Merriman order."

"You know the details?"

"All of them," Mark said flatly.

"Good. That saves some time."

If Spencer were going to indulge in recriminations, it was not at this point.

He tilted back in his chair and studied Mark a moment before he went on. "You and I are businessmen, Mark. We know the value of coming to the point instead of beating around the bush."

"Right."

"So I'm going to make you a proposition. Lay my cards on the table and offer you a deal."

Mark waited for Spencer to show his hand.

"You say you heard the details of the Merriman fiasco. Then you must know that I was in Wimbley's office when Frank cracked up. I got the whole picture, unvarnished and straight. I didn't like what I saw. Frank made a poor showing."

Mark could only keep silence. There was nothing to say. He had to admit that Spencer's attitude baffled him. He had come in here expecting a dressing down. He was ready for it and he had some idea of what he was going to say. Now Spencer was using different tactics and while it did not throw Mark off guard—he had known Spencer too long not to be accustomed to his subtlety and strategy—he had to admit he was bewildered.

Frank Muthersbaugh was Spencer's man. Spencer had brought him here over Mark's protests. For Spencer to reverse himself like this, chuck over his pride and admit Muthersbaugh was a mistake must take a pretty strong motive. Spencer had something more precious to save than his pride, that was apparent. Mark listened quietly, waiting to hear what it was.

"I've concluded that Frank isn't the man for the job, Mark," Spencer continued. "I thought he was but I was wrong. It won't be an easy thing to do but we'll have to let him go."

"Who's going to take his place?"

"I'm coming to that." Spencer moved closer to his desk and picked up a pencil. Thoughtfully, he balanced it between the forefingers of both his hands. Then he put it down and looked up at Mark.

"I've just been advised that another engineer is about to join the ranks of our family." Mark shifted uneasily and Spencer put up his hand. "I know you're dead set against what you have called our inbreeding policy, but this is different, Mark. Hear me out."

"Go ahead."

"This is a young man, two years out of M.I.T. He graduated third in his class. He's brilliant. A first-class engineer. He's been getting some factory experience. His record is excellent. He's going to marry one of our cousins next month. I'd like to suggest—with your permission, of course—that they skip a honeymoon for the time being and come over to Bradford. Let him take the chief engineer's job off Frank's hands. He's a good man, Mark, a fine engineer. I've looked him over carefully. I know."

"*With my permission*," Mark repeated what he considered the salient words of Spencer's speech. "It's a little late to be asking for that, isn't it?" Spencer's eyelids flickered. "And if I don't choose to give my permission?"

"Why wouldn't you?" Spencer rose, showing agitation for the first time. "You can look at his record for yourself. Everything I say is true. This time we've got something. What difference does it make if he's a member of our family? He's a good engineer."

"How much factory experience has he had?"

"Two years. He's done well. His recommendation is excellent."

"Has he made lathes?"

"No-o-o." A reluctant admission.

"Two years out of M.I.T. No factory experience to speak of. Never saw a lathe made in his life, I bet. You want to bring him in here as chief engineer. Doesn't it sound a little sour even to you, Spencer?"

"I don't like your insinuation. *Even to me*."

"All right. I'll take it back. Let's put it another way. You bring a green kid over here. Sure his school is good. My own school, at that. But he's raw, wet behind the ears. What does he know about handling men? What does he know about production and design and all the inspection problems? It won't work, Spencer. It won't work any more than Muthersbaugh worked."

Spencer's eyes narrowed. "What kind of man do you want?"

"I want my own man. I want Steve Emrich. Why in the name of heaven won't you give me a man with know-how and experience and real brains, someone the men in the shop can respect and work with?"

"I said I wanted to make a deal with you, Mark. I meant it. If I give you the man you want, how do I know that you'll play ball with me? What guarantee have I that you'll go along?"

"None," Mark said tersely. "I'm not interested in bargains."

Spencer walked across the room and stood looking out the window at the parking lot below. He clasped his hands behind his back, tapping one against the other for a full minute before he faced Mark again. He turned, not moving from his post by the window.

"Mark, this isn't easy to say, but it's got to be said no matter how much it hurts you or me. We're men. We know the score. Talk gets around. I've heard something of your, well, for want of a more positive word, let's call it your friendship with a certain woman in town. It's bad business, Mark. You married into this family of your own free will. You must have known what it would mean to be a Bradford. We're the backbone of the town. Half the schools in the town bear a Bradford name. We're a prominent family. The rewards are great but it carries some responsibility too. It's a matter of *noblesse oblige*."

"Speak English, Spencer. Better yet, speak good plain American, or you won't reach me."

"You have an obligation to uphold the Bradford name, the Bradford reputation. I don't like what you did this past week. You had no right to take yourself off like that without a word to anyone. It was even worse that a woman was involved. You can't do things like that, Mark. You owe it to all of us to watch your step."

"How? How should I watch my step?"

Spencer, thrown off guard by Mark's apparent nonresistance,

misinterpreted it. He moved closer, as if to set up a chumminess between them.

"I know what's happened to you and Nina, Mark. Believe me, I understand. We're men together, you and I. It happens to marriages. You can't seem to sidestep it. The time comes when the romance is gone. You wake up one morning and it's dead. You thought maybe your marriage would be different, that you could sustain the high peak of romance longer than other people, but the fact is you can't. No one can. So what do you do? You face it. You don't throw over the marriage because you don't love each other any more. You keep the home fires burning. You carry on. You ride out the storm and one day you find you're glad you did it. It doesn't matter that you aren't in love any more. You've still got a marriage. And believe me, that's important. You can't beat marriage. It's an institution we've got to have. For respectability, if for nothing else. A woman needs it, a man needs it. Even without love, even when love is dead, you're better off if you hang on."

Mark felt such a revulsion of feeling toward the man in front of him and what he was saying that his impulse was to double his fist and let him have it. For the time being he couldn't speak. Once again Spencer misunderstood and went on.

"You're fond of this other woman, Mark, I know. It's an old love affair. Those things can be very tempting. We men understand each other on that score. But, Mark"—Spencer leaned earnestly toward him—"can't you be smarter? A bright boy like you. If you must play, do you have to do it so close to home? A smart man would have gone out of town, Mark. That way there's not the gossip. What people don't know, doesn't bother them."

Mark found his voice in one great rush of fury, but he kept his tone low, remembering that there were secretaries and stenographers outside.

"Let me get this straight, Spencer. Let me be very sure I

understand you. You're suggesting that my love for Nina is dead. But that even if it is, we ought to keep our marriage intact. Live together. Put on a good front to the world in a kind of sham marriage. Then you're further suggesting that it will be all right for me to have a girl friend so long as I keep it hush-hush, far enough away from Bradford so the glorious and illustrious Bradford name won't be smeared. Right?"

"You put it too bluntly. You make it sound dirty."

"It is dirty, Spencer. Then further you offer me a deal. If I'll do this, if I'll follow this pattern of morality you've laid out for me, be a good boy and behave myself according to the Bradford standards, you'll play ball with me. You'll give me the man I want in the factory."

"Come now, the way you put it—"

Mark interrupted. "That's the deal, isn't it? In plain language, that's the deal."

"I only want what's best for all of us."

Mark shortened the distance between them. He spoke into the other man's face.

"Spencer, listen to this. Listen to it and get every word of it straight. I left Nina this morning. I walked out because there's nothing left of our marriage. You should know, Spencer. You've helped Nina choose the Bradfords instead of the Galloways. My new address is the Harrington Inn."

"You didn't."

"It's true."

"I don't believe it. I would have heard."

"You're right, you would have heard, but there hasn't been time. The grapevine hasn't got the news. Nina won't tell it herself. She's confused and upset, the way I am, Spencer. We're not all your breed. Maybe Nina isn't such a good Bradford after all. She doesn't seem to share your views on marriage. She wants love or she doesn't want anything. She's not like you. She's not a whited sepulcher."

"Don't talk to me like that."

"I'm almost finished." Mark paused, but he didn't back away. "As for your deal, the answer is no. I wouldn't touch it with a ten-foot pole. This is my day for walking out. When I leave this office I'm going straight to my own end of the hall. To dictate my letter of resignation. I'm through, Spencer. Through with everything that spells Bradford."

"You've got to eat," Spencer said. "Without the salary you got from us, how are you going to live?"

"I've got a dream," Mark said. "One I've had for a long time. Now I begin to think I should have taken a fling at it before. I'm going to open my own plant."

"You're out of your mind. What will you use for money? You can't touch your mutual securities unless Nina signs and I'll advise her not to."

"I'll get the money somehow."

The two men faced each other, silent at last. The room was filled with a great emptiness, more potent because of the clamor of the words that had filled it a few moments before. There was no sound from the outer office where secretaries and stenographers kept their silent vigil, straining to hear what the new trouble was in the Bradford family.

Spencer was the first to break the silence. "Mark, don't be foolish. We need you here. You've done a good job. Don't throw everything over for a whim. These things iron themselves out. Give them time."

Mark shook his head. "I've had a bellyful," he said. "Of everything Bradford."

"All right." Spencer was angry now. "Go ahead. Have it your own stubborn way. But you'll see I'm right. You'll never start that business. You won't be able to raise the capital."

"Thanks." Mark strode to the door but before he opened it he turned and said, "Thanks for the moral support. In your own words, *noblesse oblige.*"

Chapter 29

In the days that followed, Mark had ample occasion to recall Spencer's parting thrust. *You'll never start that business. You won't be able to raise the capital.*

It hung over Mark's head like a prophecy, for prophetic it was.

That night after he had eaten and unpacked his bags, Mark left the Harrington and drove, through a blinding snowstorm, to Steve Emrich's house. They talked until two o'clock in the morning about opening a machine shop. Steve had dreamed of such a possibility, but only after his boys were through college. That was a long way off. His capital was scanty and he had very little he could sink into a business right now. Perhaps he could scrape together a thousand dollars, and go in with Mark. He'd have to talk it over with Anne. He wouldn't want to take a step like this unless she was for it, one hundred per cent.

There was a little place out on King's Highway that Steve had been keeping his eye on. It would be a good spot for their shop. Formerly a plating shop, it had stood vacant for several years. When they got it in shape, Steve said, it would be a trim little building with enough ground around it for expansion when that happy day came.

They talked about what kind of shop they wanted. There

was no friction between them. They both agreed on a contract machine shop as the best bet. This area needed a shop like that.

"I don't see why we shouldn't make a go of it, if we can get the backing," Steve said.

"I'll take care of that," Mark told him. "I've got friends. My own money is tied up and I don't want to bother my wife about that now. But give me a few days and I'm sure I can raise all we need."

Mark did not waste any time. Early next morning he drove out to King's Highway and stopped at a farmhouse for the key to the building Steve had told him about. He took a thorough look at it, inside and out. It would make a good spot for their shop. A few carpenter jobs, some plumbing work, a coat of paint, and the place would be as good as new.

He sat in his car and jotted down a list of men who were possible sources of capital for the project. There were seven names, all gilt-edged prospects, men with whom he was on first-name terms.

They were, some of them, Nina's friends as well as his, but that did not matter. Business was business. Mark was approaching them with a sound proposition. They'd get their money back with a good profit. There might be a moment or two of embarrassment as he explained his new position, but business was not the place for sentiment. An opportunity was an opportunity. If any of these men had come to him, Mark would have written out a check for any one of them.

He decided to try Wayne Abbott, vice president of the Bradford Trust Company, first. There was some Bradford money in Wayne's bank as there was in every bank in the town, but not by any means the larger portion of it. Bradford Tool and most of the Bradfords themselves did their heaviest banking at the First National Bank.

This, however, was not the only reason why Mark chose to approach Wayne Abbott. He liked Wayne personally. Mark and Wayne had a lot in common. They were both tall men, liked by other men and highly attractive to women. They had both risen from the bottom.

As Mark entered Wayne's office this morning, Wayne smiled genially, pulling a chair for him nearer his desk.

If he's heard about Nina and me, Mark thought, it doesn't make any difference to him.

"I need some money, Wayne," Mark said, knowing that in this case the direct approach was the right one. "I quit my job at Bradford Tool yesterday. I need capital. Will you lend me some?"

"What sort of shop are you planning on, Mark?"

Mark told him, outlining his and Steve's plans as quickly as he could.

"That doesn't sound like such a big project, Mark. I thought you had quite a bit of money yourself."

"Just a few thousand in my personal checking account. Everything else is tied up in jointly owned securities. My wife would have to sign. If you could accept that as a sort of collateral, I can pay you back as soon as Nina and I talk things over."

"I should think it would be best if you and Nina got together at once. That would release your money, Mark."

"You can't rush these things, Wayne. Nina's upset. I'm upset myself. We can't talk things over until we've both cooled off."

"Are you sure Nina will sign?"

"Spencer Bradford's been talking to you."

"He called Ray Harrick yesterday afternoon."

"He didn't lose any time," Mark commented wryly. Ray Harrick was president of the Bradford Trust Company.

"This is a delicate spot I'm in, Mark. You know how I feel about you. I'd back you any day. But Ray and Spencer are old friends. Spencer has done quite a few favors for Ray over the years. Personal favors and business favors. That sort of thing builds up. You can't discount it."

"In other words," Mark said, "you've had your orders."

Wayne spread his hands in a gesture of helplessness. "I'm sorry, Mark. I'm sorry as the devil. I hate this sort of thing."

Mark looked at him, head on. "So do I," he said.

He tried Cal Jessup next. Cal owned a lumber company in Southport, the town that lay just beyond Bradford on the map. Cal was a Yankee himself. He took orders from no one. In his shirt sleeves, with an old gray wool vest buttoned around his ample middle, his thinning hair mussed up and a pencil over his ear, Cal Jessup greeted Mark in the confused mass of file cases and lumber supplies which he called his office.

Mark led into his request with greater finesse this time. "Heard any rumors about me, Cal?"

Cal squinted at Mark. "If you mean the bust-up between you and Spencer, Mrs. Jessup spilled the beans at the supper table last night." Cal cackled in appreciation. "Land sakes, I'd like to have been there to hear you tell that stuffed shirt off."

"I've left Nina, Cal. Or maybe you know."

"No!" It took a few moments to digest that one.

"I need your help, Cal."

"Go ahead."

"I want to open my own plant." Mark briefly covered the salient facts. "I know you like to sink a few thousand now and then into a new venture, Cal. You could either do that and we'll give you some shares, or lend me some money and I'll pay you back. If you don't want to go whole hog, I'm sure I can get someone else to lend me part of it. It's a good investment."

"It's a good enough investment, Mark." Cal spoke slowly. Then he was silent, twirling around a glass paperweight that lay on the shambles that was his desk. "I believe in you, Mark. Before I say anything else, I want to make that clear. You're a good man, one of the best. I don't believe for one moment that you could possibly fail in anything you ever started."

"Thanks, Cal."

"Now what I've got to say is gonna hurt both of us, Mark. You and me." He paused. "I can't give you any money, either for a loan or an investment."

"You mean you can't afford to release any?"

"Shucks, no! You know how I'm fixed. I can't give it to you, because you're Nina Bradford's husband and Spencer Bradford's brother-in-law."

"I don't get it. What's the matter, Cal?"

"I'll show you." He got a faded gray ledger from his safe.

"This is my first ledger." He turned pages as he talked. "My first account—Bradford Tool. Forty-five years ago. I remember the day." He squinted again, with the mistiness of nostalgia in his faded blue eyes. "I just opened up my shop, a shack across the road."

He looked at Mark. "Old Jared Bradford was my first customer. Come up the road in a buggy—drove it himself—on a bright autumn day. I walked out to his buggy and stood there talking to him. I remember what he said to me. 'Cal Jessup'—he had a habit of calling people by their full names—'Cal Jessup, I heard what you're planning to do here. I like your idea. I like you. You're a clean, honest boy, right-living and God-worshiping. I've come to help you out.'"

Cal Jessup came back down the years, taking his time to reach Mark. "He gave me the Bradford business, all their crating and skids for shipping. From that day on, he ordered every single bit of lumber from Jessup Lumber. Helped me in other ways, too. Gave me tips on how to run a business. Sent me every single account I had for the first five years." Cal turned the pages of the old ledger. "Southport Pump Company, Brampton Hardware, Imperial Hardware, Universal Hardware, Brampton Marine Supply, United Tool. Most of them are still buying from me. The business Jared Bradford sent me is the backbone of my company today, Mark."

"You liked him, didn't you, Cal?"

"You didn't just like Jared Bradford. You loved him. He was like you, Mark. A man among men. There aren't too many of his kind around any more."

"So you mean that for sentimental reasons you don't want to get mixed up in a Bradford squabble."

"Shucks, no. I wouldn't be caught dead doing a sentimental thing." It was a half-truth and Mark accepted it as such. "Ain't the sentiment that's bothering me. It's the business angle. You know my son, Mark?"

"Slightly."

"He's a scatterbrain. Awful thing for a father to say about a son, but it's true. Mind you, I'm mighty fond of him. But a man has to be honest even about his own children." He shoved his chair closer to Mark in confidence. "He's not the man his father was. I can admit that to you, Mark. Not any more than Spencer or Bob Bradford are the men that old Jared was. Something happens to these families. They start out all right, with good stuff back of them, but the younger generations go to pot. Get soft and weak, or worse yet, get vicious and twisted up. Like these younger Bradfords."

He got up. "I'm on your side, Mark, but I can't afford to show it. If I were a younger man, I'd be able to gamble on my convictions. I'm not a young man. I'll be seventy-five next month."

"Then you won't help me, Cal?"

"I can't, Mark. I can't." The old man sounded almost distressed in his plea to be understood. "I've got to think of my son. He needs this shop, needs it a lot more than you need my money. You'll come out of this somehow, even without my help or anyone else's, because you're Mark Galloway."

Mark got up and stood beside Cal Jessup.

"It's all right, Cal," he said. "I understand."

Cal walked out to the car with Mark.

"If you had a son, you'd be able to put yourself in my place."

"Yes," Mark said as he switched on the ignition. "I'm sure I would, Cal."

With grim determination, Mark turned to the next man on his list.

Mark found John Brill, Southport building contractor, standing ankle-deep in mud and shouting orders to a young fellow on a bulldozer. When he spied Mark, he waved and shouted over, "My headquarters is in the house at the end. Go on in and I'll be right there."

Mark walked into the brand-new house, empty except for the hollow re-echoings of his own footsteps.

Mark had introduced John Brill to Wayne Abbott, who had got the Bradford Trust Company to back John's first development project. Brill didn't need that kind of help now. He was a man well-heeled, a man who had pulled himself up by his bootstraps but who had arrived to stay. Mark was sure that at last he had come to the man who would help him.

He was standing at the picture window, with his back to the room, when he heard his name.

"Mark, you old son-of-a-gun, where you been hiding? I haven't seen you in months!" Mark turned. The man before him was rugged, built like an ox, with huge hands that had learned to use a pick and shovel. In his jacket and boots, he looked like what he was, an honest, hard-working builder. But his manner was something else again. He had acquired a certain polish in his speech. He knew the right thing to say and do.

"Hello, John. I surprised you by coming here."

"Not at all. Always glad to see an old friend like you." He clapped Mark on the back. "You know that."

"Have you heard what happened?"

"What happened?"

Mark could tell from the puzzled expression on John's face that he had not heard, so he told him.

"Nina and I have separated." Mark finished his account. "I'm living—for the time being—at the Harrington."

John was a warm man, with sympathetic responses, and Mark could see him probing into Mark's troubles and taking some measure of them upon himself.

"I'm sorry," was all he said. Then, after some more thinking, "That must be tough on both of you. Nina and you too."

Mark nodded. "I didn't come here to spill my guts," Mark said.

"If I can do anything, Mark. If there's anything *at all* I can do."

"There is. You can lend me some money."

"Sure. Sure thing. How much do you want?"

"Maybe you'd better ask me what I want to do with it."

John snorted. "Ask, my eye. I'd trust you to the end of the earth. How much do you want?"

"I want to open a factory of my own, John. Steve Emrich's going in with me. We're going to contract for machine work."

"A factory! Have you talked this over with the Bradford brothers?"

"Spencer knows."

"I'd bet my bottom dollar that he's raised the devil over it."

"He tried to frighten me. Said I'd never raise the capital."

"You won't either."

"But you just offered me any sum I name."

"That was before I knew what you wanted it for." John Brill walked over to the picture window and stood looking out upon the unfinished ground of his development. He was very quiet before he turned back to look at Mark.

"Mark, I'm a direct man. Making money is my goal in life and time is money. So I'm going to give it to you straight from the shoulder."

"Go ahead."

"There isn't a man who's got money in Bradford or Southport who isn't tied up with the Bradford family one way or another. You might as well face it."

"You," Mark said. "Nobody's got any hold on you. You've dug and shoveled your way up. You don't owe the Bradfords anything."

John Brill laughed. "That's right. I don't. But I want something from them. Something mighty important to me. Mark, listen. For almost ten years I've been trying to buy some land in Bradford. There's no development like this over there, never has been. There are fine houses on two or three or twenty acres and there are workers' houses. But nothing for people who want a comfortable home that's neither crowded nor pretentious. The Bradfords own most of the best land in the town and they won't sell. At least they wouldn't until recently. Three months ago I got an inside track with Bob Bradford and we're negotiating now for the sale of a seventy-five-acre tract."

"The Redcoat Ridge property," Mark said.

"Right. It's perfect for the kind of development I specialize in. Just far enough from the main stem. Not too far. Good high land. And dry. City water. I plan to take my time. Make it a four-year job. Put up one hundred and fifty houses on a half acre each. Sell them at a nice profit. This is the deal I've been waiting for."

"I thought you'd been doing pretty well up to now," Mark said wryly.

"I have. But I've got a big family and I want to retire one of these days. I've pushed myself all my life. I need a rest. I want to quit before I fall over."

Mark got up. John Brill detained him. "Wait. I haven't said it all. I'm not turning you down on the loan, Mark. I just wanted you to know why I can't let it get out that I'm giving you this money. If it did get out, Bob Bradford wouldn't give me a chance at the property. However, we can make other arrangements."

"I don't follow you."

"There's a lawyer in Hartford. Personal friend of mine. I figure the thing to do is transfer whatever amount you want to him. The loan will come from him instead of me. No one will be the wiser."

"Thanks, John. I appreciate the offer. But I don't want money that way."

"Why not? It's perfectly legal."

"It's not the legality I'm concerned about. It's something a little more than legality. It's you and me. If we have to sneak around corners to make a loan, I don't want it."

"Mark, you're being foolish. There's no place for that kind of talk in business. You need the money. You've got to take it the way you can get it."

"Not me, John. I'll take it the way I want it. No other way. Right out in the open or no deal." His voice was harsh and angry and he deliberately softened it as he went back to his friend. "Forget it. I'm not mad at you."

"What are you mad at then?"

"I don't know. I honestly don't know. Maybe I live in the wrong kind of world. Maybe I need to wake up and become more of a realist."

"Maybe," John Brill replied. "I think what you're looking for, Mark, is a hero. There aren't any heroes in real life. On battlefields, in jet fighter planes, on submarines there are heroes. Not in the workaday world, Mark. No heroes, no villains. Just human beings. Everyone tries to survive. The best way he can. No one can worry too much about the other fellow. He's too busy worrying about himself."

"I'm worrying about the other fellow. About you, John. That's one reason I can't accept your offer. It would get out somehow that you'd lent me that money. The Bradfords would find out. That would be bad for you."

"I'll take that chance."

Mark shook his head. "I can't let you, John."

The two men walked out. They stood on the freshly laid flagstone terrace of the new house. The lawn had not yet been graded and the grounds were a stretch of brown mud, rutted by bulldozers and trucks.

John spoke. "Mark, back there I said something that was only a half-truth. I said there weren't any heroes in this workaday world. I want to take that back. I know just one guy I've met who might fill the bill. A guy named Mark Galloway."

Mark looked away, up at the sky. He suddenly seemed very far away from the world of John Brill and bulldozers and steam shovels, of the Bradfords and their smug little autocracy.

He could hear Claire's voice talking to him. It was summer and they were driving back to River Street with its heat and smells. "Be a hero, Mark Galloway," she was saying. "Don't ever settle for anything less."

Chapter 30

By now Mark was pretty well convinced that it would be the same story wherever he went. But to satisfy himself, he tried the other men on his list. He had lunch with three of his friends at the Ocean Grill in Brampton.

Alec Forbes, Dick Johnson, and Sherm Mitchell often pooled their funds to back some promising enterprise. Because they worked and lived in Brampton, Mark thought that at last he had found his men. Alec was head of one of the Brampton department stores, Dick ran a brokerage office in the city, and Sherm managed a large electronic supply company.

Over a lunch which Mark hardly touched, he laid his plans before them. From the moment he started talking he knew that their answer would be no.

After the refusal it was Alec who walked the three blocks with Mark to the parking space where he had left his car. Alec opened up with the truth. Sherm's brother was one of the selectmen in Bradford. He had political aspirations. It would be more correct to say that Sherm had the aspirations for him. He wanted to see his brother run for governor. He couldn't run without Bradford backing.

"We have a strict policy in our syndicate to act only by unanimous agreement. I'm sorry, Mark."

"Everybody's sorry, Alec. Take a good look at me. I've got a sign across my chest two feet wide and a foot high. Know what it says?" Alec shook his head. "It says: 'Bradford Scrap. Not Wanted.' "

Mark got in his car. "So long, Alec," he called. "See you at the Governor's Ball."

There was just one man he hadn't tried and he turned his car toward this final destination, not because he had any hope but because he wished to round out the picture.

There was no man he had ever met, unless perhaps some buddy on the battlefield, who owed so much to Mark Galloway. Emerson Hayes owed him his very life itself.

Emerson Hayes was a son of wealth. Groton, Harvard, a place prepared for him in his father's firm, Emerson had never known what it was like to be without money. He owed the Bradfords nothing financially, socially, politically. He was as rich as Spencer, but he was more a man, more likable, less arrogant.

When Mark first met Emerson he was depressed, blaming himself for the failure of his two marriages, not openly, but in moments of confidential talk with Mark. His two marriages had been identical in many respects, cat-and-dog affairs with his palatial home near Turkey Hill filled with harangues from morning till night. When his second wife left him, he went to pieces.

Mark had found him in the depths one night when, in answer to a frantic call from the Hayes' housekeeper, Mark had hurried over to his friend. Emerson was preparing to kill himself and Mark had stopped him. Mark persuaded Nina to invite him to their house for a few weeks, until they were sure he was on the road to recovery. It had been at a dinner party during those weeks at the Galloway house that Em Hayes had met Cheryl Hunt.

They fell in love gradually, finding out in a leisurely way

whether they wanted each other, but once they had found out, their love never wavered. Cheryl had been the right woman for Emerson Hayes. She would have been the right woman for almost any man but that was beside the point. All Em Hayes knew was that now there was happiness in his house.

He had not forgotten that Mark was almost directly responsible for this happiness and he often spoke with gratitude about it.

He was home today, in his stables. The housekeeper sent Mark there, and Em greeted him cordially, although he of all Mark's friends must have heard most accurately the details of his separation from Nina.

"I've come after a favor, Em." Rapidly, with the facility born of repetition, Mark told his story.

When he was finished, Em Hayes spoke quickly in nervous jerks and stops. He was sorrier than he ever had been about anything in his whole life to have to turn Mark down. The truth of the matter was that Cheryl and he had come as near to quarreling over this Bradford mess as they had ever come in their years together. Someone had telephoned Cheryl earlier today and told her that Mark was looking for backing and he was sure to turn up at the Hayes' home sooner or later.

Cheryl was distraught. Nina was one of her dear friends. She didn't want Em to take sides. She insisted that he not do anything to help Mark at this point. Em pooh-poohed her attitude. He could help Mark if he wanted to and he certainly would want to if Mark came to him.

There were tears, bitter recriminations, some threats. Em had capitulated. What else could he have done? Cheryl had given him the only real happiness he had ever known. She was not a domineering woman. She seldom demanded anything. This was the first time she had taken an open stand against him.

Mark left the Hayes home and headed his car in the direction of the Harrington. He felt exhausted. He didn't blame Em

Hayes. Cheryl had, as Em had so simply and eloquently put it, given him the only real happiness he had ever known.

On the way to the Harrington Mark made a decision. He left his car out front. The lobby was almost empty. He went straight to the public telephone booth at the far end of the lobby. He dialed Nina's private number in the house on Turkey Hill and listened while it rang. There was no answer. He dialed again and still no answer. Hanging up, he tried the house phone. This time Effie answered.

"Mr. Galloway!" she exclaimed, recognizing his voice. "I'm sorry. Miss Nina won't speak to anyone."

"Tell her it's me and tell her it's urgent."

"I'll try," Effie said.

He waited a long time. When Nina finally answered, her voice was strained, aloof.

"Nina, I don't like to call you like this. It would be much better to talk things over later, after we've both had time to think." No answer. "I need some of my money. Need it badly. Perhaps you've heard what for."

A long pause. Then, "Yes, I heard."

"I'm calling to ask if you'll release some of our mutual securities, Nina."

Another pause. "I'd rather not talk about it now."

"But we've got to talk about it now. I've got to have that money right away."

"Can't it wait?"

"No, it can't. I've got to know now. Tonight." There was what sounded to Mark like a gasp. A long pause followed.

"Why must we hurry so, Mark?"

"Because this is important to me, Nina. This is something I want settled now. Tonight."

"You sound so . . . so final, Mark." It was one of the few times he had heard Nina stammer. She seemed bewildered, confused, almost terrified.

"This is a time for finalities, Nina."

She paused again. "I had hoped—" She interrupted herself. Whatever she had hoped, it would remain unvoiced. "I want to wait awhile, Mark. We've got to talk things over. Lots of things. This is one of them." He sensed a pleading in her voice, a frightened unwillingness to let him go, and it moved him, but not enough. Perhaps if he had not been through the ordeal of this frustrating day he might have acted differently. As it was, he was tired, beaten, upset. All the tenderness had been crushed from him.

"Then you won't give me your answer tonight, Nina? Yes or no."

"Please don't ask me to do that, Mark. Couldn't you come and talk it over?"

"But I don't need to see you, Nina."

There was a long pause before she said, "I see."

"All I want is an answer."

"I haven't got one, Mark," she said softly.

And without waiting for another word, Mark Galloway hung up.

He opened the door of the booth and walked over to the stairs. Grabbing the banister, he walked up slowly, pulling himself forward by grasping the polished rail. He felt old, suddenly, unaccountably old. It was an effort to reach the top. Then, with the same measured step, he walked down the hall to his room. He was surprised to see that the door was slightly ajar. When he pushed it wide open, he saw Victoria Bradford sitting there.

Neither of them spoke. He went to the window. He felt bereft, as if everything that mattered had passed out of his life. The window stood partly open and the impulse to hurl himself out swept over him. He shook it off and slammed the window shut. Then anger surged up, hot, vicious anger that wanted revenge. His hands trembled, itching to smash something.

322

There was a small china lamp on the night table. He wrenched the wire from its socket and smashed the base of the lamp against the side of the wastebasket. One blow and he had shattered it the way this day's work had shattered him.

He turned to Victoria. "I had to do it," he said.

"There's another one over there," she said. "Bigger."

He shook his head. "One is enough."

She got up and came over to him.

"Mark, how much money do you want?"

He looked at her, not answering.

"You want some money. I came here to write you out a check for all you want."

"You know what I want it for?"

"I know."

"No one in your family will ever speak to you again."

"That's a blessing I had not even dared to hope for."

He turned away, walking toward the other end of the room.

"Victoria, I wish you could have been with me today. For the first time, I tried to raise money. I went to seven men. All of them, as men go, pretty good men. They turned me down. To a man, Victoria, they turned me down. I died seven times today. Died is the word for it. And then when I came back here I called Nina up and asked her to release some of our mutual securities. Her answer was no. I feel a million years old. Can you understand that?"

"I understand, Mark."

"Now I find you here. Ready to give me all the money I want. All day I've been trying to raise money. I wanted it. I wanted it so bad I would have done almost anything to get it. Now suddenly I don't want it."

"You're tired. You'll think better of it."

"No. You've got to understand me. I won't think better of it. I don't want the money. I don't want it because it's Bradford money. You're the last person in the world whom I want to hurt, Victoria. But I can't take your money. I don't want any more Bradford money. Never. Do you hear me. Never!"

Victoria came over and put both her hands on his shoulders. "You really mean that, Mark, don't you?"

"I do."

"Good. I'm glad. You don't need the Bradford money. You never did. You'll be better off without it." She paused. "But I meant what I said. You can have as much as you want. I'm your friend."

"I know that."

"What will you do now?" Victoria asked.

"I don't know. I need time to think and it sure looks like I'm going to have plenty of it."

"Thinking is a good thing. Most of us don't do enough of it."

They were quiet, looking at each other. Victoria picked up her fur stole. She started to put it on and then dropped it again upon the chair.

"Mark." He looked up. "Money isn't as important as you think. I know that must sound fantastic coming from someone who's never been without it. I'm not rooting for poverty. A little money is a good thing so far as it will take you. But I'm talking about our kind of money, the kind of money you've been clinging to the last seventeen years." She paused. "Does this sound like a sermon? Is it more than you can take right now?"

"No. Go ahead."

"I've watched you, Mark. From the beginning. You've been almost naïve in your single-mindedness. You didn't marry Nina for her money, but once you'd got your hands on some of it, you clung for dear life. This is it, you shouted to your world. This is what counts. Believe me, brother, I didn't start with it, but now I've got it and believe me, I know. This is living."

He turned his back on her and walked slowly to the window,

where he stood looking down upon the stretch of withered lawn and the ice-fringed river. She did not stop.

"It wasn't living, Mark. It sounds anomalous from me, I know. You think I've lived that way, too. But I haven't. I've lived in spite of it. Let me say it again, Mark. I've snatched me a great big chunk of life not because of the Bradford wealth, but in spite of it. The very opposite of your credo, Mark. I've said to myself and my world, *even* if I have money, I'm going to live. I'm going to love and lose and suffer like other people. I'm going to escape the dreadful tedium of being a Bradford. That's all that's wrong with you, Mark. You're bored to death with being a Bradford. You want to live again."

"You can't sell an idea like that, Victoria, to a man who was born into poverty."

"I'm not trying to sell you anything. I'm telling you the way it's been with me. All my life I've been running away from the boredom of having too much. All the zest of life is in the challenge it flings at you. It's the fight that keeps a man going. The never having quite arrived. I've fallen in love a half-dozen times. I've written a few good poems. I've painted some bad pictures. I often think, in these twilight years, what I would have done with my life if so much had not already been done for me. I would have loved more completely. I would have written better poems, perhaps painted better pictures. Everything about a man is determined by his goal."

"You're trying to tell me I'm better off than I've been in the last seventeen years."

"Just so." She came over and turned him around. "Is that such a terrible thought to leave you with?"

"You couldn't leave me with a terrible thought, Victoria. Not if you tried."

"Thanks." She reached up and kissed him on the cheek. "I never see you, Mark, but that I regret I was born forty years too soon. I could have shown you what it meant to love a man.

There would have been no doubt in your mind. A man runs to another woman only because he's not sure of himself. I would have made you sure, Mark." She paused. "Mark, if you love this other woman, go to her. You need her now. She'll understand."

"The devilish part of it is that I'm not sure. I don't honestly know."

"Perhaps she'll help you to decide." She went over and got her stole and picked up her handbag from the desk. "Will you be all right, now?" she asked. "I won't leave unless you promise to be yourself, not to do anything impulsive or foolish."

"I promise."

"My home is always open to you, Mark."

"Thanks. That means a lot to me."

"You'll keep in touch with me." It was a polite command. "Promise to call me every few days."

"I promise."

She kissed him again. "*Au revoir*," she said. "If you don't telephone me soon enough, you'll find me here again."

He forced a smile. "Vicky, you're the world's best." He started toward the door. "I'll walk down with you."

"No," she said lightly. "I know my way. You can't afford to be seen coming out of a hotel room with a scandalous character like me." She was gone, with the quick grace that still belonged to her. He turned back to the room, less alone than he had been when he entered it. Victoria Bradford had left behind her more than the fragrance of amber and musk.

Chapter 31

MARK CAME SLOWLY OUT OF SLEEP. HE WAS CONSCIOUS FIRST OF voices, then quick footsteps and more voices. Sudden laughter. Silence.

He propped himself up, not sure where he was, fumbling in consciousness for a time and place to anchor his ego. The room was dark, full of unfamiliar shapes. Then he knew. He was at the Harrington. He reached for his watch on the night table. Nine o'clock!

He jumped up, thinking, I'll be late at the plant. He stopped.

They're not waiting for me at the plant. They'll never be waiting again.

Gradually, now, things came back to him. He remembered yesterday. The taste of it was still in his mouth, bitter, sour.

He looked around him where his clothes lay scattered on chairs. The place was a mess. After Victoria had left yesterday, he had pulled the blinds and yanked off his clothes, throwing them anywhere. Then he had dropped on the bed to sleep the sleep of exhaustion.

He walked to the windows and pulled open the blinds, letting in warm sunshine. Half-stupefied with sleep, he looked at the sunlight, letting it pour in upon the rugs, the furniture, his clothing, engulfing everything in its irritating cheerfulness.

Over the telephone he ordered breakfast in his room. He

took a shower and dressed quickly. A knock on the door told him his breakfast had arrived just as he was tying his four-in-hand.

He had breakfast by the window, looking out upon the river. Another time this might have been pleasant but this morning he enjoyed neither the setting nor the food. He ate merely to satisfy his hunger. He might have taken his time, lingering over breakfast, reading the Brampton papers that had come up with his tray, but he ate hurriedly. The urge to be out of this room, out of this building, pushed him on. He realized that he was hurrying for nothing, but he could not stop.

His car was waiting for him in the parking space and he turned it away from Bradford toward the open country, spurning the more familiar shore road or the parkway to Brampton. At first he drove at breakneck speed, in an impulse to leave Bradford behind him. Then he slowed up, thinking that since he was going nowhere it was foolish to hurry.

The country was not unexplored but it had about it a newness that baffled him. He discovered the trouble. He was seeing it through new eyes. It was he, not the scenery, that had changed. This was the first time he had ever driven out here in this frame of mind, belonging nowhere, to no person, with no destination in mind, with nothing to do when he stopped.

Claire came to his thoughts. He had intended to call her last night but the visit from Victoria and sheer exhaustion had changed his plans. He pulled into the next gas station and called the Skyline Lodge from an outdoor booth. It took a little time to locate her and when she heard his voice, she seemed pleased, with no sense of the disaster that had settled down upon him, and was sure to involve her.

"Claire," he said, "I've got some news, but before I give it to you, I want to tell you something else."

"Yes, Mark?"

"I want you to know how much I appreciate you. You've

been wonderful, Claire. Not only because of what you've done for me. But also because of the things you left unsaid. Any man should be grateful just for having known a woman like you."

Then he told her the news in as few words as he could, about Nina, about the breakup, about the quarrel with Spencer. He did not tell her about his attempts to raise money. That could wait.

She listened. She did not say, as so many persons might have, "Oh, I'm so sorry. How dreadful for you." There were none of the easy and hypocritical expressions of sympathy, warm in tone and sentiment, barren of real meaning. She said nothing until he had finished and then, one question: "Mark, are you all right?"

"I don't know. I haven't had time to think. That's what I need, Claire. Plenty of time to think. About you. About us together. I hope that's all right with you."

"Of course it is, Mark. We both need time to think. Let's not rush it."

"Let's give ourselves a chance to straighten out, Claire. There's plenty of rough going ahead for both of us. But I feel sure we'll work things out once we're clear in our own minds. I'll be in touch with you when you get back. Sunday night?" She said yes. "Don't try to call me. I'll call you." A pause. "Claire, thanks for everything. You've been wonderful."

He left the gas station and drove on. The miles clocked off on his speedometer but he paid no attention. He must be far from Bradford, going into farm country. White clapboard houses, red barns, an occasional silo blurred into indistinctness as he shot past. He slowed up and stopped behind a school bus that disgorged its crowd of shouting children. This told him it was around noon. There were several inviting restaurants along the road, but he did not pull in. He felt disinterested in food, not just because of his somewhat late breakfast but because his appetite had deserted him.

A stiffness in his arms and legs suggested how far he must have driven and he swung off the road into a secluded spot shaded by evergreens. In summer this was a state picnic area. The sign at the entrance said *White Birches* and there was the clump of trees that had given the place its name. It was deserted today, stripped of picnic tables and benches. This was a place where he could stay awhile, unnoticed, quiet, a place where he could think.

I've got to take inventory, he thought. The way you would in business. That's the thing to do. Face the facts. See what I've got and what I can do with what I've got.

To be honest, brutally, almost viciously honest with himself, that was the keynote of the moment. Nothing short of soul-stripping honesty would be any use to him now.

He was thirty-eight, almost thirty-nine. That wasn't young any more, especially in industry. He knew two things well, engineering and production. He was one of the most capable production managers in the state. But he was also Nina Bradford's husband. By now there was no doubt in his mind what it meant to be Nina Bradford's husband. He was a one-job man, and that job was in Bradford Tool. Outside of Bradford Tool, he was nothing.

Even at best it was hard enough to crack open a new place for oneself. Let's suppose he were some guy fresh out of a job looking for a place in production engineering. He'd try every possible avenue, every plant in the vicinity of Bradford. He would, quite possibly, have recommendations. Even so, time would be needed, time for probing, searching, making contacts, following them up. Maybe after a few months of searching he might find the job he wanted. That's if he had been some ordinary guy.

Who am I?

The question pounded against his temples, sending a wave of uncertainty over him.

Who am I?

Mark Galloway, in my late thirties, a one-job man who's just been eased out. Sure, I got out myself but the handwriting was on the wall. In red letters two feet high. I'm flat on my fanny and I've got no real friends. Total available assets, a few thousand dollars. How long will that last?

Who am I?

I'm a guy who doesn't belong to anyone, doesn't belong anywhere. All my bridges gutted behind me. There's Victoria and there's Claire. But Victoria is a Bradford. And Claire's a young woman with a future already sullied from meddling around with me. They've both already risked enough for me.

Who am I?

I'm a guy alone.

Alone.

The word hammered against him.

Why? he asked. Why am I alone? Because I once believed in my wife, believed that she respected me as much as she loved me. I found out different. She showed me, all right. At the slightest provocation she showed me just how little she thought of my opinion, or even of my happiness if it stood in the way of her precious Bradfords. All right, so maybe I was a little to blame too, as far as Nina is concerned. But with Bradford Tool I've got a clean slate. I gave them everything. The works. Everything I had. No one could deny that, not even that wizened-livered pinhead Spencer.

By main force he put Spencer and Nina and the Bradford tribe from his consciousness. He had to do something. He couldn't sit here all day. He had taken his inventory. He knew what he had. Now he had to take some action.

Mentally he ran through the list of firms that might need a man like him. Production engineering. There was Woodward and Gamble. Bradley Pump. Chalfonte's. Hawley and Masterson. Von Brock Engineering.

He projected his thought ahead, two or three hours from now as he made the rounds. He saw himself walk into a plant, talk to a girl in the reception office, maybe if he was lucky drop the name of someone he knew. Then, what? The solicitous inquiry about health, the ready handshake, the quick smile. Sure, Mark, we'd like a man like you. You're one of the best. We're pretty overloaded right now in every department but we'll sure keep you in mind. By the way, you might fill out this application blank. Just as a matter of form. Routine stuff. With you it doesn't mean a thing. We know your caliber.

He saw the form in front of him. Age, schools, experience, references. He knew the ropes. He had eased out many a man himself, asking him to fill out this form. It was a polite way to get rid of a guy. No one ever looked at the form again. It was filed away in the morgue. It was the business death sentence.

Pride whipped through him, lashing every nerve in his body. I'll never subject myself to it, he thought. I won't drink the dregs of humiliation. Me, who a week ago was at the top. The very top. General manager of Bradford Tool.

Me, Mark Galloway. Who am I?

The question thrust itself in again, buffeting him. It whirled in his head, pounded through his veins, churned his stomach. He felt dizzy. It was the old war sickness, riding in on the flood of dismay and loneliness, attacking him in this moment of loathing and fear.

Fear for what? For himself. For his very life. For his ruptured and embattled ego. Fear for Mark Galloway. Who was Mark Galloway? A man alone.

Who am I? Who am I?

He hunched over the wheel to stem the tide of terror.

The inrush of fear was more swift and devastating than any he had known before. The illness swept over him, turning him hot and cold in turns, gripping him, wrenching his mind apart.

As always before, he lost track of time, sitting there in his terror and aloneness. And as always before, it passed as it had come, with unpredictable suddenness, leaving him cold and shaking.

It was like all the previous spells, with one exception. It lasted longer and it was more devastating.

I've got to do something, he thought. I can't sit here waiting for something to happen. *I've got to do something.*

Do what? a voice within him mocked. You weren't just a Bradford relative, you belonged to them. You were their property. Now that you've broken with them, see how far you'll go. You'll have to begin all over again. Not the fair-haired boy this time. Just a guy almost forty, walking his shoe leather off looking for a job. That's you, brother. Face it.

Depression settled over him, crowding him, blinding him. It was so real, so powerful, it became almost a physical force pressing and pushing him.

He fought it off as if it were a live thing. It was a struggle, fierce and brutal, a battle to keep his sanity and save his life. It was a close fight but he won, temporarily at least.

He got out of the car, standing beside it, half-leaning against the door, as exhausted as if he had come from physical combat.

"If I could only know what it's all about." He said the words aloud. The scheme of things, the reason for being here, the whys and wherefores of life itself baffled him. He wanted an answer. He wanted it quick.

It's not in me, he thought. That's for sure. Whatever I've got to do now, the answer won't come from me. I've shot my bolt. Something somewhere that's bigger than I am has got to show me. Jason might have the answer. Maybe if I went to him and talked this time, instead of clamming up the way I did before, maybe we'd get somewhere.

So, because he had no other place to go, he turned his car back to Bradford and Jason.

Chapter 32

Mark had to wait in Jason's study while his wife ran over to the church to get him. Mark did not mind waiting. Time which had once seemed of such importance no longer had any value for him.

When Jason entered the room he was smiling, but the sight of Mark huddled in the chair by the fireplace sobered him.

He came over and took Mark's hand and gripped it. The very quietness of the act calmed Mark.

"I left Nina," he said. "I left Bradford Tool."

Jason put up his hand to interrupt him. "Don't try to tell me. I know all I need to know."

There was a long silence between them.

"I don't know why I came here, Jason. Except that I need help. Need it badly. I don't mean money. Not that kind of help. Nothing like that can help me now."

"What's troubling you, Mark? It's something deeper than Nina or Bradford Tool."

"It's me. I'm what's troubling me." Mark jumped up. "I came here a few weeks ago to talk about it, Jason. You remember that night." Jason nodded. "When I got here and faced you, I couldn't."

"You can tell me now."

334

Jason's soft-spoken tone acted like a sedative on Mark's frazzled nerves. The tension within eased a little.

"I don't know how to talk about it. It's something mental, I guess. Shot nerves. I don't know what a psychiatrist might call it and I care less. It started during the war but it cleared up. A few weeks ago under the strain and pressure it started acting up again. It's hard to describe. It's a kind of terror. Fear isn't a strong enough word. It comes over me fast, before I can stop it. I'm suddenly terrified of everything, things I can't name, terrified about life itself." He was talking agitatedly, walking back and forth. He stopped and faced Jason. "It doesn't make any sense to you."

"Yes, it does," Jason said with that same quietness.

Mark brushed aside the answer. It didn't matter to him whether or not Jason understood. He wanted to unburden himself now that he had started. Just the talking helped.

"When I took those few days up at Great Barrington, I seemed to find myself up there. In all that space, that vastness, a man could reach out and find himself. A man could almost know what the truth about everything was. But it didn't last. Back here, I've lost it again."

"You can't lose truth, Mark."

Mark walked over to him and stood squarely in front of him.

"What is truth, Jason? That's it. I've got to know. I've got to know the meaning of things. I've got to know what it's all about. I can't find myself. I don't know who I am or where I'm going any more. A week ago I was Mark Galloway. A man with a clear and positive identity. Mark Galloway is finished. He's dead, Jason. But I'm still here and I ask myself, Who am I? What is the truth about me and everything else? What's happened to me and to my wife? We loved each other, Jason—or I believed we did. What's happened to the marriage we believed in and worked for? Tell me, Jason." He was shaking. He looked down at his trembling hands. He felt the old terror rising as he talked, felt it pushing against him in violent resistance to the questions he was asking. What is truth? the terror screamed at him. Who are you? There is no truth about you or marriage or love or anything else. The only truth is despair, the only surety, death itself.

It swept in, encompassing him. He stood shaken and broken before Jason, trying to stem the tide of violence within him. He fought back the impulse to sob. The sobs rose inside, great wrenching sobs, and he choked them down.

This is it, he thought. This is the breaking point. I'm cracking. This time it's got me for good. I can't fight it off any more. There's no more fight left in me.

He felt himself flounder, felt his mind go gray, felt it cracking. Into the grayness that surrounded him, a voice reached out for him. It must be Jason's voice because Jason was the only one in the room with him, but he did not recognize the accents or the tone. It was merely sound, sound breaking through the gray barrier that separated him from sanity, from life itself.

The sound was indistinct at first, muttered words. Then it came more clearly. He heard snatches of sentences.

" 'I will say of the Lord, He is my refuge and my fortress; my God; in him will I trust . . . his truth shall be thy shield and buckler. Thou shalt not be afraid for the terror by night; nor for the arrow . . . by day . . . nor for the destruction that wasteth at noonday. . . . A thousand shall fall at thy side . . . but it shall not come nigh thee. . . . There shall no evil befall thee, neither shall any plague come nigh thy dwelling. . . . He shall call upon me and I will answer him; I will be with him in trouble. . . . With long life will I satisfy him, and show him my salvation.' "

The darkness about Mark gave place. He felt himself coming back. The objects in the room took shape again. The first thing he saw as he opened his eyes was Jason's desk, strewn with papers and books. Then the room took form around it, the chairs, the pictures on the walls, the andirons and fireplace tools. He saw Jason last, standing near the window, his back toward Mark, his head bent. Mark knew that he was praying and he knew that Jason was praying for him.

A cold sweat covered Mark's body and he sank down into the chair. Peace, the kind of peace he had never known before, came to him. Peace and stillness. The terror was past. He felt for that precious moment of quietness and strength, as if he would never be afraid of anything again.

His first positive thought was, I feel *newborn*.

"Jason." His friend turned. "I'm all right now."

Jason turned, coming back to him in thought before he crossed the room to him.

"Of course you're all right," he said.

"Thanks." Mark's voice was a husky whisper. "Whatever you did, it reached me. Thanks."

Jason stood beside him, hesitating. "Suppose I get you something hot. Some soup. A hot drink."

"No." Mark put out his hand to detain him. "Stay with me. I want to talk to you." He pointed to the chair nearest him. "Sit there." Jason complied. "What was that you were saying to me back there when I almost conked out?"

"It was the Ninety-first Psalm."

"Say some of it again." Jason did. Mark stopped him when he was half through. "You believe in those statements. Don't you, Jason?"

"It's a little more than belief. I think you might call it understanding."

"I mean, you know they'll work for you. And so they do."

"They work for anyone, Mark. No one's got a corner on God."

"Talk to me about God, Jason. I want to know some more. I want especially to know if He knows about me and what He knows about me."

Jason talked, quietly, without emotion. He talked about a God who loved man, a God who knew only good and who had made man in His image and likeness. He talked about justice and mercy and truth. He talked about life itself. It wasn't a tense, fierce struggle for things outside oneself. It was in its essence a calm, insistent inclusion of all that was good and fine. Couldn't Mark see that it had very little to do with success or failure, with wealth or poverty. Surely Mark must realize that the real values of life were spiritual.

Mark shook his head. "When you talk about love and justice and mercy, I can go along with you, but I'm afraid that I'm a long way off from spirit." He smiled feebly. "But thanks, I'll think about what you said." He got up, with some effort, but once he was on his feet, he seemed lighter, less depressed than he had been in weeks.

"Mark," Jason said, "you're sure it's all right now? Maybe you'd better stay here overnight."

"I'm all right. I can make it now."

Jason helped him into his coat.

"Mark, I haven't said much about joy, but before you go, let me say this one thing. I know the way looks dark to you. If you'll do one thing, turn away from the way it looks, turn your back on what seems to have happened in your life and look on the brighter side, the side ahead, you'll find your way. You're bound to find your way. Joy is a great healer, Mark. I know it seems hard now. You've got so little to feel happy about, but try it. I've seen it move mountains."

Mark nodded. "I'll think about that too."

Jason walked with him to the car. "I'll run over to see you every day, Mark," he said. "You know we're rooting for you. We haven't lost faith in you. Keep an open mind and you'll be surprised at what good can come your way. I mean it. It's not just words. I've seen it work."

Mark got into his car. He looked at Jason standing on the

curb. He was all man, big, strong, vital. There wasn't a weak spot in his whole make-up. Coming from someone else, Mark might have found this talk hard to take. But today he listened. He listened because this was all he had to turn to. There was nothing else left.

Chapter 33

MARK DID, AFTER ALL, TAKE A JOB. AFTER TWO WEEKS OF HUNT-ing and a half-dozen turndowns, he landed an expediting job with Brampton Machine Company.

Brampton Machine specialized in custom-made machinery. They designed and made printing machinery, textile machines, packaging machines, almost anything you could name that was not highly specialized.

Mark was surprised, when he walked into the plant, to learn that the vice president was someone he knew well. Ed Thatcher had, some years ago, been an accountant at Bradford Tool. He and Mark had got along well. He had left Bradford Tool to take a somewhat obscure job at Brampton Machine and had worked his way up. He was energetic and had plenty of push. Mark could understand how he had gotten where he had.

When Ed heard that Mark was there he came down to see him. Mark laid all his cards on the table. Ed Thatcher knew nothing of his break with Bradford Tool. But he seemed pleased to hear about it. He had never liked the policy at Bradford Tool himself.

He was delighted to know that Mark was available. It so happened there was an opening now. It wasn't as big a position as Mark was used to; the salary wouldn't begin to touch what he had been making. Their expediter had just moved to the West, seeking dry mountain air for his wife's health. Brampton Machine was being fussy about replacing him.

They needed a certain kind of man for a job like that. Someone who was diplomatic and could meet plant executives, particularly sales department managers in other firms, on their own level. Mark should have a pretty good idea of the work involved. It was the customary expediting, going into other plants to speed up delivery of material, parts, assemblies purchased by Brampton Machine. Mark would be a good man for the job, in Ed Thatcher's opinion. He understood manufacturing methods, knew how long it took to make stuff and what the problems of manufacturing were. He'd know how to talk turkey to top management.

If he'd like to consider it, he might look on this as an opportunity. Brampton Machine had a liberal promotion policy. If you were good you weren't likely to be lost in the shuffle. They played fair with men of high caliber. Mark was that kind of man.

The salary—and Ed Thatcher looked away as he named the figure—would be eight thousand a year to begin with. It might stay at that figure for quite a while. Mark would want to consider this very carefully. Ed had some idea of the kind of money Mark had been used to.

Mark didn't take long to consider. The salary, it was true, came as a shock to him. He had been thinking for so long in terms of thirty-five and forty thousand a year that he had forgotten that once, twenty years or so ago, he would have considered eight thousand a handsome sum. It would not be accurate to state that money now meant very little to him, but it was true enough that it meant less than it had three weeks ago.

He wanted a job. He wanted something to keep him busy. He couldn't stand waking up each morning with nothing to look forward to. This job was not the ultimate aim and end of life for him. He would take it and see what happened.

He walked out of Brampton Machine with a lighter step than when he had entered. Here at least was something that needed him.

He moved from the Harrington that night, reserving a room for a week at the Brampton Hotel, but before he left Bradford he drove out to Claire's to tell her what he had done. He and Claire sat by the fire in the room Mark had found so cozy and talked for hours. But it was not with the abandon and high spirits they had known at the Lodge. They spoke quietly, almost solemnly, and they found themselves talking of almost everything but themselves. It was as if the very fact of Mark's decision to leave Nina had made them stand off and see one another as people, not as childhood sweethearts grown up. This confirmed Mark in his feelings that he must wait. He and Claire were not ready for one another, not yet. As he left he asked Claire again if she minded waiting. She repeated what she had said on the phone: "We both need time to think, Mark. Let's not rush it."

That week end he found a place in a small apartment house on the outskirts of Brampton, not too far from Brampton Machine, not too close to the noisy center of the city. It consisted of two rooms, a tiny kitchenette, and bath. By the simple expedient of turning the living room into a studio apartment with a convertible bed, Mark could use the bedroom for a den. He could move in a drafting table and set up a place to experiment with his dreams.

He found all he needed to furnish his apartment in the numerous secondhand shops of Brampton. He stopped by at a department store for some draperies, a couch cover, the bed, and some kitchen utensils. By ten o'clock that night he had a home.

It was pleasant and attractive. There were several big lounge chairs where a man could stretch out. There was a drop-leaf table shoved against the wall with two straight-backed chairs for dining. Lamps were everywhere he needed them. The rug on the floor was secondhand but it showed little wear.

His den was the *pièce de résistance*. He had picked up a fairly good drafting table with a straight edge and a flat-topped desk with drawers opening at both front and back. He was proud of his day's work.

He entered upon a new life. His job was a busy one which kept him going nine or ten hours a day. He liked it. It was surprisingly interesting, something he could get his teeth into. He liked going into other plants, meeting all kinds of men. The same qualities that had made him a good general manager at Bradford Tool made him a good expediter for Brampton Machine. From his friend Ed Thatcher he got word that top management was pleased with the way he had taken hold.

For personal reasons, he was glad the job was such a demanding one. If he had to think, he would rather be thinking about manufacturing problems than fighting off memories of Nina.

Even from the beginning of their separation he began to miss her. At first it was just an ache of loneliness which he thought was merely part of his big readjustment. After all, things were completely different now. But as the weeks wore on he realized it was Nina he missed most of all.

Everywhere he turned, the memory of her was there to torment him. He would push through a revolving door and come face to face with a good-looking blond woman and his heart would leap and his mind would cry "Nina!" But it wasn't Nina. It was never his wife. In restaurants, in movie lobbies, in the crowds along the street, his eyes went instinctively toward every golden-haired woman, searching, looking for the wife he had lost and now wanted.

He felt the same aching loneliness for Ginger and Jill with whom he had passed so many happy years. It was not the rebellious Ginger he remembered during these empty days but the carefree Ginger of childhood.

In spite of all this, he avoided any personal contacts with Nina. If he had anything to say to her, he let his lawyer do it for him.

Jason came over to see him often. Victoria, true to her word, visited him once when in the throes of his new job he forgot to telephone her. She examined his new living quarters minutely, commenting on everything. She asked him to take her to dinner. Her interest in what he was doing was flattering. She had a hundred questions to ask about his work. Not a word was said about Nina until Victoria got ready to leave.

Then she said, "Nina's not well, Mark. She's dreadfully thin. Doesn't eat enough. The circles under her eyes would break your heart."

"I'm sorry to hear that," he said to Victoria. He wanted to say so much more, yet he did not dare. He did not dare admit even to himself how much he missed Nina, how much he yearned for his wife. A hundred times a day he was reminded of her—and the longing grew into an ache.

Claire came over once in a while, and they drove out into the country for dinner. He enjoyed the hours he spent with her and always returned feeling refreshed and happy. During the next day he would think about her frequently. But somehow his feelings seemed different now that he was free. He was as deeply attracted to Claire as he had always been. He enjoyed being with her as much as he always had. Yet now that he was comparatively free and their relationship might have deepened, it did not seem to work that way.

As time passed he began to doubt more and more that he and Claire should marry. And the more they were together the more he wondered if Claire did not share his doubt. Perhaps she did not want him for keeps any more than he found he wanted her, now that he believed he could have her.

344

But neither of them spoke of these feelings. It was as if they wanted first a few carefree hours to remind them of youth and freedom.

Jason, Victoria, his job. These were familiar, these were what served to steady him, if not to anchor him as much as possible to safe moorings in a new and strange way of life, but he made new friends too, and these were friends just at hand.

On the same floor with him, at the rear of the house, were the Hobart sisters. Boots and Jacky—he never did learn their real names—were respectively a secretary in a law office and a jewelry buyer in a Brampton department store. In their late twenties, they seemed like kids to him, and early in their friendship they took to calling him "Uncle Mark." He told them that he was married because he thought it was a good thing for them to know, although the fact seemed negligible to them. They were not interested in him romantically. They had plenty of boy friends.

He became their mentor. They told him everything that happened to them, calling to him as he passed their door and inviting him to come in for coffee and dessert while they chattered on, bringing him up to date on their romances and problems. They asked his advice and sometimes they even took it. They were amusing kids, rowdy-dow and almost brutally honest with themselves and their world. "I-don't-kid-me" was one of their favorite expressions. It was certainly their philosophy of life. Watching and listening to them, he felt in some strange way closer to his own daughter Ginger, and they made him understand and miss her. He longed to see Ginger again, to talk with her and try more earnestly than ever to bridge the gap that had separated them.

Then there was Miss Sherman, an elderly spinster on the third floor. He had made Miss Sherman's acquaintance when the building superintendent, a surly fellow, had refused to fix her windows.

345

"They stick," she told Mark. "In winter it's not so bad, but now that we're getting some spring days, I'd like them to open easily."

Mark offered to have a look at the windows, went in, took off his coat and tie, rolled up his sleeves, and in half an hour had the windows working. He found other things in the tidy two-room apartment that needed fixing and when he left, he and Miss Sherman were fast friends.

She told him her life story, and a bleak, lean one it was. She had come from the country as a girl to take a position—she always referred to her job in the pocketbook factory as her "position"—in Brampton. She had worked thirty-five years in the same place, doing the same work, sewing up pocketbooks. Two wars had come and gone, plastic had replaced leather in her shop, even the management of the place had changed, but Miss Sherman had stayed.

She was a dumpy woman in her late fifties, undistinguished except for rather remarkable eyes that had kept their sparkle. They were russet and her hair had once been that color but now it was the horrid shade of gray that reddish hair turns. She wore it as spinsters were proverbially wont to do, in a small, tight bun high on the back of her head.

When she confided to Mark that she had once been very much in love, he almost fell off the chair.

"But he was married," she said, "so what could we do? I don't think he would have made a good husband anyway. But it's nice to have been in love once. It gives you perspective. Days when I'm sitting at the machine in the shop sewing up bags, I think about love. Not especially about him. It was long ago and I doubt that I could tell you the color of his eyes, the shape of his face. But I think about love as I remember it. It was a kind of halo to me. That's what it was, a halo of light and I walked in it. Wherever I went, it went just a little ahead of me and then I stepped into the light that was waiting for me."

He liked Miss Sherman. He liked her philosophy and her cheerfulness and the way she had kept going, not losing her spunk or her character after thirty-five years of sewing pocketbooks all day.

The Reeds were his other friends in the apartment house, and they were perhaps his best friends. They lived on the first floor so that Mr. Reed, who had been crippled in an accident in a factory, could hobble out and sit in the courtyard on fine days. He walked with crutches and he was seldom without pain of one kind or another, but he was also never without a friendly word for Mark. It was through stopping to chat with Herb Reed that Mark met the rest of the family. Ellen Reed was a slender, tiny woman in her early thirties. Mark could see the traces of an earlier loveliness in the delicate features and even now, when she was not tired, she was quite pretty.

However, she was almost always very, very tired. She went to work at eight o'clock after getting the two boys off to school. She was employed as salesgirl in the cosmetic department of one of the stores. At six o'clock she came home, cooked supper for the family, did whatever household chores were waiting.

Mark took to the Reed boys from the start. Bill was the older, around twelve, with small, serious features. He was a brilliant, high-strung boy interested in everything, science, mechanics, airplanes, nature, books, sports. The younger boy, Tom, was roly-poly and a rascal, with a sly sense of humor.

Mark did as much for the boys as he could. He took them to the movies and on fine Saturdays the three of them had the best seats available at the Brampton Ball Park. Once he drove them over to the boatyard in Bradford where his sloop was in dry dock to give them a look at his boat. When Mark promised them a sail on the first fine summer day, along with some lessons in handling the boat, the boys' eyes shone.

During these weeks Mark would find himself stopping in the

347

middle of his lunch, to shake his head over some amusing foible of the Hobart sisters. He worried about Miss Sherman. He could not help wondering what would happen to her if she ever got too old to work in the pocketbook factory. He tried to figure out how well her small pension and social security would take care of her.

Bill Reed, of course, was most in his thought. He wanted to do more for the boy than buy him a few books and a new sweater. He wanted to see the boy have everything a son of his own might have had. He wanted him enrolled in the best college in the country, the way his own boy would have been. He hated to see his wings clipped by the straitened circumstances of his family. He was a boy who would go places, do big things.

He talked to Claire about him, telling her what was on his mind.

"Let him alone, Mark," she said. "Don't spoil him. Mark, see what you're doing. You want to live his life for him, to take over in Bill Reed where you left off in yourself. We can do those things for ourselves. We can't do them for others."

It was a warm Sunday in May and they had driven far north, almost to the state line. They had dinner in a charming setting on a terrace overlooking a lake. Claire was wearing that shade of violet so peculiarly becoming to redheads, a simple dress open at the throat. Her large enameled earrings were shaped like violets and tinted a deeper hue than her dress. Looking at her, Mark thought how pleasant it would be to take her in his arms.

They left the inn where they had eaten and drove out into the country, to a ridge high above the town. There they parked and spread blankets on the ground under a clump of trees. Mark took off his coat and Claire, kicking off her shoes, stretched out, looking up at the sky. He leaned down and, gathering her in his arms, kissed her. She lay in his arms a moment, veiling her eyes, smiling up at him.

"Kiss me like that again, Mark," she said. He did. She pulled away from him and got to her feet. Walking to the edge of the clearing in which they were, she stood there, visibly shaken.

With her back to him she said, "I was wrong to ask you to repeat that kiss. I should have known better." He came over and clasped her to him. He could feel her trembling.

When she could speak again, she said, "Mark, love is the strangest and most unpredictable thing in this unpredictable world. I've thought about it a lot. I've thought about us a lot. I think I've loved you more than I have any man. Yet our love, like all loves, is a thing of moods, of nuances, of lights and shadows. It's made up of the places we've been together, of songs we've heard, even of people we've seen and wondered about and laughed at. Take away one of the facets of love between a man and a woman and you spoil the gem."

"What are you trying to say to me, Claire?"

"Just that I want today to be very perfect. I want to have no one slightest thing foreign to our happiness touch this day."

"That seems a sad thing to say. It sounds almost like an ending."

"Today sad? No! Today must be all brightness and joy. Look. Look at the sky. Not a cloud on the horizon. And look around you, Mark. It's spring. You've been too busy to notice. See, yellow in everything. In the uncurling leaves and the grass. In the forsythia. Everything new and fresh. Everything beginning all over again. And you dare to speak to me of endings!"

She ran from him along the beaten path that led through a woodsy stretch. He followed her, catching up and pulling her toward him. He kissed her again and this time she did not resist. She returned his kiss, but without warmth. And Mark realized that he had been right. Claire had not kissed him with love. This *is* an ending, he thought. I've really known all along that there would be an ending. I've known ever since I left Nina. Claire and I are not made for marriage—not together. Today is like some strange interlude from the past—*our* past —the youth we've been trying to relive.

But he said nothing, and they made a day of it, stretching their happiness far into the night, riding back slowly toward Brampton where Claire had left her car, stopping along the way for supper, enjoying each other as if there were for them neither past nor future but only the exultant now.

When they reached Brampton, she asked him to drive through Seaside Park down to the water's edge. There, against the gentle surf of the incoming tide, she told him.

"Mark, when you spoke of an ending your intuition was right. This is an ending for us—if we really had a beginning. I couldn't bear to spoil today by telling you before. I'm leaving Bradford in three weeks, right after school closes. It was unthinkable that I work there next year after what's happened, even if I hadn't been politely requested to give up my job."

"You didn't tell me about that."

"What was the use? It happened weeks ago. When you were in the throes of your own troubles. It would have been one more thing to bother you."

"Where are you going?"

"I'm going to New Hampshire. To marry David."

"Claire, I don't believe it. You can't . . ."

"Wait!" She put up her hand to interrupt. "Sometimes it's important to love. Sometimes to be loved. You don't love me, Mark. I've known that all along. David loves me," Claire went on. "He's not at all the way you picture him. A man always imagines that his rival is an inferior person. In many ways he's very much like you. He's a big man and strong. I think he'll be happy with me."

"Will you be happy with him?"

"I think I will. I think for the first time in my life I'm ready for marriage."

"But way up there in the mountains!" Mark shook his head. "I can't imagine it for you, Claire."

"I can. I love the mountains. There's a strength in them. You catch it when you're there. It seems to reach out and envelop you. I'll be busy, not only as David's wife. He's going to help me start my theater. My own theater."

"The way you tell it, it would be selfish for anyone to do anything but let you go."

"It's better for both of us, Mark. You'll see."

Chapter 34

THAT SUMMER DEEPENED THE MAN. WITH CLAIRE GONE, WITH the Reed boys (through Mark's efforts and partial financial assistance) packed off to camp, with Jason taking a summer sabbatical in Maine and Victoria in Europe, Mark learned the meaning of aloneness.

He worked far beyond what his job required, letting his time spill over with no thought of compensation. It was enough that he was busy. He went to movies until there was nothing more to see. Although by now the sight of restaurant food sickened him, he ate out because this gave him some company. He drove through the park and down to the water's edge, to the spot where Claire had told him that she was going to marry David. Sometimes he went swimming here, sometimes he merely sat in the car looking out at a distant boat or up at the gulls. He thought about sending to Bradford for his sloop but with Bill Reed gone, there was little incentive and too much trouble involved in finding a mooring.

At first he dreaded the hours alone. He seemed bereft, unwanted. Then he grew used to them. He learned to think deeply, to feel things he had not felt before. Money, which had once been the driving force in his existence, seemed of very little importance. It was good to have enough to do the things he wanted, but now he wanted so much less. The almost vicious impulse to accumulate, to pile up lavish possessions, to be the Mark Galloway he had once been, left him.

In its place came a new quietness and a great calm. He reached out for serenity and found it. Strength settled down on him, a spiritual strength to which he had to become oriented. This was a new self and he realized it. It was a self that had been born anew in Jason's study on that bleak day last March, and which had been growing steadily since then and was now approaching maturity.

In these hours of being alone a new awareness came to him. He sensed the deeper meaning of everything. It was a wholly subjective experience. He no longer beat the air, screaming who am I, what is it all about? He was touching the edge of truth's garment.

Claire had gone and he might have turned to other women if he had wanted them. He had always been the kind of man to draw women's eyes when he entered a room. That had not changed. The Hobart sisters kept prodding him, telling him about the pleasant and attractive women his own age whom they knew. He met some interesting women in the plants he went to on business. A few times he asked one or another of these to dinner. Nothing came of it. They all seemed to lack something.

Nina was still under his skin. He knew that now. Whereas at first he had struggled with brutal determination to thrust her from his thoughts, he could no longer do this. He missed his wife. She was too much with him in thought for comfort.

She came back to him as the Nina he had known, smiling, radiant, beautiful. She was warm, the girl she had been. He remembered all the happy times they had had together. The bitterness, the sharp, insistent rising of strife between them was gone. He knew only that he wanted her.

Yet he could make no move to tell her so.

They continued to be in touch with each other through their lawyers. There was no talk from Nina about divorce, nor even legal separation. He offered several times to send her money, since the law of the state was that the husband must support the wife no matter what her circumstances. Nina refused his money. She had all she needed, was her answer.

The first bright blue days of autumn brought Jason back and several letters from Claire. She was apologetic about having written only one sketchy note of thanks for his wedding present during the summer. Things had been hectic but rather wonderful. The mountains were all she had expected. The farm was fascinating, especially since most of the work was done by machines. David was not the typical overworked farmer. She was afraid—and Mark sensed a note of jubilance in the admission —that she had married a "gentleman farmer." He was helping her get her theater established. He had selected the site, a huge barn in excellent condition which they were in the process of remodeling. Money seemed no object. It was overwhelming, for the first time in her life, to have plenty of it. It made her feel a little guilty. . . .

David and I love each other, Mark. It isn't true that love is something you cannot cultivate or develop. It is like some rare and beautiful flower that needs proper soil, and watering and indefatigable attention. There, you see! I am a farmer's wife already, talking about soil.

Mark, I miss you. It would be foolish to pretend I didn't. You and I will always miss each other. There is a kind of love that blossoms early and struggles for fulfillment and never quite hits the mark. This is the tragedy of loving someone who is emotionally too much like oneself. But I would not have missed this kind of love for anything. A life that has not known it is a barren life indeed.

Take care of yourself. You're precious to both of us, because

David already knows about you and he's anxious to meet you. We're expecting you to come visit us the first chance you get. I'm looking forward to seeing you because from your two letters, I sense that a new man has come through the rough experiences of the last year. I think I shall like that new man. The old Mark I loved, but this new one I feel sure I will like and respect as well.

When you see Ginger, give her my love.

Fondly as always,
CLAIRE

When you see Ginger. Mark folded the letter and slipped it back into its envelope.

You mean *if* I see her, Claire. Sometimes I wonder if I'll ever see Ginger and Jill and Nina again, Mark thought, feeling an upsurge of longing for his daughters and his wife.

I need them. I need Nina especially. How strange it is that when we're separated from those we really love we can see how much different everything might have been.

Perhaps if I had tried a little harder to see Nina's point of view, this whole heartbreaking business might have been avoided. It's strange that I had to come this far away from Nina in order to see her point of view.

You were selfish and dishonest, Mark. You've been a fool.

Chapter 35

AFTER MARK LEFT HER, NINA'S IMMEDIATE REACTION WAS ONE of shock. For days she was numb. She moved through the house on Turkey Hill like a somnambulist. Her senses were closed to the trivia of daily living that surrounded her. All her feelings were turned in upon herself, upon the tragedy within.

Then, as she began to return to normalcy, she awakened to an agony of perception in which everything jarred her almost shattered nerves.

There were times when she would wake up in the middle of the night with a feeling of utter despair. When morning came, she did not want to get up. There was nothing to get up for. For days, she could not trust herself near an open window. She never shed a tear in public. She never talked about Mark to anyone. Only once did she take Ginger aside and, as fairly as she could, present the problem to her. She spoke with frankness and honesty, because she felt this was the only right thing to do. She neither condemned Mark nor excused herself. Her talk with Ginger was impersonal and she tried to tell it as if it had happened to two other people.

Her reward was the expression of admiration she saw in Ginger's eyes. When Nina finished what she had to say, Ginger threw her arms around her.

"Mother," she whispered in Nina's ear. "I'm sorry. I'm terribly, terribly sorry, but I do understand. These things happen."

It was Ginger who stood by her during the weeks that followed. These were bitter weeks, weeks that tried Nina beyond all credulity. She had never believed it would be so hard to live without the man she loved. She had known something of separation during the war, but that had been with a difference. There was hope then. There was the great compelling force that held them together with all those thousands of miles between because they knew that one day Mark would be home again. Even the hazards of war, the hourly dangers, could not crush from Nina the expectation of having her husband with her one day.

Now, with only a few miles between them, Mark and she were being pushed farther and farther away with each passing day.

Nina entered upon a new life, and in many ways a terrifying one. For almost seventeen years, virtually all of her adult life, she had lived with a man. She had never thought about what it would be like to live without one. The smallest details of daily living took on a complicated aspect. Spencer attempted to ease some of the burden for her, but he was only her brother. When he suggested that she hire Effie's son as caretaker and chauffeur, she accepted his advice.

"You need a man on the premises, Nina," Spencer said. "If you don't hire someone, you'll have to give up the house."

I will not give up my home, she thought, with a fierceness she could not explain even to herself. She did not understand why she held so tenaciously to the big house in which Mark and she had lived so long. She knew only that she would never give it up.

Even more forcibly than the household problems, the social

complications drove home to Nina what it meant to be a woman alone.

The fact that she was still young, attractive, and endowed with much more than she needed of this world's goods made no difference in the eyes of her world. She was still a woman alone.

She noticed the immediate difference in her social status. A single woman, it appeared, was a liability. From the first days of separation, invitations that normally came via the mails and the telephone were cut abruptly off. At first she thought that this was because people were tactfully giving her time to pull herself together. In the beginning she did not care whether she was asked out or not. But the day eventually came when she grew restless with boredom. She wanted to be among people, even if only to hear other voices, to see other faces.

She found it was not an easy thing to pick up the threads. The old associations had, to an alarming extent, been shattered by Mark's going. As a couple they had been wanted, sought out, invited to more dinners, parties, teas, concerts than they cared to accept. Now only a few, a *surprisingly* few, of her friends seemed to be aware that she was still around.

Once she saw how things were going to be, she made the best of it, carving out a new way of life for herself. There were a few of her old friends who were also alone, widows or divorcees or bachelor girls, and she sought these out. She learned to do the things that two women or a group of women can do together, to go to and give luncheons, to run into town for a matinee and early dinner, to shop, to attend tea parties. She did not really enjoy any of it. She was a man's woman. She had always been a man's woman and Mark's leaving her could not change that. The pettiness and ofttimes the frightening cattiness of women together bothered her. She could never learn to be one of "the girls."

Nina found some release for her pent-up emotions in riding.

Every day she went out to the Hunt Club and got her horse and rode miles into the country, shunning the more familiar bridle paths.

It was at this point that Ginger surprised her most pleasantly, by inviting herself along on the afternoon rides.

"It's about time I went in for riding seriously," Ginger told her mother with a matter-of-factness that did not fool Nina. "Jill wrote me the other day that if I plan to be a movie actress someday then I'll be sorry I didn't learn to ride as well as you do, Mother."

"Don't you have to be at play rehearsals?" Nina asked, knowing that school dramatics had occupied so much of Ginger's time.

"I didn't try out for the play this time," Ginger answered. She did not seem to want to elaborate and Nina did not urge her. Nina knew, however, that Ginger was not running out to Claire Elliott's workshop so frequently as before. Claire had never been mentioned between them. Yet it was obvious that Ginger's interest in Claire as a person had cooled off since the separation between Mark and Nina. Sometimes Nina wondered how much Ginger had heard. She must have heard enough, Bradford schools being the gossip centers which they were. Whatever she had learned about Claire and her father, Ginger was taking it in her own stride, with philosophical quietness. "No comments," was her attitude.

These wise, wise young people of today! Nina thought. If this had happened to my father and mother I would have gone to pieces. Even Jill seems to want to reassure me, when I go to see her at Briarwood. Yet she was grateful for their fortitude. She was even more grateful for Ginger's company. It was pleasant to have a young person around her. It was good to reach out for Ginger's moral support during these months, and better to find that support there, willing, understanding, ever ready.

Ginger not only rode horseback with Nina. She made excuses to keep her week ends free so they could do things together. Once she even asked Nina to go to dinner with her new boy friend.

"He's my first older man," she said to Nina with pride. "A college junior. He's coming home this week end just to be with me."

Nina enjoyed the evening. The young man was nice-looking and affable and he seemed to bring out the best in Ginger. Ginger, on the other hand, was very anxious that Nina should like him.

"You do think he's wonderful, don't you, Mother? Because he is," she said with an enthusiasm that made Nina turn away, catching her breath, because Ginger looked and sounded so much like Mark at that moment. "He's the finest man I've ever met." Nina noticed that she always referred to this boy, Tom Edwards, as a "man."

Then, Ginger added hastily, "Well, *almost* the finest man, anyway."

Nina knew that Ginger was thinking of Mark and for a second time within the space of one minute, Nina felt that quick flash of nostalgia for Mark.

I miss him too, she wanted to cry out. I miss him more than I dare to admit to myself, Ginger. To lose a man is a dreadful thing, my daughter. Don't ever let the one you love get away from you. But even more than that. Help to keep a man's faith in himself alive. You can't do that from the outside. That must be done within yourself. You've got to believe in the man yourself, Ginger. You've got to let him know it. There's no second best in this kind of thing. You've got to go all out. You'll live to regret it otherwise. Life is nothing, nothing at all without the man you love.

Yet she said nothing. She stuffed all her grief and loneliness within her. Never a tear where anyone could see her. Never a word to let her world know how much she had lost. She wept in the solitude of her own being. And always, always, no matter where she was, in the theater, dining in some crowded place, driving along the familiar roads of Bradford, riding out on horseback into the country, in the dark, lonely hours of the night, in the bright sunshine of early morning, in the gray, sad hours of twilight, always, always, she cried out for Mark, wanting him back with her again.

There were times when she thought about the things she might have done differently but it was too late for self-recrimination now. Being sorry for the things she had done, or left undone, was not enough. It would never bring Mark back.

Chapter 36

On a Friday night in early October Mark found a cablegram waiting for him when he returned to his apartment.

ARRIVING LIBERTÉ SATURDAY AROUND FOUR. PLEASE MEET ME. I NEED YOU DESPERATELY.

It was signed with much love and it was from Victoria.

The cablegram was no surprise. All summer Victoria had been sending him cards, letters, mementos from England and France, Italy and Austria. Before she left she had exacted a promise from him that he would meet her at the pier when she got back. "You're the only one in the family I want there," she had said. "I can't abide the rest of them."

She still insisted on including him as "in the family," and he did not quibble with her about it.

It was one o'clock Saturday before he could leave Brampton, and the traffic was heavy. When he reached the Forty-eighth Street pier, the *Liberté* had already docked. Passengers were streaming off the boat into customs and he was just in time to see Victoria disembarking in all her glory. She came down the gangplank waving to him, smiling, throwing kisses. He waved and smiled back. She was still the old Victoria, the grand old girl of whom he was so fond, very slender and straight and tall, her white hair coifed to perfection, a saucy black hat perched on top of it, her suit and stole fresh from some *maison* of the Parisian *haute couture*.

She reached for his hand with her left arm and then suddenly he saw that she was reaching for another hand with her right arm. He saw that the smiles and kisses had been for someone else too. He turned to see who it was. His eyes looked straight into Nina's.

His eyes held Nina's for only a second. Victoria was undaunted, and indeed why not, since she had planned it all this way.

She led them away from the crowd toward the "B" section in customs. Then she turned to them.

"Mark, this is your wife. Nina, your husband, Mark. Why don't you get acquainted?"

She turned back to her trunks and smaller luggage, busying herself with the customs' inspectors who, sensing that Victoria was a celebrity, gave her a great deal of attention. Mark and Nina stood there, forgotten. Other friends of Victoria's appeared like so many rabbits from a magician's hat. Mark counted three artists, a sculptor, two writers, all of whom he knew by name, and a dozen other people whom he had never seen before. They hovered around Victoria, adding to the confusion.

She tore herself loose and came over to where Mark and Nina were standing in tongue-tied misery.

"Oh, dear, this is dreadful," she said. "I had no idea it would turn out like this. The newspapers gave it out that I was returning today. You see what's happened. There'll be no peace anywhere. They"—she waved toward the scores of friends who had gathered around her luggage—"are giving a home-coming party for me." She looked from Mark to Nina. "You were darlings to come down and now I feel responsible for you.

You'd have a miserable time at my party. It will be bedlamish. Mark, be a darling. Take Nina to dinner. And then drive her home or I'll never forgive myself. I asked her to come by train so she could drive out in my car tonight. Now I'll have to stay over."

Nina's eyes seemed to be pleading for him to stop Victoria's prattle, but she said nothing and he could not be sure. When he did not speak, Nina turned and walked away, searching the crowded place for a way out.

"Go after her, Mark. If you're a man, catch her now."

Even before Victoria spoke he had started to move. He did not need Victoria's goading command. He hurried through the place, elbowing and pushing his way to catch Nina before she was lost in the crowd. He saw her ahead of him; her blond hair under a small brown beret was not to be missed. When he was near enough, he reached out and caught her arm.

"Nina." She turned, and he saw relief wash the tension from her face. "Nina, do you think that just for today you could pretend that we're going the same way?"

Her smile was slow and charming. "Yes, for today I think we might pretend that."

They had dinner in a small French place of Nina's choosing. Across the table from her, he had his first good look at his wife. She was, as everyone had been telling him, looking frail and delicate, but the delicate air became her. She was, if anything, lovelier. She had the appearance of a real lady. She looked like one and talked like one. She had charm and refinement, and Mark found this appealing.

They talked about Ginger and Jill. That bridged the first strained moments of embarrassment. He was surprised when Nina asked about his new job. She seemed to be interested, she wanted to know all he would tell her about it. His apartment, too, was exhaustively discussed. He found himself telling her about the Hobart sisters and Miss Sherman and Bill Reed.

"It would have been nice to have such a boy of our own," she said, as Mark finished talking about Bill Reed.

When he questioned her about herself, she said there was not much to tell. She had kept busy. She did not say how. It seemed as if she would rather not say how. Ginger was quite a young lady now—and Mark noticed how quickly she switched the talk to their children again—she was as tall as Nina, the clumsiness and awkwardness of childhood were leaving her. She was showing the first faint tracings of the handsome woman she would be. "She resembles the pictures of your mother, Mark. She favors your family with her bold, striking good looks."

This surprised Mark as much as Nina's interest in his work. The whole tenor of her conversation was conciliatory. There was an emphasis on gentleness, on letting bygones be bygones. He detected no suggestion of rancor or resentment.

On the ride back to Connecticut, they talked little. Nina sat close to Mark and when she became drowsy her head rested on his shoulder. He turned off at Bradford. She did not waken until they were turning into Turkey Hill. Then she sat up with a start and said, "We're home! I had no idea."

He swung into the circular driveway at the front and kept his engine going while she got out. She hesitated a moment, as if to say something that was bothering her, but changed her mind and said good night, thanking him for the dinner and the ride back. As she turned to walk up the steps, he called to her.

"Nina." She wheeled around. "Suppose I were to call you up. Would you have dinner in Brampton with me?"

In the semidarkness, her face lighted with a smile. "I'd like that," she said.

"Let's make it sometime next week," he answered and drove off.

They made a regular thing of it. Once a week, Nina drove over to Brampton, left her car at one of the parking lots and joined Mark for dinner. She would meet him at the hotel. Often she would be early and as he bounded up the stairs toward the lobby, he would see her sitting in one of the lounge chairs. She was always the smartest woman in the place, in some new frock or suit, with a fur or cashmere coat thrown over her shoulders, a quite mad hat crowning her outfit, her jewels simple and elegant.

Wherever they went, people looked at Nina. "You don't look like Brampton to me," Mark would remark with a chuckle. It became a gag line before the autumn was over.

They had fun together. They did the things they had not done for years, tried every eating place, the good, the bad, the indifferent. They took in concerts and when shows were tried out in Brampton prior to Broadway, as they frequently were, they saw them.

Nina wanted to see his apartment so she came one crisp November evening and met everyone. The Reed boys were reserved until Nina smiled at them. When she produced a box of candy for each and asked Bill to show her the jet model airplane he was working on, they gave in. Nina asked Bill all the right questions.

"I never knew females could be interested in things like this," he said.

Nina smiled up at Mark. "My husband is an engineer," she replied to Bill. "We mustn't forget that."

The Hobarts went all-out for her, declaring she was the most "gorgeous creature" they had ever seen. "You'd think she was a model," Jacky commented.

When Mark took Nina to Miss Sherman's door, she took both Nina's hands and said, "I knew Mark's wife would be lovely." She asked if she might give them a plateful of apple strudel, "fresh-baked," to take up to Mark's apartment for their tea.

"Couldn't we have tea here with you?" Nina asked. "That

would be so much nicer." Miss Sherman threw wide the door, beaming.

Two days later some packages arrived at the apartment house and Mark was greeted with enormous excitement when he got home from work. There was a pair of skis for Bill and ice skates for Tom. Miss Sherman had a new toaster and the Hobart sisters jeweled caps from France.

"Look!" Boots exclaimed. "The label's right in them. *Made in France*."

Nina's card was in each package.

When Mark saw her the next week, he told her how pleased they all were. "It was sweet of you to do it," he added.

"They're friends of yours," she said. "I did it because they've been so nice to you."

"Is that the only reason?"

"No," she replied. "I did it because I liked them and because I love you."

They were sitting at a restaurant table. All he could do was take her hand and press it. "That's the nicest thing anyone has said to me in a long, long time."

That was the best evening of all. Mark and Nina had found each other again. They had learned to laugh together, to reach out for each other during the moments when they were apart. It was amazing how small a thing could bring to their love the sweetness of renewal: the clasping of hands across a table, a significant glance, the gardenia Mark stopped to buy for Nina and the way he looked into her eyes as he handed it to her. Little things, all of them, but potent enough to recall the early days of their love, and to prove to them that this renewal of affection, of mutual understanding, was what their marriage had most needed—what all marriages needed.

The year marched toward its climax. Looking back on it, Mark thought of it as the turning point in his life, his year of decision. It had been in some ways the most brutal year in his life but it had also brought him the most sure and solid happiness he had known. Reviewing it, one fact stood out above all the rest. It was the year in which he had fallen in love with Nina all over again.

Chapter 37

THEY HAD THANKSGIVING DINNER AT THE SPINNING WHEEL as they had last year, only today Ginger was with them. It had been Nina's idea to do this. When she had asked Mark if he were willing, she had said, "The children would love it."

Jill was ecstatic over seeing Mark again. She threw herself into his arms, squealing, "Daddy, it's wonderful to have you with us. I've missed you so much!"

Ginger was more dignified but no less sincere. She kissed Mark and said, "I've missed you too, Dad."

It was a good day for all of them. After dinner they drove out into the country and then swung back to the house on Turkey Hill. Mark got out, expecting to get his car and drive back to Brampton. It was Jill who said, "Daddy, aren't you coming home? Not even on Thanksgiving Day?"

Nina leaned toward him. "Yes, come in awhile, Mark. It is Thanksgiving, you know. And I have something to talk over with you."

He was surprised when he entered the house to see that nothing had really changed. His study was there, exactly as he had left it. The living room was warm and familiar with two bowls of yellow chrysanthemums beckoning him on.

Ginger had a "date." A pleasant young man whom Mark

had never seen before picked her up almost as soon as they got in. He had a good handclasp and called Mark "sir." His attitude toward Ginger was mature and possessive. It frightened Mark. He spoke to Nina about it.

"Don't be alarmed. They're not serious. He's the first 'older' man she's had. He's a junior in college. This is something she's got to get out of her system, Mark. When she's ready to settle down, she'll be able to choose the right man."

"Choose the right man!" Mark exploded. "Why, she's still just a child."

"Oh, no she isn't." Nina smiled wisely.

Mark brooded about it while Nina changed her dress to something more comfortable. He would always brood over Ginger. She was too much like him, too much a Galloway with the touch of adventure, the high and handsome independence. Today he had noticed a quietness in her that, while it was nothing new, seemed more accentuated. She had always withdrawn from them during her adolescence but today she seemed so *alone*. Then with a flash of insight he knew. She was like him. She was like all human beings. Each must reach through to the truth about himself and his universe, and an essential part of that search was loneliness.

When Nina returned, she had changed to a hostess gown of antique gold. "Victoria brought it from Italy," she said. "Do you like it?"

"It suits you," he said. "A golden dress for a golden person."

"Is that a pleasant remark?"

"I meant it to be."

"Come sit near me. I want to tell you something that will require all the coziness we can find in this big room."

"This big, imposing, formal room," he corrected.

"Yes, I suppose it is a little that way. You never discover how big and frightening a house can be until you try to live in it alone."

He got up and sat close to her.

"Mark, this is something you must let me begin and finish without a single interruption." He nodded. "It won't be an easy thing to tell you."

"I'll be on my best behavior." He smiled and she returned the smile.

"First, I want to tell you that no matter what your answer is to me tonight, I stand ready to release our mutual securities. You can have your money whenever you want it."

He waited, nodding his acknowledgment, and she went on. "We want you back, Mark. We all want you. Your wife wants you. Your children, too, and Bradford Tool. Come back where you're needed. Come back where you belong." He did not interrupt.

"I think you would like to know how much you've been missed at the plant. I went to see Steve Emrich the other day."

"You went to see Steve!"

"Yes, there were things I wanted to find out and this was my only way of learning them. The plant's not the same without you, Mark. The men are clamoring for you."

"I could never go back, Nina. You know that."

"Wait. Hear everything I have to say. You won't be coming back to the same situation, not at all. Victoria and I have had quite a few talks. Mark, she's made her will. She's leaving her Bradford stock to you."

"That's fantastic."

Nina smiled. "Victoria has always been a little fantastic." She went on. "Seriously, she wants to give you that stock now, while she's still living. She has no earthly use for it. She's got so much money she doesn't know how much. If she signs over her Bradford stock to you, and if I sign mine over to you, you'll hold the majority vote."

Mark got up. "You'd never do that, Nina."

She got up too, facing him. "I just told you that I would. If you want to come back, it's yours, Mark." She hurried on. "Lest you think this is a deal, that you're being bought, let me say something right away. I'm doing it because I learned something while you were gone, Mark. I learned what it meant to be without the man I love."

"What about Spencer? Surely he must be having a lot to say about all this."

"Yes, that's true. He's fought Victoria and he's fought me, but even Spencer knows when he's licked. Besides, he's tired. With you holding the power, he'll retire. You'll be president of Bradford Tool, Mark."

He turned his back. The impact of what she was offering was too much to take. He felt convulsive emotion rise to the surface and he clenched his fists to get control.

She was behind him, pleading with him. "There are so many things you could do. So many things you could accomplish for the men. They like you. You know what they want and what will help them most. Steve Emrich told me about some of these things. A recreation building, pensions, insurance, sick benefits, incentive systems. He put it in a strange way, in words I didn't quite understand, but I memorized them to tell them to you. 'Tell Mark we'd like to have the one guy in there who isn't afraid to come running across the catwalk in his shirt sleeves.' Maybe you understand what he means."

Mark turned. He tried to smile but his lips were trembling with emotion and he could not manage it.

"Yes," he said. "I understand."

He went over to her, taking both her hands in his. "Nina, this is a shock. If I didn't admit it, I'd be the biggest liar in the world. Give me time to think. I've got to have time to thrash it all out."

She kissed him sweetly. "It's been one of the nicest Thanksgiving Days I've ever had," she said. "Thank you for it, darling."

372

Chapter 38

HE TOSSED ALL NIGHT WITH INDECISION. MORNING FOUND HIM
limp and exhausted. He took a shower, dressed quickly and telephoned the office of Brampton Machine to say he'd be late getting on the job. Something personal, urgent, and important had
come up. He'd show up around noon if he could make it.

He got his car and drove down to the park where he had
spent so many hours alone. He tried to work it out, to know
what was the right thing to do. He hated Bradford money,
hated so much of what the family stood for. He loved Nina,
but that was another matter. He had tried living without Nina's
love and found out he couldn't. You couldn't love and live with
a woman almost twenty years and have children by her and
lose your only son together without wanting her back again.

That was one thing. Re-entering the Bradford rat race was
another. He was his own man now. He had his own dream.
During these months of separation from Nina that dream had
grown stronger. He wanted a business that he had built up himself. Nina had said she would release his money. She had
made that offer last night before she made the other proposition. He didn't suspect her of playing cagey. He admitted it
was a clever move, but Nina was not the scheming kind of
woman. She didn't calculate. She had made some mistakes in

her life. So had he, but he could never accuse her of sitting down and coldly calculating that if she did thus and thus, he might do so and so.

Nina was sincere. She was honest. She had, in the long run, acted very decently about their affairs. Besides, he loved her. It was hard to suspect a woman with whom you were in love.

But the dream stood. She could not change that. Unwittingly perhaps, she had given him the very thing he needed. With one breath she had offered to release his money. That gave him his opportunity. With the other she asked him to come back.

He looked at what she had offered him. It was a lot. A whole lot. It was what to most men would be the gift of a lifetime. To the old Mark Galloway it would have been the consummate opportunity. Mark Galloway, president of Bradford Tool. It sounded good. It sounded wonderful. It was the most terrific temptation he had faced in his life. A man could scrap a dream for stuff like that.

He turned on the ignition and started his car. He had to have another look at that empty building on King's Highway. When he faced it, he would be sure. Nina could not make this decision for him. Not her gentleness or her sweetness or the magnificence of her offer. Not her pleading. Not her promises. Not even the voice of Victoria which had run, powerful and persuasive, through all that Nina had said to him last night. None of these things could move him.

The answer was in himself. He had to go there and have another look at it and see what the answer would be.

He drove away from Brampton across country to the spot where Steve had sent him that winter morning months ago. The place was still vacant, a long, rambling shedlike structure, nothing much to look at but solidly built, a good Yankee job of building.

He got out, walked over and stood looking at it. He walked down the road a city block or so to the farmhouse where the key was kept. The farmer's wife recognized him and gave him the key on a leather thong.

He let himself in. The place was musty, a building long closed up. He threw open a couple of windows and walked through it. If ever a man saw his dream come true before his eyes, Mark Galloway did that morning. He knew what he wanted. He saw it take shape around him. He heard the whir and whine of machines. Saw men working. Heard their conversation.

This was what a man wanted out of life. A business of his own. A business that bore his own name. Old Jared Bradford would understand that feeling. He would know what Mark was facing now.

Old Jared. Mark's vision faded and another took its place. He saw and felt and heard Bradford Tool. The scream and roar of the machines, the busy stir of men running back and forth, old McGovern in the stock room, old Albie Griffin in the elevator, Wimbley, red-faced and sometimes imperious but commanding respect, his secretary whose long face and black bang reminded him of a thoroughbred horse, Joan and Jean, the Torso Twins.

He wheeled around, trying to throw it from him, but it followed him.

Now it gathered momentum, coming at him from all sides in the forms of hundreds of men milling from the plant at four thirty, hurrying across the parking lot to their cars. "Mr. Galloway." He heard his name. "Hi, Mr. Galloway. Good night, sir. Hope you get that defective lathe licked by morning. You're the one to take the bugs out of it, Mr. Galloway."

The men are clamoring for you. Tell Mark we'd like to have the one guy in there who isn't afraid to come running across the catwalk in his shirt sleeves.

He was standing again before the exhibit of the first lathe in the lobby. *One of the first Bradford lathes, manufactured and sold on this site by Jared Bradford.*

Jared Bradford. He must have been quite a guy. Strangely enough, of all the Bradford men Jared stood out most prominently in Mark's thoughts. Yet Mark had never met him.

He had been a man with vision, a man with a dream. Mark was a man with a dream, too.

It was a question of Jared's dream or his dream.

A man couldn't have both of them.

He went to the door, shutting the windows on the way. He got in his car, dropped the key off at the farmhouse and turned his car toward Turkey Hill.

He stopped to telephone Nina to say he was on his way and ask if she were free to see him now.

"I'm alone," she said. "The children are out. Come right along, Mark."

She was at one of the windows watching for him and as soon as he jammed on the brakes, she opened the front door. Her face was alive with the question that hovered unanswered between them.

"Come in, Mark," she said, and he stepped into the broad hall. She turned toward the living room but he stopped her.

"Let's talk here." He paused, but only for a moment, because he could feel the terrible tension that gripped Nina as she waited for his answer.

"I've come to say I'll do it," he told her. The instant the words were out, he felt an overpowering relief wash over him.

"Mark!" she exclaimed. "I'm so glad. So glad!" She put both her hands on his shoulders. "You won't be sorry, darling," she said. "I promise you."

"Victoria will want to know too," he reminded her.

"Yes, of course. I'll call her up. Now, while you're here."

"Don't you think we should go see her?"

She turned back. "Yes, you're right. That's better yet." She snatched her fur coat from the hall closet.

"Nina."

"Yes?" Her eyes were bright, her cheeks flushed with excitement.

"Before we see Victoria, there's something I want to say." She faced him, waiting for him to begin. "This wasn't a quick decision for me, nor an easy one. I think you should know that."

"I understand, Mark." He felt she was telling him the truth. This time she did understand. He knew he was talking to a new Nina, a bigger and deeper woman than he had walked out on all those months ago, and he felt a new respect for his wife.

"Once you called me selfish and dishonest. A fool." She glanced away but in a moment her eyes were on him again. "In a way you were right, Nina. Bradford Tool needs me. I belong there. It took a hundred dreams to make the company what it is. All that can't be wasted, not when new blood— Galloway blood from River Street—can save it. I thought at first it was a tossup between Jared's vision and my own, but now I see it another way. Old Jared's dream can become mine, too. I want it that way."

She was reaching up to kiss him, but before she did, she said, "Mark, darling, I love you. I would have gone with you no matter what you had decided to do. When you left me, I knew there would never be anyone else for me. But I found out something else. I found out that you were not only the man I loved. You were a big man." She was smiling. *"Big Mark Galloway."*

(1)